CLAIMED BY THE Desert SHEIKH

SUSAN
MALLERY

SUSAN
STEPHENS

OLIVIA
GATES

Mills & Boon, an imprint of Harlequin (UK) Limited, Eton House, 18-24 Paradise Road, Richmond, Surrey TW9 1SR

CLAIMED BY THE DESERT SHEIKH
© Harlequin Enterprises II B.V./S.à.r.l. 2012

The Sheikh and the Pregnant Bride © Susan Macias Redmond 2008
Desert King, Pregnant Mistress © Susan Stephens 2008
Desert Prince, Expectant Mother © Olivia Gates 2008

ISBN: 978 0 263 89624 4

009-0112

Harlequin (UK) policy is to use papers that are natural, renewable and recyclable products and made from wood grown in sustainable forests. The logging and manufacturing processes conform to the legal environmental regulations of the country of origin.

Printed and bound in Spain
by Blackprint CPI, Barcelona

The Sheikh and the Pregnant Bride

SUSAN MALLERY

New York Times bestselling author **Susan Mallery** has entertained millions of readers with her witty and emotional stories about women and the relationships that move them. *Publishers Weekly* calls Susan's prose "luscious and provocative," and *Booklist* says, "Novels don't get much better than Mallery's expert blend of emotional nuance, humour and superb storytelling." While Susan appreciates the critical praise, she is most honoured by the enthusiastic readers who write to tell her that her books made them laugh, made them cry and made the world a happier place to live. Susan lives in Seattle with her husband and her tiny but intrepid toy poodle. She's there for the coffee, not the weather.

Visit Susan on the web at www.susanmallery.com.

Chapter One

Maggie Collins hated to admit it but the reality was, she was a tiny bit disappointed by her first meeting with a real, live prince.

The trip to El Deharia had been great. She'd flown first-class, which was just as fabulous as it looked in the movies. When she'd landed, she'd been whisked by limo to a fancy hotel. Until then, her only other limo experience had been for her prom and then she and her date had been sharing it and the expense with six other couples.

Arriving at the exclusive Hotel El Deharia, she'd been shown to a suite with a view of the Arabian Sea. The living room alone had been about the same size as the two-bedroom house she'd grown up in back in Aspen.

She also couldn't complain about the palace. It was big and beautiful and historic-looking. But honestly, the offices where she was supposed to be meeting Prince Qadir weren't anything special. They were just offices. And everyone was dressed so professionally in conservative suits. She'd been hoping for harem pants and a tiara or two. Of course, as she'd mostly seen men, a tiara was probably out of place.

The thought of the older British gentleman who had shown her into the office wearing a tiara made her giggle. She was still laughing when the door opened and a tall man in yet another suit walked in.

"Good morning," he said as he approached. "I am Prince Qadir."

Maggie sighed in disappointment. Yes, the prince was very handsome, but there was nothing different about him. No medals, not even a crown or a scepter or some proof of rank.

"Well, darn," she murmured.

Prince Qadir raised his eyebrows. "Excuse me?"

Had she said that aloud? Oops. "I, ah…" She swallowed and then squared her shoulders. "Prince Qadir," she said as she walked toward him and held out her hand. "Very nice to meet you. I'm Maggie Collins. We've been corresponding via e-mail."

He took her hand in his and shook it. "I'm aware of that, Ms. Collins. I believe my last note to you said I preferred to work with your father."

"Yet the ticket was in my name," she said absently as she dropped her arm to her side, aware that even though she was five-ten, he was still much taller than her.

"I sent you each a ticket. Did he not use his?"

"No, he didn't." She glanced out the window at the formal garden below. "My father…" She cleared her throat and returned her attention to the prince. This was not the time to get sad again. She was here to do business. "My father died four months ago."

"My condolences."

"Thank you."

Qadir glanced at his watch. "A car will return you to your hotel."

"What?" Outrage chased away any threatening tears. "You're not even going to talk to me?"

"No."

Of all the annoying, arrogant, *male* ways to react. It was just so typical. "I'm more than capable of doing the job."

"I don't doubt that, Ms. Collins. However, my arrangement was with your father."

"We were in business together." The last year of her father's life, she'd run the car-restoration business he'd started years ago. And lost it, although that hadn't been because of anything she'd done wrong. The medical bills had been massive. In the end she'd had to sell everything to pay them, including the business.

"This project is very important to me. I want someone with experience."

She wanted to deck him. Given the fact that she was female and he was well-bred, she could probably get one shot in, what with the element of surprise on her side. But to what end? Hitting a member of the royal family was hardly the way to get the job.

"There were exactly seven hundred and seventeen Rolls-Royce Phantom IIIs built between 1936 and 1939, plus ten experimental cars," she said as she glared at him. "The earlier models had a maximum speed of ninety-two miles an hour. Problems started showing up early because the cars weren't designed to be run at maximum speed for any length of time. This became an issue as owners took their cars to Europe where they could drive on the newly built German autobahn. The company's initial fix was to tell the drivers to go slower. Later, they offered a modification that was little more than a higher-ratio fourth gear that also made the car go slower."

She paused. "There's more, but I'm sure you already know most of it."

"You've done your homework."

"I'm a professional." A professional who desperately needed the job. Prince Qadir had a 1936 Phantom III he wanted restored. Expense was no object. She needed the money he offered to pay off the last of her father's medical bills and keep her promise of starting up the family business again.

"You're a woman."

She glanced down at her chest, then back at him. "Really? I guess that explains the breasts. I'd wondered why they were there."

One corner of his mouth twitched slightly, as if he were amused.

She decided to push while he was in a good mood. "Look. My mother died right after I was born. I grew up in my dad's garage. I learned to change oil before I learned to read. Yes, I'm female, but so what? Cars have always been my life. I'm a great mechanic. If what they say is true, that classic cars are female, who better to understand them than me? I can do this. I work hard, I don't get drunk and knock up the local girls. Even more important, with my father gone, I have something to prove. You're a man of the world. You know what a difference the right motivation can be."

Qadir stared at the woman before him and wondered if he should let himself be convinced. If Maggie Collins restored cars with the same energy that she was using on him, he had nothing to worry about. But a female in the garage?

He reached for her hand and took it in his. Her fingers were long, her nails short. She was attractive, but not delicate. He turned her hand over and stared at her palm. There were several calluses and a couple of scars. These were the hands of someone who worked for a living.

"Squeeze my hand," he said, staring into her green eyes. "As hard as you can."

She wrinkled her nose, as if she couldn't believe what he was asking, then she did as he requested.

Her fingers crushed his in a powerful grip.

Impressive, he thought. Perhaps she was who and what she claimed.

"Should we arm wrestle next?" she asked. "Or have a spitting contest?"

He laughed. "That will not be required." He released her hand. "Would you like to see the car?"

Her breath caught. "I would love to."

They walked through the palace to the garage. Along the way, Qadir pointed out some of the public rooms along with a few of the more notable antiquities. Maggie paused to look at a large tapestry.

"That's a lot of sewing," she said.

"Yes, it is. It took fifteen women over ten years to complete it."

"I don't have the patience for that sort of thing. Seriously? I would have killed someone within the first six months. One night I would have snapped and run screaming through the palace with an ax."

The vivid image amused him. Maggie Collins was not a typical woman and he had met more than enough to know the difference. Although she was tall and slim, she moved with a purpose that was far from feminine. She had striking features, but wore no makeup to enhance them. Long dark hair hung down her back in a simple braid.

He was used to women using flattery and sexuality to get what they wanted, yet she did not. The change was…interesting.

"This is my first palace," she said as they continued walking down the long corridor.

"What do you think?"

"That it's beautiful, but a little big for my taste."

"No dreams of being a princess?"

She laughed. "I'm not exactly princess material. I grew up dreaming of racing cars, not horses. I'd rather work on a fussy transmission than go shopping."

"Why aren't you racing cars? Women do."

"I don't have the killer competitive instinct. I like to go fast. I mean, who doesn't? But I'm not into winning at any cost. It's a flaw." She pointed at an ancient Sumerian bowl and wrinkled her nose. "That's a whole new level of ugly."

"It's over four thousand years old."

"Really? That doesn't make it any more attractive. Seriously, would you want that in your living room?"

He'd never paid much attention to the ancient piece of pottery, but now he had to admit it wasn't to his taste.

"It's better here, where all can enjoy it."

"Very diplomatic. Is that your prince training?"

"You are comfortable speaking your mind."

Maggie sighed. "I know. It gets me into trouble. I'll try to be quiet now."

And she was, until they reached the garage. He opened the door and led her inside. Lights came on automatically.

There were only a dozen or so vehicles in this structure. Others were housed elsewhere. Maggie walked past the staff Volvo, his Lamborghini, two Porsches, the Land Rover and Hummer to the battered Rolls-Royce Phantom III at the far end.

"Oh, man, I never thought I'd see one of these up close," Maggie breathed.

She ran her hands along the side of the car. "Poor girl, you're not looking your best, are you? But I can fix that." She turned to Qadir. "The first one of these was seen in October 1935 at the London Olympia Motor Show. They brought nine Phantoms, but only one of them had an engine in it." She turned back to the car. "She's a V-12, zero to sixty in sixteen-point-eight seconds. That's pretty fast for this big a car. Especially considering how quiet the engine runs."

Maggie circled the vehicle, touching it, breathing in, as if trying to make it a part of her. Her eyes were wide, her expression one of wonder. He'd seen that look on a woman's face before, but usually only when giving expensive jewels or shopping trips to Paris and Milan.

"You have to let me do this," she told him. "No one will love her more than I do."

George Collins had been one of the best restorers and mechanics in the business. Had he passed on his greatness to his daughter or was she simply trading on his name?

Maggie opened the passenger door. "Rats," she muttered, then looked at him. "They've chewed the hell out of the leather. But I know a guy who can work miracles."

"How long would it take to restore her?" he asked.

She grinned. "How much money do you have?"

"An endless supply."

"Must be nice." She considered the question. "With express delivery and my contacts, six to eight weeks, assuming I can find what I need. I'll want to fly in someone to do the upholstery and the painting. I'll do everything else myself. I'm assuming I can get metal work done locally."

"You can."

She straightened and folded her arms over her chest. "Do we have a deal?"

Qadir had no problem working with women. He liked women. They were soft and appealing and they smelled good. But the Phantom was special.

"You can't refuse me because I'm female," Maggie told him.

"That's wrong. You know that's wrong. El Deharia is forward and progressive." She looked away, then turned back to face him. "My father is gone and I miss him every moment of every day. I need to do this for him. Because that's what he would have wanted. No one is going to care more about doing this right than me, Prince Qadir. I give you my word."

An impassioned plea. "But does your word have value?"

"I've killed a man for assuming less."

He laughed at the unexpected response. "Very well, Ms. Collins. You may restore my car. The deal will be the same as the one I negotiated with your father. You have six weeks to restore her to her former glory."

"Six weeks and an unlimited budget."

"Exactly. Someone on my staff will show you to your room. While you are employed here, you will be my guest in the palace."

"I need to collect my things from the hotel."

"They will be brought here to you."

"Of course they will," she murmured. "If the sun is a little too bright, can you move it?"

"With the right motivation." He eyed her. "I do not appear to intimidate you. Why is that?"

"You're just some guy with a car and a checkbook, Prince Qadir."

"In other words, a job."

"A really great job, but a job. When this is done, I'll go home to my real life and you'll have the sweetest ride in El Deharia. We'll both get what we want."

Qadir smiled. "I always do."

Maggie refused to think about how much per minute she was paying on her calling card as the phone rang.

"Hello?"

"Hey, Jon, it's me."

"Did you get it?"

Maggie threw herself back on the massive bed in her large suite. A suite that was even bigger than the one at the hotel. "Of course. Was there any doubt?"

"He was expecting your dad."

"I know, but I dazzled him with my charm."

Jon laughed. "Maggie, you don't have any charm. Did you bully him? I know you bullied him."

"He's a prince, which makes him immune to the whole bullying thing. Besides, I'm a nice person."

"Mostly, but you're also driven and determined. I know you."

"Better than anyone," she agreed, keeping her voice light despite the sudden tightness in her chest. Losing her dad had been the worst thing that had ever happened to her, but losing Jon had been nearly as bad. Jon had been her best friend, her first lover…pretty much everything.

"How's the car?" he asked.

Maggie launched into ten minutes of praise complete with technical details. She paused only when she recognized Jon's "uh-huhs" for what they were. Lack of interest.

"You're writing an e-mail, aren't you?" she demanded.

"No. Of course not. I'm mesmerized by, ah, the V-8 engine."

"It's a V-12 and I'll stop talking about it now. I should let you get back to work."

"I'm glad you got the job. Let me know how it goes. Or if you need anything."

"I will. Say hi to Elaine."

Jon didn't answer.

Maggie sighed. "I mean it. Say hi to her. I'm happy for you, Jonny."

"Maggie—"

"Don't. We're friends. That's what we're supposed to be. We both know that. I gotta run. I'll talk to you later. Bye."

She hung up before he could say anything else.

Despite the late hour, she was too restless to go to bed. Jet lag, she thought, knowing the twelve- or fifteen-hour time difference had messed up her body clock.

She'd traded in her pantsuit for jeans and a T-shirt. After slipping her feet into a pair of flip-flops, she opened the French doors and stepped out into the cool night air.

Her rooms faced the ocean, which was pretty exciting. Back home she had great views of the mountains, but vast expanses of water was its own special treat.

"Don't get used to living like this," she reminded herself. She'd rented out her house for the next couple of months. It was the end of ski season in Aspen and rentals still went for a premium. But once the job was done, she would be returning to the small house where she'd grown up, with its creaky stairs and single bathroom.

She breathed in the smell of salt air. There were lights in the garden below and the sound of voices in the distance. From what she could tell, the balcony circled the entire palace. Curious and eager to explore, Maggie closed her door behind her and started walking.

She passed empty rooms and a lot of closed and curtained windows. One set of doors stood open. She caught a glimpse of three girls cuddling on the sofa with a man who looked a little like Qadir.

A brother, she figured. From what she remembered reading, the king had several sons. No daughters. One wouldn't want a mere woman getting in the way, she thought with a grin. What would it be like to grow up here? Rich and pampered, being given ponies from the age of three. It must be—

"Qadir, I expect more," a gruff voice said in the darkness.

Maggie skidded to a halt so quickly, she nearly slid out of her sandals.

"In time," Qadir said, his voice calm.

"How much time? As'ad is engaged. He will be married in a few weeks. You need to settle down, as well. How is it possible I have so many sons and no grandchildren?"

Maggie knew the smartest thing would be to turn around and head back to her room. It's what she meant to do…except she couldn't help wanting to listen. She'd never heard a king speak to a prince before. She couldn't believe they were arguing, just like a regular family.

She slipped behind a large pole and did her best to stay completely silent as Qadir said, "As'ad brings you three daughters. That should be enough for a start."

"You are not taking this seriously. With all the women you have been with, you should have found at least one you're willing to marry."

"Sorry. No."

"It's that girl," the king murmured. "From before. She's the reason."

"She has nothing to do with this."

Woman? What woman? Maggie made a mental note to get on the computer and check out Qadir's past.

"If you cannot find a bride on your own, I will find one for you," the king said. "You *will* do your duty."

There was the sound of footsteps, then a door closed. Maggie stayed in place, not sure if both men had left.

She breathed as quietly as she could and was about to go back the way she'd come when she heard Qadir say, "You can come out now. He's gone."

Maggie winced as heat burned her cheeks. She stepped into

view. "I didn't mean to listen in. I was taking a walk and then you were talking. I was really quiet. How did you know I was here?"

Qadir nodded toward the plate-glass window that reflected the balcony. "I saw you approaching. It does not matter. My quarrel with the king is common knowledge. It is an argument my brothers and I share with him."

"Still, I wasn't eavesdropping on purpose."

"You seem intent on repeating that fact."

"I don't want you to think I'm rude."

"But I have already hired you. What does it matter what I think?"

"Because you're my boss. You could fire me tomorrow."

"True, but per our contract, you would still get paid."

She fought against the need to roll her eyes. "While the money is important, so is doing a good job. I don't want to leave until the car is finished. It's a matter of pride."

Maybe being über-rich and a sheik meant he wouldn't understand that. Maggie doubted Qadir had ever had to work for anything.

"Will your father really find you a wife?" she asked.

"He will try. Ultimately the choice is mine. I can refuse to marry her."

"Why would he think anyone would agree to an arranged marriage?"

Qadir leaned against the railing. "The woman in question will be marrying into a royal family. We trace our bloodline back more than a thousand years. For some, the dictates of history and rank matter far more than any matters of the heart."

A thousand years? Maggie couldn't imagine that. But then she'd grown up under relatively modest circumstances in a fairly typical medium-size town. Over the past few years movie stars showed up every winter to ski, but she didn't have any contact with them. Nor did she want any. She preferred regular people to the rich and famous. And to princes. Even one as handsome as the man in front of her.

"You must have all kinds of women throwing themselves at you," she said. "Aren't there any you want to marry?"

Qadir raised his eyebrows. "You take my father's side in this?"

"You're royal. Doesn't having heirs come with the really plush surroundings?"

"So you're practical."

"I understand family loyalty and duty."

"Would you have agreed to an arranged match if it had been expected?"

Maggie considered the question. "I don't know. Maybe. If I'd always known it was going to be that way. I'm not sure I would have liked it."

"Such an obedient daughter."

"Not on purpose. I loved my father very much." He'd been all the family she'd ever had. She still expected to see him in the house or hear his footsteps. One of the big advantages of her job in El Deharia—besides the money—was that she could escape the sad memories for a few weeks.

Qadir shook his head. "I am sorry. I had forgotten your recent loss. I did not mean to remind you of your pain."

"Don't worry about it. I'm kind of bringing it with me everywhere I go."

He nodded slowly as if he understood what it meant to lose something so precious. Did he? Maggie realized she knew nothing about Qadir beyond what she'd heard on television. She didn't read gossip magazines. Or fashion magazines for that matter. Her idea of a great evening was when *Car and Driver* arrived in the mail.

"You must have other family back in Aspen," he said. "How will they cope with you gone?"

"I, ah, I'm kind of alone. It was just my dad and me. I have a few friends, but they're busy with their lives."

"So you had no one to call and tell about your new job?"

"I called Jon. He worries about me."

Qadir's dark gaze settled on her face. "Your boyfriend?"

"Not anymore," she said lightly. "He's someone I've known forever. We grew up next door to each other. We played together when we were kids, then kind of fell in love in high school. Everyone assumed we'd get married, but it never seemed to happen."

She'd always wondered why they hadn't taken that last step. They'd dated for years, been each other's first time. He was the only man she'd ever been with and until Elaine, Jon had only been with her. She still loved him—a part of her would always love him.

"I think we fell out of 'in love,' if that makes sense. We still care for each other, but it's not the same. I think we would have broken up a long time ago, except my dad was sick and Jon didn't want to dump that on me, too."

But she'd sensed the changes in their relationship. "I ignored the obvious because of my dad dying. After he was gone, Jon and I talked and I realized it had been over for a long time." She forced a smile she didn't feel. "He's met someone else. Elaine. She's great and they're crazy about each other. So that's good."

She mostly meant that. Jon was her friend and she wanted him to be happy. But every now and then she wondered why she couldn't have met someone, too.

"You are very understanding," Qadir said. "Even if it is all a mask."

She stiffened. "I'm not pretending."

"You're saying there is no anger at Jon for replacing you so easily?"

"None at all," she snapped, then sighed. "Okay, there's a twinge, but it's not a big deal. I don't really want him for myself, exactly."

"But he should have had the common courtesy to wait a while before finding the love of his life."

"I can't agree with that. It makes me sound horrible."

"It makes you sound human."

"I'm emotionally tough." At least she was trying to be. There had been a single breakdown about five weeks ago. She'd called Jon, sobbing and trembling with pain. She'd hurt everywhere, not only from the loss of her father, but from the loss of her best friend.

Jon, being Jon, had come over to comfort her. He'd hugged her and held her and she'd wanted more. She'd kissed him and...

Maggie walked to the balcony and stared out into the night. Thinking about that night made her so ashamed. She'd seduced him because she'd wanted a chance to forget all that had happened in her life. And maybe to prove she still could.

At the time, he'd only known Elaine a couple of weeks, but Maggie had sensed they were getting serious. In a way it had been her last chance with Jon.

When it was over, neither of them had known what to say. She'd apologized, which he'd told her wasn't necessary. Things had been awkward between them. They still were.

"Life is complicated," she murmured.

"I agree."

She looked at him. "You're not going to get any sympathy from me, Prince Qadir."

"You're saying my life of wealth and privilege means I don't deserve to complain."

"Something like that."

"You have many rules."

"I like rules."

"I like to break them."

Hardly a surprise, she thought as she smiled. "Of course you do."

He laughed. "I still do not intimidate you. What was it you called me? A guy with a checkbook and a car?"

"Is reverence an important part of the job?"

"Not at all. You may even call me by my first name, without using my title."

"I'm honored."

"No, you're not, but you should be." He took a step toward her, then touched her cheek. "Do not mourn for the man unwise enough to let such a prize go. He was born a fool and he will die a fool. Good night."

Qadir disappeared with a speed that left Maggie gasping. She didn't know what to think about first. The soft brush of his fingers on her cheek or what he'd said.

She wanted to protest that Jon wasn't a fool. That he was actually a really bright guy, which was one of the things she'd always liked about him. Except she liked Qadir's attitude about the whole thing. She also enjoyed thinking about herself as a prize to be won…by a man who was not a fool.

Chapter Two

Maggie finished getting ready, then hovered by the door, not sure if she was just supposed to go down to the garage or wait to be called or what.

"Palaces should come with instruction books," she murmured to herself as she reached for the door handle. She might as well see if she could find her way to the garage and…

Someone knocked on her door. She pulled it open to find a pretty blonde about her age in the wide hallway.

"Hi," the woman said. "You're Maggie, right? I'm Victoria McCallan, secretary, fellow American and your guide to all things royal. Victoria, never Vicki, although honestly I can't say why. It started when I was little. I think I was in a mood and I haven't gotten over it."

Victoria smiled as she spoke. She was a few inches shorter than Maggie, even in her insanely high heels. She wore a tailored blouse tucked into a short, dark skirt. Her skin was perfect, her nails long and painted and her hair curled to her shoulders. She was the very essence of everything female. Maggie suddenly felt tall and awkward. Not to mention seriously underdressed in her jeans and T-shirt. She didn't want to imagine what Victoria would think about the coveralls she had in her duffel.

"You *are* Maggie, aren't you?"

"Most days."

Victoria laughed. "Welcome to the palace. It's great here."

"Is there a map?"

"If only. I can't tell you how many times I've been lost. We need internal GPS or something. They could implant us with a chip and track us." She wrinkled her nose. "On second thought, maybe not. Are you really here to fix a car?"

"Work on one. I'm restoring an old Rolls-Royce." She thought about going into more detail, but figured the other woman's eyes would glaze over.

"On purpose?"

"It's not going to happen otherwise."

"I never got the car thing."

Maggie looked at Victoria's perfect outfit. "I never got the clothes thing. I hate shopping."

"I shop enough for two so you're covered. Come on. I'll show you the way."

Victoria waited while Maggie grabbed her duffel.

"Do I want to know what's in there?" the other woman asked.

Maggie thought about her personal tools and coveralls. "No."

"Good to know. The El Deharian palace was originally built in the eighth century. There are still parts of the old exterior walls visible. I can show you later, if you'd like. The main structure is broken down into four quadrants, much like the interior of a cathedral, but without the religious implication. There is artwork from around the world on display. At any given time, the paintings alone are valued at nearly a billion dollars."

Victoria pointed to a painting on a wall. "An early Renoir. Just a little FYI, don't even think about taking it back to your room for a private viewing. It's protected by a state-of-the-art security system. However, if you insist on trying, rumor is they'll take you down to the dungeon and cut off your head."

"Good to know," Maggie murmured. "I don't know much about art. I'll keep it that way. How do you know so much about the palace?"

"I like to read. There's a lot of great history here. Plus I've been asked to fill in a few times when foreign dignitaries want a private tour after dinner when the regular tour staff has gone home."

"You live here—in the palace?"

"Just down the hall. I've been here nearly two years." She paused at a staircase. "Look at that hideous baby in the painting." She pointed to a large oil painting on the wall. "It's the easiest way to remember your wing and floor. Trust me, most of the other art is much more attractive."

"Good to know."

Victoria started down the stairs. "As live-in staff you're entitled to a whole bundle of goodies. Free laundry, access to the kitchen. I will warn you that you have to be careful with the food. You can really pack on the pounds in a heartbeat. I gained the freshman fifteen when I first moved here. Now I make sure I walk everywhere."

Maggie eyed her high heels. "In those?"

"Of course. They go with my outfit."

"Don't they hurt?"

"Not until about four in the afternoon."

Victoria led her downstairs, then along a long corridor that led to the rear garden. At least Maggie thought it was the rear garden. It looked a little like what she and Qadir had passed through the day before.

"Back to the kitchen," Victoria said. "You can call in your request at any time. They do post a menu online, so if you want to just order from that, they'll love you more. Everything is delicious. Unless you want to weigh four hundred pounds, avoid the desserts." She looked at Maggie. "Of course, you're probably one of those annoying women who doesn't have to watch what she eats."

"I'm pretty physically active during my day," Maggie admitted.

"Great. And here I thought we'd be friends." She pulled a key out of her skirt which, apparently, had a pocket, and passed it over. "You have private access. Very impressive."

She waited while Maggie unlocked the side door, then they stepped into the massive garage.

Victoria paused by the door as the automatic lights came on, but Maggie walked directly to the Rolls, stopping only when she could touch the smooth lines of the perfect beauty.

Victoria paused behind her. "It's, um, old."

"A classic."

"And dirty. And kind of in bad shape. You can fix that?"

Maggie nodded, already visualizing what the car could be. "I'm going to be searching for original parts, if I can find them. It will be a pain, but in the end, I want her exactly as she was."

"Okay, then. Sounds like fun." Victoria walked to a door. "This is your office."

Office? Maggie had expected a bay in the garage and a toolbox. She got an office, too?

The space was large, clean and fully equipped. In addition to the desk with a computer, there were bookshelves filled with catalogs and a wall-size tool organizer.

Victoria opened the desk drawer and pulled out a credit card.

"Yours. You are allowed to get whatever you need for the car. Qadir has placed no restrictions on your spending. I'm thinking you'll want to avoid a trip to the Bahamas, however. What with the whole beheading thing."

Maggie laughed. "Thanks for the tip. Is this really for me?"

"All of it. I was in here late yesterday and set up your computer. You're already connected to the Internet."

"Thanks." Maggie had been excited about the job before—working on the Rolls would be a once-in-a-lifetime experience for her. But to have all this, too, was unbelievable. "Guess I'm not still in Kansas."

"Is that where you're from?"

"Colorado. Aspen."

"It's supposed to be beautiful there."

"It is."

"How'd you end up in El Deharia?" Victoria asked. As she spoke, she rested one hip on the desk.

Maggie figured with those shoes, she would want to stay off her feet as much as possible.

"My dad had talked to Qadir about restoring the car. They were still working the deal when my dad got sick. Cancer. Things were put on hold, then he died and I decided I wanted the job."

It was the simple version of the story, Maggie thought, not wanting to tell someone she'd barely met that she had been forced to sell the business to pay for medical bills and that this job with Prince Qadir was her only chance of keeping her promise to her father about buying it back.

"I'm sorry about your loss," Victoria said. "That has to be hard. Is your mom still alive?"

"No. She died when I was a baby. It was just my dad and me, but it was great. I loved being with him in the shop and learning about cars."

"Well, I'm sure it's a handy skill." Victoria tilted her head so her curls fell. "So that's all this is about? A job?"

"What else would it be?"

"Marrying a prince. That's why I'm here."

Maggie blinked. "How's that working out for you?"

"Not very well," Victoria admitted with a sigh. "I work for Prince Nadim—he's one of Qadir's cousins. I keep waiting for him to notice me, but so far, it's not happening. Still, I have faith. One day he'll look up, see me and be swept away."

Maggie wasn't sure what to say. "You don't sound like you're madly in love with him."

"I'm not," Victoria said with a grin. "Love is dangerous and for fools. I'm keeping my heart safely out of the game. But what little girl doesn't want to grow up and be a princess?"

There had to be more to the story than that, Maggie thought. Victoria was too friendly and open to only care about money. Or maybe not. Maggie didn't have that many female friends. Most women were put off by the car thing.

Victoria glanced at her watch. "I have to get back." She bent over the desk and scribbled down a number. "That's my cell. Call me if you have any questions, or if you want to have dinner or something. The palace is beautiful, but it can be a little scary at first. Not to mention lonely. We can hang out."

"Eat dessert?"

Victoria sighed. "Yes, and then I'll have to take the stairs even more than I do. Good luck with the car."

As Maggie watched her go, she wondered if Victoria really meant what she said—about wanting to marry Prince Nadim. She supposed there were women who were more interested in what the man could provide than the character of the man himself. Not something that would interest her.

Unfortunately, thinking about men made her think about

Jon. She hated that she still missed him and that seeing everything around the palace made her want to call him. He would
appreciate what she was going through. Knowing him, he would
even understand her ambivalence about their situation now.

But calling wasn't an option. He was in love with Elaine. That
fact shouldn't mean she and Jon couldn't be friends, but the
truth was, things were different. They could never go back and
she couldn't figure out a way to go forward.

"Don't think about it," she told herself, then looked at the
credit card Victoria had left with her. She didn't enjoy shopping
for girly stuff, but when cars or car parts were involved, she could
really get into it. "So let's take you for a test drive," she told the
card, "and see what you can do."

Maggie typed in the amount, held back a wince and pushed
Enter on the computer. Less than a second later, her bid amount
showed on the page. She clapped her hands, then groaned when
someone outbid her by two dollars.

She wanted that part. She *needed* that part. Maybe she should
just offer the full price and get the stupid thing now, without
worrying about it.

Practicality battled with how she'd been raised and frugality
nearly won. It was ridiculous to pay the full amount when she
might be able to get the part for less. However, she did have to
budget her time and as Prince Qadir was incredibly rich, she
wasn't sure he would care that she'd saved him twenty bucks.

Still, it took a couple of deep breaths before she typed in the
"pay this amount and buy it now" price. She writhed in her chair
a couple of seconds before pushing Enter.

"Are you in pain?"

She turned toward the speaker and saw Prince Qadir stepping
into her office.

"Is it serious?" he asked.

"I'm fine." She hesitated, not sure if she should rise or bow or what. "I'm ordering parts online."

"A simple enough action."

"It's an auction. I've been bidding all morning. Someone else keeps topping me by a couple of dollars."

"Then offer enough to push him out of the battle."

"That's what I did."

"Good."

"I probably could have gotten the part for less if I'd waited."

"Do you think that is important to me? The bargain?"

She looked at him, at his tailored suit and blinding white shirt. He looked like a successful executive…a very handsome executive.

"No one likes to be taken," she said.

"Agreed, but there is a time and a place to barter. I doubt there is a huge market for parts for my car, but what market there is will be competitive. I want you to win."

"I'll remember that."

"But you do not approve."

"Why do you say that?" she asked.

"Your expression. You would prefer to bargain and wait."

"I want you to get your car at a fair price."

He smiled. "An excellent idea. I appreciate the fairness of your concern. Perhaps a balance of both would be easiest."

He had a great smile, she thought absently. She hadn't spent a lot of time thinking about princes, but she supposed she would have assumed they were stern and serious. Or total playboys. She'd seen plenty of those during the season in Aspen. But Qadir didn't seem to be either.

"I'll do what I can," she said. "It's just I'm used to getting the best price."

"While I am used to getting the best."

With his family fortune, he always did, she thought humorously.

"Must be nice," she murmured.

"It is."

Maggie smiled. "At least you're clear about it." She rose and walked to the printer. "Here's a list of all the parts I've ordered so far. I'll start disassembling her tomorrow. I haven't seen much rust, which is great. Once I get her into pieces, I can figure out exactly what needs replacing. For now, I've just been ordering the obvious stuff."

She handed him the printout. Qadir studied it, even as he was aware of the woman next to him. She was an interesting combination of confidence and insecurity.

He knew from personal experience that many people were uncomfortable around him at first. They did not know what was expected. He'd asked one of the American secretaries to help Maggie get settled, but only time would make his new mechanic comfortable in his presence.

He reminded himself that being comfortable wasn't required for her to complete the job.

She was nothing like the women who drifted in and out of his life. No designer clothes, no artfully arranged hair, no expensive perfumes and jewels. In a way she reminded him of Whitney. There had been no pretense with her, either.

He pushed the memory away before it formed, knowing there was no point in the remembering.

"I'll want to pull out the engine in the next couple of weeks," Maggie was saying. "You told me you could help with that." She paused. "Not physically, of course. I mean hiring people. Not that you're not terribly strong and manly." She groaned. "I didn't just say that."

Qadir laughed. "You did and it is a compliment I will treasure.

Not enough people comment on my manly strength. They should do so more often."

Maggie flushed. "You're making fun of me."

"Because you earned it."

"Hey, back off. You're the prince. I get to be a little nervous around you. This is a strange situation."

He liked that she didn't back down. "Fair enough. Yes, I have a team you can use to pull out the engine. I have several local resources. I will e-mail them to you. Mention my name—it will improve the response."

"Do you have a little crown logo you put in your signature line?" she asked.

"Only on formal documents. You may have to go to England for some of your purchases. I have contacts there, as well."

"Any of them with the royal family?"

"I doubt Prince Charles will be of much help."

"Just a thought."

"He's too old for you, and married."

Maggie laughed. "Thanks, but he's also not my type."

"Not looking for a handsome prince? Some of the women here have exactly that in mind. Or perhaps a foreign diplomat."

Maggie glanced away. "Not my style. Besides, I work with cars. Not exactly future princess material." She held out her weathered hands. "I'm more of a doer than someone who is comfortable just sitting around looking pretty."

"That is the monarchy's loss."

She laughed again. "Very smooth. You're good."

"Thank you."

"The women must be lined up for miles."

He smiled. "There's a waiting area over by the garden."

"I hope it's covered. You don't want them getting sunburned."

As she spoke she leaned against the desk. She was tall. He

couldn't see much of her shape under the coveralls she wore, but he remembered how she had looked the previous day and was intrigued. Curves and a personality, not to mention humor. How often did he find *that* combination?

A flicker of heat burst to life inside him, making him wonder how she would taste if he kissed her. Not that he was going to. He was far more interested in her abilities as a mechanic than her charms as a woman. But a man could wonder...

He amused himself by imagining his father's reaction if he were to start dating Maggie. Would the monarch be horrified, or would he be pleased to see yet another of his sons settling down? Not that it mattered. Speculation was one thing, but acting was another—and he had no plans to act.

"I come bearing food," Victoria said as she stepped into the garage. "One of the cooks told me you never get away for lunch. He assumes you don't appreciate his culinary masterpieces. Trust me, those are people you *don't* want to annoy."

Maggie straightened and set down her wrench, then pulled off her gloves. "Thanks for the warning. I've been so busy pulling everything apart, I haven't stopped to eat."

Victoria set the basket on a cart. "Let me guess. You're one of those annoying people who forgets to eat."

"Sometimes."

"Then we'll never be really, really close."

Maggie laughed. "I think you're a strong enough person to overlook that flaw. Come on. Let's go eat in my office. It's cleaner there."

While Maggie washed her hands in the small bathroom, Victoria set out their lunch. She'd brought a salad with walnuts, arugula and Gorgonzola. Several mini sandwiches on fresh foccacia bread, fruit, drinks and chocolate-chip cookies that were still warm.

"I thought I was supposed to avoid dessert," Maggie said as she took her seat.

Victoria settled in the one opposite. "It's your fault. I had to placate the cooks." She slipped off her high heels and wiggled her toes. "Heaven."

"Why do you wear those if they hurt?"

"They don't all hurt. Besides, without them, I feel short and unimpressive. Plus men really like women in high heels."

Maggie laughed. "I've never thought about being impressive. And I've never tried to get a man that way. By being attractive."

"You could in a heartbeat," Victoria told her as she speared a piece of lettuce. "I would kill for your bone structure."

The compliment pleased Maggie. She'd always thought of herself as a tomboy. Girls like Victoria usually avoided her.

"How is it working with Qadir?" Victoria asked.

"Great. He really wants me to make the car perfect, which is what I want, too. I love not having a budget. It's very freeing. The progress is going to be slow at first, which he understands. I appreciate that. He's—"

She pressed her lips together as Victoria raised her eyebrows. "What?" Maggie asked.

"Nothing. I'm glad he's an excellent boss."

"That's what you asked me."

"I meant as a man."

"Oh." Maggie grabbed a sandwich. "He's fine."

Victoria laughed. "He's a sheik prince worth billions. He's one of the most sought-after bachelors in the world and all you can say is he's fine?"

Maggie grinned. "How about really fine?"

"Better, but still. You're really not interested in him."

"Not as anything but the man who pays me."

"Interesting. Then I guess you won't be angling for an invitation to the ball."

Maggie nearly choked. "There's going to be a ball?"

"Uh-huh. To celebrate Prince As'ad's engagement to Kayleen. They've been together for a while now, but no one was supposed to know. The official announcement was put off until Princess Lina, the king's sister, married King Hassan of Baharia a few weeks ago. Anyway, the ball is where the news is made public and everyone who works in the palace is invited. Apparently when the guest list is a thousand, what's a couple hundred more?"

"I've never been to a ball," Maggie admitted. Her only frame of reference was cartoons with princesses as stars and she hadn't really been into watching them.

"Me, either, but I'm very excited. It's sort of a once-in-a-lifetime chance to wear a formal gown and dance with a handsome prince. I'll be hoping Nadim finally sees me as a person and not his efficient secretary."

"But you don't love him," Maggie said.

"I know. I wasn't kidding before—love is for suckers. But if he offered me a sensible marriage of convenience, I sure wouldn't say no. I think I could be a good wife to him. Better than some of those plastic bimbos his father parades around the palace. Anyway, my point is, you should come to the ball. It will be great fun. You can tell your grandchildren about it."

Maggie wasn't exactly tempted, although the idea was a little intriguing. She'd come to El Deharia to get away, but also to experience something new in her life.

"I'm not much of a dancer."

"They lead, you follow. I have an appointment to try on dresses. Come with me. It'll get you in the mood."

"I don't think so. I haven't actually been invited."

"You will be. Ask Qadir."

"Ask me what?"

They both turned and found the prince in her office. Victoria started to stand, which told Maggie she should be doing the same. Qadir waved them both back into their seats.

"Ask me what?" he repeated.

"I was telling Maggie about the ball celebrating Prince As'ad's engagement. As all live-in employees are invited, Maggie said she would love to come."

Maggie scrambled to her feet. "I didn't. I'm not interested in the ball." She knew Victoria meant well but she, Maggie, didn't want Qadir thinking she was using him or their relationship. She motioned to the coveralls she wore. "I'm not exactly ball material."

Qadir nodded slowly. "Perhaps not today," he said slowly. "But I see possibilities."

"That's what I was saying," Victoria told him.

Possibilities? What did that mean?

Maggie told herself not to read too much into the word. Besides, what did she care about Qadir's opinion on anything but the car? He was just some guy. Royal, but still.

"I already have some dresses ordered," Victoria continued. "I could have them send a few more in Maggie's impossibly skinny size. With her hair up and in high heels, she could be a princess."

Maggie glared at her friend. What was Victoria up to?

"I agree." Qadir nodded. "Maggie, you will attend the ball."

With that, he turned and left.

Maggie waited until she was sure they were alone, then glared at Victoria. "What were you doing?"

"Throwing you in the path of a handsome prince. My quest for a royal connection has failed miserably, but that doesn't mean you can't be successful."

"But I'm not interested in him that way." She didn't think she would ever be interested in another man. Loving and losing Jon had been too painful.

"Can you honestly look at me and tell me you aren't the tiniest bit excited by the thought of dressing up in fancy clothes and dancing with Qadir?"

"We'll dance?"

"See! You're interested."

"No. It's just I've never done anything like that."

"All the more reason to do it," Victoria told her. "Come on— it will be fun. We'll both be fabulous and the princes won't be able to resist us."

Maggie had a feeling she would always be resistible, but allowed herself to momentarily wonder what it would be like to dance with a prince.

Chapter Three

"What is the longest river in America?" the guy on the radio asked.

"The Missouri," Maggie said as she undid the first screw in the window cranks from the door. "The Mississippi is the biggest, but the Missouri is the longest."

"Ah, the Mississippi," the contestant said.

"No, that's not it."

"Ha!" Maggie crowed as she set the screw into the small labeled plastic container next to her. "You have to pay attention in school."

"Or have a mind for trivia," Qadir said from his place at her desk.

She looked at the open office door and sighed. "You can hear me?"

"Obviously."

The American radio station in El Deharia ran a quiz every afternoon at two. She'd gotten in the habit of listening. Usually she was alone.

But today Qadir had stopped by to check out the parts list she'd put together. She'd sort of forgotten he was still in her office.

At least she'd gotten the answer right, she told herself. It beat getting it wrong.

Qadir stepped out into the garage. "You'll need access to a machine shop," he said.

"Along with a good machinist. I can explain what I want, but I can't make it myself."

She was rebuilding the engine rather than buying a new one. Unfortunately time had not been kind to many of the original parts and replacements were difficult, sometimes impossible, to find. She would buy what she could and have the others custom-made.

She smiled. "I'm sure you have contacts for me."

"I do."

"I figured. The thrill of being royal."

"There are many."

"I can't imagine."

"It is all I know. But there are disadvantages. My brothers and I were sent away to English boarding school when we were eight or nine. The headmaster was determined to treat us as if we were regular students. It was an adjustment, to say the least."

"Doesn't sound like fun," she admitted, grateful for her normal life. "Were the other boys friendly?"

"Some of them. Some were resentful, and eager to show us they were stronger."

"Bullies." She went to work on the second screw.

"Sometimes. My brothers and I learned how to fit in very quickly."

"At least you had a palace to come home to."

"And a pony."

She laughed. "Of course. Every royal child deserves a pony. I had to make do with a stuffed one. It was one of the few girly toys I liked. I was more into doing things with my dad than hanging out with the other little girls in the neighborhood. I hated playing dolls. I wasn't very popular."

"Until the boys got old enough to appreciate you."

He was being kind, or assuming something that wasn't true. Either way, she didn't know how to respond. That combined with a particularly stubborn screw caused her to slip and jam the screwdriver into the side of her hand.

"Ouch," she yelped and set down the screwdriver. Blood welled up.

Qadir was at her side in an instant, taking her hand in his. "What have you done?"

His touch was warm and sure. "Ah, nothing. I'm fine."

"You're bleeding."

Still holding her hand, he led her to the small bathroom and turned on the water. "Is it serious? Will you need stitches?"

Stitches? Just the thought of a needle piercing her flesh was enough to make her woozy. "Not if I haven't cut anything off."

She pulled free of his touch and shoved her hand under the water. The wound stung, but wasn't too bad. She managed to rub on some soap without screaming too loudly, then held still as he applied a bandage he'd found in the medicine cabinet. He was surprisingly competent at the task.

When he'd finished, he took her hand again and examined it. "I think you will survive."

"Good to know." Even not thinking about the needle, she felt a little lightheaded. How strange.

Maybe it was the bathroom itself. The space was pretty tight and Qadir took up a lot of room. But even all that didn't explain the sudden thumping of her heart or the way she couldn't seem to catch her breath.

She was aware of the flecks of gold in his dark eyes and couldn't stop staring at the shape of his mouth which was, by the way, a very nice mouth. They were close enough for her to inhale the crisp, clean, masculine scent of him.

He smiled at her. "You will be more careful next time?"

She nodded without speaking.

"Excellent. I must return to my office."

He released her hand and walked away. Maggie stayed where she was, her body oddly tense, her fingers tingling despite the pain from the cut.

What had just happened? She couldn't seem to focus and the few thoughts that did pop into her brain seemed unrelated to anything. The tiny puncture wound couldn't be responsible and there was no way she'd lost a significant amount of blood. It was the weirdest thing.

She looked toward the garage to where Qadir had stood only moments before. This couldn't be about him, could it? She wasn't attracted to her boss. It was a recipe for disaster. She knew better. And even if she didn't, she was still mourning the fact that she and Jon weren't together. She wasn't interested in anyone else. She couldn't be.

Maggie stared at the rack of elegant, sophisticated, *expensive* gowns and felt as if she'd stepped into a movie star's dressing room.

"I thought they'd be like prom dresses," she admitted. "These are real gowns."

"I know," Victoria said with a sigh. "They're beautiful."

"I can't afford them."

"Neither can I. Fortunately we get a discount."

Unless it was an ninety-five percent discount, there was no way Maggie could buy one of these dresses. She needed the money to buy back her father's business. She couldn't waste a few thousand dollars on a dress she would wear once.

"Still," she murmured, not sure how to explain to her friend that there was no way this was happening.

Victoria patted her arm. "You have to trust me. I don't want to endanger my IRA any more than you do. These are to give us ideas only. Then we're heading into the back."

"What's in the back?"

Victoria laughed. "I can see you're not going to trust me. Come on. I'll show you."

They walked through the elegant boutique with the plush carpeting and soothing music. At the rear of the store, they stepped past heavy curtains and found themselves in a plain corridor. Victoria walked purposefully toward a simple door. She pushed it open and then moved to the side.

"Prepare to be amazed," she said.

Maggie stepped inside. There were dozens of racks, all crammed with beautiful clothes. Pantsuits and dresses, blouses, skirts.

"I don't get it. Why are these here?" she asked.

"Consignment," Victoria told her in a low, amused voice. "The very rich and elegant bring their barely worn clothes here where hardworking young women can buy them for pennies on the dollar. How do you think I can afford to dress like I do? I get a four-hundred-dollar blouse for all of fifty dollars. You can find anything here and the quality is amazing. I love this place. Seriously, the evening wear is discounted the most because so few people have any interest in it. The stuff is practically free."

That was a discount Maggie could get behind. "They really have ball gowns here?"

"They have everything. Because I'm short and chubby, I'll

be buying used. You, on the other hand, are tall and willowy so you can probably squeeze your tiny butt into a sample. Not that I'm bitter."

Maggie grinned. "Willowy is a nice way to say flat chested."

Victoria wove through the dozens of racks until she found one with her name on it. She quickly sorted through the dresses and handed Maggie six.

"Now we try them on," Victoria said.

Maggie took them into the large dressing room on the left while her friend took the one on the right. As she pulled off her jeans and her T-shirt, she had trouble believing she was really trying on dresses for an actual ball. Three weeks ago, she'd been attempting to sort out her life in Aspen. How could so much have changed so quickly?

Unable to find the answer, she pulled on the first dress. It was peach, with a fitted bodice and a tiered skirt that fell in waves of shimmering fabric. Victoria ripped back the curtain and sucked in her breath.

"I knew you'd look fabulous. That dress is amazing."

"It's unusual," Maggie said, facing her reflection. She had to admit that the color was good for her, but she wasn't sure about the fluffy skirt.

"It's couture, honey, and when it looks that good, you say a little prayer. I, of course, am hanging out everywhere and will have to pay to get this sucker hemmed."

Victoria's dress was black, strapless and fit her like it had been painted on. Maggie did her best not to be bitter about the curves spilling over the top. But hemming would be required. At least six inches of fabric bunched on the floor.

"Nadim won't be able to resist you," she said honestly.

"Aren't you sweet? He's managed to resist me very well so far, but I'm not going to think about that. Instead I'm going to talk you into that dress. You'll be dazzling. I know you're not interested in Qadir, but there will be plenty of handsome, successful men at the ball. You can dazzle them instead."

For a second Maggie wondered if Jon would be dazzled. Then she reminded herself she wasn't going to think about him anymore. Not that way.

In truth, she didn't want to be involved with him. She just missed him.

"Uh-oh," Victoria said as she put her hands on her hips. "What aren't you telling me? There's a guy, isn't there? I can tell just by looking at you."

"There's no guy," Maggie told her.

Victoria kept staring.

"Okay, maybe there's half a guy."

"Interesting. Which half?"

That made Maggie laugh. "I mean I'm only half involved. Or less, even. I keep telling myself Jon is just a habit."

"A bad one, I'm guessing."

"We grew up next door to each other, so I've known him all my life. In high school, we started dating. Everyone assumed we would always be together."

"Including you," Victoria said.

Maggie nodded. "Then we started drifting apart. I think we both sensed the change, but neither of us wanted to be the first one to say anything. Then my dad got sick. By then we knew it was over, but Jon didn't want to break up while I was dealing with my dad's death, so the relationship went on longer than it should have."

She drew in a breath. "The thing is, we've been best friends forever. That's the part that's hard to give up. I miss talking to him. But he's with someone else and the truth is, we're not best friends anymore."

Victoria gave her a hug. "I'm sorry. That has to be hard. You lost your guy and your dad so close together. It's okay to take the time to deal with that."

"I know. I'm just ready to be over him."

"Love sucks the big one," Victoria said firmly. "It's why I'm never giving away my heart. I want a sensible arrangement with a man who is all about security and convention."

Maggie was surprised. Victoria seemed spontaneous and fun loving. "Won't that be boring for you?"

"Nope. I want safe and practical. Did you know it's a really big deal for a prince to divorce? So they never do. I like that in a man."

"Part of Nadim's charm?" Maggie asked.

Her friend nodded. "A lot of it. Plus, my dad can be…difficult." Victoria shrugged. "Having a prince on my side would really help."

Maggie sensed there were a lot of secrets in Victoria's past, but she didn't want to pry. The other woman would tell her when she was ready.

"I'm going to think about not making a fool of myself," Maggie muttered. "Is there a book or brochure telling us how we're supposed to act and stuff, because I could use some pointers."

Victoria grinned. "I'll see what I can find. It will be practice for when we attend the wedding."

A royal wedding? "I don't think I'll still be here," Maggie told her. "I should have the car done in less than two months."

"The wedding is in six weeks. Apparently As'ad is very anxious to claim his bride. So you'll get to be there. If nothing else, you can fly back to dance at mine."

Standing in the dressing area of her suite, Maggie stared at the peach dress practically floating on the hanger. Victoria *had* been right. It was the perfect choice.

On the floor by the fluffy hem was a shopping bag containing a pair of high-heeled sandals and an evening bag, also purchased from the consignment room at the boutique.

"I'm really going to a royal ball," Maggie murmured to herself, unable to believe it was happening. She was just some mechanic from Colorado. Stuff like that didn't happen to her.

She tucked her hands into her pockets to keep herself from reaching for the phone. The need to call Jon was powerful and she wanted to resist. While they had both claimed they would always be friends, the truth was, they weren't. Not the way they had been.

Everything was different and there was no going back. Everything was—

The phone rang. Maggie jumped, then walked into the living room and picked up the receiver.

"Hello?"

"You're hard to track down."

The familiar voice stole the strength from her legs. She sank onto the sofa and tried to remember to breathe.

"Jon. Is everything okay?"

"Sure. I'm calling to check on you. I haven't heard from you and wanted to make sure everything was all right."

"I'm fine," she told him. "Everything is fine."

Which it was—so why was she suddenly fighting tears?

Probably the loneliness, she told herself. She missed her dad and she missed Jon.

"You sure?" he asked.

"Of course. Work on the car is going really well and you'll never guess. There's going to be a royal ball here, and I've been invited."

"Good for you."

"It's kind of a strange thing, but I think it will be fun. And I've made a few friends. There's a great secretary here who is also

American. We've been hanging out together." Maggie talked a little more about her life then said, "How are things there?"

"Busy. It's quarterly season and you know what that means."

She did. Jon was a corporate accountant. While she couldn't relate to his world of numbers and reports, she knew he liked it.

"How's Elaine?" she asked, because the alternative was to say that she missed him and she refused to go there.

He hesitated. "Maggie, I..."

"I'm allowed to ask and you're supposed to answer," she told him. "Don't we at least have that much left?"

"It's not that. I hate how things ended between us. I want it to be better and I'm not sure talking about Elaine is the best way for that to happen."

Heat burned on her cheeks. She knew he was thinking about the last night they'd been together. When she'd called him sobbing about her father and he'd come over, because that's the kind of man he was. Then she'd kissed him and...

She pushed the memory away. In theory, they were equally at fault. It wasn't as if Jon had said no. But somehow she always felt that she was the one to blame.

"I've let it go," she told him and realized she meant it. She still felt stupid, but she wasn't longing for a repeat performance. "You've let it go. We're moving on. So answer the question. How's Elaine?"

"Good. Great. We're spending a lot of time together."

She could hear his affection in his voice. Maybe it was more than affection; maybe it was love.

"I'm glad," she said firmly. "You deserve someone great in your life."

"You, too. But watch out for those princes at the ball. They play by different rules."

That made her smile. "I'm hardly in danger, Jon."

"You're exactly what they're looking for."

She glanced at her scarred hands and thought about the long days she spent in a garage working on cars. She doubted a lot of princes dreamed about a woman like her. "If you say so."

They talked for a few more minutes, then said goodbye and hung up. As Maggie replaced the phone, she realized she didn't hurt as much as she thought she would. That talking to him had actually been...nice.

She probed her heart, trying to figure out if she had regrets that things were over between them. There was tenderness there, but it was a whole lot more about missing her friend than missing her lover. Maybe she hadn't been lying when she'd said they'd both moved on. And wouldn't that be a good thing?

"They're not comfortable," Maggie grumbled as Victoria rolled her hair with heated curlers.

"Beauty is pain. Suck it up, honey."

Maggie eyed her friend. Victoria was a blond stunner, with her hair piled on top of her head and makeup emphasizing her beautiful features.

"So you practically had to cut off a leg to look like that?" Maggie teased.

Victoria laughed. "What a sweet thing to say. Hold on to that thought because when I'm done with your hair, I'm going to pluck your eyebrows."

"I don't think so."

"You're going to have to trust me."

An hour later Maggie stared at herself in the mirror. "Wow."

"I know. You had all that potential just lurking. Maybe now you'll take a second or two and put on mascara in the morning."

Maggie knew that was never going to happen, but she had to say she'd cleaned up a lot better than she'd ever imagined she could.

Her hair had been pinned up in a loose style that allowed a few curls to tumble down to her shoulders. Makeup made her eyes look big and her mouth all pouty. Victoria had lent her a pair of dangling earrings that sparkled, and the dress fit her perfectly, emphasizing the few curves she had.

"I like it," she said slowly, then shifted her weight and winced. "But the shoes are killing me and don't say beauty is pain again."

"You'll get used to them." Victoria linked arms with her and stared at their reflection. "Damn. I'm still short."

"You're gorgeous."

"We both are."

Her friend was being generous, Maggie thought, but she was in the mood to accept the compliment.

There was a knock at the door. The two women looked at each other.

"It's your room," Victoria pointed out. "So I'm not expecting anyone."

Maggie walked to the door, nearly falling off her high heels as she moved. She opened the door and found Qadir standing there.

"Good evening," he said. "I am here to escort you two ladies to the ball."

Maggie stared at the handsome prince in his tuxedo. He looked perfect, but then he always did. "Really? That's so nice. Thank you. We're about ready."

She stopped talking and held in a groan. *That's so nice?* Could she have said something more stupid?

He stepped into the suite. "Hello, Victoria."

"Prince Qadir. You're looking especially royal this evening."

He smiled. "Thank you. You're both very beautiful."

Victoria grabbed Maggie's arm and pulled her into the bedroom. "You know he's here for you, don't you? I'm just a pity date."

"What? No. He's not. He's my boss."

"So he's carrying on a time-honored tradition. Be careful, Maggie. You lead with your heart."

Maggie rolled her eyes. "Please. Qadir isn't here for me. He's just being polite."

"Uh-huh. Do you see Nadim being polite and taking me to the party? Qadir is intrigued and when the man in question is a prince, you need to be careful."

Maggie appreciated her friend's warning, but there was no need. Qadir would never see her as anything other than his employee. Not that she wanted him to.

The two women collected their evening bags and returned to the living room. Qadir escorted them both downstairs and led them to the elevator.

When the doors opened on the main floor, she could hear music. There were dozens of people in the wide hallway, all moving toward the massive open doors at the far end.

There were lights everywhere. Bright chandeliers and sconces illuminated the well-dressed crowd. More people pushed toward them and Maggie found herself separated from Qadir and Victoria.

She didn't mind. Victoria's well-meaning advice had made her a little uncomfortable. Qadir didn't see her as a woman and she wasn't about to get any ideas about him. Sure, he'd been great about the car and he was easy to work for, but there was nothing between them.

She pushed Victoria's words to the back of her mind and concentrated on the beauty of the ballroom.

There was a dais at one end, with an orchestra playing. There were dozens and dozens of food tables scattered around the outside of the room with an equal number of bars between them. Guests pressed together, talking and laughing.

The women were so beautiful, Maggie thought, not sure where to look first. Regardless of their ages, they were stunning in amazing gowns and glittering jewels.

She reached up and touched the earrings Victoria had loaned her. The stones were glass, the gold merely a colored finish. But that didn't matter. No one had to know they weren't real or that she'd bought her gown on consignment. For tonight, she was attending a royal ball and she planned to enjoy herself.

She waited in line to get a glass of champagne, then sipped the bubbly liquid. People stood in groups around her, talking loudly. Some of the conversations were in English, but many were not. She recognized a few of the languages.

She moved closer to a large plant and wished she hadn't agreed to the high-heeled sandals Victoria had insisted on. She'd only been at the ball a few minutes and her feet already hurt.

Maggie glanced around to make sure no one was paying any attention to her, then she eased back behind the plant, slipped out of her shoes and bent down to grab them. She'd just started tucking them out of sight in the planter when someone came up behind her and said, "I'm not sure the king would approve."

She spun and saw Qadir standing behind her. His expression was stern, but humor gleamed in his eyes.

"They hurt my feet," she told him.

"Then make sure you hide them so no one can find them."

She laughed and slipped the shoes under a couple of large leaves.

"Better?" he asked.

"Much."

"Have you danced yet?"

"No."

Before she could explain she didn't know how, he'd taken her glass from her and set it on a nearby tray, then led her toward the dance floor.

"I'm not very good at this sort of thing," she admitted.

He pulled her into his arms. "I am good enough for both of us."

He was warm and strong and held her securely. She rested one hand on his shoulder, her tiny evening bag held in her fingers. Her other hand nestled in his. He moved purposefully, guiding her with a confidence that allowed her to believe that maybe she *could* dance after all.

"See?" he said.

"Don't test me with anything fancy. Not unless you want people pointing and laughing."

He chuckled. "Are you always so honest?"

"Most of the time. I try to be."

"You are charming."

"Really?" The word came out before she could stop it. "Sorry. I meant to say thank you."

"So polite."

"It's how I was raised," she told him. "You're very nice, too."

"Less arrogant than you'd imagined?"

"Something like that. Although you have your imperious moments. Am I allowed to say that?"

"Tonight you can say anything."

Was he flirting with her? Was that flirting?

She wanted to believe it was. After spending her entire life as a tomboy, it was nice to be girly for once. Not that she would want to make a habit of all the torture Victoria had put her through.

"I like your country," she said. "The parts I've seen are very beautiful."

"The city is more modern than many parts of El Deharia. Out in the desert the people still live as they once did."

"I think I like my modern conveniences too much for that," she admitted.

"I agree. One of my brothers has chosen to live there permanently, but not me. I, too, want my conveniences."

They moved together in time with the music, swaying and sliding and turning together. She stumbled once, but he caught her against him. Then they were touching from shoulder to knee, pressed intimately as they moved.

She raised her gaze to his, not sure if this was allowed or appropriate. He was a prince, after all. But he didn't seem to mind and she found herself enjoying the contact, maybe more than she should.

It was the dance, she told herself. The night, not the man. But the faint tingles in the pit of her stomach warned her that maybe it was the man. Just a little.

"Are you homesick?" he asked.

"Not tonight."

"But other days?"

"A little. I think being here has been good for me."

"New adventures?"

She nodded. Tonight was certainly that.

The song ended. Maggie felt a jolt of disappointment as Qadir released her, followed by a distinct coolness. As if all the warmth had faded away.

She found herself wanting him to pull her close again. She'd liked being in his arms.

Victoria's words of warning flashed into her brain. While Maggie didn't agree that she led with her heart, she was smart enough to realize that regardless of how good Qadir looked in a tux and how much she'd liked dancing with him, he was light-years out of her league. All tingles aside, nothing was going to happen.

She started to excuse herself when they were interrupted by a tall, older man who looked oddly familiar.

"There you are," the man said. "I've been looking for you."

"Father, may I introduce Maggie Collins. Maggie, my father, King Mukhtar of El Deharia."

Chapter Four

K-king? As in *king?*

Maggie stood frozen, not sure if she should curtsy—not that she knew how—or bolt. Worse, she was barefoot. She couldn't meet the king when she wasn't wearing shoes.

"Lovely to meet you," the king said, not even looking at her. "Qadir, I want you to meet Sabrina and her sister Natalie. Their uncle is a duke. British, of course. Well-educated." The king moved closer to Qadir and lowered his voice. "Pretty enough, they seem to have decent heads on their shoulders. Their older sister already has two children, so we know they're breeders."

Maggie still couldn't move but the shock had been replaced by humor. She was terrified that if she did anything at all, she would break out into hysterical laughter.

It wasn't just the king's matter-of-fact description of the two

potential brides that made her want to giggle—it was the look
of long-suffering on Qadir's face.

Apparently being a prince had more than its share of stresses.

When she was sure she could control herself, she eased back,
pausing only to look at the two young women hovering just out
of earshot. They were pretty, she thought humorously, and hey,
known breeders. When one had to worry about the continuation of the royal line, that was probably important.

She was about to turn away when Qadir glanced at her.
"You're not leaving." It sounded a whole lot more like a
command than a question.

"Um, surely you want to dance with one of the duke's nieces,"
she murmured. "Sabrina is especially lovely."

"Exactly," the king said, smiling at her. "That's what I thought."

Qadir stepped closer to her and spoke quietly. "You have no
idea which one is Sabrina."

"They're both very pretty. And reasonably intelligent. What
more could you ask for?"

He started to say something else, but his father pulled him
away.

Maggie took another step back as she watched the introductions. She was willing to admit to a slight twinge of envy, but
this was for the best. Better to remember who Qadir was and
where he was going than to allow a single dance to mess with
her head.

Still, it had been a very nice dance, she thought wistfully. It
had reminded her she was still alive and capable of tingles.
Which probably meant she was nearly over Jon. A good thing,
if a little sad.

She watched as Qadir spoke with both women, then led one
off to dance.

"Good luck," she murmured. "It's not going to work."

Unfortunately as she spoke, the music faded and one of the sisters—Natalie, she would guess—flounced away.

"What is not going to work?" the king asked Maggie.

"I, ah—" She looked around frantically for a way to escape. "Ah, nothing."

"It is not nothing. It is important that all my sons marry. As they seem to be in no hurry to find a bride on their own, I am forced to interfere."

Maggie remembered what Victoria had said about the beheading and hoped the other woman had been kidding.

"You can't lead a woman to him like that," she said cautiously. "Not that your choices aren't lovely, lovely young women."

The king glared at her. "I assume you have a reason for saying that."

"Because men like the chase." Jon had told her all about it several times. They'd laughed about his friends and their disastrous love lives, secure in the comfort of their own relationship. "Did you see the movie *Jurassic Park?*"

"No."

"You should rent it. Or have it delivered or something. Men are like the T-Rex. They don't want their next meal handed to them. They want to hunt it down. By meal I mean—"

"Women. Yes, I understand the analogy." He looked out at the couples dancing then turned back to her. "You're sure of this?"

"Sort of." At the moment she wasn't sure of anything except she really wanted to be done talking to the king.

"Who is he hunting now? You?"

"What? No. No. Not at all. I work for him."

The king frowned. "Doing what?"

"Restoring a car." She held out her hands to show him the scars and calluses. "See? I'm not anyone. Really."

"For not anyone, you're very free with your opinions. Come with me."

He started walking without once glancing back to see if she was keeping up with him. Maggie entertained a brief thought at ducking away, then she reminded herself she lived at the palace. Total escape was impossible and she really did want to keep her job.

The king stopped and motioned her forward.

"Do you know any of these people?" he asked.

She looked at the unfamiliar faces, then shook her head.

What followed was a rapid set of introductions to people she'd only read about in the newspaper, including two American senators, a impossibly thin starlet and the Russian ambassador to El Deharia.

Maggie murmured greetings and tried to ignore the fact that she was barefoot. Thank God her gown trailed onto the floor and no one could see. Still, she couldn't help covering one foot with the other, as if to hide the truth.

Conversation flowed for a few minutes, ranging from a recent Grand Prix time trial to the continuing rise in oil prices. Maggie kept her mouth firmly closed and wished for someone to rescue her. Unfortunately she was on her own.

Then the Russian ambassador, a handsome older man, smiled at her. "May I have this dance, Miss Collins?"

Everyone looked at her. Maggie did her best not to blush. "Thank you, sir. It would be a pleasure."

At least she hoped it would be. If he danced as well as Qadir, she wouldn't have a problem.

He took her hand and led her to the dance floor. The music began and they were moving together. It wasn't as easy as it had been with Qadir, and not nearly as exciting, but she didn't step on him or stumble.

"You are friends with the king?" he asked.

"We've just met."

"So you are not his mistress?"

Maggie did stumble over that. She steadied herself. "No." The next word should have been *ick* but that wasn't appropriate. "I work here, at the palace, Mr. Ambassador."

"I see. You may call me Vlad."

Did she have to?

"I am a powerful man, Maggie. We could be good for each other."

Her shock must have showed because he chuckled. "You are surprised by my honesty?"

Not exactly, she thought. Was it just her or was the whole thing really tacky?

"Mr. Ambassador—"

"Vlad."

She ignored that. "Mr. Ambassador, I'm afraid you have the wrong idea about me."

She had plenty more she wanted to say, but just then Qadir appeared at her side. "Maggie. There you are. Our dance is next." He smiled at the Russian. "Do you mind if I cut in?"

Vlad stepped back. "Of course not."

Qadir drew her against him. "What happened?"

"Nothing."

He waited. She sighed. "I think he was coming on to me. I'm not sure."

"He was."

"Yuck."

Qadir laughed. "He would not be flattered by your reaction."

"I barely know the man."

"He is powerful. For many women that is enough."

Then those women needed to get a life, she thought. "I didn't know what to say."

"You can start with no. That usually works."

"I'll remember that." Not that she was likely to run into any more ambassadors. "How was your dance with Sabrina?"

Qadir's gaze narrowed. "Are you mocking me?"

"Maybe a little. But she is a known breeder."

He moved them off the dance floor and out onto a balcony. The stone floor was cool on her bare feet.

"For you this situation is amusing," he grumbled. "For me it is anything but. I do not want an arranged marriage to a sensible young woman from a good family."

"Then what *do* you want?"

Qadir didn't answer. Was it that he didn't know or was he simply not prepared to share his private thoughts with her?

"Can the king force you into marriage?" she asked instead.

"No. But he can be difficult."

"He cares about you and it's not totally crazy that he wants his sons married. I'm sure he's more than ready for grandchildren."

"You're taking his side?" Qadir asked.

"No. I'm pointing out that while his tactics are a little obvious, he means well. He cares, which should be worth something."

"If he were to turn his considerable interest on getting *you* married, I suspect you would change your mind."

"Maybe," she murmured thinking she wouldn't mind a little meddling from her own father. It would mean he was still around to bug her. Right now that sounded lovely.

"So he wants a good breeder," she said, "and you want to fall in love?"

"Love is not required. I would settle for mutual respect and shared interests."

Neither sounded very romantic, Maggie thought, but then

she wasn't royal. She wanted a lot more than that. Passion, excitement. She wanted to be swept away. She wanted a deep love that would last forever.

Qadir walked around the edge of the dance floor, both watching Maggie dance with his cousin and avoiding Sabrina, Natalie and any other woman of whom his father would approve.

Nadim danced with Maggie as he did everything in his life—with great competence and little real interest.

Nadim was sensible. In truth he lacked personality. Even as a child, Nadim had been boring.

Qadir, As'ad and Kateb had been close, always getting into trouble together, playing tricks on unsuspecting palace staff and causing their father to constantly threaten them with banishment. Nadim had always followed the rules.

Even now, as the song ended, Nadim bowed politely to Maggie, then turned away, never once noticing her bare feet or the way she adjusted her dress to make sure no one caught sight of her toes.

His gaze shifted to the left where he saw Natalie—or was it Sabrina?—glancing around the room as if searching for someone. He moved deeper into the crowd.

While he was pleased his brother As'ad was celebrating his engagement to Kayleen, Qadir wished only for the ball to be over. If he had to meet one more "appropriate" young woman, he would ride into the desert and join his brother Kateb, living in the villages, far from the palace.

It wasn't that he objected to marriage…at least not in theory. But practice was a different matter. While he wasn't waiting for the fantasy of falling in love, he wanted to feel *something* when he chose his future wife. Anticipation would be good. Pleasure.

Even a comfortable level of fondness. So far, he hadn't felt anything.

He'd been in love once, he reminded himself, and once had been enough. He wasn't interested in love, as he'd told Maggie, but he insisted on something more than simple disinterest in a marriage of convenience.

He saw As'ad bend down and say something to Kayleen. They looked happy. Not only had his brother found the right woman, but he'd managed to get their father off his back. If only Qadir could do that, as well.

What he needed was an engagement, he told himself. Or at the very least, a serious relationship. While he knew dozens of women who would be interested, he found himself not the least bit intrigued by any of them. One of life's ironies, he supposed.

He saw Maggie move toward the buffet. She ignored the caviar and went right for the tiny quiches. She popped one in her mouth, then licked her fingers.

The action was quick and unstudied, yet he found it erotic. The flick of her tongue against her skin made him think of doing the same to her himself. All over.

The heat that accompanied the thought was nearly as surprising as the image now planted in his brain. Maggie? Sexy?

She was competent and he enjoyed speaking with her. He liked teasing her and the sound of her laugh, but nothing more. She worked for him. She wasn't the type of woman who played his kind of game. She was…

Perfect, he thought as he studied her. Sensible, hardworking and not the least bit pretentious. While she hadn't come out and said money was an issue in her life, he knew she'd wanted the job because of the high fee involved. Was she willing to sell other services that might help him distract his father?

* * *

"It's almost like Christmas," Maggie breathed as she stared at the stack of boxes waiting right outside her office. She'd arrived a little late this morning. The party had gone on long into the night and she'd stayed far later than she'd expected. It had made getting up with her alarm a bit of a challenge. But now that she was here, she stared at the packages and forgot to be tired.

She wasn't sure where to start, she thought happily as she dug through her desk for a utility knife to slit open the first box. There were so many choices, so many possibilities.

"You look happy."

She turned and saw Qadir walking toward her. While the tux was gone, he still looked pretty darned good in his tailored suit.

"I love fast delivery," she said, pointing to all the boxes. "It's like a miracle. I don't know where to start. There are so many possibilities. Headlights, gears, pistons, brackets."

He stared at her for a long time. "You're a very unusual woman."

"I know. I've heard that before." She found the utility knife and moved toward the first box. It was small and light. The possibilities were endless!

She pressed the knife to the seam, then looked at him. "You want to open the first one?"

"Not especially."

"Okay." She slit the tape, then dug into the box. She pulled out the clear plastic bag within. "O-rings. Aren't they beautiful?"

Qadir laughed. "As I said—unusual. I would like to speak to you for a moment, Maggie."

"Okay."

She put the O-rings back in the box and followed Qadir into her office, where she settled on the corner of her desk and looked at him.

She told herself it was silly to be nervous. She hadn't done much on the car yet so it was unlikely he was upset about anything. Not that he looked upset. His expression was as unreadable as ever, although not in a hostile way. He looked very...princelike. And handsome, she thought absently, liking the firm set of his jaw and the way his eyes seemed to see so much more than they should.

"What do you think of me?" he asked.

The unexpected question made her blink. "Um, what?"

"We get along, do we not?"

Was that a trick question? "Yes."

"Good. I agree."

With what? What were they talking about?

"We have much in common," he continued.

That nearly made her laugh. What did they have in common? A love of fine Arabian horses? Jetsetting around the world? Hardly.

"Cars," he added. "We both like cars."

"Okay," she said slowly. "Sure. Cars."

"I mention this because I was thinking about your business back home."

The one she'd lost, she thought sadly. "It's not exactly what it was," she told him.

"The loss of your father would have changed things."

More than he knew. "It was hard while he was sick. He was in the hospital a lot and I was with him. It was hard to stay on top of things."

"Of course. When you return, you'll have more time."

She nodded, thinking she would also have a fair amount of money, although not enough to buy back the business. Still, she could start over with her own small shop. Continue the work.

"More money would help," he said.

"It usually does." A hopeful thought appeared. "You have a second car?"

"Not exactly."

"Then…"

"I have a proposition."

If she'd looked anything like Victoria, she would have assumed he was coming on to her. However, she stood there in coveralls that had been patched more than once, no makeup and her hair pulled back in an uneven ponytail.

"Which is?"

Qadir smiled. "You may have noticed my father's enthusiastic efforts to interest me in a woman. Any woman. He's determined to get all his sons married as quickly as possible."

"Typical father behavior," she said, then grinned. "Well, not counting the whole 'good breeder' part of the introduction."

"Exactly. I am not interested in being pressured. However, the only way to get my father to back off is to give him the impression I'm involved with someone and that it might be serious."

She nodded. "That would probably work."

"I'm glad you agree. So I propose an arrangement between us. We would date for a period of weeks. Perhaps three or four months, then say we are engaged. Nothing would be formally announced, of course, although there would be hints. Then a few weeks after that, we would have a heated argument, you would return to your country and I, heartbroken, couldn't possibly consider getting involved again for the rest of the year. Perhaps longer."

She opened her mouth, then closed it. His words had actually entered her brain—she knew she'd heard them. But they hadn't made any sense. He couldn't be saying what she thought he was saying.

"I… You… It's…"

He smiled. "A relationship of convenience," he said. "You will consent to be someone I become involved with for an agreed upon period of time—say, six months. I will, of course, pay you for your time."

He named an amount that made her already spinning head threaten to fall off and explode.

He wanted to fake *date?* Then get fake engaged to her? And *pay* her? All in an attempt to trick his father, the king?

"If he finds out about this, he'd kill me."

"Not in the traditional sense. He would be unhappy."

Not exactly comforting, Maggie thought. "Just go out with one of the women he introduces you to. Why won't that work?"

"None of them interest me."

"Sabrina seemed really nice."

He rolled his eyes. "You didn't have to dance with her."

"Lucky me." She stared at him. "You can't mean this."

"Why not? It's an arrangement that works for both of us. I don't have to deal with the king's matchmaking and you get to make extra money. I know the plan requires you to stay in El Deharia longer than you'd planned, but you will also earn a considerable sum for your trouble."

More than considerable, she thought, unable to take it all in.

"I'm not princess material," she said. "I work on cars."

"You are delightfully different."

If only. "I don't know how to dress or say the right things. You should ask Victoria. Nadim's secretary," she added when Qadir looked blank. "Pretty, blond, a great dresser."

"You and I get along. Spending time together would not be a hardship."

She thought of the dance they'd shared at the ball. Nope, not a hardship at all. Especially if there was more dancing. She wouldn't even object to kissing.

The image of them pressed together was so intense and so unexpected, she scrambled to the other side of the desk to put some distance between them.

"This is crazy," she said. "Let's all take a deep breath and start over."

"It isn't crazy. It's a sensible plan that benefits us both. I get peace and quiet for at least a year. You get to work on my car, then vacation in a beautiful palace, all the while getting paid. I will provide you with an appropriate wardrobe, a chance to meet world leaders. We will travel and attend conferences. In time, the relationship will end and you will return home with a much larger bank balance."

"It's a whole lot of trouble just to get your father off your back."

"You have never had to deal with a monarch as a parent."

Good point.

She was tempted. Not only by the money, but by the opportunity. When else could she have an experience like this? Plus, a teeny, tiny, shallow part of her, the part that was still ashamed of what had happened with Jon, sort of liked the idea of him thinking she was dating a handsome prince.

"We would need ground rules," she said.

"Such as?"

"You can't be going out with someone else while we're fake-dating. I don't want to be cheated on."

"Agreed. Although the same rules apply to you."

She smiled. "Not a big issue for me, but thanks for worrying." What else? "I don't want any of this in the papers. Do you guys have tabloids out here?" The idea of Jon knowing was one thing, but having a fake relationship played out in the media was another.

"We have some local coverage," he said. "It is nothing like what exists in America and Europe. I would want some minor mention of us dating to convince my father, but nothing more."

"Okay." She hesitated. "I feel like I should ask more, but I can't think of what it would be."

"You've dated before," he told her. "This will not be all that different."

Except for not falling in love with the guy.

She looked at Qadir. "Are you sure about this? You do remember I'm a car mechanic, right? I don't do the long-nail thing."

"Yes, I know and please, do not recommend your friend Victoria again. I thought of this last night at the ball. You did extremely well there. Remember, the Russian ambassador was interested."

"I don't think that's a very high bar," she said.

"Regardless, you're the one that I want. Yes or no, Maggie?"

Was she crazy to consider the offer? If she said yes, she would have enough money to buy three shops back home. She would be set for a long, long time. She would also not have to return to Aspen and watch Jon and Elaine fall deeper and deeper in love.

It wasn't as if there was any pressing reason to say no. She didn't have to be anywhere or do anything by a certain time. She was sadly free from commitment.

Maggie couldn't think of a single downside. She supposed there was the remote possibility of falling for Qadir, but honestly—what were the odds of that? He was nothing like Jon and Jon was the only man she'd ever been in love with. So she was perfectly safe.

She drew in a breath. "Yes."

"Excellent. We will meet again soon to work out the details."

"Fine."

"I will let you return to your packages."

He approached as he spoke. She straightened and started to lift her right hand so they could shake on the deal. Instead Qadir cupped her cheek, bent forward and brushed her mouth with his.

The touch was light, quick and not the least bit sexual. Still, when he stepped back she felt the burn all the way down to her toes. Something sharp and needy twisted in her stomach and made her want to lean into him so he could kiss her again and this time do it like he meant it.

Her reaction stunned her. She hoped she answered as he said goodbye, but she couldn't be sure. She could only try to breathe through the desperate need to have him kiss her again and know that she had just dropped herself into a level of trouble that she'd never been in before.

Chapter Five

Maggie spent the rest of the morning trying to figure out what she'd gotten herself into. Fake dating a sheik? That sort of thing didn't happen to anyone, let alone someone like her. Maybe Qadir had a brain disorder that left him confused. Maybe he'd been kidding. Maybe she'd imagined the whole conversation and the next time she saw him he would call her "Ms. Collins" and look right through her.

Rather than make herself crazy with all the possibilities, she opened packages, savored the thrill of her car parts, then started an inventory base. It was nearly one before she noticed she was starving. But before she could cross to the phone and order lunch, Qadir appeared with a folder in one hand and a picnic basket in the other.

"We have much to discuss," he told her. "Is now a convenient time?"

If it wasn't, did she really get to say so? "If you brought lunch, then now is fine," she told him.

"A conditional acceptance?"

"I'm starving."

"So you can be bought with food."

"Sometimes." Based on their deal, she could also be bought with money, but she didn't want to think about that.

They went into her office where she laid out the lunch he'd brought.

She eyed the white-chocolate macadamia-nut cookie and knew that if she had been alone, she so would have started with that. Next time, she told herself with a sigh, thinking one day she was going to have to go down to the kitchen, find whoever provided the daily baked cookies and give him or her a big hug.

"I had my assistant make a list of possible places and events for us to go to," Qadir said when she'd taken her first bite of the sandwich. "The choices are divided into events that are purely public and those that will be perceived as private."

Maggie nearly choked. "You told your assistant about our deal?"

"No. I asked for an updated social calendar. Then he prepared a list of restaurants where photographers were known to frequent. I'm sure he thinks we'll be avoiding those places."

She managed to swallow without killing herself. "Okay. That makes sense." They would have to be seen to convince people—meaning Qadir's father—that this was all real. "Is the king going to be upset about this? I'm nothing like Sabrina or Natalie."

Qadir smiled. "Which is a good thing."

"In your mind. What about in his?"

"He is not the one dating you."

She narrowed her gaze. "Be serious. I don't want the king hating me or ordering me out of the country because I'm not a known breeder."

"Don't worry about anything. My father will be delighted to think I am finally getting serious about someone. It has been a long time."

How long? Maggie remembered her first night at the palace when she'd overheard Qadir and the king talking about someone from Qadir's past.

He put the list on the desk between them. "I have marked several events I suggest we attend, but the others are discretionary."

She glanced from the paper to him. "I don't understand. You're saying I get a vote, too?"

"Of course. Why would you not?"

Because he was a royal and she wasn't. "Okay," she said slowly. "That's nice."

He smiled at her uncertainty. "You keep forgetting, I'm the most charming of all my brothers."

"So you say. I haven't actually talked to any of your brothers so I only have your word on this."

He grinned. "You'll have to trust me."

For reasons that weren't clear to her, her gaze dropped to his mouth. She found herself reliving that brief but powerful kiss they'd shared.

She'd reacted so strongly to the lightest of touches. It had been the strangest thing…most likely brought on by too much champagne—even though she couldn't remember having more than half a glass. Or maybe it had been because she hadn't eaten. Whatever the cause, it hadn't meant anything. Forgetting it had ever happened made the most sense. Except she couldn't seem to forget.

"Maggie? Did you want to make some suggestions?"

"What? Oh. Sure."

She glanced down at the neatly printed possibilities. There were plays, sporting events, a hospital wing opening. The shower for Kayleen and the wedding to follow were in bold.

"These are…" she asked.

"Required. The shower for you and the wedding for both of us."

If she'd been standing she would have backed up a couple of feet. "I can't go to Kayleen's wedding shower. I barely know her."

"If we are together, then you are part of the family."

"I don't want to lie to your family."

He leaned back in his chair. "Deception is the nature of our endeavor."

Most of the time he sounded like a regular guy, but every now and then he said something princelike.

"I've never been a very good liar," she admitted. "I'd hate to see that change."

He said nothing, as if giving her the time and space to change her mind. Did she want to go through with this?

She thought of her father fading away. He kept making her promise that after he was gone she would try to get the business back. He hated that his illness had caused them to lose everything. She'd never blamed him, never wished for anything except his recovery. She knew he would want her to have a financial cushion. He would probably find the whole situation with Qadir funny. Then he would squeeze her shoulder and tell her not to do anything he wouldn't do.

The memory made her both happy and sad. With her father gone, she was alone in the world. The deal with Qadir offered her a level of financial freedom she'd never experienced. She would be a fool to walk away.

"I've never been to a wedding shower," she told him. "I'm sure it will be fun."

"Excellent."

They discussed other possibilities. There was a car show in neighboring El Bahar. They both agreed that would be a good choice.

"Will you want to pick out the engagement ring?" he asked.

She stabbed her fork into the pasta salad and sighed. "I'd deliberately forgotten about that part of the deal. Do we have to get engaged?"

"If I am to be crushed by your leaving, then yes."

She tried to imagine him emotionally crushed, but her imagination failed her. Qadir was too strong and in charge.

"You know, you could make this a lot easier by just falling in love with some woman and getting married for real."

"I am aware of that."

"You shouldn't be so picky," she told him.

"Thank you for that extraordinary advice."

They returned to the list, but Maggie wasn't really paying attention. Once again she was remembering the mystery woman from Qadir's past—and wondering why it hadn't worked out.

Maggie stared at the clothes in her closet and wished desperately that she'd asked Victoria to help her get ready. She also wished she had at least a couple of nicer outfits. But dining with princes hadn't been on her weekly agenda in Aspen so her wardrobe tended toward supercasual with the odd somewhat less casual piece thrown in.

Her choices seemed to fall into two categories—long-sleeved T-shirts and short sleeved T-shirts. She had a couple of blouses, one pair of black slacks and a ball gown that seemed as inappropriate for dinner as one of the T-shirts.

"I came here to work on cars, not date a sheik," she muttered as she flipped through the meager selection again, desperately hoping to see something she'd missed the first three times.

There was actually one other choice. A simple knit dress that she'd packed on a whim. It was burgundy, plain and a little too fitted for her taste. She'd bought it a couple of years ago when she'd wandered through a mall shortly after finding out her father had been diagnosed with cancer. It had been on sale. She'd tried it on as a distraction and then had purchased it because explaining why she didn't need it required too much effort.

Maggie wasn't sure why she'd tossed it in her suitcase. Fortunately the fabric traveled well.

She pulled off the tags, then brought the dress into the bathroom and started getting ready.

Once she'd showered and blown her hair dry, there wasn't all that much for her to do. She put on a little mascara, then lip gloss. Victoria had done a lot more to her the night of the ball, but Maggie had neither the skill nor the makeup. Qadir was going to have to suffer with her natural look.

She pulled on the dress, then stepped into a flat pair of sandals that weren't nearly as pretty as the ones she'd worn with her ball gown, but were a whole lot more comfortable. Then she glanced at the clock. It had taken her twelve minutes from stepping into the shower until she was ready to go. That included four minutes blow-drying her hair. Victoria would be horrified.

Thinking about her friend made her wonder what the other woman would think about the deal. Which made Maggie nervous. She put her hand to her stomach, as if that would help settle her nerves. Then someone knocked.

She opened the door to her suite and saw Qadir standing in the hallway. He looked as he always did—tall, handsome, well-dressed. Nothing was different. Except the tension in her stomach increased until she thought she might have to throw up. Just as intense was her need to have him pull her close and kiss her.

"Good evening," he said and smiled. "You are prompt. I should not be surprised."

"No, you shouldn't." She collected her purse and followed him into the hallway. "It doesn't take me long to get ready."

"And yet the result is lovely."

A compliment? She didn't know what to say. "Ah, thank you."

He chatted about something on the walk down to the front of the palace, but between her spinning head and swirling stomach, she had no idea what. When they entered the courtyard, a limo was waiting.

"I happen to know you have regular cars," she said as he held open the rear passenger door for her.

"Agreed, but this makes a better entrance."

Right. Because this was all for show.

She slid along the leather seat and tried to catch her breath. Fake dating, she reminded herself. Nothing more. She had no reason to be tense.

She forced herself to think calm thoughts. About ocean waves rushing in, then retreating. A cool, green forest. Water flowing in a brook.

"Maggie?"

She turned to him. "Yes?"

"What are you doing?"

"Trying not to throw up."

One corner of his mouth turned up. "You are always honest."

"I try to be."

"There is nothing to be nervous about."

"My stomach doesn't agree with you."

He shifted close and took her hand in his. "We are going to dinner at a very nice restaurant. You need to be calm so you can enjoy the meal. It is unlikely that we will be spotted by a photographer, however certain people will see us and that will start the gossip. Other than nodding politely to a few diners, little will be expected of you except eating."

"I'm a good eater."

"Then you will be fine."

His voice was so deep and low, she found herself getting lost in the sound. He rubbed her hand with slow, steady movements. That was nice, too, she thought as she felt herself relaxing.

This was just Qadir, she told herself. Just dinner. Nothing more.

She raised her gaze to his and found him watching her. With their eyes locked, he brought her hand to his mouth and kissed her palm.

It was a soft kiss that probably meant nothing. It was just…just…

Tension filled her stomach, but this was a whole new kind. It was hot and tight and had nothing to do with the rest of the world and everything to do with the man next to her.

Before she could figure out what she was supposed to do now, the car came to a stop. Talk about timing, she grumbled to herself.

The restaurant was on the water, with a beautiful view and the kind of low lighting that made everyone look good. They didn't have to wait, but were immediately led to a private table in an alcove.

"Thank you so much for joining us this evening, Prince Qadir," the hostess said, eyeing Maggie with obvious confusion. "I hope you enjoy your dinner."

The young woman nodded, then left.

Maggie shifted uncomfortably, wanting to explain that she wasn't *really* dating the prince. That the other woman didn't have to worry she would one day really be a princess. One thing for sure—she was going to have to talk to Victoria about going shopping in that secret back-room boutique. Better clothes were required for this whole fake-dating thing.

Still feeling out of place, Maggie picked up the leather-bound menu. As she did, she bumped one of the three different wine glasses set at her place. There was also a waterglass and an assortment of flatware, some of which she didn't recognize. Couldn't they have gone for a burger instead?

She opened the menu and stared at the pages and pages of choices.

"Do you have a preference for the wine?" Qadir asked. "French, Spanish, Italian? They also have an excellent selection from California, Washington, Australia and Chile."

"Whatever you would like is fine with me," she murmured, knowing she could never admit that the last time she'd had wine, it had been poured from a very lovely box purchased at Target.

She returned her attention to the menu, determined to pick something, but the words all blurred. She couldn't do this—she didn't belong here.

She looked up and found Qadir watching her.

"What's wrong?" he asked.

"Pretty much everything."

He surprised her by smiling. "If it is as awful as all that, then we have many areas where we can improve."

At least *he* found the situation amusing. "I'm not the right person for this," she whispered, leaning forward so he could hear her. "You've made a mistake."

"I have not." He took the menu from her hands and set it on top of his. "You are unfamiliar with the circumstances. This will get easier."

"I don't think so."

"Let me order for you. Do you have any food dislikes?"

This was a fancy restaurant. The possibilities for disaster were endless. "I'd just like something normal. Nothing squishy like sea urchin, or gross like paté."

"Very well. How about roast chicken with vegetables?"

"I could do that."

"Then that is what I will order."

A waiter appeared. He barely glanced at Maggie before bowing low to Qadir and thanking the prince for choosing the restaurant. A fast-paced conversation followed with wine chosen, entrées, salads and either appetizers or desserts picked. Maggie didn't recognize the names, so she couldn't be sure which.

The waiter left. Seconds later another man arrived with a bottle of white wine, along with a free-standing ice bucket. The wine was opened, tasted, pronounced excellent and poured. The second man left as quickly as the first.

"One can't complain about the service," Maggie murmured as Qadir lifted his glass. She took hold of hers and raised it, as well.

"To new beginnings," he said. "Let us give them a chance."

"A sneaky toast." Still, she touched her glass to his, then took a sip.

The wine was nice. Light and maybe crisp. She didn't really know the right terms. She knew she liked it and that she would probably faint if she knew how much it cost.

"Perhaps this will go more easily if we get to know each other better," he said, looking at her over his glass. "Tell me about your family."

"There's not much to tell," she admitted. "I'm an only child. My mom died when I was a baby. Dad always kept pictures of her around, but I don't remember her. It was just the two of us." She smiled. "I didn't mind. I couldn't miss what I'd never had and my father was great. He was one of the kindest men I've ever known. He took me with him everywhere, which is where I learned about cars. I grew up playing around them. I got in the way constantly, but then I learned how to help. It was a lot of fun. I learned math by helping with invoices. My dad made everything fun."

"He sounds like a good man."

"He was. He cared about people and loved his work. We lived

in a typical middle-class neighborhood. The houses were all the same and the kids played together. I was never into dolls or playing house. I was out with the boys. That was fine when I was young, but became a problem later. I didn't fit in either place."

She still remembered the horrible summer when she'd started to get curves. As minor as they were, they still made her feel as if she didn't fit in with the guys who had always been her friends.

"Feeling out of place made me hang out at the garage even more. It was the only place I felt comfortable."

She took another sip of wine. "Things got a little better in high school. I started seeing boys as something other than friends and they didn't seem to mind that I knew more about cars than they did. I never got really close to any of the girls, though."

She'd tried a few times, but hadn't known what to talk about. Makeup and clothes didn't interest her and she'd been too shy to admit to her crushes—a conversation point that might have allowed her to bond with the female half of the population.

"I would think the girls were jealous," Qadir said.

Maggie laughed. "I wish, but no. Then I started dating Jon. He lived next door. We'd been friends for years. One day I looked at him and everything was different. He asked me out and that was it. Being a couple allowed me to fit in. He was good to me. My dad liked him. We were together all through high school and while he went to college."

"Your relationship ended recently?"

"A few months ago."

Qadir studied her. "You are still in love with him." It wasn't a question.

"I'm not," Maggie said quickly, knowing it was true. "I miss him. He was my best friend forever. It was hard losing my dad, then Jon. I miss belonging and having someone to talk to. But I'm not in love with him."

Which made her behavior that night even more unforgivable.

Stop thinking about it, she told herself. Especially here, with Qadir.

Qadir didn't look convinced so she decided to change the subject. "What about your past?" she asked. "Yours must be more exciting, what with your being a prince and all. Don't women throw themselves at you wherever you go? Doesn't it get tricky, stepping over all those bodies?"

"It can be tiresome," he admitted, his eyes bright with humor.

She leaned toward him. "I want details."

"There aren't any of interest."

"No great love lurking in your past?" she asked before she remembered the mention of the mysterious woman the night she'd arrived.

Qadir picked up his wine, then put it down. "When I was very young—still in university—I met someone. Her name was Whitney."

"Was she from here?"

"England. I went to university there, although I did some graduate work in the States." He shrugged. "She was lovely. Smart, determined. She wanted to be a doctor. We fell in love. I brought her home to meet my father. I thought everything had gone well, but when we returned to England, she told me she couldn't marry me. She wasn't willing to give up her dreams to be my wife." He glanced at Maggie. "There are...restrictions that come with being a member of the royal family."

Made sense, she thought. "Whitney wouldn't have been able to practice medicine."

"Among other things. She's now in her final year of residency," he said. "She's a pediatric neurosurgeon."

Something that never would have happened if she'd married Qadir. "You still miss her."

"No. I respect her decision and I wish her well. It was a long time ago. We've both moved on."

Maggie was willing to believe he wasn't pining for Whitney. Qadir didn't seem the type to pine for anyone. But were there regrets?

Knowing about his past made him seem more like a regular guy, she thought. But was that a good thing or a bad one?

Qadir watched the play of emotions in Maggie's eyes. She was trying to put Whitney in context. Perhaps he should not have told her, but there was something about Maggie he trusted.

She wasn't like the usual women in his life. While she was certainly attractive, she lacked a sophistication he was used to. She didn't play games. And she knew more about cars than any female he'd met.

He started to tell her that when he saw a flash of movement out of the corner of his eye. He turned and saw a photographer easing along the far wall.

"An excellent opportunity," he said as he reached for Maggie's arm and pulled her toward him.

"What?"

Instead of answering, he kissed her. He had barely touched his mouth to hers when a flash went off. There was a flurry of activity as the restaurant staff raced for the photographer, no doubt to drag him outside. Qadir hoped they didn't take away his camera.

Even though the event had ended, Qadir continued the kiss. He liked the feel of Maggie's lips, the softness, the way she yielded. At times she was tough and in control, but now, she was all female—finding the true power of giving in.

He moved his hand to the back of her neck, where her long hair teased him. She smelled of soap and an elusive female essence that made him want to explore all of her. Need stirred.

He wanted to deepen the kiss. He wanted to taste her and

claim her and hold her. He wanted to feel her body next to his, even if all they did was kiss. But this was not the time or the place. Reluctantly he withdrew.

Maggie blinked several times. "Was there a flash?"

"I saw a photographer approaching. I wanted to give him something worthwhile."

She drew in a breath to steady her pinging nerves. "You did. Definitely."

The next morning Maggie had barely pulled on her robe when she heard someone pounding on her door. She walked through the living room of her suite and pulled open the door.

Victoria stood in the hallway, one hand on her hip, the other shaking a newspaper. "Do you know what's in here?" her friend said, pushing past her and walking into the room. "Do you have any idea?"

With that Victoria slapped the paper down on the dining room table.

There, in the middle, was a clear photograph of Qadir kissing a woman. At least she was pretty sure it was Qadir—his face wasn't visible. But hers was. Even with her eyes closed, she was easy to recognize.

Victoria crossed her arms over her chest. "There has to be a heck of a story because the last time you and I talked, you were barely calling the prince by his first name."

Maggie walked over to the coffeepot and turned it on. "It's not what you think."

"I don't know what *to* think."

While she and Qadir hadn't actually discussed keeping their deal quiet, it was certainly part of the bargain. But Victoria was her only friend in El Deharia and Maggie had a feeling she was going to need to talk things over with someone.

She turned. "Qadir doesn't want his father constantly bothering him with appropriate women, so he came up with a plan. I'm going to fake dating him for a couple of months, then we're going to get fake engaged. We'll have a big fight, I'll go home to Aspen and he'll go into mourning. That's all it is. A business proposition. He's paying me and to be honest, I can use the money."

Victoria stared at her. "Fake dating?"

"Uh-huh."

"Is it a lot of money?"

Maggie grinned. "Oh, yeah."

"Well, you go, girl."

"You're not mad?"

"No. I'm bitter. I should have thought of something like that for Nadim. At least then he would have to acknowledge I was alive. Fake dating, huh? You have to make him take you to some very cool places. He's a prince. He knows the global hot spots. You can…" Victoria swore under her breath. "Do you realize what this means?"

"What?"

"With the pressure off Qadir, the king is going to try to find Nadim a suitable bride. Knowing Nadim, he'll agree and that will be that."

Maggie poured them each a cup of coffee. "You aren't in love with him. Maybe you need to let the whole prince thing go."

"Maybe. It's just I'd be a really great princess."

Maggie noticed her friend sounded more resigned than heartbroken. Maybe a distraction would help.

"I desperately need your help," Maggie said. "Would you have time to go back to that consignment place? I have a fabulous wardrobe of T-shirts and nothing else. I don't want to embarrass him. Qadir is going to be taking me places other than the garage."

"Good point." Victoria stared at her for a long time. "Sure, we can go shopping, but I have a question first."

"Which is?"

"Are you sure about this? Have you thought it through?"

Maggie didn't understand the question. "Are you saying Qadir might not want to pay me the amount he's agreed to?"

"Not at all. I'm sure the money will be transferred with no problem. I was thinking more about not getting involved."

With Qadir?

Maggie immediately thought about their brief but powerful kiss. He made her quiver with the lightest touch. She told herself it was nothing more than chemistry and circumstances. She would be fine.

"It's a business deal."

"So it seems. Just remember that princes aren't like other men. Keep your heart safely protected."

Maggie laughed. Her body she could worry about but her heart was safely out of reach. She'd been hurt too much to ever give it again.

"Don't worry about me. I'll be fine."

Chapter Six

Qadir nodded to himself as he read the screen. All was well. Not that he expected less, but confirmation was always pleasant. He saved the information. His phone buzzed.

"Yes?"

"Sir, there is a Victoria McCallan to see you. She has no appointment but insists it's very important."

Qadir's male assistant didn't sound convinced of the fact. Qadir hesitated. Victoria was Nadim's secretary. Why would she need to come here? Still, the woman had never bothered him before. He could afford to give her a few minutes of his time.

"Send her in."

Seconds later an attractive blonde walked into his office. "Thank you for seeing me, Prince Qadir. I know you're busy."

He offered her a seat, but she shook her head. "I prefer to stand."

He rose, as well. Interesting. "How may I assist you?"

Victoria drew in a breath. She was visibly nervous, although she seemed to be trying to hide her upset.

"I want to talk to you about Maggie," she said. "I know about your deal."

Any natural instinct to aid turned cynical as he eyed the woman. Maggie had innocently shared the information of their deal with someone she perceived to be friend. Now Victoria sought to use that information for herself. Typical.

His brother Kateb was right—too many women were out for what they could get.

He waited for her to continue.

"Maggie isn't going to handle this well. She's not girly. She doesn't do the hair and makeup thing. She doesn't have the right clothes."

"But you do." He wasn't asking a question.

"What? Of course I do, but that's not the point. She's blunt and funny and sweet. She cares about people. Going out with you means getting mentioned in the papers. Maggie isn't going to like that."

Women didn't often confuse Qadir, but he now found himself at a loss. "You are concerned about your friend?"

Victoria's gaze narrowed. "Of course I care about my friend. Why else do you think I'm here?"

Her question hung in the air. He saw the exact moment she realized what he'd been thinking. Her back went stiff. Her mouth thinned.

He waited for her to start defending herself or even yelling at him. Instead she sucked in a breath and continued.

"My point is, Maggie is playing out of her league. You need to make sure she doesn't get trashed in the papers. And don't spring stuff on her. She's never done anything like this. She's going to have to figure it out while she goes. This is a tough time for her. She's dealt with a lot of loss in the past few months."

Victoria obviously knew about Maggie's father. He wondered if she knew about the old boyfriend.

As he listened to Victoria talk he realized he had never considered Maggie's feelings about the situation or how she would react to being thrown into his world. He'd seen her as someone he liked and enjoyed spending time with. He knew her to be honest, which made her the perfect candidate for his pretense. He should have considered whether his plan might hurt her in any way.

"She needs a makeover," Victoria said.

Qadir stared at her. "A what?"

"A makeover. Maggie's pretty, but she's the country mouse. She needs a new wardrobe. And someone to teach her how to wear makeup and do her hair. Maggie's proud and sweet. She doesn't deserve anyone asking why someone like you would bother with someone like her."

He didn't like Victoria saying that. "No one who knew Maggie would ask that question."

"I agree, but we're not going to be dealing with people who know her, are we?"

As much as he hated to admit it, she had a point. "I will see to it."

"Good. Look on the bright side. How often do you get to meet a beautiful woman who has no idea how great she is?"

Victoria was right, although he found himself hoping Maggie didn't change too much through the process.

"There's one other thing," Victoria said as the nervousness returned.

He waited.

She raised her chin. "You can't hurt her. She doesn't deserve that. You can't use your position or power against her."

Annoyance filled him. "You challenge my integrity?"

"Among other things."

"I am Prince Qadir of El Deharia. No one questions me."

"Then this is going to be a bad day for you."

"I can have you deported."

"I don't doubt that. Maggie is my friend and I don't want you to hurt her."

She trembled. He could see it. Yet she didn't back down. She faced him, knowing she could lose her job and be sent home in disgrace.

His opinion of both women increased favorably. Victoria for being so willing to protect her friend and Maggie for inspiring such loyalty.

He wondered if Nadim had ever noticed the firebrand lurking behind Victoria's blue eyes. It was his cousin's loss if he had not.

Qadir walked around the desk and touched Victoria's shoulder. "I will not hurt your friend. Maggie is doing me a favor. I have no intention of making her regret her decision to help. We have a business arrangement. Nothing more."

Victoria shook her head. "That's what she said. It always starts out sounding so sensible, right up until someone gets hurt."

"But I don't want to," Maggie said, a distinct whine in her voice. "I don't like shopping."

Qadir laughed. "You are the first woman to ever say so."

"I'm sure there are other women who don't like to shop," she muttered, wondering if she could fling herself out the limo's rear door and survive the impact. She would probably end up with a few scars but they would be better than an afternoon spent shopping. She shuddered at the thought.

"If you are to spend time with me, you need an appropriate

wardrobe," he told her. "You came prepared to work on cars, not date a prince."

She knew he was right. She didn't have any clothes to wear to all the events he'd mentioned. She needed a decent wardrobe to be able to fit in. But shopping?

"Can't we use the Internet?"

"No."

"We could send them my measurements. Wouldn't that work?"

"No."

"But there—"

"No."

She slumped back in her seat. "This really sucks."

He laughed.

They pulled up in front of the exclusive boutique where she and Victoria had come before. Maggie had a feeling they weren't going to be checking out the consignment room.

"Not here," she told him. "It's too expensive."

He turned to her. "Maggie, do you know how much I'm worth?"

Not even a clue. "A lot?"

"Exactly."

She eyed the store. She didn't want to go in, but then she didn't want to go to any store. "Okay, but they offer a palace discount. Make sure you use it."

He was still laughing when they walked inside.

Last time she'd been here, she and Victoria had moved through the large boutique without being acknowledged by a single assistant. Now it seemed as if every employee descended.

"Prince Qadir, you are here. How lovely to see you."

"Prince Qadir, as always you brighten our day."

"How may we help you?"

"What can I show you?"

Maggie slipped behind him for protection.

Then a tall, elegant woman of indeterminate age glided toward him.

"Prince Qadir," she said in a low, cultured voice. "You honor us with your presence."

"Thank you, Ava." He turned to Maggie. "This is Ava. She owns the store. She'll be helping us today."

Ava smiled at Maggie and took her hand. "Welcome, my dear."

Maggie wanted to slink away. Ava was one of those perfect women who looked like she would never wear anything that didn't match or had a stain or was sensible.

"Maggie is very special to me," Qadir said. "But not much of a shopper. She needs a complete wardrobe. One that prepares her for anything. However, I will warn you—she will resist this process. I'm counting on you to convince her all is necessary."

Ava smiled at Maggie. "My pleasure. Come, child. We have much to do. Let's get started."

Maggie felt like the fly being led away by the spider. She wanted to yell back at Qadir not to leave her alone with this woman, but she knew he wouldn't take her seriously. He thought this was funny. Which was just like a man. Someone should pinch and poke him while forcing him to wear stupid clothes. Then they'd see how much *he* liked it.

Ava led her to a large dressing room where they both stood in front of the three-way mirror. Maggie looked and felt frumpy next to the other woman. She sighed.

"What would you say your style is?" Ava asked.

"I have no idea."

"Casual, I'm thinking. You're not the sort of person to ever really enjoy wearing a dress." She turned Maggie so she was facing the mirror sideways. "Hmm. You have a perfectly good figure, but those jeans do nothing for you. I have a couple of styles in mind that will make you look spectacular."

Maggie stared at her. "Jeans?"

Ava smiled. "Very expensive designer jeans, child. With the right accessories, a beautiful blouse and jacket, jeans can be worn many places. A casual dinner, a luncheon. Nothing with the king, of course."

Ava walked around her. "While I would normally want to put one of Qadir's young women in pretty dresses, that won't do for you. You'll just be uncomfortable. We'll do pants as much as we can, then separates. You're going to be stuck with dresses for evening wear, of course. There's no getting around it."

Maggie thought of the ball gown she'd worn and how it had made her feel. "Sometimes a dress is okay."

"I'm glad you think so."

"I can really wear jeans?"

Ava smiled. "I promise."

It was kind of funny how at that moment Ava transformed from a spider into someone really, really nice.

Three hours and Maggie wasn't sure how many outfits later, she found herself sitting in front of a mirror at a very upscale beauty salon. She knew the place had to be pricey because they'd offered her a latte, bottled water or cocktail before discussing her hair. No one had *ever* offered her a cocktail before cutting her hair. Of course the way her stomach was jumping, getting tipsy didn't seem like such a bad idea.

"Not too short," Qadir said as he stood behind the chair, next to the stylist—a short man with a ponytail. "I like her hair long."

"I agree." The stylist, whose name Maggie couldn't remember, ran his hands through her hair. "She has a natural wave. I want to layer it so we can see the movement."

Maggie wrinkled her nose. "Does anyone care that I hate my

natural wave?" It was one of the reasons she wore her hair as long as she did and always tied it back. To hide the natural wave.

"Not really," Qadir said with a smile, then bent down and kissed the side of her neck.

"But it's *my* hair," she murmured without much energy. She was too caught up in the tingles racing through her body.

It had been a nothing kind of kiss—the only kind Qadir seemed to give her. A light brush, a meaningless peck. Kisses for show. Kisses that stole her breath away and made her want to…to…to *something*. Kiss more. Kiss back. Beg. Instead she was forced to sit there quietly while they continued to discuss her hair.

In the end, they chose the layered style they'd talked about, along with subtle highlights.

"Could I be blond?" Maggie asked. "I'd like to be blond."

Qadir turned the chair so she was facing him. "You are beautiful just as you are."

Beautiful? He didn't mean that, did he? "But I'm getting highlights. Going blond is practically the same."

"Not to me."

"Should we have the whole 'this is my hair' conversation again?"

"I will not be listening."

He leaned in and kissed her. On the mouth. Firmly.

She told herself it was just so the people in the hair salon would gossip about them. She told herself it didn't matter to her at all, one way or the other. It was just a kiss.

But it felt like a lot more.

His lips were warm and firm, taking and offering at the same time. He braced himself on the arms of the chair so they weren't touching anywhere but their mouths. Still, that was enough to make her whole body sit up and take notice.

He moved his mouth back and forth before brushing her lower lip with his tongue.

Instinctively she parted for him. Anticipation made her tense. When he slid inside, she wanted to squirm closer, to take whatever he offered. Instead she lifted her hand to his shoulder and felt the strength of him.

His tongue touched hers. Sparks flew in every direction. He circled her as they began a dance so exciting, so erotic, she found it difficult to breathe.

She'd been kissed before hundreds of times. She'd made love. She'd experienced desire for a man. But nothing had prepared her for the hunger that consumed her whenever Qadir kissed her.

Wanting began low in her belly and spiraled out, filling every cell with a need that almost frightened her. She felt control slipping and worried she would beg him to take her right there, in the chair, in front of anyone who happened to be watching. She felt breathless and out of control. It was frightening…and yet she never wanted him to stop.

At last he pulled away. Something hot and bright burned in his dark eyes. She had a feeling he could see the same in her. Passion, she thought. Heady and unfamiliar, but more compelling than she'd ever thought possible.

"You are a surprise," he murmured.

"I could say the same about you. Of course it could be a prince thing. You might take special classes and be taught techniques not known to mortal man."

"I am mortal and there is no special training."

Which meant it was just him. A slightly scary thought.

"I must go. The car will return and the driver will wait to take you back to the palace."

"Okay."

"I look forward to seeing your transformation this evening."

"We're doing something tonight?" Not that she minded.

"A play."

"Right. You mentioned that. I should probably get a calendar."

"I'll have my assistant print out a schedule."

That made her smile. "I've never dated by schedule before. Maybe he should include suggestions on what I should wear. Formal, informal, strictly casual."

"If you like."

She started to say she'd been kidding, but then realized having that information would help. "Theater is dressy, right?"

"Yes."

"Okay." She thought about the clothes they'd bought earlier that afternoon. "I have a couple of things I can wear. What's the play?"

"A musical. *Les Miserables.* The king's favorite."

"Has he seen it?"

"Many times. He'll see it again tonight."

"Oh. He's going, too?"

"We'll be in his box. It will be a good opportunity for him to get to know you better. As the woman I'm dating."

With that he straightened and walked away.

The stylist returned. "He's so hot. You're really lucky. Are you all right?"

Maggie shook her head. The king was going to be there tonight? In the same box? Was she expected to talk to him?

Stupid question, she told herself. She would have to carry on a conversation and pretend to be Qadir's girlfriend and what if the king asked about her being good breeding stock? How was she supposed to answer?

"I think I'm going to be sick," she whispered.

"I get that a lot," the stylist said as he wheeled a cart close and reached for scissors. "Deep breaths. You'll be fine."

"I can't do this," Maggie said as the limo pulled up in front of the entrance to a very large, very old building. "I can't breathe,

I can't think. This was all a mistake. If I'd already accepted money, I would return it. Seriously, pick someone else. Fainting will not make the king like me."

"You're exaggerating your condition," Qadir said, not sounding the least bit sympathetic. "You said you like musicals."

She glared at him. "What does that have to do with anything? I can't meet the king."

"You already have."

"As a nobody. You're being deliberately difficult and for the record, I don't like it."

He laughed. He actually laughed.

"You'll be fine," he said as he stepped out of the limo and held out his hand to assist her.

"It's all fun and games now," she muttered as she followed him. "Let's see how amusing this is when I throw up on your expensive handmade shoes."

He had the nerve to chuckle again, then he tucked her hand into the crook of his arm and led her into the theater.

Maggie concentrated on walking in new shoes and breathing and trying not to think about the way her stomach flopped over and over and over. Look at the architecture, she told herself. Admire the clean lines, the soaring ceilings, the whatever the sticky-out parts were called by the corners.

Actually, now that she was paying attention, she realized the building *was* beautiful. Elegant and oddly feminine, if such an imposing building could be called that. There were mosaics and huge chandeliers, gilded pillars and archways. A staircase that seemed to glide up to heaven.

"What is this place?" she asked.

Instead of answering, Qadir came to a stop and turned her to her right. She stared at the handsome couple in front of them, then gasped when she realized it was them.

The large mirror showed her Qadir was as good-looking as always. Strong, tall and elegant in a tailored tux. The woman next to him wasn't half-bad, either, and the most amazing part was it was her.

The haircut had brought out the waves she hated, but somehow now they didn't look so geeky. Instead they were almost loose curls flowing to her shoulders. The makeup she'd been shown how to use made her eyes larger and mouth bigger. But it was the clothes she really liked.

True to her word, Ava hadn't tried to stick her in a dress. Instead Maggie wore white silk trousers and a white silk tank top. What transformed the outfit from day to night wasn't just the beading on the tank top, but the fact that her trousers were actually slit from ankle to thigh. While she was standing still, they looked perfectly conservative, but when she moved she flashed a whole lot of leg.

High heeled sandals made her even taller, although she was still several inches shorter than Qadir.

He put his hands on her shoulders. "You have nothing to be nervous about. You are beautiful, smart, funny and charming. The only problem we're going to have with the king is that he is going to want you for himself."

That made her smile. "I think you're safe."

For a second she thought he was going to kiss her again. There was something in his posture and the look in his eye. But then he took her hand and pulled her along toward the stairs.

Disappointment chased away the last of her nerves. She wouldn't have minded a little premusical kissing. Honestly, the way Qadir made her body go up in flames, she wouldn't mind a little anything with him. Something interesting to think about later.

They climbed the stairs and walked to the right. A guard stepped aside, allowing them to step into what Maggie assumed was a private box. She'd never been in one before.

There were several people standing around, drinking champagne and nibbling on appetizers. She had a sudden craving for those little hot dogs wrapped in pastry.

But before she could check out the food, the crowd parted and she found herself in front of King Mukhtar.

"Father," Qadir said, "I would like you to meet my date for the evening. Miss Maggie Collins. She's from America. Colorado."

Maggie tightened her grip on Qadir's fingers as she smiled at the king. "Your Highness, this is a great honor for me."

The king frowned. "Have we met?"

One of the guards came forward. "Your Highness, the photographers are here. Shall I let them in?"

The king nodded. Everyone shifted position as several men with cameras entered the booth and began snapping pictures. Maggie found herself blinded. Just when she thought she couldn't stand it anymore, the king waved his hand and the men instantly stopped.

"There's power," she murmured to Qadir. "It really is good to be the king."

"So I hear."

He gave her a glass of champagne. She took a sip.

"What am I supposed to say when he asks me what I do?"

"Tell him the truth," Qadir said.

Easy for him, she thought. He wasn't a car mechanic. "He's going to give me that look. The one that says I'm weird and that I should have gone for something more traditionally female."

"He's the king. He doesn't do looks."

"He'll have the look. Trust me."

Someone called Qadir away. Maggie eased into a corner and did her best to be invisible. She picked up a cracker with she wasn't sure what on top and had just taken a bite when the king walked over.

"This is your first time at our theater?" he asked.

She chewed quickly then swallowed. "Um, yes. Sir. The building is stunning. I was admiring it when we came in. There's something unique about the architecture." Or was there? She swallowed again but not because of any food. "At least it seemed that way to me."

"Early fifteenth century," the king told her. "One of my ancestors built this small palace for a favorite mistress. He promised to build her something as beautiful as herself. When it was completed she claimed that no woman could live up to such beauty. But she accepted the palace anyway."

Maggie grinned. "You have to respect a woman who enjoys real estate."

As soon as the words were out, she wanted to stuff them back in her mouth. There were probably a thousand different ways for someone to interpret that comment and most of them were bad.

But before she could think about throwing herself off the nearby balcony, Mukhtar laughed. "An excellent observation, my dear. Very funny."

She exhaled in relief. Time for a safer topic. "I'm looking forward to the performance tonight. I've heard most of the music from the show, but I've never seen it in person." She thought about mentioning she'd seen the performance on PBS, but maybe he wouldn't know what that was and she wasn't sure he would find the explanation interesting.

"You are in for an experience," the king said. "The music is compelling and touches one's soul."

Maggie didn't know what to say to that. Fortunately the lights flickered. Qadir returned to her side and guided her to their seats.

"I did okay," she whispered. "I didn't say anything stupid to the king."

Instead of answering, Qadir motioned to her right. She turned and saw Mukhtar sitting next to her.

She smiled tightly, then leaned to her left.

"You are so going to be punished for this later."

Qadir, of course, only laughed.

The orchestra began playing. At first Maggie was so aware of the king seated close, she couldn't relax. But eventually the story pulled her in. She found herself caught up in the events playing out on the spartan stage. When Javert killed himself, she felt tears in her eyes.

She did her best to blink them back, only to feel something soft pressing against her hand.

She looked down and saw a white handkerchief, then sniffed and looked at the man handing it to her.

"He was a good man facing an impossible choice," Qadir murmured. "His soul could only handle so much before it ripped in two."

She nodded without speaking, then wiped away her tears. He put his arm around her and pulled her close. She relaxed with his embrace, and felt safe for the first time in what seemed like forever.

Chapter Seven

Qadir stood by the office in the garage. It was his nature to take charge, to direct. Rather than give in to that need, he'd physically stepped back to let Maggie have control of the moment.

Gone was the sophisticated beauty from the previous night. Today she was all business, in coveralls and a T-shirt, her hair pulled back, her face scrubbed clean. She focused on nothing but the equipment and the men she directed as the engine was slowly lifted from the body of the Rolls.

Qadir knew he should be paying attention to the action. The engine was the heart of the car and if something happened to it then true restoration wasn't possible. Yet he couldn't seem to stop watching Maggie as she moved around the car, double-checking that everything was secure and then nodding for the men to resume.

There was something in the way she moved, he decided. Or

maybe it was knowing that she could be both this competent leader and yet feminine enough to cry because a character in a play died.

Her tears had startled him. He couldn't recall the last time he'd seen a woman cry for reasons other than manipulation. Later, as the musical had continued, Maggie had struggled for control, telling him or perhaps herself that she was fine.

"Swing it around," Maggie called out. "Slowly. We don't have any other plans for the day. That's it. Great job. Just like that."

He watched as the engine was lowered to the supports that would allow Maggie to work her magic on the aging beauty. When the engine was in place, Maggie breathed a sigh of relief and applauded her team.

"Excellent work," she told the men. "Thank you so much for your patience and attention to detail."

Qadir waited until everyone had gone to walk over to the engine.

"It could be worse," she told him without bothering to look at him. "I'll admit to a few moments of terror when it was pulled out. I thought there was more damage. But there doesn't seem to be any horrible surprises. It'll take me a few days to take everything apart and access the damage. That will really tell us where we stand."

She glanced up at him. "What? You're looking at me funny."

"You are an interesting combination of traits. You were very good with the men."

She rolled her eyes. "I've been working with men my whole life."

"These are men of my country, not yours. They do not usually take direction from a woman. Yet you established authority with them easily and offered them much praise. They will speak well of you."

"Don't be so surprised. I told you when you hired me, I know what I'm doing."

Surprise didn't describe his feelings. He was intrigued by her. Impressed. Aroused. But not surprised.

"The king likes you, as well," he said.

She pulled a rag from her back pocket and wiped her hands. "Okay, that one I don't know how to deal with."

"You should be pleased."

"Why? Wouldn't it be better if he didn't like me? We're going to break up. I don't want him mad at me when that happens."

Qadir smiled. "Fear not. I will keep him from locking you away when you break my heart."

"How comforting."

"You did very well at the theater. Our next event will be to have dinner with As'ad and Kayleen. That will be easier."

"Maybe for you," Maggie said with a sigh. "I'm not so sure. I only had to talk to the king for a couple of minutes. Dinner is a lot longer. They're going to ask questions like where we met."

"We met here," he reminded her.

"Oh. Right. Well, they'll want to know other stuff. Like what we see in each other."

A question he could easily answer, he thought as he watched her walk around the engine. Maggie was bright and funny and she spoke her mind. She was also a fascinating combination of competent and sexy. Like now. The coveralls hid everything, which only made him want to see and touch all that they concealed.

"My brother and his fiancée are within weeks of their wedding," he told her. "They have adopted three young girls. If the conversation turns too personal, ask about some detail in the planning or how the children are doing. I am confident that you'll be just fine."

"Wish I were." She walked over to the car and ran her hands along the side. "This I understand. This makes sense to me. Where art meets function. Couldn't I just stay here and work on the car?"

He crossed to her and touched her face. Her skin was soft, her eyes wide, her mouth…tempting.

"Do you wish to be released from our arrangement?" he asked, wanting her with a power that left him hungry and restless.

Her pupils dilated. "No. I just want to whine about it."

As always, she made him smile. "Then I will ignore your complaints."

"Fair enough."

"I must return to my office."

The need to kiss her was strong, but he resisted. He'd hired Maggie to convince his father he was involved. He would not take advantage of the situation, no matter how much she tempted him.

He left the garage and walked toward the palace. Halfway through the garden he realized he had not told Maggie what time they were to meet for dinner.

He retraced his steps. She wasn't in the garage, so he crossed to her office. The door was closed. He opened it without knocking and walked inside only to find Maggie changing her clothes.

She stood in the center of the room, her back to him. As he watched, the coveralls fell to the floor and she stepped out of them.

She'd already removed her boots, so she wore nothing but socks, tiny panties and a T-shirt.

Everything he'd been taught told him to retreat, to give her the privacy she expected and deserved. The blood of the desert that still pounded through his veins demanded that he take this beautiful, alluring woman.

He couldn't seem to look away from her long legs, the curve of her hip, the way she moved as she bent down to pick up the coveralls. She turned slightly, saw him and jumped.

Maggie was pretty sure she didn't scream, which was good because she hardly needed one more embarrassing moment where Qadir was concerned. Then she remembered she was kind of undressed and felt herself flush anyway.

"I...forgot to tell you what time we would meet for our dinner," he said.

"Isn't it seven? That's what my schedule says."

"Ah, yes. Seven."

She stood awkwardly, sort of holding the coveralls in front of her body, even as she tried to convince herself that panties and a T-shirt were more clothing than she wore to the beach. Only they weren't at the beach and she'd been undressing.

"I didn't mean to intrude," he said. "My apologies."

She appreciated the words, even as she noticed he wasn't leaving. That should have annoyed her. But there was something in the way Qadir looked at her that made her feel all shaky inside.

"Maggie." He crossed to her in three long strides. "Send me away and I will go."

His gaze was intense, as was his touch when he held her by her upper arms.

Sparks arced between them. She could practically see them as they singed her skin. Need grew until it devoured every part of her.

She didn't understand what it was about this man that made her react the way she did. Cosmic humor? Chemistry? Hormones? She didn't know and she wasn't sure she cared. She only knew that when she was close to Qadir, touching him, being touched, she felt more alive than she ever had in her life.

She dropped the coveralls. "That won't be necessary," she whispered.

He pulled her toward him with a force that caused her to lose her balance. Not that it mattered. She knew if she fell, he would catch her, just as he caught her now, pulling her against him, claiming her with a hot, wild kiss that threatened to steal her soul.

She leaned against him, her curves flattening against his hard chest, wrapped her arms around his neck and gave herself over to the kiss. She met him stroke for stroke. As he explored, she tightened her lips around his tongue and sucked. He stiffened.

Pleasure filled her, along with the confidence of knowing she wasn't the only one in danger of getting lost in the moment.

He dropped his hands to her hips then around to her rear, squeezing the curves, causing her to surge against him.

Her belly nestled against his arousal, hard, thick proof of what she did to him. Feeling it made her insides melt. She felt herself swelling in anticipation.

He ran his hands up and down her back before slipping one around her rib cage then up her T-shirt to her breast. Even through the layers of fabric, he found her nipple, tight and hard. He teased the sensitive point, rubbing it, circling, then brushing it with the palm of his hand.

At the same time he broke the kiss, only to nibble his way along her jaw.

He moved his free hand to her other breast. His touch was exquisite. Powerful need made her tremble. She wanted everything right that second. She wanted *him.*

He stepped back far enough to pull off her T-shirt. She quickly undid her bra and tossed it aside. Then his hands were on her bare skin.

He stroked her with his fingers before bending down and taking her nipple in his mouth. When he sucked, deep ribbons of desire wove their way down to that place between her thighs. She cupped his head with her hand, as much to be touching him as to make sure he never stopped.

His tongue danced with her, flicked against her, made her gasp and moan. Then he slipped one hand between her legs.

She braced herself for the magic of his touch and the intensity of her response. But even as he eased into place, she heard someone in the garage. A voice, then a burst of male laughter. She stiffened.

Qadir straightened. He immediately pulled off his suit jacket and covered her, then moved to the door, closed and locked it.

All that only took a second, but it was enough for her rational mind to wake up and be horrified by what had almost happened.

Qadir was her boss. They had a deal and that didn't include sex. Just as confusing was the fact that she'd never been the kind of woman who threw herself into bed with any guy who came along. There'd only ever been Jon and it had taken them three years of dating to finally go all the way.

Of course they'd been young and both virgins. Qadir was a man of the world. Which explained his actions, but what about hers? It was one thing to enjoy a man's kiss—it was another to get so swept away that she'd nearly done it in her office in the garage, in the middle of the day.

"Maggie?"

She looked at him. "I don't know what to say."

"I won't apologize."

He hadn't done anything wrong except take what was offered. "I don't expect you to."

"Would it help if you threw something?"

That made her smile. "I'm not sure. I don't feel angry. Just confused. I don't usually do this sort of thing."

"There is a powerful attraction between us."

"I got that."

He picked up her bra and T-shirt. After handing them to her, he turned his back. She set his jacket over a chair and quickly dressed. When she'd pulled on the coveralls, she said, "Doing anything…you know, intimate, would mess things up."

He faced her again. "I agree."

"I work for you."

He nodded. "Better to keep things business only."

"Yeah."

They were both saying the right words, so why did she have the feeling that neither of them believed them?

"You are all right?" he asked.

"Fine. Weirded out, but fine." She gave him a little push. "Go back to your office and do princely things. I'll be ready at seven."

"I'll be waiting," he told her and left.

Maggie watched him go. When she was alone, she sank into the chair and tried to figure out how much trouble she'd just gotten herself into.

Could she and Qadir put this behind them and pretend it had never happened?

Without meaning to, she closed her eyes and remembered how it felt to have his mouth on her breasts. Talk about amazing.

"It's just chemistry," she told herself. "Nothing more."

It couldn't be. She was here for a job and that was all. In six months their fake relationship would end and she would go home, much richer for the experience.

The trick was to not get personally involved. But for the first time she wondered if that was going to be harder than she'd ever imagined.

"Tell me about the woman," Kateb said as he shrugged out of his robes and tossed them over a chair in Qadir's suite.

Qadir poured them each a Scotch and handed his brother a glass. "What woman?"

Kateb raised his eyebrows. "Word of your involvement had even reached me in the desert, so there must be a woman."

They settled on the oversize sofas in the main living area. Qadir raised his glass in a toast to his brother. "It is good to have you back. You stay away too long."

"I find no pleasure in the city. I belong in the desert." Kateb took a sip of his drink. "But you have not answered my question."

"Her name is Maggie Collins. She's restoring the Rolls."

Kateb's expression gave nothing away. "And?"

"And she's beautiful, funny, down-to-earth."

"You say all the right things. What aren't you telling me, brother?"

Qadir grinned. "That it's a game. I'm paying her to pretend to be my girlfriend. In a few weeks, we'll get engaged. Then this will all be too much for her and she'll return home. Heartbroken, I won't be able to consider any of our father's offers for perhaps as long as a year."

Kateb nodded slowly. "An impressive plan."

"You wish you'd thought of it yourself."

"The idea has merit, although living in the desert as I do, I am well out of the king's reach."

"Lucky you."

Kateb took another drink. "You do realize the game may have consequences."

Qadir thought about his encounter with Maggie that morning, in the garage. If those were the consequences his brother was talking about, he would welcome them.

She had been all sweet fire in his arms. Her body yielding, her moans telling him she was as aroused as he had been.

"I am not concerned," Qadir told him. "I know what I'm doing."

"As you wish."

"Are you here to discuss the nomination?" Qadir asked.

Kateb shrugged. "I am not sure there is anything to discuss."

"They will name you and then what? Our father will not be pleased."

"I have never been able to please him."

"If you accept, you face him as an equal."

Kateb smiled. "The king will not see things that way."

Years ago, Qadir and his brothers had been sent into the desert, as was tradition. Young royal sons were taught the old ways, living with the nomads who roamed the deserts of the area. Qadir had endured the time but Kateb had loved it. As soon as he had finished university, he had chosen to make his home in the desert.

Tradition stated that every twenty-five years a new leader was nominated. As Kateb had become one of them, he was expected to be named.

But he was already an heir to Mukhtar's throne. Not the first in line, but still close to being king. For Kateb to accept the nomination of the desert people meant abdicating his rights to the El Deharian throne.

"What do you want?" Qadir asked.

"To stay where I belong. I am unlikely to be king here. Walking away from what will never be mine is not a hardship."

But if it was so easy, wouldn't Kateb have already made the decision?

"Apparently the kind of flowers matter," Kayleen said with a sigh. "There are rules."

"Ignore the rules," Prince As'ad told her. "You are to be my bride. Do what makes you happy."

"So imperious," Kayleen said, although she smiled at her fiancé. "It's easy for him to tell me to break the rules, but he doesn't have to face the wedding planner." She leaned toward Maggie, her eyes wide. "Do you know the president of the United States has been invited? I nearly passed out when they told me. Fortunately he can't come. They'll send someone else, which is great. I couldn't help fainting if I knew the president was there."

As'ad touched her cheek. "You are far too strong to faint."

"Maybe, but I'll sure be thinking about it." Kayleen shook her head. "I'm sorry. Hearing all this talk about the wedding must be really boring for you." She smiled. "Qadir especially."

"You are so lovely that any topic is interesting," Qadir told her.

Maggie had to press her lips together to keep from laughing. As'ad glared at his brother.

"Do not use your charm on my fiancée or you will suffer the consequences."

Qadir only looked amused. "Are you so unsure of her affections?"

Kayleen rolled her eyes. "They get like this from time to time. Sort of a royal way of letting off steam. We can pretty much send it in any direction we want. You could get insulted that Qadir is pretending to make a play for me or I could be flattered he thinks I'm worthy or we would ignore them altogether and just talk about something else."

Maggie had been nervous about the dinner with As'ad and Kayleen. She didn't know either of them and an intimate setting would require a lot of conversation. She had wondered how it would be possible to keep her fake relationship with Qadir seeming real.

But she found herself enjoying the evening very much. The other couple was easy to talk to. Kayleen especially bubbled about the wedding. They hadn't asked any awkward questions and seemed to totally accept her. Life being what it was, that made her feel a little guilty.

"Let's ignore them," Maggie said. "Tell me about your three girls. That's a lot to take on when you're just getting married."

"I know," Kayleen said, sounding totally thrilled. "But the girls are the reason As'ad and I are together. He adopted them—

it's a long, complicated story. Anyway, I was their nanny and we sort of, well…"

"Fell in love," Maggie said, seeing the truth in her eyes.

"Yes. It was wonderful. *He's* wonderful."

Maggie watched Kayleen look at her fiancé. There was so much love between them. So much caring. She felt a flicker of envy deep inside. A strong desire to have the same for herself.

She tried to remember if she'd ever felt that kind of connection before. Had it existed with Jon? She realized she wasn't sure. That their love had evolved slowly. How much of it had been proximity? Had they fallen in love because they'd both been together all the time?

She didn't have an answer, but as she considered the question she realized she wasn't sad. That thinking about Jon didn't depress her anymore.

She probed more deliberately. Didn't she miss him? Didn't she want them to get back together?

The answer came quickly. No. She still liked him and admired him, but the longing was gone. Even the simple need to talk to him burned much more quietly.

She still felt regret for that last night together. She wasn't sure how long it would take for the shame to ease. But except for that, she felt ready to put Jon behind her. She found herself genuinely happy that he'd found someone else and longed to do the same herself.

Involuntarily she found herself looking at Qadir. Was he the one?

That made her smile. Yes, the man was amazing and apparently had a direct and sexual line to her nervous system, but that didn't mean they would have any kind of serious relationship. Ever. The prince and the car mechanic? Not likely.

"Qadir is very nice," Kayleen said, her voice soft.

Maggie smiled. "He is. Not nearly as imperious as I would have imagined a prince to be."

"I think he's more low-key than the other brothers. Now Kateb is superintense. Have you met him?"

"No."

"He lives in the desert. He just got back. I talked to him for a few minutes earlier today. Wow. Talk about dark and dangerous. I kept wanting to hide behind As'ad."

"Why?"

"I can't really explain it. There's something about him that isn't completely…tamed. Hmm, that's the wrong word, but its the best one I can come up with."

An untamed prince?

"The king is already asking about grandchildren," As'ad said to Qadir.

Kayleen squeezed his hand. "But that's the fun part."

As'ad smiled at her. "You are too understanding. The king goes too far. We are not yet married."

"You could just tell him we're planning on having children fairly quickly. That would make him feel better."

"I will not give him the satisfaction."

Kayleen looked at Maggie. "See what I mean? Totally stubborn. How am I supposed to fight against that?"

"You are not," As'ad told her. He looked at his brother. "You know, if your relationship gets serious, he will do the same to you. The man is never satisfied."

Qadir reached for her hand. "Don't get scared. I'll protect you from the king."

"I'm not worried," Maggie told him. There was no way she and Qadir would ever be having the children discussion. She was here for a limited period of time. Sort of like the traveling theater. Not that she wouldn't want children one day.

She and Jon had always assumed they would get married and have kids. They'd argued about the number. He wanted three. She kept pointing out that practically, an even number was better. Then he joked about eight and they would laugh.

Instinctively she braced herself for the pain from the memories, but there wasn't any. She had truly moved on.

"It's kind of funny to have to worry about not getting pregnant early," Kayleen said. "Obviously one doesn't want to be a pregnant bride under any circumstances, but when the groom is a prince, it's a huge deal."

"It would only take one mistake," Qadir said cheerfully. "No pressure, brother."

As'ad growled some reply but Maggie wasn't listening. She found herself oddly frozen in time, as if she'd left her body and could see the party happening below her but wasn't a part of it anymore.

"No, no, no," she told herself silently. It wasn't that. It couldn't be. It had only been the one time. Off the pill, her period was never regular, so she wasn't technically late.

Fear clutched her, leaving her chilled to the bone.

One time with Jon. That single night.

As they had only ever been with each other, their only worry for protection had been pregnancy. She'd gone on the pill early in their relationship and all had been well. But after the breakup, she hadn't bothered, knowing she wasn't interested in being with anyone, at least not for a long time.

Which meant that she hadn't been taking birth control that last night she and Jon were together—and he hadn't used a condom.

"Maggie?" Qadir asked. "Are you all right?"

She nodded and tried to smile, even as she fought waves of panic. She couldn't be pregnant. Not now. Not with Jon's baby. That would be a massive disaster—one she wouldn't know how to fix.

* * *

After getting directions to the nearest couple of drugstores from Victoria, Maggie headed out first thing the next morning. She hadn't slept all night, even after telling herself that her period was late because of the stress she'd been through. One encounter did not a baby make. Or did it?

As her friend had promised, there were several shops on the street, with a drugstore at each end. Maggie went into the first one and prayed that El Deharia was a enough of a forward-thinking country that there would be pregnancy kits right there on the shelf.

She found the aisle with all the female products and breathed a sigh of relief when she saw the boxes that she had only previously seen on television. At least she wasn't going to have to ask the pharmacist.

She was about to grab one when she heard some odd whispering. She turned and saw a couple of teenage girls behind her. They were in school uniforms and carrying books.

"You're her, aren't you?" one of them said. "The girl dating Qadir. He's delicious. I like him the best. What's he really like?"

Maggie wondered if she was standing there with her mouth hanging open from shock. These girls had recognized her from those stupid tabloid pictures? Was it possible?

"Oh, hi," she said, feeling like an idiot. "He's really nice. Friendly."

"How did you meet?"

"I work at the palace."

The other girl sighed. "I wish I could get a job there. My mom says I'm not the type to do real work, but I could do something."

Her friend smiled. "He's the best. You're so lucky. Come on. We need to get to school."

They waved and left. Maggie walked around to the next aisle, where she picked up some bandages she didn't need. When she was sure the girls were gone, she returned to the first aisle and bought three different pregnancy kits. Then she went to the front of the store and paid for them.

What she didn't see was the third teenage girl lurking behind, her cell phone held high, camera at the ready. As Maggie fished money out of her wallet, the third girl started snapping pictures.

Twenty-four hours later, Maggie sat on her sofa trying to decide which was worse—the fact that she was pregnant, or the picture in the paper showing her buying the pregnancy kits.

And the speculation that the child was Qadir's.

Chapter Eight

Maggie couldn't believe it. There was her picture and she was clearly holding the pregnancy kits. Who had done that and how? Who walked around with a camera all the...

A cell phone, she thought as she sank onto the sofa and held in a groan. Those girls. Was it possible?

She looked at the grainy picture and realized it was more than possible. It had happened.

She didn't know what to think, what to feel. Remembering that last night with Jon, she knew it had to have happened then. But why did she have to be pregnant? Now? Like this?

She covered her face with her hands, ashamed, embarrassed, confused. This couldn't be real. She was asleep and she would wake up and be grateful that—.

Someone knocked on the door. She didn't want to answer, but knew she couldn't hide out in her suite forever. She would have to face Qadir. She winced, thinking about how all this was going to effect him. What must he think of her?

She stood and walked to the door, then sucked in a breath and pulled it open.

She'd been hoping for Victoria. Instead a handsome prince stood in her doorway.

"I see by your expression you've seen the morning paper," he said calmly. "May I come in?"

She stepped back, then closed the door behind him. Heat burned on her cheeks. She had no idea what to say. She'd never planned on getting pregnant in the first place, let alone drag him into the mess, with people assuming the child was his.

"I feel horrible," she said, knowing she should be the one to start the conversation. "I had no idea about this. You have to believe me."

"I do." He looked at her, his dark eyes unreadable. "Jon is the father?"

She nodded. "There was one time, a few weeks ago. I was feeling lost and alone and things just got out of hand." She pressed her lips together. Okay, not the whole truth, but she was afraid to have him think even less of her by explaining it all in detail.

"It wasn't supposed to happen," she said. "Not that, not the pregnancy. We don't love each other. He's with someone else and I've moved on." She was more sure of that by the day. "I can't believe I'm pregnant."

Qadir looked at her. "You've taken the test to be sure? There is no mistake?"

"I wish there was. I didn't just take one test, I took three of them. I'm pregnant."

She waited for a reaction. An immediate statement that their deal was over. Maybe even orders to leave the country. But when he said nothing, she didn't know what to think. Worse, she couldn't look at him.

Maybe he was waiting for her to just pack her things and go. Her previous life hadn't prepared her for a situation like this. Everything was awkward enough, but his royal status added a whole new level of embarrassment to the conversation.

"This creates a complication," he said at last.

Despite everything she smiled. "You do have a talent for understatement."

"Jon will not be expecting you to be pregnant."

"Probably not." She drew in a deep breath. Okay—fine. She could be the one to say it. "Look, I know why you're here. You want me to understand that with things being the way they are, our deal is off. I get that. In your situation, I'd feel exactly the same way. But I'd really like to finish the car. I can do a beautiful job and being pregnant isn't going to make me any less skilled. To be honest, I need the job. I don't have health insurance and once I start to show, no one is going to want to hire me."

She felt panic flaring inside of her but refused to give in to it. Under the circumstances, she felt slimy enough just begging for her job. If she had any pride—or money in the bank—she would simply walk away. If it was just her, she would. But she now had a baby to think of.

A baby?

She pressed her hand to her stomach. No way. There couldn't be life growing inside her. She couldn't sense it. She didn't feel any different. Shouldn't she have a maternal connection or at least a clue?

"Do you want to leave?" he asked.

"What? Of course not."

"I have not suggested you should go."

"But I'm pregnant."

He nodded. "And people will assume the child is mine. What does it say about me that I let you leave the country?"

Maggie sank onto the sofa. She hadn't thought about that. "You'll have to issue a statement or something. Tell them it's not your baby. Some kind of official denial. People will think badly of me rather than you." Which she hated, but how could they get around that?

"Who will believe the child isn't mine?" he asked. "We have been seen together."

"Only for a short time and the baby not being yours is the truth."

"Why would that matter?"

She opened her mouth, then closed it. Good point, she thought, feeling alone and confused. Since when was truth a priority when it came to gossip?

"I'll tell the truth," she said slowly, hating that she would be known as a slut in public. "That I was with someone else. You're off the hook."

"You don't want to do that," he told her. "You will not enjoy the attention."

"I agree, but what choice is there? You're not taking the blame for this. You can't be the bad guy. I'm responsible."

"I'm the prince."

"What does that have to do with anything?"

"None of this would have happened if I hadn't asked you to lie on my behalf. I'm the one who put you in the public eye."

"I went willingly." She'd sold her soul for money. Her father would be so disappointed with her.

Before she could give in to that blow, the door to her suite opened and King Mukhtar swept inside. He held the paper in one hand.

"Is it true?" he demanded, glaring first at Qadir, then at her. "You are pregnant?"

If Maggie had thought she would squeeze in, she would have crawled under the sofa. But before she could make an attempt, Qadir pulled her to her feet and stepped in front of her, as if offering protection.

"This is none of your business," he said coolly as he faced his father.

"It *is* my business," the king told him angrily. "Is she pregnant? If so, the child cannot be yours. Unless you were seeing her before and brought her here specifically to meet me. Which you should have told me. Qadir, I demand to know what's going on."

Maggie cringed. "Your Highness," she began, only to have Qadir shake his head.

"Is it your child?" the king asked his son. "If so, I insist you marry her immediately. I understand having the wedding *after* the child is born is very fashionable these days, but this is my palace. I will not have it so."

"The baby isn't Qadir's," she whispered, wishing she really could disappear into the floor. "I'm sorry."

Qadir pulled her next to him and put his arm around her. "Don't apologize. You are not at fault here. The blame is mine." He looked at his father. "I paraded Maggie in public. That's why the pictures were taken. It is my fault."

"But not your child."

Maggie stared at the king, trying to figure out what he was thinking. He sounded almost disappointed by the news. Had he been hoping he would have a grandchild at last?

"No, Father."

Mukhtar nodded. "Very well. Maggie, you will leave El Deharia at once."

Maggie started to nod only to have Qadir say, "No, she will not. She's staying here."

"To what end? You can find someone else to work on your car."

"This isn't about the car. This is about her."

Maggie couldn't believe it. After all this, Qadir was still going forward with the deal? Didn't he know what a disaster this all was? How her pregnancy complicated everything?

"You can't go out with her," the king said.

"Why not?" Qadir asked. "I like her."

Words spoken to prove a point, she told herself. Silly words that meant nothing. Yet she wanted to wrap herself in them like they were a blanket and she were caught in a snowstorm. She felt her eyes burning, but refused to give in to tears.

"Maggie stays," Qadir said. "We will issue a discreet statement saying the child isn't mine."

"No one will believe you. Not until the child is born and there can be a DNA test."

"Perhaps not, but we will have stated our position. No one will publicly defy us. We will be left alone. Maggie will be left alone. That is what matters to me."

Mukhtar narrowed his gaze. "She means this much to you?"

"Yes."

"Very well. I hope you know what you're doing."

With that, the king left.

Maggie waited until he was out of the room to turn on Qadir. "Are you insane? What are doing? You can't go up against your father like that. It's crazy and wrong. I'm pregnant, Qadir. With another man's child. I know you don't want your father picking out your future wife, but this is taking things too far. I can't stay. Besides, you're a handsome, rich guy who happens to be a prince. Are you telling me there isn't one other woman you can think of to play this game?"

She practically spat the last couple of sentences at him. Her eyes flashed with temper so hot, he expected to see flames. Intriguing.

"So much energy," he told her.

"One of us has to put a little energy into this," she told him. "You obviously have a head injury. I am *pregnant*."

"Despite your repetitions of the facts, I am already aware of that."

The morning paper had shocked him, but not nearly as much as his reaction to the picture. He'd felt a deep, powerful sense of betrayal. As if he'd been cheated on.

Maggie was his in name only. There was nothing between them…if one ignored the powerful sexual chemistry that drew him at every turn. So why would he care that she was pregnant by another man?

Yet he found himself caring and that reaction was so unexpected, he wanted to know what it meant. So he wasn't going to let her go. Not yet.

"A month," he told her. "Stay a month. You can finish the car. If acting as if we are dating is still too difficult, you can leave and I will pay you the full amount for both jobs."

She started to speak, then stopped. He wondered if she was going to refuse the money. If she could. He knew there were money troubles in her past. It would only take him a few minutes to get someone to find out her exact financial situation. But he chose not to violate her privacy that way. Not until he had to.

"I'll finish the car," she said at last. "I want to do that. It means a lot to me."

"And the rest?"

"I can't figure out why you'd want to continue to pretend to date me, but it's your call. For now, I'll agree."

That night Maggie curled up on the sofa in Victoria's suite and sipped the herbal tea her friend had made. Her friend's rooms were similar to hers, with a stylish living room and French doors leading out to the balcony that wrapped around the palace.

But unlike Maggie, Victoria had added little touches to make the place her own. There were a few prints on the walls, a throw that added color. Colorful masks formed a centerpiece on the dining room table.

"They're beautiful," Maggie said. "Where did you find them?"

"The local bazaar. They mostly sell food, but a few times a year they feature work from local craftsmen. I always try to go. I've picked up some beautiful jewelry, as well. There's supposed to be a place in the desert where they make the most exquisite gold. Beautiful woven patterns, like nothing you've ever seen. I have a pair of earrings I—"

She started to stand, then sank back onto the sofa. "Sorry. You're not interested in my earrings."

"Not even on my best day," Maggie admitted with a smile. "But I can pretend."

"No need. I forgot the purpose of our meeting."

"That's right. I'm expecting you to fix my life."

"I'm not sure I'm up to that," Victoria told her.

"I know. It's kind of beyond fixing." Maggie set down her mug and pulled her knees to her chest. "I feel so awful. Not physically," she added quickly. "I'm fine. In fact if I didn't know better, I would swear I wasn't pregnant. Nothing's different. Shouldn't I be throwing up or something?"

"That can come later," her friend told her.

"Something to look forward to." Maggie sighed. "I just can't get my mind around the fact that I'm going to have a baby. I've been distracted the whole day, thinking about it, but it's just words. I don't know how to make it mean anything."

"You have time."

"Nine months less six weeks," Maggie said. "I know the day it happened. The exact day."

"The last time you were with Jon."

Maggie nodded.

"So you're confused," Victoria said. "That's not a surprise. You weren't expecting to end up pregnant. But beyond confusion…is there anything else?"

Maggie tried to probe her heart. What did she feel? "Terror," she admitted. "I'm not like you. I don't know how to be a mother."

Victoria held up both her hands. "Hey, I'm about the least maternal person you know. I can't keep a plant alive."

"But you're so feminine and girly."

"Knowing how to buy shoes on sale has nothing to do with being maternal. You're confusing your definitions of feminine. From what you've told me about your past, you'll be a great mother."

Maggie stared at her. "Why?"

"Because you had a great father. He was totally there for you. He loved you and supported you and only wanted what was best for you. So you know how to do the same. No baby is going to care if you actually knitted the blanket or bought it at a store. What he or she will care about is being loved. And you're gonna love your baby."

Maggie felt a twinge of something inside. Something hot and fierce and powerful. A baby. Was it possible?

"Thank you," she said. "You've made me feel better. So that's one problem down and four thousand left. I'm pregnant."

Victoria smiled. "I know."

"This is a huge complication."

"It usually is."

"I'm going to have to deal with Jon at some point."

"True."

"This isn't going to make him happy."

"You'll figure something out."

Maggie wasn't so sure, but she didn't want to think about Jon just then. "I felt bad about that picture being in the paper. It was incredibly humiliating for me, but I also felt awful about Qadir. That he got dragged into this."

Victoria sipped her tea. "An interesting way of looking at things. A case could be made that he dragged you into things by offering up the deal in the first place."

"He didn't know I was pregnant. He never would have said anything if he had."

"Agreed. My point is that he started things going by wanting to pretend to date you."

"Maybe. I just hate that now he has to deal with my problem."

"Because you like him."

"Of course I like him. He's a great guy. He defended me to the king."

Maggie still couldn't believe how Qadir had stood up for her. While she hated to cause trouble in the family, she couldn't help feeling safe and protected, even just for the moment.

"I find it fascinating that he still wants to see you," Victoria said. "Even after knowing you're pregnant by another man."

"I know. I don't get it, either. I told him we should break things off. That the public would totally understand him dumping me." She shivered slightly. "I'll admit I hated the idea of being branded a slut in the press, but I'm responsible for what I did, so it was only fair that I was the one who got stuck. I said I really wanted to finish the car, but nothing else."

"He didn't agree."

"I can't figure out why. What's in it for him? There's going to be speculation about the baby no matter what anyone says. I wonder if I made a mistake in agreeing."

"Isn't the bigger question whether or not Qadir made a mistake in asking you to stay."

Maggie didn't want to think about that, but she knew her friend was telling the truth. "Probably."

"But that's not the most interesting part," Victoria said. "What I find intriguing is that Prince Qadir of El Deharia, who could admittedly have nearly any woman he wanted, has chosen you."

Maggie straightened. "What?"

"He picked you to play the game for a lot of reasons. You're pretty, he thought he could spend time in your company without going crazy, that sort of thing. But it was a deal. A monetary transaction. Yet suddenly, it's more than that. When faced with trouble, instead of running, he's standing by you."

"He's just that kind of person."

Victoria laughed. "I promise you, if Nadim and I had the same kind of arrangement and I had turned up pregnant, he would have kicked me to the curb so fast there would be skid marks."

"Then why would you want to marry a man like that?"

Victoria sighed. "Good question. I had these big plans to marry for money and spend the rest of my life totally secure. But apparently I picked the wrong prince. The more I look at how Qadir is with you, the less I like Nadim. I've been working with him for two years and he hasn't noticed me. What kind of idiot is he?"

"One you should forget about. Do you really need to marry for money? What about love?"

"Love is for fools," Victoria said firmly. "I will never be a fool for love. But you're right about me forgetting Nadim. He may be a prince, but he's a boring twit of a man and I'm so over him."

Maggie grinned. "That would be a more impressive statement if you'd ever actually cared about him."

"I know." Victoria drank more of her tea. "Maybe I can find a nice diplomat in the foreign office. Someone who comes from money."

"Would you get off the money thing?"

"I can't. You don't know what it's like to be afraid you're going to lose everything. That's how I grew up. There were plenty of nights I watched my mother go hungry because there was only food for one. I vowed that I would never be like her— never give my heart to a jerk who walked on it and used her, thinking only of himself."

Maggie didn't know about her friend's past. "I'm sorry," she murmured. "I'm sorry you went through that."

"Me, too." Victoria sighed. "Wow—talk about getting carried away. I didn't mean to shift the conversation that way. We were talking about you. Have you considered that he defended you because he doesn't want you to leave?"

Maggie blinked several times. Victoria's words floated through her brain, forming images, then fading, but never disappearing completely.

"It can't be that," she said at last.

"Why not?"

Because… Because…

"He's just being kind."

Victoria wrinkled her nose. "He's a sheik, honey. Kind isn't one of the descriptors. Arrogant, powerful, determined. Those all work. But kind? No way."

Maggie knew her friend was right, which did leave that interesting question on the table. Why hadn't Qadir just dumped her when he'd found out about the baby?

"He wants his car finished."

"I don't mean any disrespect when it comes to your skills," Victoria said, "but couldn't he just hire someone else? You're good and all, but do you have a totally unique talent?"

Maggie wanted to defend herself, but she understood the other woman's point.

"Then I can't explain it," she admitted.

"Oh, I can," Victoria told her. "I would say you have a sheik who's interested."

"I don't think so," Maggie said automatically, even as she found herself almost wishing it were true. Qadir? Interested?

She knew there was a powerful attraction between them, but that was just one of those weird, unexplained things. He might want to sleep with her, but getting emotionally involved was very different. There had to be another reason.

"Trust me," Victoria told her. "I've seen male indifference. He's not showing it."

"I can't believe he wants anything from me but the deal we'd arranged."

"I don't know where he's going with this, either," Victoria told her. "But I do know one thing. If he wanted you gone, you would be. The fact that you're still here tells me he wants something more from you. The trick is going to be figuring out what."

Chapter Nine

Maggie worked carefully to pry the door panel from the door. The fit was perfect, which made her job more difficult but would allow the end results to be spectacular.

After a day of confusion and worry and not knowing what all she was going to do with her life, it felt good to be back with the car. Here the world was clear and everything made sense. She knew what to do and how to do it.

She turned back to the body of the vehicle and ran her hands along the sides.

"You're going to be stunning," she murmured. "Men will want you, other cars will want to be you."

"She's going to get a big head," Qadir said as he walked into the garage. "I'm not sure that's a good idea."

Maggie smiled at him, trying not to notice the funny feeling in her stomach or the way her heartbeat suddenly tripled. "I think you'll be able to handle her even if she gets conceited."

"Perhaps."

"I'm taking the doors apart. We'll be able to see if there's any interior damage. Then they can get repaired, replace any missing little parts, sand, prime and paint."

"Are you sure you should be doing all this?" he asked.

Huh? "It's part of my job. Not fixing the doors will make the rest of the car look funny."

"I was referring to your pregnancy. Is it safe for you to work here now?"

Oh. That. "I'm still the same person I was yesterday," she told him firmly. "I'll be careful about chemicals. I wasn't going to paint the car, anyway. I'll want to do some of the sanding by hand, but I'll wear a protective mask so I don't breathe in the particles. I'll avoid solvents. Otherwise, I should be fine. I'm just pregnant—I haven't morphed into an alien."

"If you are sure."

"I am." The last thing she needed was him having second thoughts about her doing the job. She desperately needed the money.

"Now you see why it is so much easier to hire a man," he said.

She narrowed her eyes. "If you weren't royal and my boss, I swear, I'd sock you for saying that."

He grinned. "Is it true."

"It's not true. Men have issues. They come in drunk, aren't responsible, pick fights."

"A lot of generalizations."

She smiled. "You mean like assuming a pregnancy is going to get in the way?"

"Point taken."

She leaned against the car. "So is yours. My dad would never have admitted it, but I know he would have agreed with you. We used to argue about treating men and women equally. He kept saying they were different halves of the same whole. Yet he didn't mind my being in a nontraditional job. I think he was even proud of it."

"I'm sorry I could not meet him."

"Me, too. You would have liked him." She smiled as she remembered her father meeting various clients. He never cared about how rich they were or how important. To him, everyone was the same. "I still miss him."

"You have a lifetime of memories to draw upon."

"I know. That helps."

"Would he have enjoyed knowing he would be a grandfather?"

"I hope so," she admitted. "I know he would have been disappointed by the circumstances. I'm hardly proud of them myself. But he would have been there for me and in the end he would have been happy about the baby. He liked kids a lot. He would have been a great grandpa."

"Did he like Jon?"

"Yes. They were close. He always thought we'd be a good match. I think that's part of the reason we stayed together through his illness. Even when things weren't great between us, we didn't want to disappoint him." And Jon hadn't wanted to leave her alone.

She'd sensed that perhaps even before he'd been able to articulate the problem.

"Jon stood by me through the end and at the funeral. His parents also helped with so much."

The two families had been connected. That had been part of the problem, too. She and Jon had been walking away from more than just each other.

"When will you tell him?" Qadir asked.

Maggie folded her arms across her chest. "I don't know."

He didn't say anything. He didn't have to. She could give herself the lecture well enough for both of them.

Jon was the father of her child. He deserved to know there was a baby. He was a good man and he hadn't done anything wrong. She owed him the truth. But...

"I don't want to mess up his life," she admitted slowly. "Knowing about the baby is going to change everything. He's happy with Elaine. This is the last thing either of them need."

He continued to study her. She sighed.

"I know, I know. I'll tell him."

"What do you think he'll say?" he asked.

"I have no idea. He's big on family. I don't think he can just walk away."

"Is that what you want?"

"It would be easier for all of us if he would."

"Life is rarely easy."

"Agreed. It's just...a baby will connect us forever. How are we supposed to get on with our lives while we're so closely tied together?"

"Because you are still in love with him?"

"No. I'm not. I'm long over him." She'd been over him before that last night together. She just hadn't realized it yet. "But it creates tension and pressure. No matter who he marries, there will always be this child between them. She may be the first wife, but she won't have the first child. That will be forever taken from her."

"Does that matter?"

"I don't know. I think, for a man, his first child is very important. There's the whole pride thing. Telling the world he procreated. It's different for women."

"Having a child with someone else would still be significant for you?"

"Yes."

"Perhaps it will be so for Jon, as well."

"I hope so," Maggie said. She just wished she didn't have to deal with this at all. She got a knot in her stomach every time she thought about having to make that phone call.

"I wish he would just walk away," she murmured.

"Will he?"

"I don't think so."

How ironic. A few weeks ago she would have done anything to get him back in her life. Now she had the perfect opportunity and she wasn't interested.

"But you would like him to."

She nodded.

He moved forward and put his arm around her. "If there is anything I can do, you must tell me."

He was warm and strong. Talk about tempting, she thought, fighting the need to throw herself against him and beg him to handle everything. She knew he was more than capable. But this was her problem and she had to fix it herself.

"Thank you. You've already done so much."

He smiled at her. "I have done very little."

He released her. She forced herself to step away.

"There is a museum opening next week," he said. "I would like you to come with me to the event."

She took a second step back. "I don't think that's a good idea."

"We have a deal."

"One you should be rethinking. Honestly, Qadir, you don't want to go there."

"The longer we are together, the more serious the relationship will appear."

She pointed to her stomach. "Do we have to have the 'baby on board' discussion again?"

"Once you leave, people will believe the child is not mine. That will solve the problem." He looked determined. "I want to see this through. You promised to give me at least a month. I will hold you to that, Maggie."

She nodded slowly. Her reluctance came not only from the potential embarrassment to herself, but also from a tiny ache deep inside. She knew that Qadir was only using their relationship to fake out his father. Nothing more. Having him talk about that shouldn't bother her.

But it did. It hurt and for the life of her, she couldn't say why.

"And if I order you not to see her anymore?" the king demanded.

"I do not think that is a conversation you wish to have," Qadir told his father.

"What is the point of this? Why her? Find someone else. Someone who isn't carrying another man's child. What will happen if things progress? Will you marry her? Am I to accept that child as a grandchild?"

"As'ad is adopting three daughters," Qadir said. "You have no problem with them."

"That is totally different."

"Why?"

"It is. Everyone knew of the girls before. They are charming."

"Perhaps Maggie's baby will be charming, too."

His father glared at him. "You are being deliberately difficult."

"I am not, despite how it seems to you. Maggie is important to me. She is someone with whom I enjoy spending time. She is charming and amusing. She does not annoy me."

"An important consideration," the king said.

"Very. She is also not interested in the trappings of my position. My being a prince does not impress her."

"Like Whitney."

There were very few people who were allowed to speak that name. Unfortunately the king was one of them.

"Like Whitney," Qadir agreed. "But with one important difference. I do not love her. I like her. I respect her. But she does not possess my heart."

No one would again, he reminded himself. Once had been enough. He had loved Whitney beyond what he thought was possible and in the end, she had left him.

He'd been stunned by her decision and the emotional pain that had followed. He'd vowed then that no woman would ever bring him to his knees again.

"A sensible match between compatible parties makes the most sense," his father said. "But this woman? What about the child? He or she can never be heir."

"I am not the eldest son."

"Perhaps not, but if Kateb walks away, you will be next in line."

There was bitterness in his father's voice, and perhaps sadness. "Kateb means no disrespect. He has taken a different path."

"Into the desert. He belongs here."

"I do not agree." Qadir knew his brother could never be fully happy in the city. The desert sand ran in his veins. He was only truly alive when he was there.

"You seek to defy me at every turn it seems," Mukhtar grumbled. "I am disappointed in you, my son."

Qadir looked at his father and smiled. "You are not. You are annoyed by my refusal to do as you say, but you are secretly pleased that I will stand up to you fearlessly. It reminds you that you are an excellent father and monarch."

One corner of the other man's mouth twitched. "Perhaps. But that does not mean I approve of your relationship with Maggie.

You will get distracted by her, then decide she will not do. By then it will be too late. You will be interested. So when you send her away, you will not be interested in another woman for months."

"I do not see that happening," Qadir said, lying cheerfully. With luck, his plan was going to work perfectly.

Maggie sat in the gardens, her eyes closed, her body absorbing the heat of the sun. It was still early spring, so the temperature wasn't too hot. Compared to what the weather would be like back in Aspen, with snow and slush everywhere, this was paradise.

Unfortunately her reluctance to go inside had nothing to do with the pleasant surroundings and everything to do with what would happen when she got back to her room.

Before she could persuade herself not to put off calling Jon for another minute, a tall man in traditional clothing swept into the garden. He moved purposefully, taking long strides, his robes swirling behind him. While he was handsome, there was a deep scar on one cheek and an air of power about him. He was not the sort of man Maggie would want to argue with.

When he saw her, he came to a stop.

"An unexpected flower in my father's garden," he said.

That made Maggie laugh. "I'm not feeling especially flowery today, but thank you."

"Who are you?"

"Maggie Collins."

"Ah, yes. The woman who restores cars."

While they were guessing identities, she said, "And you would be Kateb, the mysterious brother who lives in the desert."

Kateb bowed low, then straightened. "Does my brother still speak of me with awe?"

She laughed. "Not so I'd noticed."

"Then you must listen harder."

He sat on the stone bench across from hers. Although they were outside and, in theory, not lacking in space, he seemed to fill up an excess of area.

"You are enjoying your time in El Deharia?" he asked.

"Yes. The country is beautiful. I haven't seen that much of it, but I hope to soon."

"Perhaps Qadir will show you his favorite places."

Maggie eyed the other man. Did he know about her deal with Qadir?

"Perhaps," she murmured.

"Do you often come out to the garden?" he asked.

"No. I'm avoiding something I know I have to do. Not my most mature decision of the day."

"But you will do what has to be done?"

She sighed, then nodded. "Yes, I'll do the right thing."

Kateb stared at her. "Do you always?"

"It's usually a goal. Is it the same for you?" she asked, knowing she probably shouldn't but wanting to ruffle Kateb's steely composure.

"When it suits me."

"How convenient."

"It is. I am Prince Kateb of El Deharia. I do as I please."

She laughed. "My father would say you're the kind of man whose mouth is writing checks the rest of him can't cash, but in your case, I'm going to guess you're telling the truth."

"Your father sounds like a sensible man."

"He was." She stood. "It was nice to meet you, Prince Kateb of El Deharia. If you'll excuse me, I have a phone call to make."

"The one you've been avoiding?"

She nodded.

He rose and bowed again. "I have enjoyed our conversation, Maggie Collins. My brother is more fortunate than he realizes."

* * *

Maggie watched the clock, then at the appointed time, she picked up the phone and dialed a familiar number. She and Jon had e-mailed back and forth to set up the call. She'd told him speaking with him was important but hadn't said why.

"Maggie," he said when he answered. "What's wrong?"

"Nothing. I'm fine."

"I've been worried."

"I said everything was okay."

"I know, but I couldn't think of why you'd need to talk to me unless something was wrong. Is everything all right there? Do you need anything?"

She needed to be able to turn back time and undo that single night, she thought sadly. Or did she? Although she was terrified about being pregnant and had no idea what the next seven and a half months would bring, she couldn't bring herself to regret the baby.

"I'm doing great," she told him. "Work on the car is going well. I'm enjoying the country. It's different but wonderful. Plus I'm living in a palace. How often does that happen?"

"Are you sure? I could probably get some time off and come get you."

She frowned. "Jon, I can take care of myself."

"I'm not convinced."

Wait a minute. How long had he seen her as incapable? She sure didn't like that.

"You should be. I'm a big girl. All grown-up. Let's change the subject. How's Elaine?"

There was a moment of silence. She wasn't sure if he didn't want to let go of how she might need him or if he was uncomfortable talking about Elaine.

"She's fine."

"You're still going out?"

"Yes."

"Come on, Jon. Details. Are things getting serious?"

"Sort of." He drew in a breath. "They are. She's funny. She wants a cat. She's wanted one for a long time, but her roommate was allergic. The roommate got married a couple of weeks ago, so Elaine has the apartment to herself, but she still hasn't gotten a cat. I finally asked her why and she said she wanted to make sure it was okay with me. I told her it was her cat."

Men weren't always as bright as they could be, Maggie thought humorously. "She wants to make sure you like cats, too."

"Yeah, I got that later. It was kind of cool, you know, that my opinion mattered that much."

"Is she getting the cat?"

"We're going to pick one out over the weekend."

"I'm glad."

Maggie said the words, then braced herself for a twinge. She and Jon had never gotten to the pet-sharing stage. But all she felt was pleasure for him.

"Sounds like things are getting serious," she said. "That's good. I hope you two are really happy together."

"Maggie, I…"

"Jon, don't worry about me. I'm fine. We're over. We were over a long time before we ended things. I wish we could have seen that. I know we stayed together because of my dad and while I'm sure he appreciated the gesture, we weren't doing ourselves any favors."

"I don't want to hurt you."

"I'm not hurt. We had a great few years and I'll always be grateful but we're growing in different directions." She knew he liked taking care of people and hoped Elaine enjoyed being taken care of by him.

Unfortunately things were not going to get easier for any of them.

"I want to talk to you about that last time we were together," she said, hating that she had to bring it up.

"Maggie, don't. We're both to blame."

"Me a little more than you."

"I didn't have to come over."

"I made a pass at you," she said, wishing it wasn't true. "I seduced you."

"I let myself be seduced. I guess we both wanted that one last time. My only regret is if it hurt you. Otherwise I'm glad we were together."

Maybe he had been, but all that was about to change.

"You're beating yourself up over nothing," he continued. "Maggie, you have to let it go."

"I wish I could," she said softly. "But it's not that simple." She drew in a breath. "I'm pregnant, Jon. After we stopped seeing each other, I went off the pill. I wasn't expecting anything to happen, so why bother? I just never thought about it."

She paused to give him a chance to speak but there was only silence on the other end of the phone. She knew him well enough to imagine the shocked look on his face.

She decided to say the little speech she'd prepared while he was trying to figure out what the hell had just gone wrong with his life.

"I know this is totally unexpected," she said. "Neither of us ever imagined this happening. But it did. I also know that you're a total good guy and you'll feel responsible. Jon, you're not. I'm the one to blame and I'm the one who is going to deal with this."

Now came the hard part. "I don't want anything from you. I mean that. You have a life, a great woman and a future. Having a baby with me will only mess that up. I told you about the baby because you have the right to know, but that's the only reason. I have no expectations. What I'm really hoping is that you'll walk away and live your life. You don't have to be involved. We can find a lawyer to write up some papers. You sign away all your rights and I promise to never come after you for money. Considering what has happened between us, it's really the best decision."

She paused again and there was still silence. She couldn't figure out what that meant.

"I know you need time to think about all this. You've been blindsided by something really huge. Fortunately we have time." She sighed. "I'm so sorry. I never meant for this to happen. I didn't do it on purpose."

"I know that," he said at last, his voice low and thick with emotion. "Dammit, Maggie, are you sure?"

She winced. "I took three different pregnancy tests. They all came out positive. I'm sure."

"I'm not blaming you," he said. "Either of us could have walked away. I meant what I said before. I wanted that last time with you."

"Just not the consequences."

"I didn't say that."

He didn't have to. In his position, she would be angry and confused. What to do? Where to go? What about Elaine?

"You need to think about what I said," she told him. "About just walking away. I know it won't be your first instinct, but it's the right thing to do. I'm perfectly capable of raising a child on my own."

"You need to come home."

Uh-oh. Was he going to get all parental on her? "I'm fine. I'm perfectly healthy. If you're worried about the baby, I can find a doctor here."

"You need to come home," he repeated. "Not for the doctor, but so we can get married."

Chapter Ten

Qadir walked into the usually quiet garage and watched as Maggie threw tools into the large open box on the floor.

"Just so damn *stupid*," she muttered. "Does anyone care about my opinion? *Noooo*. I just want to beat him with a stick."

She threw more tools as she grumbled, her expression tight with annoyance, her movements jerky. She was on fire and he found himself attracted to her temper.

"Someone has annoyed you," he said.

She turned and glared at him. "Yes, someone has. A man. You probably don't want to be here today, what with you being a man and all. I'm angry enough not to be picky about who I yell at."

He laughed. "You do not frighten me."

"Because I'm a woman, right? What is it with you men that you think you know better?" She pointed to his crotch. "It's just excess flesh, you know. It's not the great repository for all knowledge. Since when did being a man make you an oracle?"

She was all fire and rage. Both her passion and beauty excited him.

"I did not claim to be an oracle," he told her. "I said I am not afraid of you."

"You should be." She picked up a large wrench. "I could do a lot of damage with that."

"Yes, you could." He walked over and removed it from her grasp, then set it on the desk. Still holding her hand in his, he rubbed her fingers. "What happened?"

"I talked to Jon."

Qadir did not respond. Better for Maggie to tell him in her own way.

She drew in a breath. "He's just so annoying. His stupid superior attitude. Like he has all the answers. I hate that."

"And him?"

"I don't hate him, but I want to smack him upside the head. He's convinced he knows best. Since when does he get to be in charge of my life? Hello, it's my life. Mine. Not his. But will he accept that? I'll give you one guess on that question."

Qadir had not been pleased to know that Maggie would have to tell the other man about the baby, but there was little choice in the matter.

She looked at him. "He wants to marry me."

"He is an honorable man," he told her, enjoying a brief image of crushing Jon like a bug. "That should please you."

"Well, it doesn't. It really pisses me off. Okay, fine. I'll accept he wants to be a part of his child's life. Knowing him, I shouldn't be surprised. I still think it would be better if he walked away, but he won't. That's just so him. But marriage? Did he notice the new-century thing, because here we are. It's a shiny new world and by God, no man is going to marry me just because I'm pregnant with his child."

The marriage proposal did not come as a surprise, but Qadir did not like it.

"He doesn't even care that it's not what I want," Maggie continued, still fuming. "No. It's all about him and the baby and what's right." She turned on Qadir. "How is this right? How is two people making themselves miserable right? Wait. It's not two people. It's three. What about Elaine? I think they're falling in love and he's going to toss that away because of the baby? This is just so typical. Do you know he doesn't think I'm capable? I never got that before, but he just about said I couldn't do this on my own. That really, really annoys me."

She jerked free of his touch and stalked around the car. "It's a guy thing, right? The need to assume women are just a little bit less? Why is that? Do we threaten you so damn much? Oh, I'm just so mad I could spit."

Despite potential risk to his person, Qadir chuckled. She turned on him.

"You think this is funny?"

"I think you are beautiful and full of life. Jon is a fool for ever letting you go, but that is his loss. He must deal with it now."

Her eyes widened. "That was good," she breathed. "Seriously. I feel almost disarmed."

"How unfortunate, as I like you armed. Go to your office and get changed. I will take you to lunch and then shopping. You will feel better when we are finished."

She rolled her eyes. "And here I was starting to like you. Do you get that I'm not the shopping type?"

"I haven't said what we're shopping for."

"Oh. Well, if it's cars, I'm so there."

He smiled. "Go get changed."

"Okay. It would probably be better for me to get out than to stay here."

"Agreed. I do not want you taking out your temper on my Rolls."

She laughed, then closed the door behind her. Qadir stayed where he was, careful not to move because if he did, he would join her in her office and this time when he touched her, he would not stop.

An impossible situation, he told himself. At first Maggie had intrigued him with her humor and lack of pretension. He had enjoyed her company, but nothing more. Recently, though, he thought they might become lovers. The chemistry between them would make their time together pass very quickly. He had considered discussing that with her, but now everything was different.

She was pregnant and the father of her child wanted to marry her. Qadir knew he could not stand between them, even when his gut told him Jon was not the one for her. Jon had let her get away. What had the other man been thinking, to prefer another woman over Maggie? Impossible.

Not that he would be having that conversation with Jon anytime soon. But it gave Qadir pleasure to imagine the other man's fear when faced with a powerful sheik.

He wondered if Maggie could be convinced to accept Jon's proposal. He did not think so, but what did he really know of a woman's mind? Perhaps she secretly longed for her old lover.

He didn't want to think about that, about her being with someone else, so he pushed the image away. For now, and for as long as he wanted her, Maggie was his. Yet he had only bought her time. Did Jon still possess her heart?

"Better," Maggie said as they walked out of the restaurant. "That was exactly what I needed."

"You have an impressive appetite," Qadir said.

"I know. It gets embarrassing. I've always thought that if my work weren't so physical, I would blow up like a balloon. Which, at this moment, I don't care about."

For the first time since her uncomfortable conversation with Jon, she felt as if she could catch her breath. Maybe it was that big, juicy hamburger sitting in her stomach. A burger, fries and a shake had been exactly what she'd needed to change her mood.

"Thank you," she told the man at her side.

"You are welcome. Although I enjoy watching you throw things, I like seeing you smile, as well."

She looked up at him, at his dark eyes, his handsome features. "You're really smooth."

"I know."

"It's a prince thing, isn't it?"

"Some of it is me. My cousin Nadim is also a prince, but he is completely lacking in personality."

"I talked to him at the ball. He was a lot more formal than you."

"A kind way of ignoring his shortcomings."

Maggie hadn't been impressed, either, which made her wonder why Victoria would even consider marrying him. Yes, he was a prince and all, but marriage was forever. Especially a royal one.

Qadir put his arm around her and pulled her close. "I, however, have a wonderful personality and you are completely charmed by me."

"That's true," she said with a laugh, even as she leaned into him. She liked it when he held her or touched her. Her body melted as little nerve endings began a "touch me" dance in the strangest places.

She wanted to turn to him and have him kiss her. Deep kisses like before with lips and tongue and hot breath. She wanted to be swept away and taken and…

Oh God. She was pregnant. Pregnant with another man's child. She couldn't have erotic thoughts about Qadir. It wasn't right. It was borderline icky.

He was totally the wrong man and even if he wasn't, her being pregnant made her the wrong woman.

The good news was her attraction to him was purely physical. It wasn't as if her heart had gotten involved at all.

They headed back for the car. Qadir had driven and parked at the end of the block. But before they reached the gleaming Mercedes, she caught sight of a window display.

Last week she never would have noticed it, but today she slowed as she took in the pale green blanket draped over the white rocking chair. The small-scale dresser had painted rabbits playing together on the drawers. A toy box stood open with stuffed animals spilling from it.

Maggie slowed, then stopped. "I've never been in a baby store before," she whispered.

"Would you like to go in now?"

It probably wasn't the shopping he'd had in mind, but she nodded anyway, then hesitated before stepping through the open door.

"Is this okay?" she asked.

"Yes."

She could see displays set up like rooms, with cribs and tables. Changing tables, she told herself, having no idea where that information had come from.

He dropped his hand to the small of her back and gave her a little push. She stepped through the door.

The space was huge and filled with clothes and toys, supplies and furniture. Maggie walked in a few feet, then stopped, not sure what to look at first.

"I don't think I can do this," she murmured.

Qadir came up beside her. "You do not have to do anything today. That should make things easier. We will walk around and get some ideas. Later, you can decide about what you need. Think of this as the first visit to the showroom. You're not buying a car today."

The analogy was perfect and helped her relax. She smiled at him. "Did I mention you're good?"

"Several times, but it is praise I enjoy so feel free to say it again."

Without thinking, she leaned against him. He wrapped his arms around her and kissed her cheek. She raised her head for a real kiss, hoping he would—

"Prince Qadir, what an honor. I am Fatima. Welcome to my store."

The speaker was a pretty woman in her thirties. She beamed at both of them, clasping her hands together. Maggie's stomach knotted and she instantly regretted the hamburger.

"It is a pleasure to meet you," Qadir said smoothly.

Maggie stepped back and cleared her throat. What was she supposed to say? Her pregnancy had been reported in the newspaper and showing up here, like this, would only cause people to think Qadir really *was* the father.

"We, ah, were just looking around," she said, wishing she didn't sound so lame.

"Of course. Please. Explore. If you have any questions I will be at the front desk."

Fatima gave a little bob, then hurried away. Maggie watched her go.

"I'm sorry," she said, feeling awful. "We shouldn't have come in here."

"Why not?"

"Because of what people will think."

"You are having a child."

"But not *yours*," she said, trying not to shriek. "That's what they will think."

"We know the truth."

He sounded so calm. "You're not upset?"

"No." He took her hand. "Come on. Let us explore, as Fatima suggested. Based on all I see here, an infant needs far more than his size suggests."

She thought about pointing out all the potentials for disaster, but knew Qadir would understand them far better than she. If he could be calm about this, then she could, too.

"Just to be clear," she told him. "I'm having a girl."

"You are confident about that?"

"Yes. I sense my body would reject boy sperm."

"Then Jon is weak for not overpowering you."

"Or sensible for not trying."

They walked around the various displays. One showed a room done in trains, with everything from an adorable loco-motive border print to stuffed train pillows. There was also a car room and one done totally in pink with a ballerina motif.

"If you're having a girl," Qadir said, pointing at the dancer.

Maggie glared at him. "Don't make me hit you in public."

"You are not as tough as you think."

"Cheap talk while you're safely around other people."

He smiled slowly. "You do not intimidate me in any way, Maggie. We both know how easily I could take you."

She wasn't sure if he was referring to his superior strength or the way her body responded every time he touched her and she wasn't sure it mattered. He was right—he could take her without breaking a sweat. The only news in that was how much she wanted him to.

"Maybe this is better," he said, pointing to a display done in shades of yellow. The teddy bear theme wasn't too sweet and she liked the border print with the teddy bears playing different sports.

"I could live with this," she said, walking around the area, touching the crib and running her hands across the top of the dresser. "The yellow is nice. I'm not a huge fan of green and we all know I'm not doing a pink-on-pink room."

"You're going to have some explaining to do if the child is male."

She smiled. "I know, but I'll be very smug when it's a girl."

"I would have sons."

"Oh, please. Is this also a prince thing?"

"No. Biology. My aunt is the only female child born in several generations."

"Oh. I hadn't thought of that." But this wasn't Qadir's baby, so she didn't have to worry.

They wandered through the rest of the store. Maggie started to hyperventilate when they stopped in front of a wall of baby items and she had no idea what they were for.

"Do they come with instructions?" she asked in a whisper.

"I am sure they do."

She pointed to a small container with a cord and a plug. "A baby wipe heater? Their wipes have to be heated?" She hadn't known that. What if there was a power outage and the wipes were cold? Would that hurt the baby?

Panic filled her. "I can't do this," she said, placing her hand on her stomach. "I'm sorry, but I really, really can't do this. I don't know how. I'll do a lousy job. What if I don't like children?"

Qadir put his hand on her shoulder. "You will be fine."

"You're just saying that because you don't want me hysterical. You don't actually know."

"I know you are intelligent and caring and you will love your child. What else matters?"

"Heated baby wipes, for one thing. What else don't I know?"

"You will learn as you go."

"Maybe. But what if I don't? What if my child is the only one with a cold butt?"

His mouth twitched. She balled up her fist and socked him in the arm. "You'd better not be laughing at me."

He chuckled, then pulled her against him and kissed her. His mouth brushed hers once, twice, then he released her.

"You are a unique woman," he told her.

"Uniquely unqualified to be a mother."

He took her hand and led her to the rows of books. "If you do not know what to do, you can learn about it."

"Oh, right. Books." She picked up one and scanned the title. "I need one for women who have no experience with children. Something like—'You've never had a baby before, but that's okay.' Do you see that title?"

He held up several that weren't even close, but she grabbed them all. Something to fill her nights, she thought.

Qadir insisted on paying for the books—which was only going to fuel speculation, she thought as they left. When they were back in his car, she turned to him.

"Thank you for being so nice," she said. "You're really easy to be around."

"You are, as well," he told her. "I enjoyed our outing."

"Even though there's going to be an article or two in the paper tomorrow."

"Even though."

She told herself to say something else, to look away, to make a joke. But she couldn't. She seemed caught up in his gaze, in the power of the man. Breathing was difficult and thinking was impossible. What on earth was wrong with her?

"You were brilliant," Maggie told Victoria as they walked back to their rooms. "I had no idea what to get a princess for her wedding shower. The lingerie was beautiful."

Victoria had suggested they go in together for Kayleen's present and had offered to do the shopping.

"She didn't register, which was probably about her marrying a prince. I'm guessing the royal set would see that as tacky. Plus, hey, what could a princess want? Cookware? So I went with the easy gift. Something sexy."

"More than sexy." The lace and silk nighties had been stunning. "Kayleen looked happy."

"An important consideration," Victoria teased. "One wants to stay on the good side of a future royal."

Maggie knew her friend was right, but the whole situation was beyond imagining. "A month ago I was in Aspen working for a friend in his garage. I'd never been out of the country. I'd barely left the state. Now I'm here, having just attended a wedding shower for a future princess. We're in a palace. There is a seriously surreal quality to my life these days."

"I know," Victoria admitted as they took the stairs to the second floor. "Most of the time I'm totally used to all this, but every now and then I look around and wonder how a girl like me landed here. It's a question I haven't answered yet. Of course, I don't have your complication."

Maggie knew what the other woman was talking about. "Qadir isn't a complication."

"Oh, really. What would you call him?"

"My boss."

"Whom you're pretending to date, while pregnant."

A good point, Maggie thought.

"Just be careful," Victoria told her. "Watch yourself."

Maggie knew that was good advice. A couple of weeks ago she would have brushed it off. Be careful for what? She was fine. But now...

Victoria paused on the landing and looked at her. "What?" she asked sharply. "You're not telling me I'm worrying for nothing. You're not saying he's just your boss."

"He's just my boss."

"Oh, that was convincing."

Maggie climbed the rest of the stairs. Victoria followed. Once they were in the corridor, Maggie shrugged. "He might be a complication."

"Okay. Why?"

"I don't know. I feel funny when I'm around him."

"Funny as in slightly sick to your stomach mingling with a strong need to throw yourself at him and beg to be taken?"

"Maybe."

"Oh, man, that's not good." Victoria looked at her. "You like him."

"He's a great guy. I enjoy his company, that's all. It's just that I don't have a lot of friends here."

"Great. He turns you on *and* you're trying to rationalize the situation. That is never good. I was going to say you're falling for him, but I think it's too late for that. You've fallen and hard."

Maggie wanted to protest that wasn't possible, but there was a sense of rightness in her friend's words. A rightness that scared her down to her bones.

"I can't fall for him," she whispered. "It would be a huge mistake. He's a prince. I'm pregnant. Worse, I'm a mechanic. Guys like him don't marry women like me. They marry socialites and beauty queens."

"Get out while the getting is good," Victoria told her.

"I can't leave. I need the money. My dad's cancer totally wiped us out financially. I have nothing in the bank. I need the money from restoring the car to help me get through the pregnancy and beyond. I won't be able to work right after."

"I have some money saved," Victoria began.

Maggie smiled at her friend. "Thanks, but no. You've worked hard for what you have. I just have to be sensible. I can pull back. I wasn't paying attention with Qadir. He's funny and caring and I let myself get sucked in. I won't do that anymore. I'll be on guard."

"A good plan," Victoria said slowly. "There's only one problem. I've never heard any of the princes being described as funny and caring."

"Maybe I'm seeing a side of him he keeps hidden."

"Or maybe you're in more trouble than you thought."

That night Maggie couldn't sleep. There was too much on her mind. Every time she thought about her conversation with Jon she got annoyed all over again, which didn't help with relaxing. But when she tried to think about something else, her thoughts wandered to Qadir.

She appreciated Victoria's warning. Maggie hadn't realized she was in danger. Now that she understood the problem, she could do a better job of protecting herself emotionally. No more long lunches or shopping trips. She would be his mechanic, nothing more.

Around midnight, she gave up pretending she would doze off, pulled on jeans and a T-shirt, but no bra, and stepped out onto the balcony.

The night was clear and balmy with a hint of the summer heat that would soon follow. She could see stars and smell the sea. There were sounds in the distance, but the palace grounds themselves were quiet.

She moved quietly through the night to one of her favorite spots—a seating area that jutted out over the water. During the day there were often people there, drinking coffee, talking, but at this time of night, the space was empty.

Maggie ignored the cluster of chairs and walked to the railing. She leaned against it and stared down at the dark, swirling water. The sound of the sea soothed her. It reminded her that whatever her problems were at the moment, life went on. She could ride the tide or she could fight it, but in the end, the tide would win.

"We're going to figure this out," she whispered to the tiny life inside her. "Don't you worry. I'm working on a plan."

"Do you need help with it?"

She turned and saw a tall man behind her. It was too dark to see his features, but her heart recognized him all too well.

"Qadir."

"I could not sleep," he told her. "When that happens, I come here."

She didn't know what to say. They were having a fairly normal conversation, so words should come easily. But her recent talk with Victoria had changed things. She was aware of her possible growing feelings, of how she no longer thought of Qadir as just her boss. She was afraid her interest would show and he would be kind. Sometimes kindness could be the worst.

He stepped closer. "Are you all right?" he asked.

She nodded.

"What troubles you?"

"Nothing," she murmured. "I'm fine."

A light wind blew a strand of hair across her face. He reached out, probably to tuck it behind her ear. But the second his fingers brushed against her skin, she felt her whole body go up in flames. Need pulsed through her, a heady rhythm that blocked out the sound of the sea.

She stared at him, wanting to get lost in his dark eyes. While he didn't promise to be a safe haven, she knew he would protect her for as long as she was in his arms. Right now that seemed like more than enough.

She wanted him to touch her, to hold her, drawing her close, taking her with a passion that would leave them both breathless.

He cupped her cheek. "In a foolish attempt to be honorable, I will tell you that I am no longer willing to walk away from the temptation you offer."

Meaning she should be the one to leave. That if they started something, they wouldn't stop.

Her heart fluttered and her skin burned. Anticipation swept through her making her melt from the inside out.

"Maggie."

He said her name with a low growl that made her shiver.

Two clear choices. Be sensible or give in. She knew what she *should* do and what she *wanted* to do. In the end, it wasn't a choice at all.

Slowly, carefully, so there could be no question of her intent, she rose on tiptoe and kissed him.

Chapter Eleven

Maggie waited what seemed like a lifetime before Qadir responded to her kiss. She was just starting to think she'd made a huge mistake when he drew back and stared at her.

"I don't want to hurt you," he admitted.

Relief was as sweet as it was intense. "I can handle it," she said with a smile.

"So you claim."

"Test me."

He took her hand in his and led the way to an open French door halfway down the long balcony. They stepped inside what she assumed was his room, but didn't get much of a chance to explore.

The second the door closed behind them, he pulled her close and claimed her with a kiss that burned her down to the soles of her feet.

His lips took all she offered and more. His tongue swept

inside, exploring, claiming, urging. She met him stroke for stroke as need grew, filling her, making her ache and want.

He touched her everywhere, first up and down her back, then down her rear where he cupped the curves. She moved against him, feeling his erection, loving how hard he felt, wishing he were inside her already.

He broke their kiss long enough to pull off her T-shirt, then he cupped her bare breasts in his hands.

Even as his fingers worked their magic on her sensitive nipples, he kissed her all over her face. His mouth moved along her jaw, then down to her neck where he licked and nipped and made her gasp.

Liquid desire poured through her. She was already wet and swollen and when he bent down to suck on her breasts, she gasped her pleasure.

She touched him where she could. His hard muscles rippled in response to her caress. She was about to tell him to take off his shirt when he dropped to his knees. At the same time he unfastened her jeans, then jerked them and her panties down to her ankles.

She was trapped by her clothing, unable to step away or spread her legs very far apart. Still he kissed her stomach, then parted her with his fingers before kissing her intimately.

The feel of his lips and tongue was exquisite. She had to hang on to him to keep from falling to the floor. He found her center and licked it over and over again as he moved his hands behind her and squeezed her curves.

"Qadir," she breathed, wanting what he was doing to go on forever, but needing more. A bed, she thought frantically. A sofa. The floor.

Still loving her between her thighs, he helped her out of her shoes, then eased her clothes from her body. She opened her legs more, giving him access, desperate to give in to the building pressure.

She put her hands on his shoulders and hung on for the ride. But just as she was about to surrender and lose herself in pleasure, he stood.

"You can't stop," she gasped.

"I'm just getting started."

He led her down a hallway, into a large bedroom. She had a brief impression of dark, masculine furniture and a bed that could sleep twenty. Then Qadir pulled back the covers, turned to her and began to touch her.

"You are so beautiful," he murmured, stroking her back. "All of you. It's maddening to watch you prance around in your coveralls with those little fitted T-shirts. I have dreamed about you in that T-shirt and nothing else."

Heat filled her as his words aroused her to the brink. He'd fantasized about *her*? Was that possible?

"I don't prance," she said, trying to tease rather than give in to unexpected tears. She couldn't figure out why on earth those words would make her want to cry, but they did.

"You excite me beyond what I can say."

He was doing a pretty good job of exciting her, as well.

She reached for the buttons on his shirt, but he pushed her hands away. As she watched, he undressed, revealing his hard, honey-colored skin.

As he pushed down his briefs, she saw his arousal—all jutting maleness that called to her. Her pulled her close and they tumbled onto the big bed, a tangle of arms and legs and need.

Even as he took her breast into his mouth, he reached between her legs and stroked her.

He found that one sensitive spot instantly and circled it. She didn't know what to think about first—his mouth or his fingers. Both were exquisite, pushing her higher, driving her closer to her release.

The steady rhythm—his sucking, his touching, her body pulsing—threatened to push her over the edge. She held back, not wanting to give in so quickly. Then he shifted so he was between her thighs, kissing her with his tongue again. He pushed a finger inside of her, circling, thrusting, rubbing and she was lost.

Her release carried her to the edge of the world and let her go. Every muscle shuddered with pleasure, making her cry out. On and on until she floated back to earth, back to his bed where she opened her eyes and found him watching her.

Despite the fact that she might never be able to move again, fire still burned. Without saying anything, she held open her arms. He eased between her legs, his hardness filling her, stretching her, making her cling to him.

He made love to her like a man starved. Deep thrusts claimed her as his and she held on for the ride of her life. His excitement pulled her along, making her hungry, as well. Her body tensed and ached and when he stiffened, she, too, cried out, feeling more satisfied than she'd ever been before.

Later, when they were together under the covers, her body pressed against his, his hands stroking her head, he kissed her.

"I am sorry," he said. "I tried to hold back. I did not want to hurt you."

"You didn't."

"I took you roughly."

He wouldn't meet her gaze, as if he was ashamed.

She rolled on top of him, pressing her body to his, then kissed him. "Qadir, didn't you feel me responding? I'm not saying I want to be hurt. Your passion excited me. Isn't that how it's supposed to be?"

"I should have more control."

She smiled. "No, you shouldn't."

He put his hands on her hips and eased her down. He was hard again. She slid over him, taking him inside of her. She gasped at the pleasure of it.

"Perhaps if you were in charge," he told her, need once again burning between them.

She braced herself on the bed. He reached for her breasts, then lightly teased her nipples. Sensation shot through her. She rode him up and down, then moving faster and faster. They both groaned.

It was, she thought as her body clenched in anticipation, going to be an amazing night.

Maggie supposed that technically she walked back to her room the next morning, but in truth it felt like floating. Her whole body seemed to hum with contentment as individual cells continued to sigh their pleasure.

Qadir sure knew his way around a woman's body. She felt as if she'd stepped onto a new plane of sensual pleasure and she couldn't wait to go back again.

"Not a good idea," she told herself as she stepped through the French doors and back into her room.

Last night had been amazing and fifteen kinds of a mistake. She'd been determined to hold her heart safely out of reach. Making love with Qadir for hours on end was not going to help her cause.

She couldn't get over how concerned he'd been about hurting her. He hadn't, of course, but the worry had been sweet. And the passion had been mind-altering.

"I am a mature woman," she told herself as she headed into the bathroom. "I can handle this."

She didn't have much choice. Despite how amazing the love-making had been, nothing had changed. She was still who she was and Qadir was still a prince.

She showered, then dried off and dressed. After combing out

her hair, she reached for the blow-dryer, but before she could turn it on, someone pounded on her door.

She moved through the living room and opened it. Victoria stood in the hallway.

"There you are," her friend said. "What is going on with you? I've been calling and calling and knocking and you haven't..." Victoria's blue eyes widened. "Oh my God. What happened?"

Maggie felt herself flush even as she said, "Nothing."

"It's not nothing. There's something totally different about you."

Was that possible? Did last night show?

"I have no idea what you're talking about," she lied.

Victoria leaned closer and stared into her eyes. "I swear, there's something. It's—" Her mouth dropped open. "No way."

The flush increased. Maggie stepped away from the open door and returned to the bathroom. "I have no idea what you're going on about."

"You are so lying. You were with Qadir last night. You were with him big-time."

As she spoke, Victoria trailed after Maggie into the bathroom. When Maggie tried to turn on the blow-dryer to drown her out, Victoria simply pulled the plug.

Maggie looked at her in the mirror. "It just happened," she admitted. "It was probably crazy, but I can't regret it."

"I want details," Victoria said. "Even more important, I'm here for you."

"I appreciate that, but I feel fine."

"You won't for long." Her friend took a deep breath. "Jon is here. He arrived in the middle of the night and he's been raising hell downstairs, trying to find you."

Maggie wished she were the kind of person who could faint on command. This seemed like an excellent time to pass out. But she stayed annoyingly conscious as Victoria led her to the private room Jon had been assigned.

"How much hell?" Maggie asked, not sure she wanted to know.

"When we couldn't find you right away, he started accusing the palace guards of holding you prisoner. They didn't know who he was or what he wanted. When he started on the 'I'm an American' rant they called me. I assured him you were fine, which he almost believed, but then I couldn't find you, either. Honestly, I never thought to check in Qadir's room. I thought you were with the car, or taking a midnight jog or something."

"I can't believe he's here," Maggie muttered. "I can't believe he's here *now*."

"At least your life isn't boring."

"I wouldn't mind boring," Maggie said, refusing to feel guilty for what had happened with Qadir. She was sorry everyone had been put out because they couldn't find her, but she had the right to a life. Jon had sure moved on. She could, too.

"I can't believe he didn't tell me he was coming," she said.

Victoria stopped in front of a door and pointed. "Good luck."

Maggie didn't want to go inside by herself. "You could come with me."

"I could, but I think you need to do this on your own." She hugged Maggie, then hurried away.

Maggie stared at the door. She had a feeling she knew why Jon had arrived in El Deharia. After last night, she would have said gathering the energy to fight was impossible, but knowing Jon as she did, she was going to have to get her mad up or he would be making all the decisions. The last thing either of them needed was a situation that would impact the rest of their lives. Of course the pregnancy had already done a good job of that.

She knocked once and the door flew open. Jon stood there, looking as he always had.

"Where have you been?" he demanded. "I got here hours ago and no one could find you. Are they keeping you hostage somewhere? What's going on here, Maggie?"

She stepped into his room, a space much smaller than her own. It faced the garden rather than the sea.

She looked at him, at the kind brown eyes, the mouth that curved into a crooked smile, the unruly brown hair he kept cut short so it didn't get too wild.

This was Jon. He'd been the boy she'd grown up with, the man she'd fallen in love with. She deliberately remembered good times they'd shared and buried herself in those memories. She dug through her heart and felt…nothing.

Until that moment she thought it was over, but she hadn't had proof. She did now. Whatever she and Jon had once shared had changed and faded until there was only a friendship she hoped would never go away.

"I'm sorry you were worried," she said. "I didn't know you were coming."

"It was a last-minute decision," he admitted.

She thought about pointing out that there were no direct flights to El Deharia. That he had to stop somewhere and he could have easily called. But he had obviously wanted to surprise her. Which he'd done.

"I'm here now." She crossed to the sofa and sat down. "Why don't you tell me why you're here."

She spoke calmly, hoping she was wrong in her assumptions.

"You're pregnant, Maggie," he said as he paced in front of her. "I'm here to bring you home. You don't belong here. You should be home. With me."

"Married to you," she clarified.

"Yes. We'll get married."

She wanted to hold on to her temper. Getting angry wouldn't help either of them.

"I'm not leaving anytime soon," she told him. "I came to El Deharia to do a job and I'm going to complete it."

He looked at her, impatience tightening his features. "It's just a car."

That really pissed her off. Her hands clenched, but still she held on to her calm. "It's my work," she corrected. "It's what I do. Prince Qadir is paying me a lot of money to restore his car and I will finish the work before I leave."

"I won't allow it."

That got her to her feet. "Fortunately it's not your decision to make."

"You're having a baby. You shouldn't be around cars."

"That's ridiculous. I'm restoring a car, not working in a toxic waste dump."

"Come home with me now."

"No."

They stared at each other, a small coffee table between them. But the distance felt much greater.

Had Jon always been like this? she wondered. Had he always tried to boss her around? Why hadn't she noticed before?

Her anger faded as sadness took its place. "This isn't what I want," she said quietly. "If nothing else, we have to stay friends."

"I'm not interested in being friends." His voice was a growl. "I'm here to marry you."

"You keep saying that and I keep telling you no." She walked around the coffee table and touched his arm. "Jon, just stop. We don't have to be like this. I'm only a few weeks pregnant. We have months ahead of us. No decisions have to be made today. I appreciate your concern, because I know what this is about. You want to do the right thing. That's the kind of man you are. But there are a lot of different right things we can do. Let's explore them. Take a breath. Go home. I'll be back in a month or so and we can figure out what we want to do."

"I want to marry you."

She held in a scream. "I don't remember you being this stubborn before."

"You were never carrying my baby before. Getting married is the right thing to do."

"Right for who? Do you really want to spend the next eighteen years tied to me? You don't love me. I appreciate that you're concerned about the baby, but how happy will this child be knowing his or her parents don't want to be married to each other?"

His stubborn expression didn't change. "We were in love before. We'll be fine."

"No, we won't. We'll be miserable. I won't do it. I won't marry you because of the child. You can't make me."

"I'm not leaving until you agree."

Maggie thought longingly of the dungeons Victoria had mentioned. "Then we have a real problem because I'll never agree."

Whatever he was going to say was lost when someone knocked on the door. Victoria stepped inside.

"I'm sorry to interrupt, but there's been another twist in your life."

She held the door open and Qadir entered, leading a young woman Maggie had never seen. She was petite, with dark blond hair and features that were probably pretty when they weren't blotchy. Tears filled the woman's eyes when she saw Jon.

"I had to come," she told him.

Elaine, Maggie thought, wondering how the situation could get worse. Then she met Qadir's gaze. What must he think of all this? Of her? Last night had been so perfect, but this morning was a disaster. Did he think she wanted to marry Jon? Was he feeling that she had simply used him?

Too many questions that she had no way to ask.

Elaine hurried over to Jon. She clutched his arm. "Don't do this," she pleaded, tears spilling down her cheeks. "Please, don't do this."

"It's the right thing for the baby."

"How is that possible? How can something that hurts this much be right?"

Maggie looked away, feeling as if she were intruding on a private moment.

"Don't you love me anymore?" Elaine asked, her voice trembling.

"Elaine, please." Jon sounded strained.

"Just tell me the truth," she pleaded. "Tell me I don't matter."

"I can't do that."

Maggie wanted to crawl into a hole. While she knew in her head she wasn't the only one to blame for the disaster, she felt the heavy weight of responsibility in her heart.

Still not looking at Jon or Elaine, she hurried out of the room and into the hallway.

Someone came after her. She half expected it to be Victoria, but then she felt strong hands settle on her shoulders.

"Who needs daytime television when they can just watch what's going on in my life," she said, trying to make light of the situation.

Qadir turned her to face him, then pulled her close.

"I can't believe this is happening," she said as she snuggled into his chest. "I can't believe Jon is here and Elaine followed him. He wants to marry me."

"I expected no less. If you were carrying my child, I would not let you get away."

Words to make her tremble, she thought sadly. If she were carrying Qadir's child, she wouldn't want to get away.

"I'm not going to ruin all our lives because I'm pregnant. You saw Elaine. She loves him desperately. He's wrong to push for a marriage with me."

"He's a man who is trying to do the right thing. His conscience wars with his heart."

"His heart better win."

Victoria slipped into the hallway. "I'm going to find Elaine a room. Apparently she's staying, at least for now."

Maggie winced. "Here? That can't be okay. We should all move to a hotel."

"The palace has many rooms," Qadir told her. "Your friends are welcome."

They weren't her friends, but there was no point in getting into that. And she sure didn't want to think what the staff must be thinking about her.

"This is all my fault."

Qadir touched her cheek. "It is not."

Elaine came out of the room and looked at Maggie. "He wants to talk to you."

Maggie nodded. "I'm sorry. I didn't want any of this to happen."

"I believe you. I wish things were different."

Victoria led the other woman away. Maggie stared at the half-open door. "I guess I need to go back inside."

"I will come with you," Qadir said.

"No, that's okay. I can handle Jon."

Qadir hesitated, as if he wasn't going to give her a choice. Then he nodded. "If there is any trouble, you will get in touch with me."

It wasn't a question.

"I promise," she told him.

He bent his head and brushed his mouth against hers, then walked away. Maggie braced herself and walked into Jon's room.

He stood by the window, looking out onto the garden. His

body was stiff, but his shoulders seemed bowed, as if they carried too heavy a weight.

"I didn't know Elaine would follow me," he said without turning around. "I'm sorry about that."

"I'm impressed. She obviously loves you very much and isn't willing to let you get away."

"She doesn't understand."

"She understands perfectly." Maggie waited until he turned to face her before continuing. "She understands that you're willing to throw away everything important to you for no good reason. She understands that while no one would have chosen this situation, it's here now and we have to deal with it. But what she doesn't understand—and I have to say I'm with her on that—is why you think there's only one option."

"Because there is. There's the right thing to do and there's everything else."

Had he always been this stubborn? "Is it because I suggested you give up the child altogether?" she asked. "Did that make you feel like I was cutting you out and pushing you away? Is that why you're so insistent?"

He didn't say anything and she couldn't read him anymore. Their intimate connection had been broken.

"I'm sorry," she said. "I shouldn't have gone there. Maybe it is the right thing for both of us, but it was wrong of me to assume anything. We need to come to a decision together. Maybe the three of us should talk."

"This doesn't involve Elaine."

"Of course it does. It's her future, too. Her life. Chances are, she's going to be a stepmother."

"You and I are the ones getting married."

Maggie rolled her eyes. "Listen to me very, very carefully. I will not marry you and you can't make me. I don't love you. You don't love me. In fact, you're in love with someone else. Now quit being an idiot and start looking at other alternatives."

"No."

"Then rot in this room. I'm done talking to you. When you're ready to be rational and reasonable, come find me. Otherwise, I don't want to see you again."

By seven that night, Maggie had a pounding headache and a deep desire to ride into the desert and never be heard from again. She sat alone in her room wondering how on earth she was supposed to fix the disaster that was her life.

She heard a light tapping on her French door. When she stood, she saw Victoria standing there with a pint of ice cream in each hand. Maggie hurried to let her in.

"I'm sneaking around," her friend admitted, holding out the cartons. "I don't want to see anyone or talk to anyone. Except you, I guess. Which one do you want?"

Maggie grabbed one of the cartons without checking the flavor, then frowned. "What's wrong?"

Victoria's blue eyes were swollen and red, her mouth puffy. "I've been crying. Me and Elaine. It's our day. Neither of us seem to be pretty criers. I'm hoping you won't be judgmental."

"Of course not. But what's wrong?"

"Nothing. Everything. It's so stupid. It's not like I really care. It's just I had this plan, you know. Then I tell myself I never thought it would happen, so what's the big deal? I mean, who am I kidding? A prince? Marry me?"

Maggie led her to the sofa and urged her to sit. "I have no idea what you're talking about."

Victoria scooped out some ice cream and licked the spoon. "I hope you appreciate that my escape of choice would be margaritas. But I hate to drink by myself and you're pregnant, so I'm stuck with ice cream."

"Still confused."

She sniffed again. "Nadim is engaged. His father found him a perfectly nice young woman. She comes from a respectable family with little in the way of financial success, but the lineage is impressive enough on its own. They apparently met last week, spent the weekend away to determine if they were compatible. All went well and now they're engaged."

Tears filled her eyes. "I know it's ridiculous. Who wants to be with a man who is that emotionally disconnected? He can't know if he likes her or not after a damn weekend. It's just I had this silly dream, you know? One where I could be financially secure and not have to worry, like I did when I was growing up. But who am I kidding? Stuff like that doesn't happen to women like me."

Maggie didn't know enough about Victoria's past to know what she was talking about. She only knew that her friend was in pain.

"Nadim is really engaged?"

"They're going to make the announcement in a couple of weeks, after As'ad and Kayleen's wedding. They don't want to take away from the happy event." She wiped her face with the back of her hand. "He didn't even tell me directly. I found out because he gave me some letters to type and they mentioned his engagement. He doesn't even know I'm alive."

"Then he's not worth even one of your tears," Maggie said. "Come on. You didn't love him. I'm not even sure you liked him."

"It wasn't about liking. It was about being safe."

"You are safe. You have a great job, you live in a palace."

"Until I get fired."

"Why would Nadim fire you? Don't you do a good job?"

"Yes."

"You have savings?"

"Uh-huh. I'm a big saver."

"So you're okay. Nadim was never the man for you. Maybe it's time to go out and live life."

"No, thanks. Life hurts." She jabbed at her ice cream. "I suppose the bright side is at least you got a proposal today."

"From someone I don't want to marry."

"It's the thought that counts," Victoria said, then started to laugh.

Maggie joined in. The two of them leaned back on the sofa and laughed until they started crying, then they tuned the TV to a shopping channel, leaned back and ate their ice cream.

Chapter Twelve

Jon showed up in the garage the next morning. Maggie put down her tools, knowing whatever he had to say, she had to listen, then convince him why he was wrong.

"You've been avoiding me," he said.

"Under the circumstances, it seemed the smart thing to do."

"You don't want to marry me."

She wasn't ready for relief. She couldn't tell if he'd really gotten it or was just testing her. "I don't want to marry you."

Jon shoved his hands into his pockets and walked around the car. "I talked to Elaine last night. All night. She pointed out I can't force you to. Even if I could, it would only lead to disaster."

Maggie had a feeling she was going to like Elaine. "I have to take a lot of the blame," she said. "I should never have mentioned you walking away from the child. That's not who you are. I'm going to guess that made you think I planned to shut you out, which you reacted to."

"I didn't like it," he told her. "This is my child, too."

"I know. I'm sorry."

"It's okay." He looked at the car. "It's not much to look at now, but you're going to make it beautiful."

"That's the plan."

"We went out to dinner. The city seems nice."

"I like it."

He stopped in front of her. "I love her," he said with a shrug. "I really love her. It's different, Mags. I can't explain how it's different, but it is. I want to be with her every second. I think about her when we're apart. It's exciting and new, but it's also comfortable. We're the same in ways you and I never were. I love her and I want to be with her always."

Maggie swallowed. "I'm happy for you," she said, and meant it. The only hint of pain came from the voice inside that said she would like that, too. Not with Jon, of course, but with someone.

She thought of Qadir and how the handsome prince had stolen a piece of her heart. The problem wasn't her feelings for him but his for her. Did he have any? Things had changed for her but she had a bad feeling they were exactly the same for him.

"I won't cut you out of the baby's life. I swear. If that's not good enough, and I understand it might not be, then I'll sign something. We'll figure out a plan. You can have summers or weekends or whatever works best. But don't lose the love of your life over this."

"You're right," he said, words she couldn't ever remember him speaking.

"I know I'm right," she teased, to keep the mood light. "Now go find your woman and take her until she's boneless. Then tell her you're sorry and that she's the one you really want to marry."

"I will," he said, and hugged her.

She stepped into his embrace. Everything about it was familiar but none of it was what she wanted.

"If you need anything, I'll be there for you," he said when he released her.

"I know." She stepped back and smiled at him. "Thanks for being willing to do the right thing. Even if it was totally crazy."

He smiled. "You have to admit, I have style."

"Oh, yeah. Now go find Elaine and tell her she owes me."

"Love you, Mags."

She believed he did love her, the way she loved him. Like an old friend. Jon was a warm memory from her past and she would never forget him. But he wasn't the one.

"I love you, too."

She watched him walk away. Elaine would be waiting, praying that she wasn't about to lose the man of her dreams. They would talk and kiss and make love. If Jon was smart, he would propose and they would fly home blissfully happy. It was what Maggie wanted for them. She sure didn't want Jon for herself. But that didn't make her feel any less alone.

Maggie spent the day feeling restless. She gave up working on the car early in the afternoon and went for a walk in the garden.

There were hundreds of different plants, trees and shrubs and she doubted she knew the names of any of them. Still, their beauty calmed her spirit and the perfume of their combined scents helped her relax.

She walked along the various paths, taking turns she never had before. She found herself next to a high wall. A soft cry came from behind the stone. Someone was in trouble!

"It is not what you think."

She turned and found Qadir standing behind her. Her reaction was, as always, instant and powerful. She gave in to the need and rushed into his arms.

He held her tightly against him, rubbing his hands up and down her back. "Fear not," he told her. "I am here. I will slay your dragons."

If only that were true, she thought as she held on, never wanting to let go. "I'm sort of dragon free right now," she told him.

"Should that change, my sword is at your disposal."

She stepped back and looked at him. "You have a sword?"

He raised his eyebrows, which made her laugh.

"Not that," she said with a smile. "Do you have a real sword? You know, made of metal and all sharp and shiny."

"Of course."

"Then I'll let you know the next time I see a dragon."

He took her hand in his and led her closer to the wall. "The crying is not what you think."

"It sounds like a kitten is lost inside. Or someone is in trouble."

"Sometimes it sounds like a child. Instead there are two old parrots. The last of them. These walls hide the harem garden. Many years ago, when my great-grandfather kept women here, parrots lived in the garden. Their cries concealed the voices of the women so no man would be tempted to climb the walls and claim what could never be his."

She stared at him. "There was a harem here?"

"Of course."

"Women kept against their will?"

"Dozens of the most beautiful women in the world."

"That's disgusting."

"Not for the king."

She glared at him. "Don't you dare become a sexist pig. I swear, I'll stab you in your sleep."

"Pregnancy has made you violent."

"Maybe I've always been this way."

"Perhaps." He leaned down and kissed her nose. "You need a good taming. Time in a harem would do that."

"I'm not really harem material. I would rebel and escape."

"Perhaps your master would so satisfy you that you would not want to be anywhere else."

The way Qadir had satisfied her? "I'm not the type who takes to confinement well."

"I would agree. You are far too independent."

For a harem or for him?

She told herself that she was only making herself crazy. Qadir had never hinted he wanted anything but the bargain they'd agreed upon. The fact that her feelings were changing didn't shift reality. She supposed the only question she had to deal with was whether or not she could stay and pretend to be involved with him when, for her at least, it was no longer a game.

"I'm glad there isn't a harem anymore," she said. "Knowing there were women locked up would really annoy me."

"I am not so sure. At times I miss the old ways."

She looked at him and saw the humor in his eyes. "You're really flirting with danger here. Just because you're a prince doesn't mean I can't take you."

"You cannot take me. Not in the way you mean. But there are other ways to bring me to my knees, Maggie, and those you know well."

His words made her tremble, then step closer so they could kiss.

His mouth was firm without being hard, offering as much as it took. She kissed him back with a passion that burned so hot she knew she would carry the scars forever.

When he led her back toward the palace, she went with him.

Yes, there was a risk in being with Qadir over and over. But she would face the pain later. For now, building memories would have to be enough.

"I love weddings," Victoria said as they walked along the hallway. "Which is strange when you think about it. I'm so opposed to love. But I guess I don't mind other people making emotional fools out of themselves."

"You're such a romantic," Maggie teased, wishing they weren't going so fast. She still wasn't comfortable walking in high heels.

Although As'ad and Kayleen's wedding was in the morning, it was still a dressy affair.

"Thanks for helping me get ready," Maggie said as she smoothed the front of her dress.

"No problem. I loved playing dress-up as a kid. You look beautiful, which is important. There will be lots of press hanging around. They won't be allowed in the ceremony, of course, but expect to have your picture taken."

Not an exciting thought, Maggie told herself. "I guess a small, intimate wedding just for family is out of the question."

"When the man you're marrying is a prince, then yes. By royal standards, this is small. There are also different traditions. No attendants. While As'ad's brothers will sit up front, they won't stand with him." Victoria smiled at her. "Which explains why you'll be there with Qadir and I'll be in the back with the other rabble."

"I'd rather sit with you," Maggie said earnestly. At least with Victoria, she wouldn't feel like a fraud.

"You'll be fine. There's really nothing to do but smile and be happy for the lucky couple. Don't worry. I'll watch all the famous people coming in, then catch up with you at the reception and let you know what movie stars are here. There will also be the usual foreign dignitaries, which is less interesting. They even got Kateb, the mystery brother, to come in from the desert for the event."

Maggie looked at her friend. "I've met him. He seems nice."

Victoria shook her head. "I don't think anyone has ever used that word to describe him. He's dark and mysterious. A man of the desert, which means he's ruled by emotions. Too passionate for me. Give me a prince like Nadim who doesn't know how to feel. Kateb is nothing but trouble."

Victoria sighed. "Not that it's an issue anymore. I'm giving up on princes."

"Really?"

"Uh-huh. I thought about what you said before. I can take care of myself. I'm well paid working here and I don't have any expenses except for clothes and vacations. I've done some traveling but always on the cheap and you've seen where I shop. I guess you can take the girl out of poverty but you can't take poverty out of the girl. Anyway, I have a fairly big savings account. I've decided to come up with a new plan."

"Which is?"

"I'm going to work here another year and keep saving, then I'm going back to the States and opening my own business. I don't know what it will be yet, but I have time to figure it out. I don't need a prince to be happy. I can avoid men at home just as easily as I have here."

"Good for you," Maggie said, not sure it was good. Having Victoria recognize that she was capable of taking care of herself was excellent, but cutting herself off emotionally wasn't exactly healthy. "And you might meet someone nice."

"No, thanks. I have no interest in getting married for the sake of it. With Nadim, I was looking for security. Now that I don't need that, I'm going to avoid men. All men."

They walked down the stairs to the main level and heard the crowd of waiting guests before they saw them. Victoria pointed toward a side door.

"Go through there. You'll find Qadir and the rest of the wedding party. I'll see you at the reception."

Maggie opened her mouth to protest that she wanted to stay with her friend, but Victoria gave her a little push. Maggie walked toward the door, then opened it and went through.

Members of the royal family were gathered around. Maggie recognized a few of them, while others were unfamiliar. She saw Qadir's aunt who was now Queen of Bahania, along with Qadir's brothers. The king was there, as well.

She circled the room, avoiding the monarch, looking for Qadir. Maybe she could explain it would be easier for everyone if she simply sat with Victoria.

A servant walked by with a tray of champagne. She shook her head as she eased back into a corner. Seconds later Qadir found her.

"Why are you hiding?" he asked by way of greeting.

"I'm not hiding, exactly." She looked around. "I don't belong here. I'm a fraud."

"Perhaps, but you are my fraud."

"You're not taking this seriously."

"Because you are taking it too seriously." He picked up her hand and kissed her knuckles. "You look beautiful. Elegant and unapproachable. Yet I know the woman inside, the one who cries out my name."

She cleared her throat. "Yes, well, that woman is busy today. I'm here in her place."

"I find this one charming, as well."

"Good to know." She looked around. "I've never been to a royal wedding before."

"They are much like others you have attended. Long and filled with tradition."

Would his wedding be like this? she wondered. When he finally found the woman he wanted to marry? Speaking of which...

"Jon and Elaine have left," she told him.

"I had heard that. All is well?"

She nodded. "They're still together and in love. Jon and I haven't figured out what we're going to do about the baby, but he no longer thinks we have to get married. We'll figure out the details later. Maybe weekends or summers. At least that's what we discussed. I was wrong to suggest he give up his child. I think that freaked him out. He reacted in the only way he knew how."

Kateb approached. "Ms. Collins, how nice to see you again."

Qadir frowned. "How do you know Maggie?"

"We met in the garden," she told him.

"I am not sure I approve."

What was it with these imperious men? "I'm not sure I care about your approval."

Kateb laughed. "It is too bad you are not involved with this one," he told his brother. "She has much to recommend herself."

Maggie knew Kateb meant his words as a compliment, but they still cut through her. The reminder that this was all a game to Qadir hurt more than it should. Not that she was surprised to be the only one who had fallen in love.

The orchestra had come from London, the flowers had been flown in from around the world. The church itself, a cathedral built in the 1600s, seated at least six hundred. Maggie sat next to Qadir in a hand-carved pew that dated back over five hundred years.

While she wouldn't want to admit it to anyone, she'd imagined her own wedding many times. For years she'd assumed she would marry Jon in a short ceremony, with her father giving her away and people she'd known all her life around them. She'd wanted a summer wedding so the days were long and the nights warm. She'd wanted to dance until she was exhausted, then drive to a secluded cabin in the woods for a week-long honeymoon.

Simple dreams, she thought now as they rose in anticipation of Kayleen walking down the rose-petal-covered aisle. Dreams that had been altered by so many unexpected turns. The loss of her father. The ending of her relationship with Jon and now falling in love with Qadir.

She might be foolish enough to fall for him, but she wasn't stupid enough to think anything would come of it. The prince and the mechanic? Who thought that was possible?

She looked down at the dress she wore. It was beautiful and expensive. Nothing she would have picked for herself. It was part of the role she played, as Qadir's girlfriend. But it wasn't who she was. She was Maggie Collins, who wore jeans and didn't bother with makeup and expected an ordinary life.

But what happened when a regular woman fell in love with an extraordinary man? How could she find happiness?

Under different circumstances she might have tried to talk herself into making things real with Qadir. But he was in line to the El Deharian throne and she was pregnant with another man's child. What was the point in telling him the truth? He would only pity her.

The first of the three girls Kayleen and As'ad had adopted stepped into view. The girls were pretty and obviously thrilled to be a part of the ceremony. They walked slowly, one after the other. Then the bride entered the church. A veil covered her face, but it was sheer enough for Maggie to see the love shining in her eyes. A radiant bride, she thought. Love made everyone beautiful.

Kayleen continued down the aisle, where an equally smitten As'ad waited.

Maggie's heart ached. She wanted this for herself. Not the fancy wedding, but the love. She wanted someone to love her forever, to hold her and never let her go.

She glanced at Qadir. She couldn't find that with him, but was it possible with someone else? The congregation sat. Qadir reached over and took her hand in his.

It was just for show, she told herself, even as she desperately wanted it to be real. Just a game. A game that was going to break her heart into so many pieces, she was unlikely to ever find a way to make herself whole again.

Maggie sanded the fender with a piece of fine sandpaper. She wanted the finish perfect, which meant doing the details herself. The work was tedious, but she didn't mind. Focusing on the car was a kind of mental vacation from the weirdness of her life these days.

She adjusted the mask she wore, wishing it weren't so hot. But she didn't want to risk breathing in any of the particles. Not while she was pregnant.

The things I do for you, kid, she thought with a smile.

Someone tapped her arm. She jumped and turned, then jerked off the mask as she recognized King Mukhtar.

"Your Highness," she said in surprise, setting down the sandpaper and wiping her hands on her coveralls. "I didn't hear you come in."

What was she supposed to do? Bow? Curtsy? Offer to shake hands?

"Stealth is important for a monarch," he said without smiling. "Might I have a moment of your time, Ms. Collins?"

That didn't sound good, she thought grimly. "Yes, of course. My office is through here."

She led the way and motioned to a seat. But the king remained standing so she did, as well.

"I will get right to the point," he said, gazing directly into her eyes. "It is time for you to leave El Deharia. You are far too pretty a distraction for my son."

Maggie didn't know what to say. The king's attitude wasn't a surprise, but she didn't think he would be so blunt.

Mukhtar continued before she could think of how to respond.

"I didn't object to the relationship initially," he told her. "Times are changing and fresh blood is always a good thing. It is not as if there are an excess of princesses or duchesses around for my sons to marry. While your circumstances are modest, so are Kayleen's and she is an excellent match for As'ad. However, recent changes in your circumstances have convinced me you are not suitable for Qadir."

Maggie stiffened, but didn't back down. He was talking about her pregnancy. She doubted anyone expected a virgin bride, but she'd gone a little to far over the line.

"Qadir needs to be available to find someone suitable. He will not look as long as you are around. Perhaps this sounds harsh to you. Unfortunately I have more to consider than most fathers. I have a country and a responsibility to my people. As does Qadir."

She'd been willing to offer a protest right up until that last bit. But how was she supposed to ignore the needs of an entire country? The king was right—she didn't belong.

"I will not ask you to pack your bags immediately," he told her. "But I would like you to begin making arrangements."

Maggie found her voice. "I have another three weeks' worth of work on the car," she said. "I don't need to stay to see it finished, but I have a few more things I must do. I'll stay through the end of the week."

"Thank you for understanding. It is most unfortunate.

Under other circumstances…" He cleared his throat. "I wish you well, child."

The king left.

Maggie stared after him. Her nature was to stand up for herself, to fight for what she wanted. But how could she? The king had told the truth. She wasn't right for Qadir and she didn't belong here. It was time for her to leave.

Chapter Thirteen

"He is an impossible old man," Qadir said as he paced the length of his living room. "Impossible."

"Agreed." Kateb lounged on one of the sofas, smoking a cigar. "Unfortunately he is the king."

"Perhaps, but he has no right to interfere."

"You are his son."

"A matter of no consequence," Qadir muttered.

Kateb merely raised his eyebrows.

"It is not his place to say who is to be in my life," Qadir continued.

"You have much energy over a matter that is very small," his brother pointed out. "Maggie was merely a convenience. You hired her to act as your girlfriend, Qadir. You were not actually with her. Why are you so angry at our father's interference?"

Qadir couldn't answer. "It is the principle of the matter," he said at last.

"Ah, well then. You must do as you see fit. But to me, the simpler solution is to let her go and find another woman to hire. What do you care who plays your pretend lover? Isn't one woman as good as the next?"

Qadir turned on his brother. The need to strike out, to punish, was as powerful as it was unexpected. Kateb studied him through a cloud of smoke, his dark gaze deceptively lazy.

"I do not want another woman," Qadir said. "Maggie suits me." She understood him. She was easy to talk to. Why would he want to start over with someone else? "She is the only one I want."

Kateb nodded slowly. "That is more of a problem."

"You will not leave," Qadir said imperiously.

Maggie was more than ready to stop being dictated to by men. First Jon, then the king and now Qadir. Of all of them, only the king made her nervous, probably because she didn't actually know how much power he had. There were still rumors of a dungeon downstairs—a place she didn't ever want to see.

"Your father wants me gone," she said as she sat on the edge of the sofa and resisted the need to bury her face in her hands. "What does it matter? Someone else can finish the car."

"You care so little for your work?"

"No, but in the scheme of things it matters a whole lot less than it did before. I've done most of the hard stuff. I'm staying through the end of the week, then I need to go." She drew in a breath. "Qadir, I know you had your plan all worked out, but it isn't going to work. Not with me." She hated saying that, but it was true.

"The reality is, you can hire someone else," she continued. "Someone who isn't pregnant." Maybe someone who would be smart enough not to fall in love with him.

She couldn't think about that, she reminded herself. That was her vow. That she wouldn't allow herself to get into her feelings until she was safely on a plane back to Aspen. Then she would have a small but tasteful breakdown and really feel the pain. It would probably frighten the other people on the flight, but they would have to deal with that.

"I do not want someone else. I want you."

His words settled on her like a warm, cozy blanket. She held them close, hardly able to believe that he was actually—

"You are easy to talk to. We share a sense of humor and excellent chemistry. I am unlikely to find that again and it will not be convenient for me to look."

She leaned back against the sofa and closed her eyes. Not only did he know where to slide in the knife, he knew exactly how to twist it for maximum effect.

Not that she should blame him. Qadir had no clue as to her real feelings so he couldn't know how he was hurting her.

"Qadir, I really think that I—"

"I have decided there is only one solution," he said, interrupting her. "We will be married."

Maggie sat up. "Excuse me?"

"We will be married. My father wants me to be married and I have no interest in someone he will thrust upon me. As I have stated, you and I get along well. I understand this match will have many advantages for you, which is also a good thing. It will be more difficult for Jon to see his child regularly, but you mentioned he could have the child for summers and I would not object to that."

"I... You..." She stared at him, too stunned to form sentences.

"It is a great honor," Qadir said kindly. "You are surprised at my generosity. I am confident we will both be happy in this marriage. While my father may take a while to convince, he will be pleased that you are a known breeder."

Her brain was blank. Totally blank. Which was probably a good thing because if she had actual use of her functions, she would be forced to hit him over the head with a lamp.

"A known breeder?" she ground out.

He smiled. "That was meant to be humorous," he told her. "What do you say, Maggie? It is an excellent solution for both of us."

"Solution? To what problem? You're the one who has to get married, not me. No one is pressuring me to take a husband."

She hurt all over. She *loved* him. She could imagine nothing more amazing than having him say he cared about her and wanted to be with her always. But that was just a fantasy. The reality was Qadir wasn't interested in being emotionally connected to anyone. He wanted a companion he liked and someone to have great sex with.

"Why are you angry?" he asked. Damn him, he actually looked confused. "I am doing you a great honor. I am Prince Qadir of El Deharia, Maggie. You would be my princess. A member of the royal family. Your children with me would be part of our history."

"Not bad for a car mechanic from Colorado, right?" she said bitterly, then held up her hands. "Never mind answering. I know you don't get it. Most of the time you're almost a regular guy. I started to forget the whole prince thing. But that's a part of you, too."

His gaze narrowed. "Are you saying that is something you do not like?"

"It's not my favorite characteristic."

Too late she remembered his ex-fiancée, Whitney, who wouldn't marry him because she didn't want to deal with the restrictions of being a princess.

"It's not just that," she said quickly. "I'm not going to marry you to better my financial situation. That's not who I am. And I'm not going to marry you because it's convenient. I wouldn't marry Jon and he thought he was doing the right thing."

"Do not compare me to him."

"Why not? You're both interested in getting me to marry you for reasons that have nothing to do with me and everything to do with yourselves. That's not what I want."

She hurt all over. Her chest ached when she breathed and she just wanted to be alone.

She stood and walked to the door. After pulling it open, she shook her head. "Look. I know you think you're doing me this big favor, but I don't see it that way. I want something different. Something you can't give me. And I'm not going to settle for anything less." She opened the door a little wider. "You should go now."

Maggie lay curled up on the bed, crying so hard, her whole body shook. She knew she should stop, that this much emotion couldn't be good for the baby, but she didn't know how.

"It's all right," Victoria said, stroking her back. "I'll go online and find someone to beat the crap out of Qadir. That will help."

"Not much."

"But a little. Right?"

Maggie reached for another tissue and blew her nose. "I can't believe he did that. I can't believe he proposed that way. What was he thinking?"

"He wasn't. I have no idea. Men can be really, really stupid. Even princes."

"Especially princes. He told me it would be an honor for me to marry him."

"What a jerk."

Maggie nodded and looked at her friend. "I love him."

Victoria gave her a sad smile. "I figured that out. Unfortunately he didn't."

"I don't want him to know. Then he'd only pity me. It's better that he doesn't understand me. At least that's what I keep telling myself." More tears filled her eyes. "I just don't know how to get through this."

"One second at a time. You keep breathing, keep putting one foot in front of the other."

"I want to go home. I have a doctor's appointment tomorrow. I want to make sure it's okay for me to fly with the baby and all, and then I'm gone."

"I'll miss you," Victoria said.

"You're leaving soon, too, aren't you? Come to Aspen. It's beautiful and there are lots of rich, powerful men hanging around the slopes."

"I'm done with rich, powerful men but I will come visit you. I want to be there when the baby is born."

"I'd like that." Otherwise Maggie would be alone. She knew Jon would offer to be with her, but that would be too weird.

At least he could be talked out of it. Qadir would not. He would storm into the delivery room and demand to be a part of things. She started to cry again.

"I wish I didn't love him," she said. "I didn't want it to be like this. I didn't want to be one of those women crushed by a man."

"You're not."

"Look at me."

"You'll get over this and be stronger for it."

Maggie didn't believe her. "Why couldn't he love me?"

"Men like him don't fall in love," Victoria told her. "They take what's offered and move on. They don't have to give their hearts. It's never required of them."

Maggie wanted to disagree and say Qadir wasn't like that, only he was. After all, he'd been the one to come up with the idea of them pretending to be involved. He was also willing to marry her even though he didn't love her.

"I want a man who loves me passionately," she whispered. "I want to matter more than anything."

"Not me," Victoria told her. "Love is messy."

Right now messy looked pretty good.

"Tell me the pain will get better," she said.

"You know it will. You're going to heal and move on. One day you'll look back on all this and be grateful you got away when you did."

Maggie hoped her friend was right, but she had her doubts.

The doctor's office was in a modern building next to a hospital. Maggie showed up a few minutes early for her appointment to fill out paperwork.

Victoria had found the female doctor by asking around at the palace and then had even phoned to make the appointment. Maggie was going to miss her when she left.

After checking in for her appointment, she took the clipboard over to one of the comfortable seats and began filling in the information. She hesitated at the line that asked for her home address, then wrote in that of the palace.

In a few days that wouldn't be true anymore. She already had her ticket home to Aspen. Once there, she would find an apartment to rent until she got her house back, then start looking for a job. She would have to put away as much money as possible before the baby came.

She answered all the health questions. She had no symptoms of anything unusual and so far, no problems with her pregnancy. Still, a part of her hoped to be told she couldn't fly for a few more weeks. Which was just dumb. What did she think? That more time would make Qadir realize he was madly in love with her? Like that was ever going to happen.

With the paperwork completed and turned in, she flipped through a magazine before she was called in to the exam room.

Dr. Galloway was a friendly woman in her late forties. They discussed her due date, prenatal vitamins and Maggie's new dietary needs.

"While everyone wants to eat for two," Dr. Galloway told her, "you're currently eating for yourself and something the size of a rice grain. It's better for you and the baby if you can keep your weight down. The more you put on now, the more you'll have to take off later."

"I'll keep that in mind," Maggie said, knowing lately she was too sad to eat. She would have to force herself to stay healthy for the sake of the baby. "Is it all right for me to fly?"

"Sure. There aren't any problems in the first few months."

"Thanks." Maggie tried not to sound disappointed. It appeared there was nothing keeping her in El Deharia.

The doctor smiled at her. "It's a little early, so I can't promise, but would you like to try to hear the baby's heartbeat?"

"Yes. Of course."

"We'll get set up in a—"

There was a commotion in the hall, the sound of footsteps followed by a woman saying, "You can't go in there. Sir, you can't."

"I am Prince Qadir. I may go where I like."

"Sir, there are *patients*."

"Then tell me where she is."

Dr. Galloway rose. "What on earth is that?"

Maggie sat up. "Um, he's with me."

The doctor stared at her. "He's the—"

"No. Not the father. Just someone I know. He's…" She

shrugged, not sure how to explain about Qadir's imperious proposal and impossible assumptions.

"You can let him in," Maggie said. "It's okay."

Dr. Galloway left to get Qadir while Maggie tried to figure out what he was doing at the doctor's office. How had he even known about her appointment? Then she remembered the date book on her desk. Had he looked there?

She knew better than to be happy about the invasion. Qadir was here for his own reasons, but they were unlikely to be overly thrilling to her.

The door to the exam room flew open and he stalked inside. "You did not tell me about your appointment."

"I know."

"I wish to be informed of these things."

"Why?"

"Because it is not right for you to keep this information from me."

She sat up on the examining table and did her best to look dignified while dressed in a thin cloth gown that tied in the back.

"This isn't your child," she reminded him, refusing to get lost in his dark eyes or remember how good his mouth felt against hers. "You have nothing to do with my pregnancy."

"I want to marry you and be a father to your child. That makes me involved."

"I didn't accept your proposal. Weren't you listening?"

"You weren't saying anything I wanted to hear." He reached for her hand. "Maggie, why are you being difficult?"

She snatched her fingers away before he could touch them. "This isn't difficult, Qadir, it's real. I'm not willing to be a convenience in your life. I want more."

The door opened and a young woman wheeled in a monitor. She paused. "Should I come back?"

"Yes," Qadir said impatiently.

"No," Maggie told her as she scowled at him. "I want her to stay. I might be able to hear the baby's heartbeat."

His expression softened. "So soon?"

"We can try," the technician told him.

"I would like to stay and listen."

Maggie thought about fighting him, but what was the point? She lay back down and was hooked up to the monitor. A few minutes later, a soft, steady beating filled the room.

It was the most beautiful sound she'd ever heard and it terrified her to the bone. There really was a baby. She was going to be a mother and responsible for the life growing inside her.

What if she wasn't any good? What if she messed everything up? Then she remembered her father and how much he'd loved her. She wanted that for herself and her child.

She turned to look at Qadir, to see if he understood the wonder of the moment and was crushed to find he had slipped out when she wasn't paying attention. Apparently he hadn't cared as much as he claimed.

"It was the sound," Qadir said as he once again paced, but this time in his brother's quarters.

"A heartbeat?" Kateb sounded unimpressed.

"Yes, but more than that. I cannot explain what it was like. There in the room. Proof of life."

"You know this isn't your child," Kateb said.

Qadir dismissed the information. "Not the child of my body, but we are still connected. I will forbid her to leave. It is within my power."

"Not without reason," his brother reminded him. "You could always drag her into the desert. I know places where you will never be found."

"Maggie would not enjoy the desert," Qadir said, wondering why she had to be so difficult and how he could convince her she had to stay. "There must be something I am not saying to her. Something she wants to hear."

His brother looked at him. "You're not serious, are you?"

"What?"

"You really don't understand why she's not happy with you?"

"And you do?"

Kateb stood and faced him. "She's a woman. She wants to be loved."

Qadir stiffened. "No. I will not."

"Because you loved Whitney and she walked away?"

Qadir ignored the question. He would not speak of her with his brother. The pain was too—

He paused. There was no pain. Whitney had been many years ago. Perhaps she was the reason he was reluctant to fully engage his heart, but he no longer cared for her in any way. But to risk loving again...

"Whitney didn't stay because she couldn't face what being your wife meant," Kateb said. "Is that Maggie's problem?"

"No. She is fearless." Feisty and determined. She challenged him. He enjoyed her challenges, especially in bed.

"So the problem seems to be you."

Qadir glared. "I have proposed. She has refused. The problem is hers."

"Did you tell her you love her?"

"No."

"Did it ever occur to you that you should?"

He started to explain to his brother that the problem was he didn't love Maggie, but he couldn't seem to speak the words. Why was that?

Did he love her? Was that why he'd wanted to grind Jon into the dust? Why he didn't want to let her go?

"I do love her," he announced. "I love Maggie."

Kateb smirked. "Then you should probably go and tell her."

Maggie left the palace in a cab. She supposed she could have gotten one of the limo drivers to take her, but somehow that didn't seem right.

She had the driver wait for a few minutes, hoping Victoria would show up to say goodbye, but she did not. Her friend had disappeared, leaving only a note saying her father had unexpectedly arrived and that she would try to stop by if she could.

Finally Maggie got in the cab and they drove away.

She stared out at the passing city, trying to take in the beauty of it all. Anything to keep her mind off her sadness. She'd come to El Deharia with high hopes and was leaving with a broken heart. She would miss her friend. Even more, she would miss the man she loved.

Alone, near tears, she admitted to herself that she had hoped he would at least try to talk her into staying. She'd hoped for one more annoying conversation where he told her what to do and she refused. At least then she could see him one more time. But he hadn't bothered.

She told herself she would get over him, even as a part of her knew that she was going to love him forever. Eventually she might be able to find a man she could like a lot, but the arrogant prince would always have her heart. Unfortunately he was too stupid to appreciate that.

Once at the busy airport, she paid the driver and walked into the terminal. She stood in line to check in. When it was her turn, the clerk took her electronic ticket and her passport and typed into the computer. The young woman frowned.

"What's wrong?" Maggie asked.

"There seems to be a problem, Ms. Collins. I'm going to have to ask you to speak with one of our security officers."

"What?"

Before she could find out what was going on, she was whisked into a small room with a single desk, two chairs and no windows. An official-looking little man stacked her luggage in the corner before facing her.

"Ms. Collins, I'm very sorry, but I'm going to have to arrest you."

This couldn't be happening, Maggie thought. It was a joke. It had to be.

"For what?"

"Violating El Deharian law. You are pregnant?"

"That has nothing to do with anything."

"I'll take that as a yes. It is illegal to remove a royal child from the country without permission from the king. You have no such permission."

She sank into the chair. Disbelief warred with despair. Wasn't her life sucky enough without this happening?

"The baby isn't Qadir's," she said, not looking at the little man. "I know what the papers said, but they're wrong. If you would just call him, he'll tell you that and you can let me go."

"That is the one thing I cannot do."

That voice!

Maggie stood and saw Qadir had entered the small room. He walked to her and took her hands in his as the security agent left.

She didn't know what to think. "Why are you here?"

"Because you left before I could speak with you. Because if you leave, I will only follow and that will make us both look foolish."

His dark gaze burned down to her soul. "Maggie, I have realized what is wrong. Why you won't stay and marry me."

"I doubt that."

He smiled. "You are difficult and stubborn and I never wish to tame you."

"I'm fairly untamable."

"Even for the man who loves you?"

Time froze. She couldn't breathe, couldn't speak, could only stare into Qadir's face.

"I love you," he said firmly. "I want you to stay so we can be together. I want you to stay so I can be a father to your child. I want you to stay because we belong together. Be my wife."

The words were magic but a little surprising. "Have you had a recent head injury?"

Qadir laughed, then pulled her close and kissed her. "I have been a fool. Many years ago, I gave my heart. When it was broken, I vowed to never love again. I did not recognize what had happened until it was almost too late."

Joy filled her until she thought she might float. She flung herself at him and held on as hard as she could. Qadir squeezed her tight until she shoved him away.

"I can't," she told him. "This will never work."

"Why not?"

"I'm a mechanic. I can't go from that to being a princess."

"Why not?"

"You need someone else. Someone more in keeping with your place in society."

"I want you. Only you. I want to make you so happy, you feel pity for all other women."

A great goal. She was so tempted. She loved him. This was her dream come true.

"I'm scared," she admitted.

"Of me?"

"Of how much I love you."

"We can face our fears together, sweet Maggie. I love you."

She went to him then, because she didn't have a choice. He already had possession of her heart. He might as well take the rest of her, too.

"Forever," he promised before he kissed her. "Now will you stay?"

She smiled. "Just try to get rid of me."

* * * * *

Desert King, Pregnant Mistress

SUSAN STEPHENS

Susan Stephens was a professional singer before meeting her husband on the tiny Mediterranean island of Malta. In true Modern™ romance style they met on Monday, became engaged on Friday and were married three months after that. Almost thirty years and three children later, they are still in love. (Susan does not advise her children to return home one day with a similar story, as she may not take the news with the same fortitude as her own mother!)

Susan had written several non-fiction books when fate took a hand. At a charity costume ball there was an after-dinner auction. One of the lots, "Spend a Day with an Author", had been donated by Mills & Boon author Penny Jordan. Susan's husband bought this lot, and Penny was to become not just a great friend but a wonderful mentor, who encouraged Susan to write romance.

Susan loves her family, her pets, her friends and her writing. She enjoys entertaining, travel and going to the theatre. She reads, cooks and plays the piano to relax and can occasionally be found throwing herself off mountains on a pair of skis or galloping through the countryside. Visit Susan's website: www.susanstephens.net—she loves to hear from her readers all around the world!

For all the wonderful people of Liverpool, who breathed life into Beth Tracey Torrance.

CHAPTER ONE

SHE was hiding in a rock pool, watching a naked man stride out of the surf. Beth Tracey Torrance, good girl, quiet girl, shop girl, Liverpool girl, pressed up against warm rocks in a foreign land beneath a blazing sun. And not just any country, but the desert kingdom of Q'Adar, where men rode camels and carried guns! Her stay-at-home self would say she was mad to be sitting here, frozen to the spot like one of the mannequins in the store—her friends would put it somewhat stronger—but she was drawn to this man. Just call it essential research. Well, she had to give a full report of her trip when she got back home, didn't she?

Beth leaned forward cautiously to take another look. If she'd thought the lash of sea on rock was elemental, the man leaving the ocean was even more stunning. Under different circumstances she would have turned away, because he was nude, but nothing seemed real to her here in Q'Adar—not the fabulous riches, the glamour, or the beautiful people.

Where was the camera when you needed it? With his lean, muscular frame and regal bearing, she was sure this man must be a member of the proud Q'Adaran race. And it wasn't every day you got the chance to stare at a man so beautiful he took your breath away.

Her colleagues at the luxury department store, Khalifa, would never believe this! She had amazed them once already with the news that her prize for being voted Shop Assistant of the Year for the Khalifa luxury group included not just a trip to the desert kingdom of Q'Adar, but a fairy-tale gown to wear to the Platinum and Diamond Ball—being held to celebrate the thirtieth birthday of the country's ruler, as well as his coronation, or whatever it was called when a man was voted Sheikh of Sheikhs. And this was the same man whose extensive business-portfolio included the Khalifa brand.

She had never met her boss, Mr Khalifa Kadir, the legendary founder of the international chain of luxury stores, but was stunned to think he would now be known as His Majesty. His full title was His Majesty Khalifa Kadir al Hassan, Sheikh of Sheikhs, Bringer of Light to His People. It sounded like something out of a fairy story, Beth thought as the man walked up the beach and disappeared behind some rocks.

And now she, Beth Tracey Torrance, was going to meet the Sheikh of Sheikhs when he handed her the trophy she'd won. So, should she bow or should she curtsey? Beth wondered, distractedly chewing her lip. There wasn't much room for manoeuvre in her tight-fitting dress, so maybe she should just make a small bow when she met him... *When she met him!* When she, an ordinary girl, met the Sheikh of Sheikhs! It was all she had dreamed about for weeks now. And yet that dream had just been eclipsed by some man on a beach.

Pressed back against the rocks, Beth closed her eyes and inwardly melted. Forget the sheikh. This man would be branded on her mind for ever!

He felt rather than saw the intruder. His training in the special forces had served him well. The sixth sense he had developed during army service had saved his life on several occasions, and had also proved a handy tool when it came to developing his business instinct. His profits now rivalled those of oil, and Q'Adar was rich in oil. Most sheikhs didn't work, but where was the challenge in spending oil wealth when that precious resource seeped out of the ground? And where was the satisfaction in paying experts to earn money for him? Where was the sense of achievement in sitting back while others did the work for him? He was always restless, always seeking the next challenge, and now he had accepted the greatest challenge of his life: to rescue his country, Q'Adar, from the brink of disaster.

Throwing back his head to embrace the warmth of the molten sun, the Sheikh of Sheikhs, His Majesty Khalifa Kadir al Hassan, rejoiced that he was more than strong enough for the task as he luxuriated in the seductive heat of his native land.

He was gorgeous, absolutely gorgeous. And if he'd just turn a little to the right…

No.

No!

What was she thinking?

Beth's thoughts flew into a frenzy as the man's naked body was fully revealed. She exhaled with relief as he turned his back. She didn't want him to turn around again or she'd be damaged for life. She'd never find his equal. *Never!* He'd been close enough for her to see *everything!* And there was an awful lot of everything to see. He wasn't even covered by a towel, though she could see one neatly folded on a rock. Thankfully the rock was some way away, which meant he wouldn't have to pass her hiding place when he went to get it. Which meant she was safe to go on staring at him. Well, she had to remember every bit of this in detail to tell her friends, didn't she?

* * *

To an untrained observer he might appear oblivious to the dangers around him, but he never took anything for granted, especially his personal safety. He had made his life outside Q'Adar, and was still weighing up the risks here. He had returned to his homeland at the request of the other sheikhs, who had asked him to lead them, and he was ready to serve. His life experiences had prepared him for most things—with the possible exception of the unfathomable workings of a woman's mind. His portfolio of business interests had achieved global renown, and he had no personal issues to distract him; no taint of scandal touched him. As a stranger, to emotion he doubted it ever would. His sense of duty was all-embracing, and, having accepted this challenge, he wouldn't let his fellow sheikhs down by carelessly offering himself up for slaughter.

As he moved steadily along the beach Khal caught sight of a flash of glowing hair. It confirmed his earlier analysis of the situation—the risk was small. An agent would have made her move by now. Paparazzi? The direction of the sun would have flared off their camera lens. No, this was a sight-seeing expedition by an amateur.

Burying his face in the towel he'd left ready for when he quit the sea, he took his time, knowing this would lull the young woman into a false sense of security. He could wait all he liked; she couldn't get past him. He was between her and the palace, and with the ocean in front of her, and thousands of miles of unseen desert surrounding them, she wouldn't be going anywhere.

Plus she would be growing increasingly uncomfortable in the heat, while he felt refreshed—and not just in the body, but in the mind; the sea had cleansed him. He swam every day, either in the pool at one of his many homes, or in the ocean. It was one of his few indulgences. It allowed him to step

outside himself—outside his life. Pitting his strength against
the ocean gave him something else to think about other than
balance sheets and treachery. He needed that space. Q'Adar
had grown fat and lazy in his absence, and he intended to
change that by setting up a strong infrastructure and wiping
out corruption. It was a daunting task, and would take many
years to achieve, but eventually he would reach that goal; he
was determined to.

The fact that someone had managed to elude his security
guards was an example of the general sloppiness he had uncovered, though for now good business-practice required him
to hold back on reprisal until he had a chance to assess all the
players involved. For what was a country, other than a
business to be managed efficiently for the good of its people?
It was ironic to think his business acumen was one of the
reasons his fellow sheikhs had voted him into this position of
supreme power over them, but he didn't kid himself it had
been a popularity poll—they knew his reputation. The financial press dubbed him ruthless and unforgiving, and where his
employees were concerned that was correct. He didn't take
the livelihoods of fifty-thousand people lightly. He defended
them as sheikhs of old had defended their territories, and if
that meant cutting out the dead wood, and neutralising the
competition, then that was what he did.

But for now his interest lay in tracking down this young
woman. He would use her as an example of how the security
forces were deficient, and stealth was his weapon of choice.
His angle of approach would make her think he was walking
away from her, when in fact he would be coming closer with
every step.

As he prowled closer he was forced to shut out the seductive beauty of his homeland. There was much in Q'Adar to
tempt the senses, and it would be easy to slip into self-indul-

gent ways. A panorama of exquisite loveliness tempted him to lower his guard and linger. When he returned to the palace he would be greeted by sights of unimaginable splendour—every wall at the Palace of the Moon was decorated with gold leaf, and the doors were studded with precious stones. Beguiling perfumes would lure him into thinking of erotic pleasures, while music would thrum a constant siren-song through his senses.

The only sticking point for him at the palace was his mother. Hoping he would marry soon, she had assembled the world's most beautiful women for his perusal. Every royal house was represented—and there was no doubt her efforts had pleased the corrupt sheikhs, who didn't care about his choice of bedmate just so long as he was distracted and left them alone. What they had failed to realise was that his mistress was work, and that here in Q'Adar there was much to do.

Beth watched the man bury his face in the towel with a mixture of apprehension and fascination. There was something about his stillness that warned her to be wary. She couldn't shake off a feeling of uneasiness. Maybe he did know she was here, watching him. Maybe he wasn't just burying his face in a towel, but quietening his body in order to listen to his senses. As he lifted his head the onshore breeze caught his thick black hair and tossed it around his face. He was magnificent. She'd never seen anyone like him before, and she held her breath as he fixed the towel around his waist.

He started walking—thankfully, away from her. Cutting at right angles to the beach, he disappeared out of sight behind some more rocks...

Letting out her breath in a ragged stream, Beth relaxed. What an experience that had been! She wished there had been a sculpter on hand, or an artist, someone capable of capturing his likeness and sharing it with the world…

Beth shrieked as something cold and hard pressed into the back of her neck. *Was it a gun?* She was too frightened to turn and find out.

'Get up,' a clipped male voice instructed. 'Get up slowly, and turn around.'

She did as he asked, stumbling in the sand, only to find the man on the beach confronting her. 'I was told I would be safe here,' she blurted out. 'The new Sheikh has reserved this beach for his staff.' Beth knew that she was rambling as tears of fright filled her eyes. She couldn't see the gun, but knew it must be somewhere. 'I've got a permit…' No, she hadn't! She had changed out of her jeans into a sundress without pockets. 'Don't you speak English?' she blurted, wondering if those few phrases were all he had.

'As well as you, I imagine,' the man replied in a voice that was barely accented.

Beth found herself confronting the hardest, coldest eyes she'd ever seen, set in a face of savage beauty, but affront had taken the place of her anger. The man was twice her size, and much older than she was. She firmed her jaw. He had no need to threaten her with a gun. 'Is it usual to intimidate guests to your country?'

She had guts, he'd give her that, but she had been spying on him, and she mustn't be allowed to think him an easy target. 'Do you make a point of invading other people's privacy?' he snapped back.

Her cheeks turned an attractive shade of rose, telling him that emotion came easily to her. In that they were very different. But the moment of embarrassment swiftly passed, and now this barefoot intruder with her wind-tangled hair and flimsy beach-dress was shooting fire at him from crystal-blue eyes. She was much younger than he had first thought, and her skin had the texture of a downy peach. She was new to the unforgiving Arabian sun, and instinctively he took a step forward to back her into the shade.

'Don't you come near me!' she warned him, holding out her tiny hands to ward him off.

She was frightened, but still determined to put up a fight. And then he noticed that her small, straight nose had a sprinkling of freckles across the bridge...

Irrelevant. He was surprised that he'd noticed such a thing. Where had she come from, and how had she slipped past his guards? She wasn't part of his world or she would have been recognised him immediately. She must have drafted in to help with the celebrations. But, if that was the case, why was she sunning herself while everyone else was working? 'Does your supervisor know you're here?'

'Does yours?'

He recoiled at her impudence. Then he recognised the accent. Natives of Liverpool weren't noted for holding back. 'I asked the question first,' he said evenly. 'Have you considered the possibility that your supervisor might be worried about you?'

A crease appeared between her upswept taupe brows as she considered this. 'It seems to me that yours has more cause to be worried about you.'

'How do you work that out?' he said, deciding he would play along.

'Do they know you bring a gun to the beach?'

'A gun?' He had to hold back his astonishment as well as his amusement. Holding out his hands, palms flat, he showed her he had no weapons—concealed or otherwise—unless she felt like searching under his towel, of course. 'I was merely attempting to attract your attention,' he told her.

'Oh, I see,' she said, catching on. 'With one sea-cooled finger?' Her mouth firmed into an angry line. 'So you don't use a gun, but you do assault guests to your country—well?' she demanded. 'Don't I deserve the courtesy of a reply when you've frightened me half to death?'

He was still adapting to this radical change to the way people usually addressed him when his attention was drawn to her full rosebud-lips, and the difficulty she was having keeping them pressed flat in an expression of affront. He wanted to smile, because she was so young and so indignant, but he knew better than to prolong the encounter. 'My apologies,' he said mildly. As he spoke he touched his right hand to his breast and then to his forehead. 'You are right to feel distress. As a visitor to my land you are of course my honoured guest...' As the silky words worked their ancient magic, he saw her eyes darken with more than interest. She wasn't so keen to get away now.

'Apology accepted,' she said. 'So, you work here too?'

Rather than answer he watched the flush rising on her cheeks. Her slight frame and pert breasts had made his senses stir. 'That's right,' he said at last. 'I just got here.'

'Oh, like me,' she cut in, forgetting to be angry with him. 'I expect you've come for the celebrations.' She glanced towards the palace. 'They told me a lot of new staff had been hired.'

'Did they?'

She gave him a long, considering look, and then decided to trust him with a little more. 'Q'Adar's the most beautiful country, isn't it?'

He could only agree. The sea was jade green with a white-lace frill, and his Palace of the Moon had turned rose pink in the mellow light of late afternoon.

'But it's not the flash that makes it so lovely, is it?' she demanded bluntly. 'Though there's plenty of that around, from what I've seen. Thing is, ostentation's commonplace when you can see it on the telly any time you want.'

'Ostentation?' He had thought the palace overblown when he'd returned to it after an absence too, but he wasn't sure how he felt about hearing criticism of it from a stranger.

'It's the scenery that gets you, isn't it?' she went on, gesturing around. 'I think it's a combination of beach, sea, and the warmth of the people that makes Q'Adar so special.'

She was making it increasingly hard for him to find fault with her, especially when she added, 'I think it's the people most of all.' She stopped then and blushed, and started fiddling with her hair, as if aware that she was keeping him. But then wariness shaded her eyes as she took on board the fact that she shouldn't be engrossed in conversation with a man she didn't know—a man who might even pose a danger to her...

'I won't hurt you,' he said, lifting his hands.

She shrugged, a little defiant gesture to cover for the predicament in which she found herself, he guessed. And then a horn sounded somewhere in the palace, and she jumped. 'What was that?' Still gasping for air, she stared at him for answers.

'That was the Nafir—'

'The what?'

'The Nafir,' he said again. 'It's a horn.' He was finding it harder every moment to remain aloof from her infectious cheeriness. 'It's a big horn about three metres long made of copper. It utters a single-note.'

'That's not much use, then, is it?'

He drew himself up to his full height. 'On the contrary. The Nafir is sounded on ceremonial occasions and will be played tonight to herald the start of the Sheikh's birthday.'

'So that was a dress rehearsal?'

'I expect so.'

She gave an exaggerated sigh. 'Well, that's a relief! I was thinking *Walls of Jericho*—you know? We wouldn't want that lot tumbling down on us, now, would we?' Hugging herself, she pulled a face as she stared up at the gigantic structure.

The Palace of the Moon had stood for centuries as a symbol of Q'Adar's pre-eminence in the Arab world, and he'd never heard anyone make light of it before. He didn't know what to make of this young woman—except, to say, she interested him. 'Don't you think you should be getting back?' He was conscious that she must have duties, and he didn't want her to get in trouble.

'Shouldn't you?' Cocking her head, she levelled a cheeky stare at him.

'Oh, I'm all right for a bit longer.'

'And so am I,' she said. 'There's ages to go before the ball.'

'So you're a waitress?'

She laughed out loud. 'Goodness me, no! Can you imagine it? Canapés flying everywhere and drinks all muddled up? I'd never be asked to do something like that!'

'So, you're a guest?'

'There's no need to sound quite so surprised,' she scolded him. 'Actually,' she confided, touching his arm in her eagerness to make *him* feel at ease. 'I'm halfway in between.'

He felt her touch like a brand, and had to refocus to ask her, 'Halfway in between what?'

'Halfway in between being a servant and a guest,' she told him blithely. 'I do work for the Sheikh, but I'm insignificant.'

'Insignificant?' he queried. Of all the adjectives he might have used to describe this young woman, 'insignificant' was not one of them. 'I wouldn't call you that.'

'That's very kind of you,' she said sincerely. 'But, I'd better tell you right away, I'm only a shop assistant.'

'Only?' He thought about all the other sales assistants who

worked for him at his luxury stores worldwide. They were the lifeblood of his business. He considered them to be the front line, and this girl was the best of them, he realised now as the mystery unravelled in front of him. 'Tell me more,' he said, wanting to hear her version of events.

'I won best Shop Assistant of the Year for the Khalifa group, and this is my prize,' she said, gesturing around in a way he guessed was meant to encompass everything she had seen since arriving in Q'Adar.

'And do you like it?' She had already said she did, but he wanted to delve deeper into that quicksilver mind of hers.

'I love it. Who wouldn't? And they say the Sheikh's gorgeous!'

'Do they?' he said with surprise.

'I won't be able to pass an opinion on him until I see him tonight, but I'll let you know.'

'Would you?' he said, containing his amusement. She was so very young, he was surprised when she leaned forward to confide in him.

'You know, I feel sorry for that sheikh...'

'Do you? Why?'

She stood back a pace, and her face turned solemn. 'You probably think he's got everything, but a man like that is a hostage for life, isn't he?' And, without waiting for him to answer the question, she breezed on with concern. 'He can never do what he wants, can he? He can only do what's right for everyone else.'

He realised now that the inevitable question with its confident answer was part of her Liverpool charm. 'Can't they be one and the same thing?' he said, marvelling at the fact that he was entering into a discussion with her. But, then, he couldn't believe he was standing here at all with a woman he didn't know.

She stood and thought about it for a while. 'He'd have to

be really strong to run a country, the Khalifa business, *and* find time for a private life.'

'And you feel sorry for him?' He felt faintly affronted.

'Yes, I do,' she said candidly.

Before he could argue with her premise, she shook her head. 'It must be hideous, having people bow and scrape around you all day without knowing who to trust.'

'Maybe the Sheikh is shrewder than you think.'

Her face brightened. 'I agree. He must be, mustn't he? Look what he's done with his business, for a start—and the other sheikhs wouldn't have voted him in if he wasn't exceptional. I like that, don't you?' she demanded without pausing for breath.

'What do you mean?'

'The way all the other sheikhs voted for him. And, of course, we couldn't be more thrilled back home that it's *our* sheikh that's going to be the ruler of Q'Adar. Except we're all worried now that he might sell off the Khalifa stores.'

'Why would he do that?'

'He might lose interest in business when he has the running of a country on his mind.'

'There's no danger of that.'

'You sound very sure.' Interest coloured her voice. 'You have the inside track, don't you?' And, when he didn't answer, she pressed him eagerly. 'You're someone important, aren't you?'

'I hear things on the palace grapevine,' he explained with a dismissive gesture.

'Of course you do—and it's the same for us back at the store. We always get to hear what's going on. What he's like?' she said after a moment's pause.

'The Sheikh?'

'You must know him if you work for him. I was off with flu last time he visited Khalifa in Liverpool, worse luck. Is he stern?'

'Very.'

'He's not mean to you, is he?'

'We have a good working relationship,' he reassured her.

'Oh, well, I'd better get a move on,' she said, heading off in the direction of the palace. 'Thanks for the chat. Are you coming?' she said, turning to face him. 'Only, I have to go now and put my glad rags on.'

'For the Platinum and Diamond Ball? Of course…' He had almost forgotten. He had allowed himself to be distracted by a pair of slender legs showing their first hint of tan, along with fine-boned hips and a hand-span waist. The unaffected friendliness in the young girl's eyes was so refreshing, he allowed himself another moment's indulgence. 'Are you looking forward to the ball, Cinderella?'

Her face turned serious. 'Don't call me that. I'm not Cinderella; my name is Beth. Beth Tracey Torrance.' And then, taking him completely by surprise, she held out her tiny hand for him to shake. 'And I'm not waiting around for some fairy godmother to come and save me. I make my own luck.'

'Do you indeed?' he said, releasing her hand, which was soft and cool in spite of the heat, and delivered a surprisingly firm handshake. 'And how do you go about that?'

'Hard work,' she said frankly. 'I read something once written by Thomas Edison. You know—the light-bulb man? I've never forgotten it, and it's become my motto.'

'Go on…' His lips were threatening rebellion, but he managed somehow to control them and confine himself to a brief nod of encouragement.

'Thomas Edison said, "opportunity is missed by most people because it comes dressed in overalls and looks like work".'

'And you agree with that?'

'Yes.' She drew the word out, as well as up and down the vocal register, for even more emphasis. 'It's worked for me. But then I love my work.'

'You do?'

'I love people,' she said, eyes gleaming with enthusiasm. 'I love seeing their faces when I find something in the store that's going to make a difference to their lives. Maybe it's a gift, or a treat they're buying for themselves—it doesn't matter. I just want to see *the look* transform their faces...'

And now her face was transformed with a smile. 'So *the look*'s your secret of success?'

'Oh, there are others on the floor just as good as me,' she told him. 'Sales figures are all a matter of luck, aren't they?'

After what she'd told him, he very much doubted it. The horn sounded again, and this time she didn't jump. 'Isn't this romantic?' she said instead.

They both gazed up at the towering ramparts, where pennants were being raised in his honour. The sun had sunk low enough to turn the walls of his citadel a soft shade of rose madder, which, yes, he supposed could be called romantic by those with a vivid imagination and time enough to look.

'Imagine having this much fuss made of your birthday,' she said, drawing his attention again. 'I thought I was lucky, but—'

'Lucky?' he interrupted, wanting to know more about her.

'I have the best family on earth,' she assured him passionately. As she laughed, he presumed all the happy reminiscences must be flooding in. 'They do all sorts of batty things for me on my birthday. Wonderful surprises...' Her eyes turned dreamy. 'You know the type of thing?'

Actually, no, he didn't. His parents loved him, but duty had always coloured his life. There had been little time to party, and much to learn. If he hadn't been voted Sheikh of Sheikhs, he would still have returned to Q'Adar to serve his people at some point.

'I expect the Sheikh's up there now,' she said, shading her

eyes as she gazed up to where the bursting flames of the dipping sun were reflected in the windows. 'There'll be champagne corks popping right now, I'll bet.'

They would be anxiously awaiting his return. He had been gone for far too long. The plans for this celebration had been rigorously planned minute by minute, and unlike the celebrations she had described there would be no surprises. The Platinum and Diamond Ball would not conform to any of the wacky images Beth had conjured, but would be stiff with ceremony, and fraught with pitfalls, especially for an innocent like Beth Tracey Torrance. 'Is someone taking care of you tonight at the ball?'

'Taking care of me?' she slanted him a coquettish look. 'Why? Are you offering? Because, if you are, I think it's time you told me your name.'

'I'll be working,' he reminded her.

'Oh, don't worry,' she said, flipping her wrist. 'I was only teasing you. I know you must have lots to do, and most probably hundreds of gorgeous women in your harem—' Her hand flew to cover her mouth. 'Sorry! *Sorry!*' She looked mortified, and her accent broadened as she exclaimed in horror, 'I didn't mean that! I hate stereotypes, don't you?'

'No offence taken,' he assured her. 'And, as for my name, you can call me Khal…'

'Khal as in *Khalifa*?' she interrupted. 'Now, that *is* a coincidence…' As she stared at him her face changed and grew pale beneath its scattering of freckles. 'No, it isn't, is it?' she said.

CHAPTER TWO

THREE things happened in quick succession. His bodyguards appeared out of nowhere, Beth screamed as one of them shoved a gun in her face, and he launched himself in her defence, seizing the gun so fast the man reeled back. 'Leave her!' he commanded in a shout.

Beth's face was twisted with fear as he reached out to reassure her. His men had stormed in—using unnecessary force to make up for their earlier negligence, he deduced—but Beth was young and a stranger to violence, and they had terrified her. 'Come,' he said, beckoning her closer with his outstretched hand.

Shaking her head, she refused to look at him. He sensed her fear, but above that he sensed her determination to maintain control. Even so, inwardly he gave a curse directed at his men. She had been so full of life only moments before, and now that life had been crushed out of her. She had been like a breath of fresh air, but her innocence had been trampled. She had come to Q'Adar with some romantic notion of what life would be like in a desert kingdom, and couldn't be expected to understand the harsh realities. He lost no time dismissing his men, and then asked her, 'Will you walk back to the palace with me, Beth?'

Hugging herself, she shook her head. He couldn't blame her for feeling the way she did when the ugly threat of violence was still hanging in the air. It would be so alien to anything she was used to, she'd have no coping strategies.

'Is that how it is here?' she said at last.

He was surprised to see her clear blue gaze had turned to steel.

'If you mean the guards—'

'And the guns.'

'They are a necessary precaution.'

'To protect you from your people?' Pressing her lips down, she shook her head in disapproval. 'Then I really do feel sorry for you…' Still hugging herself, she stalked away.

He had pulled her CV from the pile and was studying it in the bath, allowing the eucalyptus-scented steam to clear his head. Beth certainly had the gift when it came to selling, and along with the bare facts he found several glowing references—not just from her line manager, but from her colleagues too. They said if she had a fault it was that Beth Torrance didn't know how good she was…

He smiled as he thought about this, about Beth—and he rarely smiled, because life was a serious business. She was so unspoiled, but then she was only twenty-two… Yet she was confident enough to stand her ground and fight for what she believed in. The Sheikh and the shop girl were as one in that, he reflected wryly.

He turned back to the folder to look at her reports from school, where she'd captained the hockey team and led the first-aid group, generally showing a solid performance in all her academic studies. From school she had moved straight into a management-training course with Khalifa, which involved working in every department over the course of five years, and was not an easy option. Her reason for doing this, he read, smiling again as he imagined her writing it, was because she had wanted 'to get stuck into something right away'. She didn't mince her words.

Beth Tracey Torrance, aged twenty-two, might be a small problem in the scale of things he had to deal with, but he wasn't about to set her adrift in a sea of sharks. Calling up his mother, the Dowager Sheikha, he asked for one of her trusted attendants to be assigned to their visitor. 'She's a young girl in a foreign land, and we must ensure that her stay is—' he chose his next words with care '—comfortable and safe.' Ignoring the suspicion in his mother's voice, he ended the call.

The young girl sent to help Beth dress for the ball was a good listener. Beth was still fretting as she helped her with her make-up. What would her friends say when she went back to Khalifa and they realised she'd let them down? 'I promised them all I'd put the trophy in the staff lounge,' she explained as the young girl pinned a fresh orchid in her hair. 'I wanted everyone to share it. But now I won't have a trophy to put there, will I? The Sheikh will never give it to me now…'

The girl shook her head.

'Well, it's no use looking on the black side, is it? I'd better get that dress on because, trophy or no trophy, I am going to that ball.' At least if she attended the ball she'd have something to share with her colleagues, Beth thought, feeling nervous as she thought about it. None of this had seemed real while she had been chatting away—not this magnificent suite of rooms in the Palace of the Moon, or the beach with the man on it, or the guns… But now it did, and she had to go to the ball all alone.

When she got up from the stool, and looked at the silvery ball-gown shimmering on its hanger next to the dressing gown she'd just discarded, her heart went wild. But she wasn't going to turn tail and run, Beth determined, though that was exactly what she felt like doing. No. She was going to this ball, and she was going to face up to the amazingly glamorous and stunningly endowed Sheikh—and if there was even the smallest chance that she could come away with that trophy then she would. 'Could you help me, please?' she said, knowing she couldn't fasten the dress unaided. As the girl passed her the dressing gown, Beth, still thinking distractedly about Khal, said, 'No, I meant the dress—' But then she noticed the girl had blushed a deep shade of red, and the penny finally dropped. 'You don't speak English, do you?'

'I am *sorree*,' the young girl managed in a halting accent.

'No, I'm the one who should be sorry,' Beth argued. 'Rabbiting on like that and you not understanding a word of it. And that's not the first mistake I've made today—if only!' Beth exclaimed, pulling a face with a laugh. 'Come on,' she said, smiling as she put her arm around the other girl's shoulders. 'Let's do this together.'

Taking the dress down from the padded hanger, Beth handed it to the maid. 'You've done me a favour, you have. You've woken me up—and about time too! It's time to put my foreign-travel head on and snap out of this. "Ooh, the sun's shining, and I left my brain behind in Liverpool". Don't worry if you didn't understand a word of that,' she added, giving the startled girl a hug. 'You didn't miss much—and that's a whole lot more than can be said for me!'

Beth grimaced as she caught sight of herself clattering along the fabulous corridor in her five-inch heels. There were floor-to-ceiling mirrors set into the golden walls, so there was no escaping the truth. No escaping her bodyguard, either! They had sent a fierce-looking woman to collect her. Did she wear a gun too? Beth wondered as she struggled to keep up. Shoes that had seemed such a good idea back at the store were killing her now. She might be short, but she always wore flats so she could scoot around finding things for her customers. Heels this high demanded the skill of a tightrope walker—skill she definitely didn't possess. 'Can you slow down a bit, please?' she begged as her stern-looking companion put on a spurt of speed.

The woman didn't answer, and as she had introduced herself as one of the Dowager Sheikha's personal attendants Beth thought she had better not push it. Personal *scary person*, Beth decided—definitely not someone you'd want to get on the wrong side of. The woman couldn't have made it clearer that she was used to escorting royalty.

'While I feel like a chicken in a bandage,' Beth muttered, using her head to propel herself along. Graceful didn't come in to it. Majestic? Forget it. She was a shop assistant at the palace under sufferance, and the Sheikha's attendant wasn't going to let her forget it any time soon.

The pace they were walking at made Beth's heart beat even faster. Her hair had started to fall down, and fronds of it were sticking to her face. As if that wasn't bad enough, she had chatted up the Sheikh of Sheikhs as if he were a beach boy. *And* she had seen him naked! What would the Dowager Sheikha make of that? How was she supposed to look at His Majesty now? What if she couldn't control herself? What if she started giggling?

As they stopped in front of two gigantic doors, men dressed in flowing robes opened them. Beth acknowledged them both with a smile and a cheery greeting, which only brought a stony look of disapproval to her chaperon's face. That was the least of Beth's worries. The ballroom was crowded, and was she imagining it or had it gone utterly silent at the sight of her? No, she wasn't imagining it. Everyone had turned to stare. There must be spies everywhere in a palace, Beth thought, noticing servants whispering together. This was a real international gathering with 'high and mighties' from every land, and enough diamonds flashing to sink a ship. Had one of these people seen her on the beach with the Sheikh, or had their servants reported her? Did they think there was an ulterior motive to her being here? Did they think her win was a fix, just a ruse, to bring her to Q'Adar so the Sheikh could enjoy her?

Beth shivered at the thought of what must be going through people's minds. But as the woman swept ahead of her she knew she must pull herself together fast. Tossing back her ruined hair, she firmed her jaw, sending the fresh flower the maid had so carefully fixed tumbling over her eye. She brushed it back and tipped her chin, and started forward again. Beth couldn't know that a keen black gaze was fixed on her with interest from behind a gilded screen.

She had been sitting at a dark table in a forgotten corner of the ballroom for nearly an hour. And she wanted to chat with someone. She didn't want to be stuck away like this, like last week's dirty washing, as if she was something to put out of the way and forget—and with the Dowager's Sheikha's sidekick glaring at her if she so much as crossed her legs. She *needed* to chat. If she was going to work off her nerves, she needed to move about. Why had they invited her if the organisers couldn't even be bothered to check up on her and see that she was okay? She would have arranged things differently in Liverpool—everyone would have got a proper welcome.

As yet another waiter studiously ignored her Beth decided enough was enough; she was parched, and if she didn't have a glass of water soon... She was not going to sit here a

moment longer and be ignored. She was an ambassador too—
for the Khalifa stores—and as such she had no intention of
hiding in the shadows feeling sorry for herself.

Beth would have carried off her intentions brilliantly had
she been accustomed to wearing five-inch heels, but as it was
she tripped at the edge of the dance floor, right in front of an
amazingly tall and pretty princess. At least, Beth assumed the
girl *must* be a princess, judging by the group of people standing
around her tutting, and the fact that Beth was blinded by
diamonds when she looked up. 'I'm so sorry...' She tried
scrambling to her feet, but only made it to all fours with her
rump sticking high in the air because her stiletto heels stubbornly refused to find purchase on the marble floor. Meanwhile
the princess and her attendants skirted round her, as if she was
a dog's doodle, before sweeping off. It took a young girl who
had been watching all this to help her to her feet.

'Thank you,' Beth said gratefully, brushing herself down
as the girl steadied her.

'Are you sure you're all right? You're more than welcome
to join us at our table...' The girl pointed to where a group
of young people were sitting. 'We've been watching you,'
she admitted. 'We hated the way everyone stared at you
when you came in—'

'Don't worry about me,' Beth said, pretending her nose
wasn't stinging with the threat of tears. 'I'm fine...' I can do
this, she was thinking, though her ballgown was ripped now,
and the flower from her hair was lying crushed on the floor.
'But thank you for coming over to help me,' she said, finding
her customary grin.

'Well, if you change your mind...?'

'I'll remember,' Beth promised. 'And thank you, again...'
Composing herself, she looked around, and this time no one
returned her gaze. It was as if she had become invisible. No

one wanted to get involved with a nobody, Beth gathered, except for her new friend. They shared a smile before the girl sat down again with her companions.

Blowing the hair out of her eyes, Beth wondered what to do for a moment, and then decided that watching would probably teach her more than anything. Her first thought was that the scent of wealth was stifling, and she could tell that Khal's guests had really gone to town on the platinum-and-diamond theme of the ball. But strip all the glitz and glitter away and they were just people the same as she was, probably with many of the same worries and concerns. At least that was what she thought, until she noticed people talking behind their hands and jostling for position in the final minutes before Khal arrived. Some of the women were licking their bottom lip and adjusting their dress to show more cleavage in preparation for His Majesty's arrival—which made weird feelings jostle inside her, almost as if she was feeling protective of Khal.

Which she did, Beth realised. What did Khal see in all this? What did it mean? What did it add up to? As far as she could tell everyone was after him for something, and this ball was just another opportunity for people to advance themselves.

Being an outsider, even of this shallow group, wasn't nice. There was only one table where people were having fun for its own sake, as far as Beth could see and that was the table where the young girl who had rescued her was sitting. Beth wished now that she had accepted the invitation to go and sit with them. As it was, she felt like leaving to start packing for her return home. But she wouldn't, because she was here to represent her colleagues at the Khalifa stores. She would hold her head up high and remember that the owner of those stores might be the Sheikh of Sheikhs in Q'Adar, but he was also her boss—as well as the driving force behind the Khalifa brand—and this employee had no intention of letting Khal or her co-workers down.

CHAPTER THREE

HAVING surveyed the ballroom from his private viewing-area and seen what he wanted to, he dismissed his entourage and walked alone in the gardens. He always centred himself before an appearance, and tonight he craved that inner calm more than ever. Because he had allowed himself to be distracted by some young girl newly arrived from England, and however hard he tried to concentrate his thoughts kept returning to Beth Tracey Torrance.

She was more than the breath of fresh air he'd first thought her, much more. He might have known she would turn up to receive her trophy in spite of her embarrassment at the beach. He'd even had to admit to a rush of pleasure when he spotted her—as if emotion of any kind was possible for the ruler of Q'Adar. But Beth was a one-off, an original, and she had made him smile. She was plucky and unsophisticated, and completely untutored in the ways of the world. His lips tugged harder when he pictured her marching away from him. Who did that? Who ever turned their back on him? For all her youth and innocence her passions ran to the extreme, and she wasn't afraid to show them, which was a novelty. But now he must put her out of his mind. He was about to put on a show of strength, and couldn't be distracted by thoughts of relationships for which he had no time. If and when he formed an alliance some time in the future, it would be with someone from a similar background, someone who understood the pressures of royal life, and who had been schooled in that role since birth. That certain someone would have to possess the confidence to appear regal and unflustered at his side in every situation.

But would he ever get that picture of Beth Tracey Torrance and her cheeky smile out of his head? He couldn't forget the way she had turned her head to look at him while the onshore breeze had played with her shimmering hair. Nor would he forget those full lips, and how they firmed, or the crystal-blue eyes that could so quickly turn to ice if he said something she disapproved of. He would like to soften those lips and turn that ice to fire, but he had to put those thoughts out of his head now because duty was calling him and he had to go.

Beth was still standing at the scene of her embarrassment when the orchestra quietened and a hush fell over the room. As all the elegant couples on the dance floor began to make their way back to their seats, she used the crush of perfumed flesh to escape the beady eye of the Sheikha's attendant and cross to the table of young guests where her friend was sitting. There was no point in remaining stubbornly alone. They had asked her to join them, and she'd have more to tell her friends that way.

As Beth had hoped the table of young people welcomed her, and quickly drew her into their conversation. They were an international group, Beth soon discovered, who had been to school in England and had only recently been summoned back to Q'Adar by their families to show support for the new leader.

'This is it!' Jamilah, the young girl who had rescued Beth, excitedly informed her. 'The Sheikh will be here any minute…'

As Beth nodded her throat dried and her heart went crazy.

A fanfare of trumpets announced the opening of the golden doors. Even the most seasoned diplomat and jaded royal was riveted, she noticed, and no wonder. Surely none of them had ever seen such splendour before? But then Beth smiled secretly to herself, remembering that the boss of the world's most prestigious chain of luxury stores would know a thing or two about presentation.

As the lights in the ballroom dimmed, the spotlight on the golden doors grew brighter. Into this pool of light strode a tall, imposing figure clad in flowing black robes which were heavily embroidered with gold thread. 'The master of ceremonies,' Beth's neighbour discreetly informed her.

The man dressed in his robes of office stood for a moment before walking deeper into the hall. The stream of light followed him, and at his signal it widened to encompass the entire dance floor. Onto this stage strode four musicians, carrying slim golden trumpets. They wore the crimson, black and gold livery of Khalifa, with the black hawk, that was the personal symbol of Khalifa Kadir al Hassan, prominently displayed. The same image was shown on the tasselled flags falling from their instruments, and as they raised them to their lips the hawks undulated as if the Sheikh's birds of prey were indeed flying.

The musicians' cheeks filled, and a silver sound cut the silence. It echoed on and on, and as it died away a party of stately men entered on silent, sandaled feet. Their robes fluttered as they lined up against the jewelled walls. Beth guessed these must be the senior members of the royal council, and she thought them a magnificent sight. Some were wearing belts studded with lapis lazuli that glinted as they walked, while others had golden scimitars flashing at their side, and a few had links attached to the belts at their waist from which dropped their keys of office. But for all their grandeur these powerful men formed up like a flock of well-trained doves to await their Sheikh of Sheikhs.

Beth's heart swelled with pride at the thought that, wherever in the world the Khalifa name appeared, it reigned supreme, and she could hardly wait to see what came next. And this time the surprise was even greater. Everyone gasped as a youth galloped into the arena on a fiery stallion, and, though Beth thought him nowhere near as imposing as his master, there was no doubt that his horsemanship was outstanding. As he brought the stallion to a skidding halt he surveyed the audience, while his mount's polished hooves pawed the floor. He was carrying a small bright bugle, and, urging his horse to rear up, he sounded it. This was a signal for a band of horsemen to join him. Each of them was mounted on a magnificent Arab stallion, and all wore the black howlis around their heads, which covered their faces so that just their fierce black eyes showed beneath the folds of cloth. Long knives glinted at their waist, and their manner spoke of a warrior past and an allegiance to their new leader. Beth's heart was thundering painfully as she watched them bring their restless horses in line, and now there was only the sound of the animals snorting and their bridles chinking as a deep hush fell over the ballroom.

It was into this silent assembly he came, towering over every other man in the room, and proving that he had no need of personal show, or horse, or even fanfare to herald his arrival. His Majesty Khalifa Kadir al Hassan, Sheikh of Sheikhs, Bringer of Light to his People, had the power to command attention with his presence alone. And as his gaze swept the room everyone rose to their feet

Except for Beth, who remained frozen to the spot. Seeing Khal like this had sent her heartrate off the scale. Dressed in the simple robes of a Bedouin warrior he needed neither gold nor weaponry to stamp his authority on the room. Power flowed from him, caressing her with the promise of his strength and virility, and, backlit like this, his magnificently toned form was clearly visible beneath his fluid robes. It would take a very foolish man indeed to challenge Khal's right to the title Sheikh of Sheikhs, Beth thought, longing for him to look at her. He was the man every woman would want for their lover, the man they would crave for their protector, the father of their child.

And this was not the time for daydreams, she told herself sensibly. But how hard was it to be sensible when your imagination was running riot?

More than anything Beth had always wanted a family of her own; the family she always talked about was a fiction she used to make her feel she belonged. She realised now she was secretly on the lookout for the ideal man—and, though she'd found him, her daydreams involving Beth Tracey Torrance and the Sheikh of Sheikhs was just another fiction. A man like Khal would marry for the good of the state and the benefit of his people; love wouldn't come into it. She only had to watch the other women reacting to him to know that. They all wanted Khal, and eventually he would choose one of them. He certainly wouldn't be taking his chances with Beth Tracey Torrance from Liverpool!

'Khalifa Kadir al Hassan…' Beth sighed, then jerked alert, realising Khal's name was in her head because the herald had just introduced his master to the assembled guests, and that everyone was standing. Except for her! She almost knocked her chair over as she quickly remedied the situation.

He saw her at once, and not just because she was the only person in the ballroom who didn't rise the moment he entered the room. He saw her because they seemed joined by some invisible thread. And that was not just inconvenient, it was a situation that could not be allowed to continue. If the only way to deal with it was to see Beth privately so he could reassure himself that she was an unsuitable distraction, then that was what he would do.

He turned from her. It was time to forget Beth Torrance and concentrate his powers of intuition on everyone else attending the ball. In a country enduring birth-pangs, there were always those who would stand in the way of progress so they could hold on to their old, corrupt ways, and it was these people he intended to root out. But each time his gaze raked the hall it found Beth.

He'd looked at her. He had. She wasn't imagining it! The Sheikh of Sheikhs had remembered her and had looked at her. At least he hadn't forgotten her. Beth Tracey Torrance had made an impression on a sheikh! She couldn't wait to tell her friends.

But then Beth started fretting. Was it the fact that she had turned her back on him on the beach and stalked away that made him remember her? Maybe she shouldn't be feeling quite so thrilled—maybe he had a dungeon waiting. And she didn't have her hands on that trophy yet—the trophy she had promised her friends she wouldn't return home without. But, if the ruler of Q'Adar forgave her and went ahead with the presentation, she'd have to say something and look at him, and that was almost worse.

She'd just have to make sure she didn't blurt out something completely inappropriate, Beth thought, starting to panic. She definitely mustn't say, 'I hardly recognised you in your clothes.' Biting her lip as she settled back in her seat, Beth told herself to relax and concentrate on the speeches.

* * *

His good intentions were shot to hell. Try as he might to focus on the speeches, all he could think about was Beth Tracey Torrance and the fact that she was staring at him. He should have her taken away and locked her up for her own safety. He realised now that everyone else was paying close attention to the proceedings, and just the two of them were distracted by each other. And now it was his turn to speak. He made it short and sweet, and when it was time for everyone to stand and bow before him he signalled more impatiently than he had intended that they must sit down again. He blamed Beth. He needed her out of his eye-line.

Beth gave a little jump as a cheer went up, and then realised that the Sheikh of Sheikhs' guards of honour had raised their weapons in a salute to him and were roaring their approval. And she hadn't even noticed them walk in. She had been too distracted by their leader. And how he had looked at her. She wasn't imagining it. And that look was well worth a night in the dungeon—for the ruler of Q'Adar stood centre-stage, backlit as if by Hollywood, with testosterone flying off him like sparks from a Catherine wheel. In this land of fierce, hard men, His Majesty Khalifa Kadir al Hassan was the hardest of them all. And she wanted him like mad, Beth confided to her inner self, glancing round guiltily in case there were any mind readers on her table. Who was she to look at their sheikh? Except to say that she knew another side of their ruler—the boss of the Khalifa group ran a company that held the best record for pastoral care of its employees in the world.

Which was why she was here. The trophy was just another example of how highly Khalifa Kadir regarded his employees. Thought it was hard to credit him with any gentleness now, when he appeared to be everything a warrior sheikh should be and more.

* * *

He was aware of her every second. Seated on the raised dais with the other members of the royal family, he told himself that this distraction was nothing more than his natural concern for an innocent abroad. He wanted to be sure Beth was safe; of course he did. He was concerned that the attendant his mother had sent at his request to look after Beth had abandoned her when she'd joined the table of young people. Beth worked for him, and therefore Beth was his responsibility.

Beth. Beth… She had eaten up too much of his time already. His body's responses to her were nothing more than an adrenalin rush brought on by this occasion. The fact that he could feel her clear blue gaze burning into him meant nothing. She was looking at him so she could report to her friends back home, and that was all. She would report that she had stared boldly at the Sheikh, and that he had stared back at her.

She was over-excited and needed to calm down. Beth gazed longingly at the exit. The girl seated next to her took her chance to ask if they could swap plates. Beth had hardly touched her food, and the chocolate pudding did look delicious, she noticed now it was too late. 'You can have it,' she said, smiling. She knew that feeling—the hole in the stomach that only chocolate could fill.

'Sure?'

'Positive.' Beth tore her glance from the Sheikh, welcoming the distraction. 'I'm overwhelmed,' she admitted, exchanging plates. 'I can't face eating. It isn't every day I find myself in a place like this.'

'Lucky you!' the girl exclaimed, laughing. 'Imagine having to dress like this on a regular basis.' Coming closer, she confided, 'I'd far rather be galloping across the desert.'

'Wish I could,' Beth agreed, thinking how romantic that sounded.

'You will if you stay here for very long,' her new friend promised, forking up a mouthful of cake.

'I'm going home soon,' Beth explained.

'Then you'll just have to come back, won't you? Oh, look!' Beth's new friend exclaimed, swallowing hectically. 'I think they're calling you.' Grabbing Beth's arm, she drew her attention to a stern-looking man, dressed in the royal livery, who was beckoning to Beth in a stiff and impatient manner. 'You didn't tell me you were someone special!' she exclaimed again.

'I can assure you, I'm not,' Beth said, shaking her head wryly.

'Well, good luck anyway.' The young girl touched her arm.

'Thank you. I'm going to need it!'

'So, that's your little shop girl,' Khal's mother commented as Beth approached. 'She's a pretty little thing, but I'm sure she's feeling quite disorientated here. Why don't I go and reassure her?'

'You, Mother?' Khal's eyes narrowed. His mother would let nothing and no one stand in the way of her ambitions for her one remaining child. He had never been under her thumb, but it worried him that her sights might be set on Beth now. He couldn't expect Beth to know how to handle his mother, and he half rose from his seat in order to intercept the Dowager Sheikha.

'You seem to have forgotten, Khal,' his mother said, waiting impatiently for him to move aside. 'That I was a no-one when I came to this country; I know how it feels to be a stranger in a foreign land.'

He had not forgotten, but he wondered at her mention of it. 'Beth's flight home is already booked.'

'Beth?' His mother gave him a long, searching look.

'Mother,' he murmured, leaning close. 'You're not as subtle as I remember.'

'That's because I'm growing more desperate, my son. I want you to find a bride and settle down.'

'Is that why you invited every eligible female you could find to decorate these celebrations?' And when she lifted her chin and refused to answer him he added, 'I may indeed settle one day, Mother, but I will never settle for second best.'

'Like a shop girl?' His mother stared at him keenly.

'Are you worried about Beth?' He laughed it off. 'I promise you, you will have the grandchildren you long for—just not yet.' Having seen his mother comfortably settled again, he raised her jewelled hand to his lips.

'I love you, Khalifa.' His mother stared into his eyes. 'Which means I only want the best for you.'

'I love you too, but I despair when you're fooled by gilt and tinsel…' He gave a meaningful glance at the row of compliant princesses all leaning forward in an attempt to attract his attention. 'I'll find a bride in my own time,' he assured his mother. 'And now, if you will excuse me…?'

His mother didn't attempt to impose her will on him a second time, and he was just gathering his robes around him in preparation to return to his seat when a shriek made him turn. There had been a collision at the foot of the stairs. Some clumsy oaf had spilled a tray of drinks over Beth, and now her ballgown was ruined. Beth had frozen and was uncertain what to do.

'Shall I remain seated, my son?' his mother whispered at his ear. 'Or would you have me go to her and help her?'

He ground his jaw in frustration. It would have suited him better to keep the two of them apart.

'You can hardly be the one to usher her out of the hall and have her return some time later in a new dress, now, can you?' his mother pointed out.

'I'm not sure what you're suggesting,' he told her with

matching guile. 'But I can assure you I am above gossip, Mother.'

'But Beth's reputation would be ruined.'

His lips tugged in wry defeat as his mother arched her brows.

'Let me go to her, Khalifa, and I promise to bring her back to you unharmed…'

He weighed the facts. Beth's misery had only increased as she'd attempted to scrub at the stains with a napkin someone had handed her. Her evening was on the point of ruin. 'Go to her, and be sure that you do bring her back to me unharmed. Be gentle with her,' he stressed, standing aside to allow his mother and her attendants to pass. 'And please remember that Beth has a trophy to collect, so don't keep her long. She must receive her award before the festivities can begin.'

'If you ask me,' his mother murmured dryly on her way past him, 'the fun has already started.'

He feared for Beth as he watched his mother descending like a galleon in full sail, with her flotilla of hard-nosed females in close formation behind. But somehow he thought Beth would cope, and either way his mother was doing him a favour taking Beth out of his sight. Beth Tracey Torrance had proved far too much of a distraction as it was.

CHAPTER FOUR

'THANK you, Your Majesty. This is really too good of you!' Beth exclaimed, blushing furiously as she sank into the first proper curtsey of her life. The Sheikha had brought her into a part of the palace Beth had never thought to see, the Dowager Sheikha's private apartment, and now they were surrounded by silks, satins and French perfume, in the most sumptuous lace-trimmed room. Unfortunately she spoiled the moment as she made her curtsey when the seams of the ruined dress finally gave way.

The Sheikha, to her credit, appeared not to notice the ugly ripping sound.

'Nonsense!' she exclaimed with a flick of her wrist. 'Any friend of my son's—'

'Oh, we're not friends,' Beth blurted frankly, her cheeks turning hotter still when she heard the chorus of disapproving clucks rising from the Sheikha's attendants because she had interrupted the royal personage. 'I mean, your son's my boss, and that's all.'

'Your *boss*?' The Dowager Sheikha said, savouring the word.

Okay, so maybe she had protested a tad too heartily, Beth thought, hurrying to explain. 'That's right. We hadn't even met until today. I was away last time he called at the store. I'd never seen him before we ran into each other at the beach.'

'On the beach? You met my son at the beach?'

So the Sheikha was aware Khal swam naked. Could her cheeks grow any hotter? Beth wondered. 'I didn't look at him. I mean…I didn't stare…'

'I should hope not,' the Sheikha agreed, delicately dabbing at her nose with a fine lace-handkerchief.

'And we barely spoke at all,' Beth hurried to reassure her, but Khal's mother had already turned away, hiding who knew what thoughts.

'Bring out the star dress,' the Dowager Sheikha commanded, turning from her.

Beth's glance flicked from attendant to attendant as they gasped, but when she saw the gown the Sheikha had chosen for her to wear she thought she understood why they were astounded. It was stunning, and must have cost a fortune. 'Oh, I couldn't,' she gasped, unable to tear her eyes away from a dream of a dress shimmering in the light. Composed of silver chiffon, it was embroidered over every inch with tiny diamanté stars.

'You think it a little old-fashioned?' Khal's mother demanded.

'Oh no, I love it,' Beth's said impulsively. Her gaze slid round the room. It appeared her honesty hadn't gone down so well with the Sheikha's attendants. 'I mean, I'm not worthy…'

'I'm not so sure,' Khal's mother argued, waving her attendants forward. 'Help this young woman to dress,' she commanded.

When Beth was finally turned out to everyone's approval, she spun round to show the Dowager Sheikha, who had seated herself in a chair to watch.

At first there was silence, and then the Dowager Sheikha observed, 'You look quite beautiful, my dear, and I hope you enjoy wearing the dress. It belonged to my daughter—'

As the older woman's voice choked off, Beth felt a change in the air. It was as if there was some history behind the Sheikha's comment that everyone but Beth knew about. 'Your Majesty,' Beth said softly, not wanting to intrude on the Dowager Sheikha's private thoughts. 'I'm overwhelmed by your generosity, and I promise to take good care of the dress.'

The Sheikha gave her the briefest of nods, and Beth suspected Khal's mother didn't trust herself to speak, because something else had joined them in the room. Grief, Beth thought, wondering at it. 'I've taken up enough of your time already,' she said to excuse herself. 'I'll bring the dress back to you in the morning.'

'That won't be necessary,' the Sheikha said, tipping her chin in a way that reminded Beth of herself when she tried fighting off uncomfortable memories. 'I'll have someone collect it from your apartment after breakfast. And now, if you're ready, my ladies will escort you back to the ballroom.'

With the faintest of smiles the Dowager Sheikha signalled that the doors should be opened and everyone should leave her now. She was desperate to be alone with whatever pain had come to join her from the past, Beth sensed.

'You remind me of myself at your age,' the Dowager Sheikha murmured as Beth prepared to leave the room. And as Beth made her final curtsey their gazes briefly met and held.

When Beth entered the ballroom this time everyone turned to stare, including His Majesty Khalifa Kadir al Hassan, Sheikh of Sheikhs, the ruler of Q'Adar. And she did feel a little buzz of excitement, Beth admitted to herself. Okay, a roar. But who would have thought it? Here she was, Beth Tracey Torrance, at the royal court in Q'Adar...

Get over it! Beth told herself firmly, *and remember to pick your feet up this time.*

Beth held her head up as a pathway cleared for her across the vast floor. She should enjoy this moment. It wasn't every day you got to wear a fairy-tale gown and parade in front of all these worthies. She walked steadily and then made her way carefully up the steps. She was determined not to fall and ruin the precious dress, which meant no one must be allowed to distract her, not even the man towering over everyone else on the royal dais.

'Ms Torrance…'

Khal's deep, husky voice ran shivers down Beth's spine. It took all she had to blank her mind at where they'd met before, or what she'd seen on that occasion. But that wasn't easy when the scent of his sultry cologne was washing over her, and naughty thoughts were making it hard not to break into nervous giggles.

Making a fool of yourself isn't an option, Beth Tracey Torrance, Beth's inner voice insisted. *Think of your friends back home.* It was true. They were all waiting to hear her news, and she couldn't let them down when any one of them would have loved to be here in her place.

'Your Majesty…' Beth surprised even herself by managing a perfect curtsey, but the only problem with that was that it brought her into close proximity with an area of the Sheikh's body it was far safer not to think about. Thankfully, Khal chose that moment to reach for her hands and raise her to her feet, but when she looked up into his face his expression was grim. What had she done wrong this time?

His mask almost slipped when he saw the dress his mother had chosen for Beth to wear. Why that dress? Why his sister's dress? Was it because it was the only dress suitable for Beth to wear in his mother's wardrobe? He realised his face was growing increasingly fierce as he fought off emotions he had battled so long to subdue, and he could see the confusion in Beth's eyes. This wasn't her fault, but he couldn't explain to her, not here. Nor could he explain to Beth that when his mother sent her arrows flying her aim was invariably accurate. This was her way of telling him that he had grown cold and unfeeling since the tragedy, and that it was time for him to rejoin the world.

He shook himself out of the painful reminiscences, remembering this was Beth's moment, not his. And no one, not even his mother, was going to spoil it for her. Having introduced Beth to the assembled guests, he handed her the trophy. 'Congratulations, Ms Torrance,' he said formally.

Khal looked so grim, but she had no option but to shake his hand and say thank you. She *had* to. Tilting up her chin, Beth met the gaze of the ruler of Q'Adar, a man who would have been stunningly sexy under any circumstances. But here, with the full weight of his power surrounding him, he was a devastating sight. Yes, except for his lack of emotion he was just about perfect. So why was he so cold? Beth wondered, as Khal stood back, allowing her to take the applause.

It was better for her if he disapproved, she concluded. Did she want him noticing her, smiling at her, wanting her? No, of course not; in fact, she was relieved.

Liar! Beth's inner voice accused her as she turned to face her audience. Still she managed a smile and then thanked everyone politely. 'And before you start dancing again...' Silence cloaked the room. She was not supposed to say anything else. Firming her jaw, she continued. 'I'd just like to say—' A gasp of astonishment greeted this. Ignoring it, Beth ploughed on, 'That this trophy isn't just for me.' She waved it in the air. 'But for everyone who works at Mr Khadir's stores.' Another gasp, much louder than the last.

'Yes, I realise you all know him as His Majesty, but to us he's the best boss ever.' It was Beth's turn to gasp as someone took firm hold of her elbow. She exclaimed out loud when she realised who it was. 'Sorry,' she said, but the words just kept on tumbling out. 'I bet you can't wait to get rid of me.'

'On the contrary,' the ruler of Q'Adar murmured in her ear. 'I'd just like to save you further embarrassment.'

'Well, you don't need to, thank you very much,' Beth said, swallowing back her fright as several royal attendants stepped forward to take her into custody. 'Do I look like a threat?' she whispered angrily to Khal.

He waved them off. Beth was more of a threat than she knew, Khal thought as he inclined his head towards her in a polite gesture of dismissal. 'Enjoy the rest of your evening, Ms Torrance...'

She did, as it happens—enjoy the rest of her evening, that was. She was determined to. She had every intention of delivering a full report on the Platinum and Diamond Ball when she returned home, and no one was going to spoil it for her friends. She was going to keep their dreams intact even if the truth, as she had discovered, was somewhat different. But here at this table it wasn't so hard to find things to report on, because everyone was so nice. Which made a change from the man frowning at her from the royal dais. That was, when Khal could spare a moment from spending time with each of the princesses selected for his attention. Khal's mother would have made a good personal shopper at the store, Beth decided. The Dowager Sheikha had a real knack for bringing tempting selections for the customer to choose from. 'How much would one of those cost?' Beth asked her friend Jamilah impishly.

Angling her chin in the direction of Khal and his bevy of princesses, Jamilah hazarded a guess. 'Those tiaras probably cost a cool million each, just for starters.'

'No, I mean the whole package.' Now she had started, Beth couldn't suppress her mischievous Merseyside humour.

'You mean the cost of one princess?' Jamilah said, grinning as she got the joke.

'A country and a camel,' someone across their table discreetly offered.

'Ten camels.'

'Any advance on ten?'

Their table was now in such uproar that Beth noticed they were attracting disapproving looks. She guessed the young people had never been so outspoken before, and it was all her fault.

'I think we've outstayed our welcome,' Jamilah confided in Beth. 'We're going back to our family encampment for the fireside celebrations. Would you like to come with us? There'll be dancing.'

'Dancing?' Beth couldn't have been more surprised. It made Q'Adar sound like Liverpool, when she was sure the life here for young people couldn't be more different. 'Where are you camped?'

'Just outside the palace walls, right on the beach. My relatives will be there and I'm allowed to bring a friend. Everyone's agreed they'd rather have you join us than one of those sacrificial lambs at the royal table.' And, when Beth looked askance at her, Jamilah explained. 'We all know those girls on the top table have been selected for their beauty, and are only here on approval for the Sheikh to take a look at. His mother can't wait for him to get married and give her grandchildren.'

'But that's rather sweet of her, isn't it?' Beth said, not sure quite how she felt about it.

'Not for the sacrificial lambs.'

'Point taken,' Beth agreed, discreetly slipping away from the table to follow her new-found friends.

'I suggest you get changed out of that dress and leave your trophy in your suite,' Jamilah said as they hurried out of the ballroom. 'I'll go and find you something suitable to wear, and then I'll come back for you, otherwise you're bound to get lost in the palace—it's such a maze.'

Beth's heart lifted as they scurried along the grand, vaulted corridor as fast as their high heels would allow. It looked as if she was going to have something good to tell her friends about after all.

He watched her leave, and knew where she'd be heading when he saw who had befriended her. He was pleased for Beth. He was glad she had found some companions of her own age to make her stay a happy one until she left Q'Adar. And it would be a wonderful experience for her to mix with his people without all this pomp and ceremony getting in the way.

No. He wasn't pleased, Khal decided, frowning. Jamilah's male relatives would be present, along with every other hot-blooded man in the palace who had been invited to take part in the open-air celebrations. Chaperoned or not, there would be opportunities for the sexes to mix, and Beth was impressionable.

He stood. It was a signal for everyone else in the grand ballroom to stand too. He gestured that they must all sit down again, and then he used the microphone to wish them an enjoyable evening. An evening he would no longer be part of. He ignored his mother's scandalised glances as he left the dais. The Sheikh of Sheikhs wasn't required to give a reason when he decided the entertainment on offer no longer held sufficient appeal. He had done his duty by the princesses, having reviewed the parade of hopefuls, and now those painted dolls could return home and take their greedy black eyes with them. He'd made enough deals in his life to know when he was being duped.

* * *

Back in her glamorous palace accommodation Beth was excited. It was good to finally be part of something where she was welcome—not that she had ever envisioned being drawn into the royal circle, of course. The Dowager Sheikha had been extremely kind to lend her the dress, Beth thought as she carefully hung it up on a padded hanger. Then she went red, remembering her speech, and Khal dragging her away from the microphone. How had she dared to speak out like that?

She had dared, and it hadn't been all that bad, Beth thought, sharing a twinkle with her reflection. Maybe what this country needed was some down-to-earth action. There was far too much la-di-dah bowing and scraping going on, from what she'd seen. And she was pretty sure Khal wasn't comfortable with it either.

When had she started thinking of him as 'Khal'? Beth wondered. On the beach, she realised—when he'd been naked with nothing but a towel to cover his country's assets! And now she must try not to think about him at all. About how hot he'd looked in his simple Bedouin robes... They had clung to his body as he'd strode purposefully about, prompting all sorts of wicked thoughts. If she ever saw him in a pair of snug-fitting jeans she'd probably faint clean away! But as sheikhs didn't wear jeans she was safe, Beth concluded with relief as she showered down under tepid water. Having brushed her hair, she wrapped a robe round herself and waited with suppressed excitement for Jamilah to come back for her.

A few minutes later Beth stared at the outfit Jamilah was holding out to her. 'Oh, but I couldn't possibly...'

'You don't like it?' Jamilah's face fell.

'Oh no,' Beth quickly explained. 'I mean, it's so beautiful I couldn't possibly wear it.'

'Unless I insist, and assure you I'll be deeply offended if you don't?'

As both girls laughed companionably, Jamilah helped Beth

dress, arranging the floating chiffon of the Arabian gown to best advantage. In subtle shades of powder blue and silver, the yards of fabric took a lot of taming. 'I'd never have managed it on my own,' Beth admitted, staring at herself in amazement in the mirror. 'Would you take a picture of me?' she said, thinking of her friends as she snatched up the camera.

'Of course I will. You look really beautiful.'

'I certainly look different, but it's your beautiful dress that makes the difference,' Beth argued in her usual down-to-earth way.

'Just one final touch,' Jamilah told her, draping a panel of the flimsy headdress across Beth's face.

Beth's eyes widened as they approached the encampment. She had never seen anything like it in her life. With the fire blazing high into the sky in front of the ocean, and the musicians beating their Arabian drums and strumming even more exotic instruments, it was like the setting for a film. Jamilah's family tents were vast and decked out with pennants and gold hangings, with the symbol of a hawk prominently displayed next to something written in Arabic script.

'Khalifa,' Jamilah said, noticing Beth was looking at it. 'Though it's a reference to my family's loyalty to the Sheikh of Sheikhs, and there are no designer shoes other than mine in our tent, unfortunately.'

Beth laughed at the reference to the Khalifa luxury brand. Would she ever get used to this mix of East and West? It couldn't have been more starkly illustrated. But as the warm breeze caressed her face she forgot the comparisons. 'It's so beautiful here,' she breathed, moving closer to the ocean on sandaled feet. The night breeze was making the ruby satin curtains outside the tents dance, and the susurration of the waves breaking on the shore was so soothing she barely noticed Jamilah slipping away and someone else taking her place.

* * *

He could move freely in the dark, and as yet his face was not widely recognised. His title meant nothing now, and the usual restrictions did not exist here in this temporary tented city outside the palace walls. He headed away from the music, following silently in the footsteps Beth was leaving on the sand. He waited as she slipped off her sandals, admiring the way she looked in traditional dress. She wore it well, with all the grace of a true Q'Adaran, and he could tell she was enchanted by the romance of wearing the flowing robes of an Arabian princess. She didn't even know Jamilah was his cousin, or that Q'Adaran women could be as subtle in their matchmaking endeavours as their Western counterparts. And for once he was grateful to the mischievous Jamilah, for no one but she knew he was there.

Khal in snug-fitting jeans? No, she must be dreaming.

'Khal?' Beth swallowed hard, rooted to the spot as the music started up again and drowned out her voice. What should she do now? Should she carry on walking out along the beach, or… It didn't matter what she did, Beth's sensible self insisted, since the Sheikh of Sheikhs could hardly be here to seek out her company. But as Khal blocked her way Beth realised she was wrong.

'You shouldn't be walking along the beach on your own.'

'Jamilah told me I'd be safe here.'

'There are so many people…' Khal gazed out across the tented city, while Beth's throat tightened to the point where she doubted she could speak at all.

'Do you dance?' he said, turning to her.

'Do I dance?' Beth repeated foolishly wondering if that really was a touch of humour tugging at the corner of Khal's mouth. And in his eyes… The dance was already inside her, she realised, and it was both an erotic and an irresistible temptation. 'Of course I dance,' she said. 'Don't you?'

This time he really smiled; there was no doubt about it. 'Shall we?' he said, offering her his hand.

Where had that attractive crease in his cheek come from? 'Do you mean you want to dance with me?' Beth gazed at Khal's outstretched hand.

'That's the general idea.'

Beth Tracey Torrance dances with the Sheikh on the beach! No toes broken—thanks to being barefoot! That would be her headline. But did she trust herself to hold Khal's hand?

Khal took the decision for Beth, drawing her to him and yet holding her at arm's length so that they were barely touching. But it wasn't enough to make her resist the seductive rhythms of the Q'Adaran music. 'Do you come here often?' Beth whispered cheekily, still wanting to pinch herself in case this was a dream.

'Never quite like this,' Khal admitted, playing along. 'But that could change.'

'What would it take to change, Your Majesty?' Beth glanced shyly up.

'Khal,' he murmured, holding her gaze until Beth thought she might never breathe again. And his smile was back. *Please let it last this time*, she silently begged. She didn't want him to change; she wanted this moment to last for ever.

When the music stopped they stood together in silence, and when it started up again in a much slower rhythm His Majesty Khalifa Kadir al Hassan, Sheikh of Sheikhs, Bringer of Light to His People drew her so close she could feel his heart beating against her breasts. Her nipples grew instantly taut at the subtle stimulation. Surely he must feel the change in them? There was no doubt in her mind that Beth Tracey Torrance had turned into a wanton hussy.

A wanton hussy with precious little common sense, Beth told herself impatiently, pulling away.

As Khal pulled her back again Beth knew she was on the point of stepping over a boundary from which there would be no turning back. So she must resist. Of course she must resist! But the lure of her surroundings combined with her need to feel wanted made it hard—no, impossible—to resist. And so she rested against Khal's hard, warm body, knowing the strength to pull away had completely deserted her. She was on fire for him, and could feel every inch of him pressed up hard against her, while streams of sensation went pulsing through her veins...

The report to her friends would have to end here, Beth decided as Khal's hand settled in the hollow at the small of her back. With his fingers splayed across the top of her buttocks, and her body pounding with desire, the rest of the night would be X-rated, and as such it would have to be censored.

CHAPTER FIVE

SEX With A Sheikh was a cocktail, not an option, Beth reminded herself as Khal took hold of her hand and drew her with him. As the lights of the campfire faded behind them, and the laughter and conversation subsided beneath the rush of the surf, she was cloaked in awareness as he stopped walking and brought her to face him.

Was this was really happening, or should she pinch herself? Her hand felt so safe in his, as he drew her inch by inch towards him, she didn't even pretend to resist. Beneath a rich blue velvet sky studded with diamonds, this was so magical her throat had closed with emotion. Things like this didn't happen to her; no one had ever treated her as if she was precious and fragile before. Khal could take his pick from any number of women, but he had chosen her. Closing her eyes, she inhaled his cologne. It was the most wonderful fragrance, but more intoxicating still was the man holding her. And, when she finally allowed her muscles to soften against him, Beth knew she was more aroused than she had ever been, and that was dangerous.

How long had it been since he'd held a woman like this? Had he ever held a woman like this?—as if she might break? By this stage he would expect any play mate to be pressing themselves against him as though they were on heat, telling him without words what he could take and what it would cost him. But not Beth.

Beth...

He should pull back now. He should recognise the way he felt about her for the warning it was and pull back now. But as he took a step back she reached out to him. He looked at her outstretched hand. It was so tiny, she was so tiny. What he should do now was throw her a careless smile and tell her he'd enjoyed the dance, before sending her back to the encampment and Jamilah, where she'd be safe. 'Shall we walk a while?' he said instead.

'Okay, if that's what you want,' she said lightly. Her chin lifted as she spoke, and a rogue breeze tossed her hair across her face. As he reached out to remove the strands from her lips, she moved too and their hands caught and tangled. Instead of snatching hers away, she let it rest in his and held his gaze. The fact that she trusted him enough to do that resonated strongly with him. And so he pulled away. She was young, and he must bring this to an end now.

She saw the change in his eyes right away. 'What's wrong, Khal?'

He said nothing, but she felt him distancing himself from her.

'Am I such a threat to you? To Q'Adar?'

'Don't be ridiculous.'

'No, I'm not being ridiculous. You're pushing me away."

And with that she picked up the skirts of her eastern dress and ran away from him down the beach, with her sandals in her hand. That should have set the seal on his determination to let her go, but instead it just etched a deeper groove in his mind for her to occupy, and so he went after her.

Beth quailed when she heard Khal coming after her. Her

chest was burning and her legs had turned to jelly. There were so many feelings exploding inside her, she was confused. She wanted a moment—and there was no time. He was here. He was right here behind her.

'Beth…'

His voice called softly, but the call reached deep inside her and made her turn. 'Khal…' She had the rest of her life to find out who she was, the rest of her life to be Beth Tracey Torrance with no one's expectation weighing on her shoulders. Couldn't she spare a moment for him, a moment for His Majesty, just to say goodbye and thank him for his hospitality?

Beth uncurled her fists, releasing the tension in her fingers. She wouldn't run from him. Maybe Khal needed a moment to talk to an ordinary person.

She looked so adorable, and even more beautiful than usual in the floating gown. But it was more than her innocence and beauty that captivated him. Beth had made him see things he hadn't noticed before, she made him think a different way; she made him question everything he had always believed in. As he stood in front of her he leaned forward, meaning to brush her cheek with his lips, but then she took a step towards him and turned her face up so he brushed her mouth instead.

Her eyes closed, but she didn't move or speak, and then the warm breeze gave them its blessing, bringing her another step closer, until all thoughts of resisting the temptation of kissing Beth had fled from his mind. She tasted sweet and warm, and the scent of wildflowers rose from her hair, invading his senses until he could no longer think. He barely touched her; she seemed so fragile, so tiny. It was a whisper of a kiss, or at least that was how it started. But Beth was innocently demanding, surprising him with the depths of her passion, a passion he guessed was new to her and that she had

no idea how to curb. It made her bolder than he had antici-
pated, as well as sweeter and more fragile, and as she wrapped
her arms around his neck, clinging on tight to tell him fiercely
that she needed him as much as he needed her, he wanted so
badly to believe it was true. As Beth's words poured into his
soul, his world expanded with possibility. It was as if they
knew each other already, and had merely been separated for
a while. How easy it would be to pick up where they had left
off… If he could just switch off his conscience.

But it had already kicked in, reminding him of all the
things that stood between them—duty, honour and Beth's innocence, the barrier he would never cross. And so on the very
point of deepening the kiss he drew back.

'Why did you do that?' she said.

'I apologise,' he said formally. 'I forgot myself.'

'You forgot how to kiss?' Her eyes were sparkling; even
now she couldn't help the humour. Plus there was some unfathomable bond between them that, incongruous and
unlikely though it might be, refused to break.

'Are you saying I'm too much for you, Khal?' she teased
him gently.

Her brand of innocent humour made him smile. Too much
for him? She was sensational. Naïve? Yes. She was also tiny,
blonde and vulnerable—but it was her inner fire that warmed
him through. But that was not his fire to take comfort by, it
was for some other man in Beth's future, a man who could
offer her all the things she deserved. 'How old are you?' he
said, meaning it as a gentle rebuke.

'Old enough,' she assured him cheekily in a way that told
him she knew nothing of the effect those words could have on
a man.

'That's a dangerous thing to say, Beth Tracey Torrance.'

'But not to you,' she said, with trust that touched him

deeply. 'And anyway,' she said. 'I've done with safe.' She paused to brush the hair out of her eyes as the wind tossed it about. 'And I wouldn't be here in Q'Adar if I'd wanted boring, would I?'

He recognised the voice of innocence speaking, and, stamping down on his desires, he made no reply.

'It's that duty of yours again, isn't it?' she said. 'Not that I'm criticising you—far from it.' Mashing her lips together as she thought about it, she said bluntly, 'I think you're wonderful. And I think the people of Q'Adar are lucky to have you. I trust you, which is why I know your people can trust you. You put duty above everything, and that's what makes you so special…' Breaking off, she started to frown again. 'But it must be a burden sometimes, mustn't it?'

He tensed as her frown turned to compassion. Beth's incessant questioning challenged him at every opportunity, and in that they were the same. When did he not question the status quo? Yet at the same time Beth and he were so far apart. 'Duty?' He gave her a wry smile. 'Duty is never a burden, Beth. You can't always have everything you want in life.'

'And *you* can never have it.' she protested, 'Because your fate is tied in to your kingdom.'

'Exactly.'

'Well, I'm going to have it all,' she said passionately.

'You are?' He felt a stirring of unease. Would she disappoint him now?

'Yes!' she exclaimed. 'I'm going to have kids, family, love, job, happiness—everything!'

Her eyes blazed with such certainty, it was a lesson in just how wrong he'd been to doubt her. She hadn't worked out the finer details yet, but nothing daunted her. Disappoint him? She had only increased his passion for her tenfold, plus he envied her, he admired her, and most of all he wanted her. He wanted for just a moment to share in Beth's freedom, and in her belief in a future full of so many wonderful things.

The look she gave him now turned the heat inside him into a raging inferno, and when he dragged her close this time he had no intention of letting go. He felt her legs give way as he swung her into his arms, and knew as he did so that he had never felt like this before, and that he never would again.

So this was what it felt like to be held as if you mattered to someone. And even if it was only for one night she was going to treasure every single second of it. Khal rounded the point to his own private beach where he told her they wouldn't be disturbed. Not even his security forces were allowed to trespass here, though there were men patrolling the perimeter. He carried her into the cool of the shadows beneath the rocks, and, dropping his towel, spread it out for them on the sand. Lowering her gently, he lay down at her side and kissed her again.

Khal kissed her deeply, teasing her lips apart with his tongue, and that together with the heat and taste of him drew a moan of approval from somewhere deep inside her. This was a dream, it had to be. How else could she play with fire and feel so safe?

As she reached up to cup his face, Khal took her hands and laced their fingers together in a gesture of closeness and trust that made her heart squeeze tight. Then he drew back, and, resting on one elbow, stared into her eyes. She had a feeling of being small, of being no one, while she was lying here with a man who occupied such a huge space on the world stage.

'Don't look so anxious,' Khal murmured, kissing her so amazingly she was quickly reassured.

He stroked her with the lightest of touches, enjoying the sight of her quivering with desire. He shivered too, internally, as restraint took its toll. But as her eyes drifted shut and she murmured his name he cupped her face in his hands and kissed her…

'Kiss me again,' she whispered the moment he released her. She had no idea how she was torturing him or she wouldn't wind her arms around his neck like this, breathing his name so it sounded like a feather on a breath of wind, a feather that had the power to travel to his heart and pierce it like an arrow.

She pulled him back when he pulled away. 'Don't leave me,' she begged him in a way that pierced his heart a second time. But when he kissed her now, and felt her shudder of desire through every part of him, he knew it would soon be beyond his mortal powers to hold back. He tried hushing and soothing her, as he might have calmed a restless colt, but trying to hold Beth back while she in her innocence was trying to hurry him on only upped the level of torture for them both.

'Khal, I know I'm not what you need…'

As she began to excuse and explain how she felt he was so incredulous, so defensive on her behalf, that all he could think was that Beth was exactly what he needed. And so why was he holding back? With all the riches of Q'Adar at his disposal, he felt blessed that fate had brought her to him. 'You're special,' he told her. 'And don't you ever forget that, Beth Tracey Torrance.' He was staring deep into her eyes, into her soul, when she answered him with perfect logic.

'Then, if you don't care who I am, what's standing between us? Because there is something, isn't there?'

'Yes,' he admitted. 'My concern for you. I care about you, Beth. I care about you very much indeed.'

She thought about this for a moment, her face serious and intent, and he saw then that beneath all Beth's light-hearted talk she was a deep thinker who, even now after so short an acquaintance, longed for something he could never give her—a family and exclusivity. How could he do that when the very thought of it was out of his reach? And even had they known each other longer he was married to his country. They both knew that whatever happened between them now was for today, and only for today, because his life and all he was belonged to Q'Adar.

The thrust of Khal's tongue was so bold Beth felt a wild urge to tear off her clothes and offer her breasts for his approval. Her innocence prevented her doing more than imagining how that might feel, but she was aching for him so badly in secret places she hardly dared to think what it would be like to have him touch her intimately…

Some force must have taken her over, Beth reasoned. This force, as elemental as the sea and as powerful as the man lying next to her took no account that she was inexperienced. It was a power that acknowledged no master, and only one goal…

The erotic daydream came to an abrupt end. Could Khal have changed his mind? Beth wondered as he sat up suddenly. 'There isn't room for both of us on the towel…' Uncertain of her ground, she tried to make it sound like a question.

Khal didn't reply at once, and instead brushed the sand from his thighs—which drew her attention to his powerful legs, legs she could so easily imagine wrapped around her. And then he firmed his lips as if he had made his decision.

'Don't…' She didn't want to hear whatever it was he had to say. She couldn't bear to hear him say he didn't want her. 'Don't stop now,' she murmured self-consciously, closing her eyes against the expression on his face. 'Or I shall think you don't want me.'

Khal's answer was to sweep her into his arms so she could feel every inch of him intimately. His energy surrounded her, softening her, empowering her… This felt so right, and yet Khal must have sensed some small remaining doubt inside her and, instead of growing more passionate, he eased her down onto the ground at his side. 'Beth, if this is all too fast for you...'

'No.' She breathed the word short and fast, closing her eyes, willing him not to pull away. She couldn't bear anything to come between them—not his duty, and certainly not her fear. If this was all they had, this short time together, then she embraced it wholeheartedly. 'Kiss me...' *Kiss away my fears*, she begged silently, rejoicing when she felt Khal's warm breath brush her face.

As the shadows gave way to the moon they matched their strength against each other. Khal was always careful, always tender, so that Beth's trust in him could only grow. She in turn grew bolder and more confident, learning to laugh and to relax in his arms. She enjoyed the simple pleasure of being close to him, and for now she wanted nothing more. She clutched his chest and rubbed her face against his naked skin. She loved the sure touch of his hands on her, and the hot words he was whispering to her in a language she didn't understand. She even found the courage to loosen the waistband of her chiffon skirt when the fabric became twisted round her legs. And when she arched her back this time Khal's hands slipped down to cup her buttocks, and she whispered, 'Yes...' Smiling against his lips, she repeated, 'Oh yes...'

Beth's spirit and her growing confidence made him smile, made him realise there was a lot more to his feelings for her than he had first thought. While he was examining them, she tugged off the rest of her clothes. 'Tease,' he accused her softly, filled with happiness because she was so happy. She was so impulsive, full of life and mischief. She lifted the weight from his shoulders and made him feel young again. And how could he fail to notice that without a bra her breasts were magnificent? His first impulse was to lose himself in them, but again he drew back.

'What's wrong now?' she said, proudly displaying them.

She was so beautiful, and had no idea of the power under her command. He wanted her to discover the mystical powers a woman possessed slowly and completely. But Beth was so inquisitive and fearless. He was many things, but not a saint, and as her tiny hands closed around him, stroking insistently and persuasively, he hardened into steel.

She was fast losing focus. She couldn't hide her hunger for stimulation and release much longer, but Khal was more experienced than she knew, and he couldn't be led. He would set his own pace, Beth realised when she tried to guide him. 'What must I do?' she whimpered, half to herself. She could see him smiling.

'Be patient.'

'What do you mean?'

'Lie back and you'll find out. Look at me,' Khal instructed her softly when she finally relaxed back on the ground. 'And lie still…'

How was she supposed to relax and lie still while he was slipping one powerful thigh between her legs? She couldn't stop moving when she was so excited and aroused, but as Khal feathered strokes down her body she slipped into a delicious lethargy, and lay still to enjoy each spine-tingling sensation. He broke her trance by hooking his fingertips beneath her lacy briefs, to which she responded by wriggling furiously to help him get them down.

'Lie still; I thought I told you,' he murmured, smiling against her lips.

Still? Was he crazy? She had never felt so sensitive and aware before. Every single part of her was wired for pleasure, and with every ragged breath she took she was moving closer to desperation.

'Don't rush me,' Khal insisted wickedly against her lips.

She was telling him about tender, throbbing places waiting to be pleasured, but he wasn't going to rush, he had every intention of savouring this. Seeing her naked beneath him, palest gold against his bronze, made him want to do more than have sex with her. He wanted to taste, stroke, and watch Beth's eyes darken with pleasure when she pressed her cushioned softness against him. The sight of her made him greedy, but for the sake of her innocence he would wait.

Beth wondered at her emotions. This was all so new and dangerous to her, and the feelings inside her had far more to do with love than mere physical pleasure—and that was scary. 'I love it when you kiss me,' she told Khal softly. She was experiencing feelings so new and tender she couldn't bring herself to speak them out loud—and so instead she reached for him, arching her back and aching for release, longing for reassurance, and needing more commitment than she was sure the ruler of Q'Adar could give.

CHAPTER SIX

As Beth arched her back, resting her hands above her head in an attitude of innocent sensuality, Khal found the urge to bring her pleasure overwhelming. But still he held back, knowing delay would bring its own rewards. He gave her lingering kisses on her lips and on her neck. He suckled her nipples until she writhed helplessly beneath him, begging for more. He lavished his attention on her soft, warm belly, and was impatient to discover if this cushioned perfection extended to every part of her.

While they were kissing he removed his shirt, and the sensation of naked flesh on flesh hit him like an electric shock. The one thing he hadn't bargained for was Beth releasing the fastening on his jeans while he was recovering. It made him laugh at her audacity, it made him hold her in his arms and transmit all that he was feeling into her eyes. It felt so right, so good to him, and as they wrestled playfully he discovered they fit together perfectly, even though he was so much bigger than she was. She was like a tiny, tender kernel at the heart of a ripe fruit and as she strained towards him, drawing her legs back in anticipation of even more pleasure, he teased her with the tip. Almost at once the pleasure waves threatened, and as she bucked towards him, exclaiming in excitement, he drew back. 'Not yet...'

'Why not?' she demanded, eyes wide as she struggled to understand the complexities of love-making.

'Because I enjoy teasing you.'

'Then I'll have to take matters into my own hands,' she threatened, though he knew she would wait for him to set the pace. Escaping her grasp, he moved down, tasting and teasing her, preparing her and laving her with his tongue until she rolled her head from side to side, gasping with excitement. There was no awkwardness between them now, just hot, hungry need, and as he eased her legs apart even more she gripped his shoulders and stared into his eyes, showing him how much she trusted him. Pouting, silky warmth greeted him, a playground in which to lose himself, a welcoming cushion where he could sink.

'Now,' she begged him. 'Now!' she cried out more insistently. 'I want more of you… I want all of you…'

He sank into her like coming home, wondering if he had the willpower to endure such pleasure. Beth's fingers bit into his shoulders while he moved carefully at first, and then firmly and rhythmically to give her the satisfaction she craved. He plunged deep and then withdrew, so that it was like taking her for the first time over and over again, and she cried out with increasing pleasure at each stroke. He was sorry when it was over for her too soon, and realised it was a measure of her inexperience, but as she cried out his name he used all his wiles to prolong the pleasure for her. He wanted her to enjoy every moment. And when she quietened he continued to move gently and insistently, kissing her all the while until he felt her respond.

'You're amazing,' she whispered, starting to work her hips against him. How could she be ready for more? But she was. Incredibly, she was. He had awoken something in Beth that matched his own hunger, and it touched him to see her blossoming into a woman in his arms.

Khal never tired. How could that be? He was at her service, pleasuring her until she couldn't stop herself, and until all thoughts of control had vanished from her mind. She was greedy for him, and he was offering her a feast. When he withdrew briefly one time she weighed him in her hands, marvelling at his size, and wondering at the pleasure he could give her. She was on the point of asking him directly where his stamina came from when he moved behind her, bringing his leg over hers, and trapping her in the most deliciously receptive position imaginable, telling her, 'I think you'll enjoy the Q'Adaran way now…'

'I'm sure I will,' she agreed, gasping a little when Khal pressed her forward and took her again. He moved so deeply he stretched her, and, at the same time as setting up a regular rhythm, the hand that wasn't pressing her forward was playing a delicate game with fingertips that brought such extremes of pleasure she could only moan her appreciation in time to each stroke and thrust.

'Yes?' Khal husked against her back.

Did he expect her to speak? She could only make a sound like an animal urging him on. How many times was it now? So many times. And this time was so powerful she must have passed out for a moment—because the next thing she knew she was safely nestled in Khal's arms, and he was stroking her and kissing her, lulling her to sleep.

'Can't we stay here for ever?' Beth asked Khal later, impulsively, when they emerged hand in hand from the sea. They had made love again beneath the stars and the moon, and with the ocean bathing their limbs in warm, limpid water.

'For ever is a long time.'

His words sent a shiver down her back. Only minutes before she had been resting on a pillow of undulating water with her legs locked round Khal's waist. His feet had been firmly planted on the sea bed, while she gazed at the stars and dreamed of 'for ever'. Now it seemed her cries of release had mingled with the surf and carried those dreams away. She had spoken carelessly. It sounded foolish and childish to her now, and as Khal let go of her hand Beth felt he must think so too. Returning to dry land was a return to reality for both of them. The sheikh and the shop girl's relative positions in life had been firmly re-established. Making love with Khal had been the most extraordinary experience of her life, as well as the most deeply moving...for her. *But for him...* Was it over now?

'I'll take you back when you're dressed,' Khal said.

'I'd like to go straight back to my room, if you don't mind?' Beth said, proud of herself when her voice remained as steady as his. She still had her pride. 'I need to shower all this salt off me.'

'Of course.'

Khal's matter-of-fact tone spoke more clearly than any words could about the wedge between them, and it was growing wider all the time. The fairy-tale was over, Beth thought, casting a wistful glance behind them at the ocean.

The clock struck as they arrived back in the courtyard outside Beth's room. Was it possible she had only been with Khal so short a time? It had felt like a lifetime of growing closer and learning to trust, until the doubt had set in. Beth paused with her hand resting on the rough stone archway, watching Khal stride away. He was purposeful now, moving on to the next part of his life. They had parted with the briefest of caresses—just a touch of his hand on her face. If she closed her eyes she could still feel it...

'Ms Torrance.'

Beth gasped guiltily and swung around to see the Dowager

Sheikha approaching. 'I'm sorry, Your Majesty, have you been looking for me?'

The Dowager Sheikha took a step back, and her gaze swept over Beth. 'I missed you in the ballroom. They told me you had left the palace, and I wanted to be sure you were safe. I want you to leave Q'Adar with happy memories. You have enjoyed your stay, Ms Torrance?'

'Oh, yes, Your Majesty!' Beth exclaimed, her honesty bursting through the need for caution. Beth blushed deep red, realising she had almost betrayed herself. Had the Dowager Sheikha seen her son leave the courtyard?

'You're a sweet child, and I can tell that my son is very much taken with you.'

'Oh?' Beth bit down on her lip, acutely conscious of how tender and swollen it was after all Khal's kisses, and she knew that her cheeks must still be red from the rasp of his stubble.

'You don't have to pretend with me, Ms Torrance. Hard as it may be for you to believe, I was young once, and I too met a sheikh under unusual circumstances...'

Beth wished she could think of something to say to allay the Dowager Sheikha's fears. Having seen the beautiful princesses, she knew Khal's mother had high hopes for her son's marriage. But what could she say? It wasn't her way to lie or fudge an issue, and she could hardly confess the truth. *The truth*. The *truth* was burning its way through her heart. She dipped into another curtsey. 'I'm sorry if I disturbed you, Your Majesty, it's very late, and I'm sure you must be tired.'

'Time means nothing here in Q'Adar, Ms Torrance. It is measured in millennia, rather than hours or minutes, and if you come with me now I would like to show you something that will open your eyes to the scale of things here in my country.'

Beth wondered what the Dowager Sheikha could possibly mean as she followed her across the courtyard. She climbed behind her, up the steep stone steps leading to the ramparts, where they could see for miles over the surrounding desert. Beth gasped as she took it all in. As far as the eyes could see campfires lit the darkness. She hadn't realised how far the tented city extended when she had been down on the beach. 'There must be thousands of people down there,' she breathed.

'Hundreds of thousands,' Khal's mother confirmed, turning to face her. 'Now do you understand the weight my son carries? Do you see now why he is wedded to duty? These people have come from all over His Majesty's kingdom to greet him on his birthday. They have come to swear their loyalty to him, Beth. May I call you Beth? And thousands more will be here by tomorrow, all wanting to bask in the strength and the hope that is His Majesty Khalifa Kadir al Hassan, Sheikh of Sheikhs, Bringer of Light to His People. They believe in him, Beth. Look at them...' The Dowager Sheikha's gesture encompassed the whole desert encampment. 'All these people rely on my son to lead them out of darkness and poverty into a new, brighter future. Would you have him distracted from the path of duty? Would you take him from Q'Adar?'

'I would never do that!' Beth exclaimed.

'Not intentionally, perhaps. But because I loved his father so deeply I know when love is all-consuming, and when there is no space in your heart for anything else. My son loves Q'Adar, and that is how it must remain.'

'There's no need for you to worry.'

'There is every need,' the Dowager Sheikha insisted. 'I have seen the way you look at my son, and I have seen the way he looks at you.'

'But we hardly know each other...' Beth bit her lip, hating the lie, hating every second of this deception.

'How long does it take to fall in love, Beth? Is there a prescribed time?'

'Of course not, but—'

'I ask you again,' Khal's mother said gently, turning her face into the wind so she could stare out across the tented city. 'Would you take my son from his people?'

'Of course not. I would never take something that didn't belong to me.' But her voice had started shaking, betraying emotions Beth hadn't even admitted to herself. She wasn't prepared for this, how could she be? 'I do like—the Sheikh,' she admitted haltingly. She loved Khal more than life itself, Beth realised now. It had happened in an instant, the moment she'd first laid eyes on him. 'But I know who he is, and I know who I am.'

'And I think you underestimate both yourself and my son, Beth.'

'So what do you want me to do? I'm leaving tomorrow.'

'And if he should try to stop you?'

The possibility that Khal might do that was so far from Beth's thinking she couldn't even answer.

'You're a good girl,' his mother told her, patting Beth's cheek. 'And I think you are standing here with me now with only the very best of intentions in your heart.'

'Oh, I am,' Beth insisted, wishing she could think of something to say to reassure Khal's mother.

'Forgive an old lady her concerns, but since the death of his sister, Ghayda, Khal is my only child…'

As the Dowager Sheikha's features crumpled into grief, Beth realised this was why she'd sensed some deep-rooted sadness in both Khal and his mother. She remained silent, allowing the woman to talk, and wishing she could think of something to say to Khal's mother that might help.

'Since Ghayda's death, my son has been like ice. I have

seen him come to life in the past few hours, because you have my beloved Ghayda's warmth and spirit, and Khal sees this. He believes himself responsible for his sister's death, Beth, and nothing I can say to him will change his mind. But they were both so young and beautiful at the time of the tragedy, both so reckless and irresponsible. They both knew the dangers of the desert, and they were both equally to blame,' the Dowager Sheikha said with finality. With a ragged sigh, she turned towards the steps.

Beth followed, wondering why Khal's mother had chosen to trust her with this precious revelation. It was almost as if the she was giving her the seal of approval. And, after hearing it, all Beth wanted to do was rush to Khal and put her arms around him so she could hold him close until the pain went away.

She had to hold on to reality, Beth told herself, and remember that what had happened on the beach with Khal was one isolated incident. It might have been life-changing for her—she would remember that first time for ever—but for Khal it had meant nothing, and she could hardly expect to see him again after tonight. So, whatever secret hopes his mother might be harbouring, they were just daydreams like her own wistful thoughts. 'You're very kind, Your Majesty, and I wish I could say something that could express my sadness for your loss.'

'Your being here and allowing me to talk to you like this is the kindness,' the older woman assured her. Reaching out, she touched Beth's face. '*Ma'salama*, Beth Torrance. Go in peace, my child...'

CHAPTER SEVEN

MONTHS had passed since she had left Q'Adar, and yet here she was, still struggling to accept the freezing rain falling day after day in the north of England. The sunshine in Q'Adar seemed a million miles away, and her time with Khal a distant dream. Dipping her head into the wind, Beth pulled up the collar on her coat, and walked as fast as she could towards the store. It threatened to be a busy morning, what with the planning meeting for the Christmas window-display. She was representing her department at the annual meeting for the first time this year, and had been up at dawn polishing her ideas.

Beth stopped abruptly as she turned the final corner, everything inside her twisting as she stared foolishly at the low-slung limousine with its blacked-out windows. Who else travelled with outriders and merited their own special-force-officers clutching guns? Beth held tight to the latest selection of magazines she'd brought to scan in her lunch hour a little closer. Since Khal's spectacular party, the press had been rife with speculation about when the most eligible bachelor in the Arab world would get married. The gossip about him had even overshadowed the uprising in Q'Adar. You could hardly open a magazine without seeing a picture of Khal blazing from it. The whole world including Beth knew that the ruler of Q'Adar must take a bride—the only questions were who, and when...?

Well, it wouldn't be a Liverpool shop-girl, would it? Beth told herself, starting forward again. And this Liverpool shop girl had a job to do. Tipping her chin at a determined angle, Beth walked briskly towards the staff entrance. The doorman welcomed her with his usual banter, and when he made some comment about their visitor Beth replied calmly, 'Ah, well, we all knew we were due a visit one day, didn't we? I missed him last time he was in Liverpool.'

'But you must have met him in Q'Adar?'

She was always bright and breezy, but today she didn't want to stop and chat. All she could think was: *Khal's here?* But she had to say something, because everyone and his wife knew she'd been to Q'Adar and had met the Sheikh. 'Briefly,' Beth agreed, hating the lie as she turned for the lift. 'I met him briefly.' She stared up at the floor numbers on the panel above the sleek steel doors, wishing the lift would come quickly so the doorman couldn't see her cheeks were on fire.

She survived walking into the boardroom and having the Managing Director introduce each of them in turn. She survived the all-pervading, and oh, so familiar scent of him: wealth, sandalwood, and warm, clean man. She even survived the sight of Khal in a dark bespoke suit that skimmed every inch of his powerful frame, enhancing it almost more than his Arabian robes. She even managed to keep her cool when Khal chose to sit in the centre of his team directly opposite her. She survived all that. But Beth wasn't sure she could endure Khal's penetrating stare for very much longer.

'Ms Torrance?' he invited, in a voice that warmed every part of her, a voice that was entirely professional and emotion-free. 'Would you like to give us your suggestions now?'

She had a few for him, Beth thought, feeling hurt rise up inside her. How could Khal have just walked away after everything that had happened between them? And she didn't just mean the sex—they'd drawn closer and seen inside each other's minds; they'd made love. Well, she had. And he hadn't even said goodbye to her before she'd left the country.

What was the point in going over everything in the past? This was the present, this was business; this was real life, and not a fantasy of her own making in Q'Adar.

Khal had taken over the room with the sheer weight of his presence, and as he sat forward attentively Beth knew she had to be as professional about this meeting as he was. She was good at presentations when she believed in something, and she was here to represent her team. She had no intention of letting them down.

He had invented the flimsiest of reasons to be at a meeting he knew she would attend. No one had questioned him; no one had dared. He had taken over the Managing Director's office for the day, and now he was forced to sit here as if he had nothing more on his mind than the Christmas window-displays at Khalifa, when the truth was he wanted Beth. He had tried and failed to put her out of his mind, and so he had come for her.

But as the meeting progressed he found himself drawn in and captivated all over again. He had always thought Beth younger than her years, but in this formal business setting he was seeing another side of her. He could understand why she excelled at her job now. This presentation was thorough, disciplined and innovative. Beth had researched her subject well, and had the statistics to hand to prove her case, as well as an impressive line in persuasion. She would get the budget she requested; favouritism didn't come into it. Where was the need, when Beth's proposal succeeded on two fronts: origi-nality and sound business-sense?

'You've got it,' he said, refocusing when she displayed her final budget calculations. She looked at him then for the first time, straight in the eyes.

'I have?' She flushed, unable to hide how thrilled she was. For him that was pure Beth. His senses stirred as he realised when he'd last seen that sort of colour on her face.

The meeting concluded without any suspicions being aroused as to why the owner of the Khalifa brand had decided to make a surprise visit, and later Beth brought her portfo-lio of ideas to the office he was borrowing as he'd asked her to. The secretary had already left for lunch, and so it fell to him to take them from her. 'You can leave them with me…' For her sake he had meant to keep it brief, but he had for-gotten how she affected him. She walked past him and went to stand in the furthest corner of the room, with her back turned to him.

'How could you do that to me?' she said, without turning.

'Walk away?' he said, thinking back to Q'Adar. 'I needed time to think. We both did.'

'I don't mean in Q'Adar. I mean just now in the boardroom.' Slowly, she turned. 'First you arrive without warning anyone, and then—' She stopped, clearly fighting back emotion.

'And then?' he prompted gently.

'Why did you look at me like that?' she asked him in a small voice.

'I thought I was being extremely professional.'

She shook her head. 'Couldn't you see what you were doing to me? I couldn't speak, I couldn't breathe.'

And how had he felt? 'Stunned' didn't even begin to cover it. He could never have been prepared for seeing Beth again, he realised now. 'You made a great presentation.'

She ignored his attempt to return to safer ground. 'I couldn't think straight...not with you staring at me.'

'I was listening to you.' He was trying to stay calm, but for the first time in his life something inside him snapped. 'Do you think I want to look at you? Do you think I want my mind full of you when I should be thinking about my country? Do you think I should be here, while my people wait for me in Q'Adar?'

'So why *are* you here, Khal?'

'I think you know.'

Pressing her lips together as if she didn't trust herself to speak, she shook her head.

'I'm here for you,' he told her bluntly, tiring of the act.

'What? You're here for me? Oh, Khal, please!' She gave a short, angry laugh that spoke of all the hurt inside her. 'What happened to all those other women?'

'Other women?'

'Here, look at them.' From under the pile of documents, she took a magazine and thrust it at him. 'Take a look at that and then tell me again why you're here.'

He only had to look at the first one. 'When tensions began to heighten in Q'Adar, my first thought was to divert attention from you. Clumsily, now, it seems.'

'Yes,' she said, sounding bitterly hurt. She glanced at the headline on the cover and read it out loud to him. '"Princess Layla comforts the ruler of Q'Adar on one of his rare breaks from leading his army against the insurgents"... Or what about this one? "The Sultana Lydia enters negotiations for an arms deal with the warrior sheikh"... A clever play on words, don't you think, Khal?' Snatching the magazine from him, she flung it on the floor at his feet.

'What better way is there to get a message across than through the media?' he said grimly. 'I was trying to protect you, and I could hardly make an announcement on the news. Those women were nothing more than props.'

'*Props?*' Beth's mouth worked. 'And what am I, Khal?'

'You're the woman I want.'

'Just like that—you decide? After all these weeks, *you* decide?'

'You…' He searched for words that properly expressed his feelings. 'Preoccupied my mind.'

'You mean you want sex?'

'No!' The word exploded from him. 'Don't demean yourself. I left a country enduring the birth pangs to come here for you. And I came the first moment I could get away.'

'So now you want me—as what?' she said in a small voice. 'As your mistress?'

He stared at her intently. 'And you don't want that?'

She flinched. 'No, I don't want that.'

'But I want you. Only you…'

It was as his mother had told her, Beth thought helplessly; she could be as strong as she liked, but the invisible bond between the ruler of Q'Adar and the Liverpool shop girl would never break. Closing her eyes, she inhaled sharply, and when Khal reached for her and slowly pulled her towards him she didn't resist. She was strong enough for most things, but not for this. As heat rose up inside her he backed her oh, so slowly towards the door. She was sure her legs would crumple beneath her before they reached it, and when they did she gasped with relief, hearing Khal slip the lock. He started kissing her, gently, tenderly, on the brow and on the eyes, and on the lips and on her neck, keeping her moving all the time, backing her towards the desk until she felt the smooth wood pressing against the top of her legs.

The desktop was at the perfect height. Grasping the lapels of his jacket, she pushed it from his shoulders. As it fell to the floor she reached for the buckle on his belt, and unfastened it. Loosening his tie, she freed the buttons at the neck of his shirt, excited even more by the sight of the familiar smooth, bronze skin with its shading of dark hair. Moving on, she released the catch on his pants and undid the zip. That was the signal for Khal to drag her to him and kiss her with a savage intensity that matched her own. When he released her she tugged his trousers down and wriggled free of her briefs. He nudged his way between her thighs before they even hit the floor. She felt him grow bigger, harder, in her hands.

'How much of me do you want?'

'All of you,' she commanded hoarsely, throwing back her head. 'I want all of you,' she gasped as Khal plunged deep.

It was so much more pleasure than she remembered. It was amazing. She screamed out, not caring who might hear her. And once wasn't enough. Once wasn't nearly enough. She moved fiercely while Khal worked his hips, just as she wanted him to, until finally she slumped exhausted in his arms. 'You don't need me?' he said.

She didn't answer.

They took a long, warm shower in the small private bathroom, but even there they couldn't keep away from each other. She was frantic for him, like a man without water in the desert who had found a well. With Khal's arms braced against the tiled walls, and her legs locked around his waist, their shower had turned cold without them realising it, and she was trembling with exhaustion again by the time Khal lowered her to the ground.

'Finished?' he teased against her lips.

'It has to be enough, I've got work to do.'

'Work?' His voice changed. He pulled away. 'Work will have to wait.'

'It can't wait.'

'I haven't come all this way to stand in line. You've got the rest of the day off.'

It was a stark reminder of who he was, but she wasn't up for being steamrollered. 'I can't. I've got a duty.'

'To me,' Khal cut across her flatly.

'No.' Beth shook her head as she stepped out of the shower and took the towel he handed her. 'I won't just disappear, Khal, and let people down. I'm expected.'

'Don't worry about it. Everyone knows you won't be available for the rest of the day.'

'You told them that?' Beth pressed her lips together angrily. 'I can't believe you just arrived and took over my life.'

Rather than rise to her anger, Khal's lips tugged wryly. 'I know no other way. You'll have to teach me...'

She was stopped in her tracks. Khal had taken the wind right out of her sails. But was he serious? And then his hard face softened even more. 'Won't you show me round your city, Beth?'

He never got the chance to do anything ordinary, she realised. 'Really?' she said, still suspicious of his motives. 'The guided tour?'

'If you'll take me.'

As he smiled, she softened. 'Just you and me?'

'Absolutely.'

'No outriders?'

'No limousine, no outriders, no Sheikh. Just Beth Tracey Torrance and Khal from Q'Adar.'

'Like normal people?' Beth made a small huff of disbelief.

'It's not impossible, is it?'

Impossible? No. It was sad, Beth realised. She showed nothing on her face, but she was thinking—one of the most powerful men in the world was asking her to show him what 'normal' was, and what ordinary people did on an ordinary day out. There would be no yachts or helicopters, and no armed guards, just an open-top bus and the two of them. She could fight Khal all she liked, but the idea he'd put forward was irresistible to someone who cared about him as much as she did. 'If you're sure you really want to…'

'I really do,' he said, and the look he gave her made her heart melt. Having made her decision, she tipped her chin and looked him over. 'In that case, I'd better find you something comfortable to wear…'

'So what does his Majesty think of the open-top bus ride?'

'Khal.'

As he prompted her, Beth tried to ignore the feelings in her heart. This was going nowhere—except to the bus terminal—and it was time she faced up to that fact. But finding a way to stop her heart hammering with love for him was another thing.

She was so lovely it almost blinded him to look at her. He had wanted this time alone with her. He counted it as precious, private time away from other people, and valued it more than Beth would ever know. However hard he'd tried, he couldn't let her go. He *wouldn't* let her go. She wasn't interested in his wealth or his position, or even the fact that he was one of the most powerful men in the Arab world and beyond. She was tender and true, and quirky. She was also the hottest thing on two spectacular legs. Bottom line—if he wanted Beth Tracey Torrance, he had to play at least part of the game by her rules.

She grinned at him, and then the rain hit them both in the face.

'Okay, so maybe we'll get off here,' he said, tugging off the jacket she'd found for him in the store to drape it round her shoulders. The jeans and shirt she'd picked out for him wouldn't come to harm, but he didn't want Beth getting wet.

He ushered her off the bus when it reached Albert Dock. He knew she wanted to look round the Tate. She stood entranced in the gallery in front of some stunning, contemporary Chinese art. The trip was a great success, and she was relaxed by the time he took her for lunch in the café. She had a hearty appetite in all departments, but it was her enthusiasm for life that attracted him the most. As she dabbed her lips with the napkin, she drew his attention to how deliciously full they were, and how much he wanted to kiss her again.

'That was delicious, and I'm stuffed,' she claimed happily, without a care in the world.

'Wonderful,' he said. 'I only want to see you happy.'

Before he had chance to say any more, she interrupted him. 'I can't believe I managed three courses. I never do that. But deep-fried potatoes with chilli sauce are my absolute favourites.'

'Along with tuna Niçoise, and chocolate pudding with chocolate sauce, I assume?'

'Absolutely,' she agreed. 'Sorry, I interrupted you. What were you about to say?' She gazed at him intently.

'I've got something to show you,' he said. 'Not that,' he murmured when she gave him a look full of mischief.

'What is it? Will I like it?'

'You'll just have to come with me, if you want to find out…' And this time when he held out his hand to her she took hold of it trustingly.

CHAPTER EIGHT

'WHAT are you doing?' Beth said when Khal flipped out his mobile and started punching in numbers. They had stopped outside the entrance to the Tate.

'Calling the cavalry…'

'You promised me no outriders.' She felt her stomach sink. 'I thought this was going to be a normal day?'

'And so it is,' he assured her.

'For you or for me?'

'Don't get mad, or you won't get your surprise.'

'Okay.' Beth bit back on her disappointment. 'I'll give you a chance, but only one, mind.'

With a grin that made her stomach lurch, Khal silenced her before speaking in Arabic to his driver.

'So, where are we going?' she asked him as the limousine pulled up at the kerb.

'To my penthouse in the city.'

'You are full of surprises.'

'You don't have to come with me,' he said, reaching for the door handle.

'But you're sure I will,' she commented dryly as Khal waved his chauffeur aside and helped her into the car. 'I suppose it won't hurt me to see where you hang out.'

'And maybe linger a while?' he suggested, climbing in beside her.

'You always have the best ideas,' Beth agreed, wondering if it would always be like this between them, the sexual tension reaching danger-levels constantly—but with a man driving them that wasn't good. She noticed both she and Khal were making sure they kept a good space between them on the spacious back seat.

Khal's penthouse was fabulous. A massive, high-ceilinged, oak-floored entrance hall complete with life-sized sculptures led through to a modern and sophisticated open-plan living area. There were panoramic views across the city and the estuary to the Welsh hills beyond, through the floor-to-ceiling window. As far as Beth was concerned every superlative she had in her head was totally inadequate to describe it, and so she settled for, 'Wow!'

'So you like it?'

'And I thought I'd seen everything in Q'Adar!' she exclaimed, turning full-circle. 'What's not to like? How big is this place?'

'Around five thousand.'

'Square feet?' Beth demanded in astonishment. 'And you keep this just for when you visit Liverpool?' When Khal didn't answer her right away, alarms bells started ringing in her head. She noticed now that there was none of the usual personal stuff around. She decided to probe a little. 'I love it, but it's not exactly what I'd call a home,' she said innocently.

'Not yet,' Khal agreed, 'But you could soon change that.'

'I could change it? Go on!' Beth gave a short laugh. 'You're kidding me.' The idea of her putting her stamp on a place like this was beyond even her wildest flights of imagination.

'No. I'm absolutely serious,' Khal assured her. 'Would you care to tour the master suite?'

Her body was still throbbing from his love-making, and it didn't take much to turn her thoughts in the direction of the master suite. Time to put her suspicions to one side. The time they'd spent apart had made her greedy for Khal. As if sensing this, he touched her, running the knuckles of one hand lightly down her arm, and then he reached for her so that now she was operating on a purely sensual plane with no thought of where this was leading. Burrowing her face in his strong, warm neck felt so good and so right, and the next thing she knew Khal had swung her into his arms. Shouldering his way through one of the doors, he took her into the most amazing bedroom—though she hardly had time to notice all the blonde wood, glass and mirrors before he laid her gently on the bed and stripped off her clothes. Joining her without a suggestion of embarrassment, he stretched out next to her. 'You have an incredible body,' she said, running her fingertips over his smooth, bronze skin.

His face softened as he looked at her. 'And you're beautiful,' he said, kissing, stroking, and reassuring her.

He wanted Beth to feel like the most cherished woman on the face of the earth, which was how he felt about her. Yes, he wanted her, but each time he brought her into his arms it was as if his world exploded with possibilities. Kissing her tenderly, he cupped her face and stared into her eyes, and what he saw there told him she felt the same.

They made love until the setting sun had thrown its last dart into the estuary, and reflection off the glass had bathed the room in crimson light. They slept a little, and when Beth finally woke it was to find Khal staring down at her. 'What?' she murmured, groggily, reaching up to touch his face.

'I was just thinking,' he said softly, 'that I can't wait for you to take a proper look around the apartment, and see if you could be happy here…'

Frowning as she tried to compute Khal's words, Beth tried to stop him getting out of bed. 'Do we have to do that now?'

'I'm impatient,' he said. 'I just want to be sure you like it before I sign it over to you.'

'Before you *what*?' She was fully awake now.

Khal looked at her. 'Why are you so surprised?'

'I would have thought that was obvious,' she said. 'I don't want a penthouse. I don't want anything from you.' She could tell from the expression on Khal's face that she might have been talking gibberish, but then he never had seen the gulf between them. Slipping out of bed, she grabbed a robe. 'You can't hand over a property to me as if it's a sweater you're tired of!'

'I'm not tired of it, I bought it for you.'

'You bought it for *me*?' Beth clutched the top of her head as if she had to contain all the confused thoughts jostling inside there. 'Are you mad?'

Khal ignored this. 'It's a good investment,' he said, swinging out of bed. 'But, if you don't like it, we'll look for something else.'

'I don't want anything else—I don't want this—'

'You must have somewhere suitable to live.'

'Why must I?' Beth's hackles rose as the penny dropped. 'What do you mean "somewhere suitable", Khal?' she said tightly. 'I already have a house.'

'And where is it?'

As Khal's drew himself up, she felt like stamping on his toes to bring him down to earth. Okay, her small modern townhouse wasn't a palace or a penthouse like this, but it was her home. And there were special reasons why it meant so much to her. She had received a surprise legacy on her twenty-first birthday from the father she'd never known. She had stared at the cheque when it had arrived from the solicitors for a long time, knowing she would have given it back in a second to know her father, and that it was too late. She wasn't about to throw that away as if it meant nothing. 'My home might not be what you're used to,' she told Khal. 'But it's all mine. Well, mine and the mortgage company's.'

'And this penthouse could be yours without a mortgage.'

'If I agree to what?'

She stood there with a look of anger and disappointment on her face. 'For goodness' sake, Beth! I'm giving you a penthouse. How much more can you ask of me?'

And there was the rub, Beth thought sadly. Khal wanted to give her so much in the monetary sense, but in her eyes his gift was valueless.

'If you want something bigger—something with a proper garden—'

'Khal, stop this! I don't need expensive gifts from you. That's not what I want—' Beth stopped in case her feelings for him poured out.

'Then what do you want?' he demanded with exasperation.

They were so far apart in outlook, in everything that really mattered, he would never understand. She settled for, 'My house suits me fine, and I don't need anywhere else to live.'

'We'll discuss this when you've calmed down.'

'No, we won't,' Beth said firmly. 'Where I live isn't up for negotiation.'

'But things have changed now.'

'What's changed? What do you mean, things have changed *now*? Oh, I see,' Beth said as the penny dropped. 'You're assuming that wherever I live can't possibly be upmarket enough for the ruler of Q'Adar to visit when he's in town...'

'That's not what I said.'

'It's what you meant, though.' Firming her lips, Beth

turned away. She didn't know when she had felt so hurt. 'If you think I'm going to become your mistress—'

'Think again?'

Khal's face had turned colder than Beth had ever seen it, and though she could never agree to this it was a stark reminder that people devoted their lives to the ruler of Q'Adar, and considered themselves fortunate to be able to do so.

She only had herself to blame for falling in love with him, Beth thought, hugging herself unhappily as she turned away. And she was twice the fool for imagining Khal might love her. 'I can't do this, Khal.' She could never agree to become just another one of his possessions. 'I can never be the woman you want me to be.'

Beth wondered why it was so quiet, and why Khal hadn't answered her. When she turned, she saw he was on his way to take a shower. She felt a chill pass over her as he paused and turned to face her at the door. 'There's another bathroom over there,' he said, pointing across the room. 'Use it and then let yourself out.'

Her jaw dropped. For once she was lost for words. She was stunned, angry, hurt, bewildered…and, most of all, full of grief and loss. How could a life that had felt so full only moments before feel so empty now? How had this happened? How had she allowed this to happen? How in her wildest dreams had she imagined the ruler of Q'Adar could ever love her as she loved him? Burying her head in her hands, Beth realised that her overriding feeling was shame. Everything in Khal's life came easily to him, and she had made herself available like all the rest. So much for all those brave thoughts at the ball—she had fallen into bed with him as eagerly as any of the other women there might have done. And now…? It had taken a single act of defiance on her part for Khal to discard her like a pair of ill-fitting shoes.

* * *

His timing was out. Everything was out. His world was off-kilter. How else could he explain exiting his bathroom at the same time as Beth? He was still battling his internal demons, wondering where he'd gone wrong. He'd bought her the best property in the whole of Liverpool and she'd rejected him. *She* had rejected *him*. 'My apologies,' he heard himself say stiffly. 'I thought you would have gone home by now.'

'It's usual in Liverpool for a host to make sure their guest gets home safely,' she told him tightly, with not one iota of her courage stripped away. 'Can you call a taxi, or shall I?'

Her steady gaze shamed him. He was so accustomed to having a car at the kerb everywhere he went, it hadn't occurred to him to call a taxi for Beth. And it was dark outside now. What had he been thinking? 'Of course I'll call a taxi for you.' His voice reflected anger with himself, but she wasn't to know that. 'Or you could use my car.'

One taupe brow rose. 'A taxi will be fine for me, thank you.' Her lips pressed together as she held his gaze.

For once he didn't know what to say and just made the call. He had been confident of her enthusiasm for his scheme. He had believed this to be the perfect solution. 'What's wrong with you, Beth?' he said as soon as he finished the call.

'What's wrong with me? No, don't answer that,' she told him. 'I know what's wrong with me. I'm naïve—and that's just for starters.'

'You must have known—'

'Why you brought me here? You're right, I should have known. I should have expected it, because that's all I am to you.'

'Beth,' he warned.

'Don't "Beth" me!'

'Look what I'm offering you…'

'You're offering me nothing,' she said angrily. 'And the saddest thing of all is you can't see it. You've killed off any hope of a future we ever had today. You've suffocated my love for you beneath your gross gift of a fabulously expensive penthouse, when an ice cream would have made me happy.'

'Don't be so ridiculous! I'll buy you anything you want.'

'But not this!' She gestured wildly, crying now. 'You're trying to buy me, Khal, and I can't be bought. You think you're offering me a million-pound home, while I think you're trying to turn my life into a theme park for you to dip into whenever you feel like playing at being an ordinary person. But when you tire of that, Khal, when you don your crown and forget about me, what am I supposed to do then?'

'I'll never forget you. And your life won't change.'

'My life won't change?' She spoke slowly and deliberately, annunciating each word as if she had to be sure of his meaning. 'You're even more cut off from reality than I thought.'

'And you're overreacting,' he said impatiently, turning away. He had never felt like this, his insides churning. He had never felt so unsettled and dissatisfied before. They waited out a tense silence until the bell sounded on the intercom. 'That will be your taxi,' he said unnecessarily, walking her to the door.

'Don't bother coming down with me,' she said in a clipped voice. 'I'll be just fine.'

He didn't doubt it, but would he?

If she had slept for even a second she might have thought twice before lifting the phone when it started ringing.

'Beth?' The voice was expressionless, but unmistakeable.

'Yes, it's me…' She held her breath and then said what had to be said. 'I haven't changed my mind, Khal, and I think it's better if we don't see each other again.'

'You took the words right out of my mouth.'

'Oh…' Somehow she wasn't prepared for that. Biting her

lip, Beth squeezed the phone until she had proper control of herself. 'Why are you calling, then?'

'I just wanted to set your mind at ease before I leave the country, and tell you that whatever happened between us will not impact on your future with Khalifa.'

She remained silent. If he'd expected enthusiasm, he was out of luck.

'Yes, in fact I have recommended you for promotion.'

'I wish you hadn't.'

'This has nothing to do with us. You're the best person for the job, and that's all there is to it.'

'Thank you.' She felt numb.

'Well, that's it... Maybe I'll see you next time?'

'Maybe...'

There was just the suggestion of a pause, and then the line went dead.

CHAPTER NINE

GRIPPING on to the cold white porcelain in her small *en suite,* Beth wondered if she was going to be sick again. As the moment passed, and she was capable of doing things again without worrying she was going to faint, she ran a basin full of cold water and dunked her face in it. Emerging spluttering, she felt clean, fresher, and more determined than ever. She knew what she had to do; she wasn't the type to let things hang.

She called into the chemist on her way to work, and then took refuge in the staff bathroom to carry out the simple test and wait for the result. She emerged from the bathroom a different person from the woman who had gone in; something deep inside her had just adjusted to a new orbit.

She was excited and scared and overwhelmed by the complications and consequences of carrying Khal's baby. But more than anything love was everywhere, bursting out of her, exploding in a cascade of shimmering light. If only she'd had someone to share it with. The love she felt for the baby they'd made was overwhelming, and her love for Khal was constant. Fate had played a cunning hand. Khal could never legitimise their relationship, but they were tied together now for the rest of their lives. She must do the right thing and let him know.

She tried first to contact him through the embassy, but no one would release his private telephone number, even when Beth explained in a small white lie that she was a member of his staff.

It was too late now to wonder why she hadn't asked for his number before, Beth reflected as she replaced the telephone receiver in its nest. And far too late for shame at the thought that if she had asked Khal for his number he probably wouldn't have given it to her, even though in every other way they'd been intimate. Even so, it was a miracle she had become pregnant. She wasn't on the Pill, but Khal had always been careful to use contraception.

It was no use looking back, Beth told herself firmly, and about as much use blaming the manufacturers of contraceptives as it was panicking about the future. This was her baby and her responsibility, and she would cope as she always had. She adored her baby already, and felt fiercely protective of it; she would guard it with her life.

Full of resolve she rang the embassy again, and this time left a message for His Majesty to call her back. It drew a sharp intake of breath from the person on the other end of the line, and wasn't really satisfactory for Beth—but she could hardly blurt out the fact that she was pregnant by the ruler of Q'Adar to a stranger. The only person she would give that news to was Khal. And she'd have to do that discreetly. She had seen enough in the gossip magazines to know how young women were derided for pointing the finger at wealthy men. And Khal was more than wealthy. She had nothing to lose, but what about her baby? No child of hers was going to be exposed to ridicule.

For now she would go back to work, Beth decided. It was crucial she brought in an income. There was the future to think about, a future in which her child might not grow up to know the trappings of great wealth, but they would know love. It would be safer for them to live quietly and anonymously, so that was what she would do.

Beth did everything required of her that day at work and more. If what Khal said was true and she was in line for a promotion, then she was determined to prove herself worthy of that promotion ten times over. She was dead on her feet by the time a phone call came through for her. She took it by the till in the store, expecting it to be one of her loyal customers wanting her to put something aside for them.

'Ms Torrance?'

Beth's heart stopped. The accent if not the voice was unmistakeable. 'Yes…?'

'I am calling from the Q'Adaran embassy, Ms Torrance.'

If she could have fast-forwarded the conversation she would have done—right up to the part where the man said, 'His Majesty regrets…'

He regretted? Regretted what? Beth shrank inside. What now? She had to make herself concentrate on what the man was saying to her. 'Keys?' she said in confusion. 'I don't know about any keys.'

'To the penthouse, Ms Torrance.'

'I'm sorry?'

'His Majesty has signed over the deeds of a property, which I believe you have viewed? I'm arranging to have the keys couriered to your home address.'

Beth recoiled. 'I don't want it.'

'I'm sorry, Ms Torrance, but that's something your lawyer will have to take up with our legal department.'

'I need to speak to him—to Khal—to His Majesty, I mean. It's really important.' Beth hardly knew that she was nursing her still-flat stomach in a protective way as she spoke. 'Can you give me a number where I can reach him?'

'I'm sorry, Ms Torrance, I'm not at liberty to release that information.'

'Then can you put me through to someone who can get a message through?'

'I'm sorry, Ms Torrance,' the caller repeated patiently. 'That won't be possible.'

'If someone could just tell him that I called…'

'In the event that you called, His Majesty has already left instructions that no thanks are necessary.'

Beth had to silence the hysterical laughter bubbling up inside her. And now it was too late, because the line had cut. Khal couldn't have made it any clearer that he didn't want to talk to her, and, whether she wanted it or not, he had given her the penthouse as a pay-off. And also as a reminder, just in case she had forgotten, that the ruler of Q'Adar pulled everyone's strings.

There was nothing she could do about it, Beth realised, firming her lips. She felt angrily defensive on behalf of her baby. Khal wasn't going to pull their strings. She would bring up their child without his help, and in her own home, and not one of his choosing. She would call a lawyer now, because she needed someone to advise her on the best way to rent out the penthouse and invest the money for her child. She wouldn't touch a penny of the money it brought in, but it would provide security for her baby in the future.

'It's about time you went home, isn't it?' the elderly doorman joked as Beth smiled goodbye to him. 'You look terrible.'

'Thank you,' Beth replied wryly. Wasn't that what she needed to hear after the day she'd had? But, not being the type to cower in a corner, she came straight out with it. 'I probably look pale because I'm pregnant.'

To his credit her old friend barely missed a beat. 'It can hit

some women like that in the first few months. If you need any
advice, I'll put you in touch with my wife—she's had seven.'

'That's really kind of you, but my mother—' Beth swallowed hard and carried on with the deception '—can't wait
to share her experiences with me.'

'There's nothing like having your family behind you.'

'No, there isn't, is there?' Beth smiled brightly, knowing
it was better for the sake of discretion if everyone thought she
had everything firmly under control.

Hana Katie Torrance was born smiling after a relatively easy
birth, and went on to become the first baby to enter the new
crèche at the luxurious Khalifa store in Liverpool. Hana
meant 'happiness' in Arabic, which was how Beth had felt
about her baby from the first moment she had discovered she
was pregnant. And that feeling had developed wings since the
day she'd felt her baby stir inside her. Hana's birth had been
the brightest day of her life. And life was good for Beth's
small family in her cosy, loving home, a family that now
included Faith, a friend from school, who had come to Khalifa
in hope of a position as a nursery nurse at the new crèche. It
had made sense to both girls for Faith to move in with Beth
and Hana and work part-time at the store.

Yes, life was good, Beth reflected with a sigh, as she
prepared for work that morning. And she couldn't think of one
way to improve it, other than to rid herself of the longing in
her heart, the longing that had never lessened, even though it
had been over a year since she'd last seen Khal.

Longing for things she couldn't have was a bad habit she'd
have to lose, Beth told herself firmly as she packed Hana's
bag for the day. 'Baby wipes, nappies, food and toys—all
present and correct,' she told Faith, glancing distractedly at
the television news. There had been more troubles in Q'Adar,

where the corrupt old sheikhs were unwilling to let go of their power. The news reporter said everything was quiet now, and that the ruling sheikh was firmly back in control. Beth bit her lip as she worried about Khal. She would always worry about him, even though she hadn't heard from him in all this time. Did he know he had a baby daughter? And, if he did, would he care? Surely someone must have told him? Glancing at the clock, Beth realised it was time to leave.

There were no happy endings outside of fairy tales, Beth reminded herself on the way to the store. The ruler of Q'Adar would hardly be interested in a Liverpool shop-girl when he had the ruling of a turbulent country on his mind.

'Shall I take our little princess?' Faith asked, jolting Beth back into the real world, their world, as they walked along the road. She hadn't told Faith the whole story, and thankfully Faith had never pushed for information, sensing something of Beth's inner grief.

'Hana *is* our princess, isn't she?' Beth said, smiling. She thought back to the hours immediately after childbirth when she'd been alone. She'd picked up a hand mirror and seen this fat, frumpy, plain woman, and had thought to herself that Khal had had a narrow escape. But plain or not she was going to throw everything she had into making Hana happy. And look what he was missing, Beth thought as she stopped to tenderly transfer Hana into Faith's arms at the door of the store. All the money and power in the world couldn't compare to this precious gift.

Beth thought a lot about Khal that day, and the dangers he was facing. She knew he would quell them, because she knew Khal. She knew he would never give up or back down, and that the wellbeing of his people meant everything to him. But when everything was back to normal in Q'Adar she wouldn't want to be part of that glittering, empty world, and it wasn't what she wanted for Hana either. And then a thought struck Beth that chilled her to the bone. What if, when the country was settled, Khal decided he wanted Hana in Q'Adar? What if he married one of those haughty princesses and then wanted Hana with them? His glamorous new wife was bound to look down on the daughter of a shop girl...

Beth couldn't bear to think about it. She couldn't bear to think of Hana being treated like a second-class citizen, or joining a family where she wasn't wanted. It must never come to that, she determined, and while she had breath in her body it never would.

He couldn't pretend he was back in Liverpool more than a year down the road just to tour the store. He didn't give a reason. He didn't need to. This was more than a business visit, it was an imperative. When he'd taken over in Q'Adar he'd had no idea how far the bribery and corruption had spread. In the absence of a strong leader, intrigue had spread like a malignant disease. No one had expected him to stamp down on it so fast when he came to power. The corrupt sheikhs had underestimated him, and they had underestimated his response. He had a kingdom and a people to defend, and he would do that in spite of threats against him and his family. He refused to be intimidated, but this was the first chance he'd had to get away and bring the rest of his family under his protection. Beth was part of his family now, whether she chose to be or not.

He left the limousine a few blocks away from his destination, telling his bodyguards to keep their distance. He needed space and time to think, luxuries usually denied him. He knew everything there was to know about Beth Tracey Torrance and their baby daughter, Hana. He'd had daily reports delivered to him whenever he'd been in Q'Adar. He'd known almost to the hour when Beth had discovered she was pregnant, and had set up a protection squad to keep her safe. The enormity of his responsibilities in Q'Adar had kept him there, but he had followed his baby daughter's progress with the keenest interest. He was pleased that Beth had called their daughter Hana. Even a little thing like a name would make his daughter's transition into her life as an Arabian princess that much easier.

Noting the undercover agents as he walked past them, he quickened his step. He was eager to see his child…eager to see Beth. And more than anything he was eager to get them both back to Q'Adar where he could ensure their safety. The uprising was over, but he couldn't protect them from renegades who might seek them out in England. And there was another reason. His people had placed their trust in him, and he wanted to repay that trust by marrying a suitable woman and providing his people with continuity—which meant providing them with an heir. It was essential that Hana was settled in Q'Adar before he married. Her presence in the palace would establish her as a member of the royal family, making her position in his affections clear before his new bride came to live there.

A year was a long time. He felt a rush of excitement as he entered the store. Surveillance photographs had told him something about Beth, and he was sure her resilience and humour were still in place—but what changes in her would he find, if any?

For instance, would motherhood soften her attitude towards becoming his mistress now that concern for baby Hana must override her pride?

He had dreamed of this moment for months, Khal realised, choosing to run up the escalator rather than wait for the lift. But would his feisty little Beth take to life in Q'Adar, even once he was married? He knew the answer to that before he even asked her the question.

He winced as he caught sight of his reflection in a mirror as he strode through her department, longing for a glimpse of her. How would she feel about seeing him battled-scarred and hardened? How would Beth feel about him?

Settling Hana in her cot at the crèche, Beth felt the change in the air before she saw anything, and the shiver down her back confirmed she was right to be frightened. Her first instinct was to reach for Hana, pick her up, and hold her tight.

'Beth…'

As she froze he thought the image of Beth holding their baby would never leave him, and he felt a great swell of emotion seeing them together for the first time. Her instinct was to shield her baby, and as she turned he saw the fear in her eyes. But, even so, she surprised him with her quick thinking and composure.

'Ring me if you need me,' she said calmly to a girl in nurse's uniform who was obviously on duty that morning in the babies' darkened sleep-room.

'Don't worry, I will,' the girl said, looking curiously at him.

Beth braced herself and turned around. 'Hello, Khal…' Nothing could have prepared her for seeing him again. All the warnings in the world wouldn't have been enough. In essence he was the same, but there were lines of strain around his eyes and his mouth, and recent scars on his face. Had it only been just over a year? A year in which her world had been turned upside down—but then so had Khal's, and in a different, ugly way.

'May I?' he said.

She recognised that tone in his voice. It echoed her own sense of wonder whenever Hana was in view. 'Of course,' she said. She would never stop him seeing his daughter, but she had feared this moment most of all. 'So, you knew...'

'Of course I knew,' Khal murmured, nursing his daughter.

Of course he knew. That was the power he wielded. And as Khal stared into Hana's face Beth feared that this was not the tender lover she'd known who had returned on a visit—but a warrior fresh from a war, a man who had come to claim his child.

CHAPTER TEN

THERE were so many unanswered questions, but all Beth was aware of was a creeping sense of dread. There was such intensity in Khal's gaze as he stared down at their baby daughter. She understood it, but it frightened her. There was a sense of loss too, lodged in the pit of her stomach like a heavy weight. Her feelings for Khal were unchanged, but that sense of loss was for something that had never been hers.

Oblivious to these undercurrents between her parents, Hana woke. The bond between father and daughter was instantaneous. Stretching out her tiny hand, Hana claimed Khal, curling her palm around his index finger. The look on his face transformed him, and when he smiled back at Hana Beth knew for certain that all their lives must change for good now. Instinct drove her to take up position on the opposite side of the cot to Khal, where she remained like a lioness in defence of its cub. Since Khal's shock appearance she hadn't been thinking straight, but she was acutely alert now. She had to keep her wits about her. Khal was supremely powerful, and used to wielding that power. If he decided to walk out with Hana, what could she do? And if he took their baby to Q'Adar would she ever see Hana again? The only thing left to her was to open a line of communication between them. 'Say hello to your daddy, Hana,' Beth said, hoping this might touch Khal's icy heart.

'Hana's a baby,' he said impatiently, 'and she can't speak yet.' Lifting his head, he gave Beth an admonishing stare. 'And when you address a royal child you should remember that baby-talk is inappropriate.'

Beth recoiled inwardly. Was this something he'd learned in the royal nursery at Q'Adar? She couldn't imagine it had come from his mother: from a nurse, perhaps. But didn't a baby love the tone of its parent's voice, and couldn't it hear the affection and love? Was that wrong now? As Khal turned his back on her Beth felt like she had been slapped in the face. She didn't have a model for parenting, and had done her best using instinct. That instinct was telling her now that Khal had just reinforced their respective positions in life, and that he was going to take Hana to the opposite side of the great divide. She spared a reassuring glance for Faith, who was doing her best to seem invisible, and then moved deeper into the shadows where she and Khal could talk discreetly. She beckoned him over. His dark eyes queried her impertinence at ordering him, but she stood her ground until he joined her. She told him straight. 'Please don't inflict your cold, unfeeling ways on Hana.'

Khal's eyes were like black diamonds, hard and unmoving. 'You'll do as *I* say where our daughter is concerned.'

'*Our* daughter,' Beth whispered, trying to remind him that she had a say. But she also had to remember that this was a man who had lived his entire life without emotion, a man whose world was not a cosy home but a palace, a man who had come here fresh from subduing his opponents. She had to find a way to make him see that this was a very different situation, and to do that she had to swallow a bucketful of pride. 'Khal, I'm begging you...'

'Not here.' He glanced at Faith. 'In my office; five minutes.'

Inwardly Beth was furious, but she would show none of that in front of Hana. She might be a mouse confronting the hawk of the desert, but when it came to their child Khal must learn that she would fight. 'I'm going to settle Hana back in her cot first,' she said, reaching for her, 'and then I'll come to your office.'

'Can't the nurse do that?'

Beth didn't answer. She remained where she was with her arms outstretched, waiting for her child; she wasn't going anywhere until Khal passed Hana over.

'There can be no agreement between us while you make these insane demands,' Beth argued. She was standing rigid with disbelief in the office Khal had taken over for his visit. He had insisted she must return immediately with him to Q'Adar and forget her life in England. 'I can't just throw everything up. I have a job here, responsibilities—'

'Yes,' he cut across her. 'Responsibilities, to me and to your daughter.'

She knew she didn't count, but the expression on Khal's face cut Beth out of the picture completely. He wanted his daughter, and if he couldn't part Beth from Hana then she must come too; that was what it amounted to. Her heart ached for the closeness they'd known, and for Khal too, but this was not the time for her to soften. It was crucial to meet Khal's steel with steel, or she'd go down. No chance *that* was going to happen with Hana to protect. Khal might be a slave to duty and cut off from emotion, but she was a mother devoted to her child. 'You can't uproot Hana on a whim. She has a routine.'

'Which can be reinstated in Q'Adar—and this is not a whim. I'm here because the safety of our daughter is at stake.'

'Hana's safety?' Beth felt sick. The world as she knew it was disintegrating, and taking its place was something frightening and unknown. The rights and wrongs of going with Khal were irrelevant. Her whole concentration was focused on keeping Hana safe. 'What do you mean?' she whispered.

'I intended to explain that to you on our flight back to Q'Adar.'

'You thought I would come with you meekly and without question?'

'I thought you would trust me.'

Beth's gaze flickered. 'It's not enough, Khal. I must know what you mean before I make a decision like this for Hana.'

'The situation in Q'Adar is turbulent and unpredictable.'

'All the more reason for staying here.'

'No,' he said firmly. 'I cannot guarantee Hana's safety when she's so far away from me. The troubles in Q'Adar are like the random thrashings of a mad dog in the final throes of its agony. We are close to stamping it out, but there are those who bear grudges and would try to slip away to try and distract me from my purpose. They would stab me in my heart,' he said bitterly.

'Your heart?' The look in Khal's eyes stopped Beth making any more remarks along those lines. Hana had released something inside him he had been frightened of admitting, even to himself—that not only did Khal have a heart, but he was capable of love so instant, so deep and lasting, it had taken even him by surprise.

'There can be no delay. I have made my decision.'

'*You* have made a decision?' Beth said, refocusing. 'Hana has two parents.'

'What are you doing?' he said, snatching a phone out of her hand.

'Calling my lawyer.' Thank goodness she had appointed

one, along with all the other precautions she had taken, like obtaining a passport for Hana so they would never be trapped anywhere by anyone.

'And alert my enemies? There isn't time for you to call a lawyer and book an appointment for some time next week. This is an urgent matter.'

'For you, but I must consider all Hana's options. I need time to think.'

'There is no time to think. We don't have that luxury. I can assure you I wouldn't have come unless there was real and pressing danger. I came to you the instant the situation in Q'Adar was under control, but when you're here I can't protect you both properly.'

'If you'd told me, if you'd explained, if you'd even given me some warning…'

He made a dismissive gesture. 'I don't expect you to understand. You're still living in your small, safe world— or at least that's what you think. That world can change horribly and in an instant, Beth. Do you want to be alone when it does?'

For the first time Beth wasn't sure what to say.

'You must accept that our daughter inhabits the same world stage as her father.'

'From which I am excluded?'

'You don't face the same risks,' Khal said flatly.

And would she put Hana at risk? Her options had dwindled to nothing, Beth realised. Hana's safety was paramount. Did she have any alternative but to go with Khal? 'If you can keep Hana safe,' she murmured tensely, speaking her thoughts out loud.

'I can,' Khal told her. 'If she returns with me now to Q'Adar. But I cannot secure the rest of the world for you, Beth. You must come back with me.'

Closing her eyes for a moment, Beth begged for guidance.

'Then I will,' she agreed on a shuddering breath. She could only pray she'd done the right thing.

And do what when she arrived in Q'Adar? Beth wondered as she packed their day bag hurriedly and explained as best she could to Faith. Would she live out her life in Q'Adar as a second-class citizen, the ruling sheikh's embarrassing little secret? How would that affect Hana's future? Would Hana grow up estranged from her in a different part of the palace? Would she be forced to endure taunts and insults in later life because her mother was deemed unworthy? Beth bit her lip at the thought of Hana suffering in any way. 'There's no other alternative to this, is there?' Beth confirmed with Khal as they left the building. 'You couldn't leave more guards here to keep Hana safe?' She hesitated outside the limousine with Hana in her arms.

'You think you live in a warm, safe nest,' Khal told her. 'But what you forget is that violence can follow you everywhere. It can seep through the cracks of your happy life and steal everything you care about away.'

'Is that meant to frighten me into coming with you?'

'Beth…' Khal's jaw worked as he fought back his feelings, and for just a second Beth thought she saw his eyes change too; they seemed to soften with understanding. 'I wish that was all it was with all my heart.'

Gazing at Hana, Beth knew she couldn't remain stubbornly obstinate; she had to do what was right for her baby.

Trouble started on the journey to the airport when questions bombarded Beth's brain and she couldn't keep quiet. 'How can your enemies be so sure Hana is your child?'

Khal didn't speak for a moment, and then he reached inside his breast pocket and drew out a document. 'They may have had sight of this. People talk…'

'What is it?' Beth said fearfully.

'It's the proof that Hana is my daughter.'

'Proof?'

'Don't look at me like that, Beth. Our daughter is a royal princess. I had to be certain. And now we both know that Hana is a member of the royal house of Hassan—'

'And I'll never be allowed to forget it, will I?' Beth said, turning the official-looking envelope over in her hands. She didn't need to read it, she had guessed the contents.

'Why don't you open it?' Khal said.

She pulled out the single type-written sheet and paled as her worst fears were confirmed. 'There is only way you could have got this, and that's by having someone come into the labour room while I was recovering from Hana's birth and take samples from her.'

'It was a necessary precaution.'

'You think that sending an intruder into a labour room is acceptable?'

'I deemed it necessary.' He shrugged. 'But there was no intruder, because that person was already there.'

Beth gasped as the implication of Khal's cool statement hit home. *'Who?* Who did this, Khal?' Beth's eyes filled with tears as she thought back to her lonely vigil in a room full of strangers. She had been strong then for Hana's sake, but her sense of betrayal now was overwhelming. She was in such turmoil, it was a struggle to remember every face and name of the medical professionals who had been with her in the birthing room.

'Don't be so naïve, Beth,' Khal said impatiently as she bit down on her fist to stop the tears. 'As soon as I knew you were pregnant my team moved into action.'

'Your *team?*' It was worse than she had thought. He hadn't even handled this personally. But then why would he, when the ruler of Q'Adar had someone to carry out even this most personal of all tasks for him?

'I didn't take any chances,' Khal explained as if this were reasonable. 'I ordered a daily report on your progress.'

'From your spies?' Beth bit back.

'Do you imagine I would leave the birth of a baby that was almost certainly mine to chance?'

'Yes, Hana's your child, Khal,' Beth reminded him, stung more than she could say by the fact that he thought there could have been doubt over Hana's parentage. 'Your *child*...' She wondered if Khal had any understanding of what it meant to be a parent.

'I had a war to fight,' he reminded her coldly, so distanced from her now they were like two strangers. It seemed to her that after a few moments of humanity Khal had slipped back into his old, hard ways.

You could have called me.

'Are you suggesting I should have given my position away, along with that of the men fighting with me? Isn't it enough to be separated from my child without having you lecture me on what I should have done, when I did all I could to keep you and the men in the desert with me safe?'

'But the way you went about it.'

'Ensuring Hana was my child? This is a big thing, Beth. We're not talking about any ordinary child.'

'No child is ordinary,' she fired back at him.

He bowed his head in acknowledgement that this time she was right. 'But all the same I had to be sure. And for your safety and my peace of mind, that was *my* doctor, *my* anaesthetist, *my* nurse, and *my* paediatric specialist with you when Hana was born. You should be thanking me instead of this. You surely didn't think I would turn my back on you when you were carrying my baby?'

'They could have told me.' The subterfuge was getting to her. She accepted his explanation regarding the need for discretion, but Khal's calculating actions almost made her wish he *had* abandoned them. The fact that Hana was a royal child deserving of some special treatment made Beth feel like a convenient womb, and made Hana sound like nothing more than the result of a successful and very privileged breeding programme. 'Stop…stop it,' she begged him, covering her ears with her hands. 'Don't say another word. I can't bear to hear you talking about Hana like this.'

'Like what?'

'As if she wouldn't be so precious without royal blood running through her veins.'

'Before you judge me, examine your own conscience. How long would you have waited before trying to contact me again?'

'The Q'Adaran embassy refused to give me your number.' Before Beth had a chance to say any more, the limousine drew up outside the VIP entrance and, taking Hana from her arms, Khal got out of the limousine, leaving Beth to scramble after him.

Beth was stunned to find Faith waiting for them in the VIP lounge.

'You mentioned Hana's routine, and so I had your attendant brought here,' Khal told her as he handed Hana over.

'Faith isn't my attendant, she's my friend. But, thank you…' She looked at him properly and saw the lines of tension on his face. She would forgive him his comment about Faith, because that was just a symptom of Khal's distance from her life. It was something that, if she stayed with him, she would have to change. But for now she was worried about him. 'Is there somewhere we can sit down?' she said, extending an olive branch. For a moment she thought he would, or maybe he wanted to, but then he shook his head.

'When I've introduced Faith to members of my staff, and greeted all these dignitaries…'

She saw them then, lined up and waiting for him. However tired he was, and whatever the demands on him personally, Khal would always do his duty and do it well.

He was gone some time before he could join her in the private lounge. 'Do you have everything you need?' he asked, swinging back into the room in a flurry of sandalwood and energy.

'Everything, thank you,' Beth said, wishing they didn't have to be so stiff with each other. She patted the seat beside her and a after a moment's hesitation he joined her. 'You asked me in the limousine why I didn't take action when Hana was born. I didn't want anything from you, Khal, and that was why. I just didn't see the point.'

'You were entitled to my support,' he said, turning his proud face towards her.

She was so relieved they were communicating again she didn't want to break the mood, and knew this wasn't the time to admit she had feared rattling the cage of Khal's formidable legal-team, and had buried her head in the sand to some extent. 'I wouldn't have kept on working at Khalifa if I'd been trying to hide from you.'

'Or maybe you had nowhere else to go,' Khal suggested, getting up to pour them both a soft drink.

'I've got my family…'

He noticed how she flinched at the lie, and he flinched too, but inwardly. He didn't want this, but perhaps it was better if the truth came out. He knew more than Beth thought he did. His investigations hadn't concentrated solely on her pregnancy. 'Why didn't you go to your family?' He turned to face her. 'Why didn't they come to you, Beth?' He knew this was cruel, but it had to be said. He couldn't live with deception any more, he'd had enough of it in Q'Adar.

Seeing he knew the truth, she looked away. 'Well?' he pressed. 'Isn't it time you told me about your family, Beth? From what you've said about them I imagine they must have been thrilled to hear about the baby. No? Is that the reason you haven't gone near them while you were pregnant...or when you had the baby?'

Her blue eyes filled with tears, but still she raised them to meet his gaze. 'You know about that too, don't you, Khal? You know all my talk on the beach was just that—talk. I don't have a family. Or at least I didn't have a family until Hana was born. I had the store, I had Khalifa; that was my family. And that's why my job means so much to me,' she admitted huskily.

He remained silent. He'd known for some time that Beth's stories on the beach had just been her sad little daydreams, and now he had trampled them it didn't make him proud.

As always she rallied fast. 'I might not have a family, and a fancy support-structure like you, but I can still appoint a lawyer to act for me, and—'

'And I will fight you,' he assured her, instinct driving him. Launching a defence against every threat that came his way was bred into him.

'I expected that,' she told him tensely. 'I expect you to stop at nothing to get your own way, Khal.'

'Don't you think Hana deserves to know both her parents? I want her to enjoy her birthright both as my daughter and as a princess of Q'Adar. Surely as her mother you would want that for her?'

'I want Hana to be happy, and that's all I care about.'

'And I want that too.'

'No, Khal, you want to take Hana from me and bring her up believing that money and power is everything, and love doesn't matter.' Was he even listening? Beth wondered.

'If you fight me,' he warned, 'I'll apply for full custody. Are you prepared to lose Hana?'

'Don't threaten me.' But just the thought of losing Hana was so terrible her voice was shaking, and all the bravado and cheerfulness that had always lifted her had gone. And for the first time in her life Beth felt beaten.

'All I want is my legal entitlement as Hana's father, a father who can provide the type of life Hana deserves.'

'The life Hana deserves?' Beth repeated, shrinking inside.

'Try to understand that the difference in our circumstances dictates—'

'Dictates *what*, Khal? That with your fabulous wealth and immense power you can buy a lawyer, buy a judge, buy a child?'

'It isn't like that, Beth, and you know it. You're distraught.'

'You bet I am!'

'Your choice is simple. You can stay in Liverpool and take your chances, or you can come to Q'Adar with me and Hana.' He glanced towards the runway where his private jet was waiting. 'Either way, Hana goes with me.'

Put so starkly, Beth could only think about Hana's safety. In the final analysis it was the only thing that mattered to her. 'Are you sure you can keep her safe?'

'Decision time, Beth…'

'I won't be your mistress.'

'I'll make the necessary arrangements for you to board the flight.' Khal cut across her without emotion.

And that was it. She felt grief for what they'd lost, but this fast decision-making and brevity of speech fit the dangerous times through which Khal was living, and she knew she could expect nothing more. With Hana always first in her mind, she thanked him and said they would be ready to leave the moment they were called.

'Tell Hana's nanny that she will also be made welcome in Q'Adar.' It wasn't much, but he wanted to give Beth something. It had never been his intention to crush her, or to have her return to Q'Adar under duress. As he held her gaze, something tugged at his heart, and instinctively he made the Q'Adaran gesture for a blessing that he had made so many times before to so many people, but never to the one person who needed it most.

While Beth went to see to Hana he sat heavily on a chair, staring through the panoramic windows, seeing nothing. He was still reeling from the shock of holding his baby daughter for the first time, and seeing Beth again. She challenged him every step of the way—but did he want the mother of his child to be a lioness or a milksop? He couldn't guarantee their safety in England, but Q'Adar would always be turbulent; it was the nature of the people. She would have to be strong, and deep down he knew she would cope, because Beth was an exceptional woman. She challenged everything he believed in—his views on life, and even his role in it. No one had ever done that before; no one had ever dared.

He'd always known she wasn't malleable mistress-material, but that didn't stop him wanting her in his life. If there was a solution to this, he couldn't see it. He couldn't marry Beth, and she would never agree to be his mistress. And so he must be content. Bringing Beth and Hana back with him to Q'Adar where he could keep them safe was the result he had aimed for when he'd come to England. He had succeeded in that, and it would have to be enough for him to know they were under his protection now.

He *was* content, Khal told himself...or as content as he ever could be.

CHAPTER ELEVEN

THE ruler of Q'Adar's preferred mode of transport wasn't a small private jet, but a full-sized airliner with the royal crest of a hawk emblazoned on its tail, and the royal standard flying from the nose of the plane. Beth was standing with Hana in her arms on the tarmac, and they were being escorted to the plane by security staff. This was how it would be from now on, Beth realised. Khal was still making his way down the line of dignitaries, and looked magnificent in his flowing Arabian robes.

'Where's Faith?' he asked the moment he could get away.

'She received a phone call to say her father has been taken ill. I took the liberty of asking your driver to take her home. I hope you don't mind?'

'You did the right thing,' Khal told her, and then instead of sweeping in front of her he paused at the foot of the steps. 'Shall I take Hana for you?'

It didn't take a flock of royal attendants hurrying to her side to tell Beth how incongruous this offer was. She couldn't imagine many sheikhs took their baby, the baby no one had previously known about, into their arms in full view of everyone. 'I can manage, thank you,' she said, staring up to where the flight attendants were waiting to greet them, in what was to all intents and purposes Q'Adar.

Aware of Khal close behind her, Beth mounted the steps with Hana in her arms. Behind Khal came a contingent of his office and security staff. She had to wonder what they made of their leader's ready-made family. To his credit Khal didn't seem in the least bit concerned.

'Would you like to put Hana in a cot?' he suggested as they entered a reception area on board the plane. 'I've made sure there are several cots on board,' he told Beth, when he saw the surprise on her face.

She held Hana a little more closely, feeling overwhelmed now she was here.

'I'll show you round so you know where everything is.' She looked very small and very young, clutching her child close to her, but he could understand Beth's apprehension. She had made a brave decision, and could sense that she was in Q'Adaran territory now. He led the way into a comfortable lounge, as spacious as anything she might find in a luxury hotel, hoping to reassure her. 'If you need anything, you only have to ask.'

'Thank you,' she said politely, with a face that was carefully expressionless.

'No one will disturb you, but if you require anything you only have to ring this bell.'

Her eyes widened and then quickly became masked again. 'If you show me where everything is, I can help myself…'

As she stopped speaking and looked at him, he saw she knew that he didn't know where anything was. He only had to ring a bell and whatever he wanted came to him. He had never had to go looking for a thing in his life. 'The staff will do that for you,' he said. 'You don't want to insult them by refusing their help, do you?'

'That's different, then,' she agreed as he tried not to notice her delicate perfume.

He showed her more rooms located off a long and luxuriously carpeted corridor, conscious that this was the first time in his life he had ever acted as a tour guide. She started talking to Hana, explaining things to her, showing complete disregard for his instructions about holding conversations with a royal baby. 'And just in case you need a doctor,' he said, indicating another room, 'this is the medical centre.'

'I sincerely hope we won't need a doctor.'

'And there are two bedrooms at this end of the plane, each with cots. Feel free to choose whichever you like. I have my own quarters at the front of the aircraft, so you won't disturb me.'

'I wouldn't dream of it.'

He continued on as if he hadn't heard her. 'And my support staff will be at the rear of the plane in a completely different section, so they won't disturb you.'

'That's reassuring, isn't it, Hana?'

'There are three bathrooms, all with a shower and whirlpool bath.'

'And a good stock of towels?'

'Of course.'

'Have you ever thought of going into real estate?' she said.

'And there's a cinema in here.'

'No swimming pool?'

He stopped, and turned to face her.

'Do you have a cot for Hana in the lounge?' she said innocently. 'Only I didn't see one.'

'I'll have one brought in for you. And there's a professional nanny on board. I would have ordered two if I'd known Faith couldn't be here.'

'You'd have *ordered* one?—like pizza?'

He looked down at her.

'Not like pizza, like people you value, Khal, because they're part of our team.'

'*Our* team?'

She blushed. 'I don't need a nanny, thank you very much. No offence to the nanny.'

'And none taken…by the nanny.'

He flew the plane too. Couldn't he delegate anything to other people? Beth wondered as Khal left her in a swirl of robes that cast up the scent of sandalwood and amber. That was how she would always think of him, Beth realised as her heart lurched, the rugged warrior sheikh with his darkly glittering glamour, and his dangerous, cold black eyes.

The flight was smooth and uneventful, and when the landing gear went down Beth was surprised to find she was excited by the prospect of returning to Q'Adar. Gazing out of the window, she realised things were starting to change for the better under Khal's rule. In the time she had been away, and even taking into account the uprising, he had managed to transform large tracts of desert into a garden of crops. She wanted to congratulate him, but when they landed and the plane drew to a halt on the tarmac she was disappointed to see a limousine waiting for her, while a smaller, faster car sped away with Khal at the wheel.

This was how it would be, Beth realised: the ruler of Q'Adar on a faster and more demanding track, while his illegitimate baby daughter and her mother slipped into the shadows behind tinted windows. But she couldn't help feeling a sense of anticipation at the thought of making things work out for the best for Hana in Q'Adar. At least until Khal told them it was safe to go home. She would never think of Q'Adar as home, would she? Beth reflected as the limousine slid past the soothing sight of orange groves, packed with ripe fruit glowing like tiny Halloween lanterns in the fast-fading sun.

* * *

Gunning the engine of his Ferrari until it threatened to take flight, Khal was still debating how exactly Beth was going to fit into court life in Q'Adar. Pure instinct had made him bring her here without any of his usual thought and planning, but when there was a threat to those he cared about he acted fast and decisively. He had never brought a woman to the palace before, and yet here he was with a ready-made family. He'd have to find something to keep Beth busy and out of his way...

'This is our life for now,' Beth whispered to baby Hana as the limousine slowed in front of the grand entrance of the palace. She was taking comfort in the warm baby-scent, with her face buried in Hana's downy black curls, but when she saw the Dowager Sheikha waiting to greet them at the top of the steps her head snapped up. 'Oh, great,' Beth breathed with genuine pleasure, her face lighting with enthusiasm as she remembered how kind Khal's mother had been to her on her previous visit. All the plans Beth had been making on the way to the palace— To achieve any one of them she'd need an influential supporter.

Oh, great, Beth thought, biting her lip as she began to lose confidence. She couldn't imagine Khal's mother would feel much like playing fairy godmother when the clumsy shop-girl from the ball returned to the palace with a royal baby in her arms...

Beth's stomach was performing cartwheels by the time the Dowager Sheikha, minus her usual entourage, came purposefully down the steps. But the driver was opening the door, and there was nothing for it but to get out with Hana and face the music.

'Welcome to Q'Adar, my dear!'

Khal's mother swooped on them, enveloping Beth and

Hana in a flurry of floating lavender fabric, delicious scent and tinkling jewellery. Was it possible she had changed so much the Dowager Sheikha didn't recognise her? Beth wondered. 'Well, hello again.' She dipped into a curtsey, fully expecting the bubble to have burst by the time she rose to her feet.

'No need for that, dear.' The Dowager Sheikha put her hand beneath Beth's elbow to support her as she rose again, and her perfume made Hana sneeze. 'Oh, she's adorable! May I hold her?'

'Of course…' Beth was still trying to accustom herself to the warmth of her welcome.

'This is what we need in Q'Adar,' Khal's mother confided as they walked up the steps together.

'What's that, Your Majesty?'

'Young blood,' the Dowager Sheikha insisted. She paused at the top of the steps to give Beth a quick once-over.

And how did she rate? Beth wondered, thinking back to all the glamorous princesses Khal's mother had assembled at the ball for her son's approval. It was hard to tell what the older woman was thinking behind those penetrating, raisin-black eyes.

'Shall I hand Hana over to the nurses for you? My son has engaged an army of support staff.'

Beth recoiled. 'No.'

'No?'

The last thing she wanted now was a disagreement with the nicest of women, but, like her son, the Dowager Sheikha wasn't used to hearing the word 'no', unless it came from her own mouth. 'No.' Beth spoke more gently this time. 'Hana won't be needing an army of support staff, but what she does need is rest after such a long journey. We're not used to being separated, you see—'

'Not even at the store?' the Dowager Sheikha interrupted. 'I understood that when you're working Hana is in the crèche?'

Exactly how much had Khal told his mother? Beth wondered. 'I'm on hand all the time, and a very good friend of mine—a school friend who lives with us—works at the crèche and is with Hana every moment.'

'I see.' Khal's mother considered this. 'You seem to have it all under control.'

Beth kept her thoughts on that to herself.

'I admire you, Beth Torrance.'

'You do?'

'Yes.'

Touching Beth's cheek, the Dowager Sheikha smiled at her, and for the first time since leaving England Beth felt a little glow of confidence blossom inside her. Maybe she would achieve a few of the small things she hoped to, things she believed she could offer Q'Adar in the short time she would be have. With Khal's mother on-side, the future didn't seem so bleak. But she would never get used to this, Beth thought, as servants bowed and doors opened in front of them as if by magic.

'I chose the garden suite for you myself,' the Dowager Sheikha informed Beth, drawing to a halt in front of a pair of exquisite gold-filigree doors. 'I think this apartment enjoys one of the most beautiful aspects in the palace, plus the courtyard and gardens have plenty of shade for baby Hana.' She stared longingly at Hana, asleep in Beth's arms. 'When she wakes—'

'I'll see that you're informed immediately.'

'Oh, would you?' Khal's mother turned grateful eyes on her. 'It's been a long time since we've had a baby at the palace, and I'd like to read to her, and maybe sing to her a little…'

And what would Khal make of that? Beth wondered. Would he dare to disapprove? Her eyes twinkled at the thought of this double-pronged rebellion by the women in his life.

Any thoughts Beth might have harboured about being stuffed away in an attic somewhere out of sight were immediately obliterated when she walked into the cool tiled hallway of her new home. 'It's next door to my own apartment,' the Dowager Sheikha told her as she bustled ahead. 'I planned it this way, hoping I might catch glimpses of baby Hana in the garden...'

As she turned, Beth saw the same longing in her eyes again. 'You can sit with Hana, or push her round the courtyard, any time you want.' Did dowager sheikhas do things like that?

'I'd love to!' Khal's mother exclaimed, dispelling Beth's fears.

Judging by that response, Beth guessed Khal's mother was pretty much like herself and didn't mind starting new trends when she had to.

'I'm going to leave you now, and give you chance to settle in,' she said. 'I expect you'd like a little time to get used to your new surroundings.'

She would never get used to them, Beth thought, acting like a tourist already, turning circles to stare up at the gloriously ornate painted ceiling.

'You'll have your own household, of course,' Khal's mother added at the door.

'My own household?' Beth repeated incredulously. 'Why would I need that?'

'Enjoy your temporary status as a member of the royal family,' the Dowager Sheikha insisted with a mischievous twinkle.

'You're very generous, Your Majesty,' Beth said, remembering her manners as she bobbed a curtsey. 'But it really isn't necessary.'

'Nonsense, you'll enjoy it. And I shall make the introductions myself,' Khal's mother decided on impulse, beckoning to the staff hovering outside. 'It's better if you don't confide too many details,' she murmured confidentially, returning to Beth's side.

Beth's eyes widened as she gazed down the line of neatly uniformed staff. 'But, if all these people are going to be looking after Hana and me, surely they deserve to know the situation?'

'You have a lot to learn, my dear.'

'Don't we all?' Beth sighed. Then, quickly remembering herself, she added, 'Well, obviously not you, Your Majesty.'

CHAPTER TWELVE

HE WAS on his way to the stables when he saw his mother hurrying towards him.

'The baby's adorable!' she exclaimed, clasping her hands together in delight. 'And I've seen your little friend settled in as you requested.' As he turned to go, she put her hand on his arm. 'Won't you stay a little while and talk with me, Khalifa?'

'I'm not in the mood to talk, and Beth is not "my little friend". Hana's mother is called Beth Tracey Torrance.'

'But I may call her Beth on your instruction, is that it, Khal? Too kind...'

'Sarcasm doesn't suit you, Mother.'

'And neither does this aloof manner suit you, Khalifa. And I hope you're not thinking of riding out without guards.'

'There's a storm brewing, enough to keep the troublemakers in their burrows. Don't be concerned about me,' he added, seeing his mother's concern. 'I can read the desert.'

'Can you, Khalifa?'

He looked at his mother's hand on his sleeve, saw the tension in her face, and knew she was remembering. 'I must have some freedom.' As her hand relaxed, he firmed his resolve and bowed to her. 'If you will excuse me...'

'You won't find an answer to your Beth in the desert.'

'She is not *my* Beth, and I am trialling a horse,' he said with as much restraint as he could muster.

'Whatever you say. Be careful, my son.'

As Beth had suspected Hana wanted nothing more than to sleep after her long journey. The facilities in the nursery were incredible, and the girls on duty were graduates of a college that had been at the forefront of childcare training for over a hundred years. After chatting with them, Beth felt confident enough to leave Hana in their care and take a look around.

The Palace of the Moon was on such a mammoth scale it took Beth a few minutes to reach her private garden. She hadn't been invited to visit this more secluded and very special part of the palace on her last visit to Q'Adar, so when she entered through a gate she gave an exclamation of delighted surprise. It was just like finding the secret garden, she thought, remembering one of her favourite childhood books. The stone walls held the scent of the flowers, intensifying it, and there were colonnades around the perimeter which offered shade along narrow pathways. The sultry temperature of late afternoon was made bearable thanks to the central fountain, which cast plumes of twinkling water high into the air. Having showered and changed in her fabulous bathroom, Beth was wearing a pair of loose-fitting lightweight trousers and a shirt, and felt refreshed, but it was still tempting to perch on the raised lip of the pool and throw her head back to catch the spray.

Dressed for riding in breeches and a shirt, he watched her from the shadows. A new stallion awaited him, the finest of his kind. It was a gift from a neighbouring sheikh, and under normal circumstances nothing could have delayed his inspection. The horse had recently knocked a couple of seconds off the fastest recorded time on a measured track, and he had yet to try him out. That should have been enough to blank everything else from his mind, but it appeared Beth was an exception, and his senses roared as she turned her face to the sky and sighed with pleasure. There was one answer, and that was exercise—fierce and hard.

'Khal…?'

He paused mid-stride. Had she sensed his presence? She certainly hadn't seen him, and he was moving away from her on silent feet. Was it possible they were so finely tuned that she'd known all along he had been watching her? He stepped out of the shadows and strode across the courtyard. 'I trust your quarters are acceptable?'

'My quarters? If you mean my fabulous apartment, it's great!'

He had to stop himself smiling. How could he have forgotten the effect she always had on him? 'Great?' he said dryly, thinking of the kings and presidents who had stayed there before her. 'Well, as long as you're satisfied and have everything you need.'

'Oh, I do,' she assured him, turning her attention to some rose petals floating on the pond. 'Does someone toss these into the water each day?'

'Why? Would you like the job?'

She looked at him, and he saw the surprise in her eyes at the flash of humour. He agreed with her, it was ill-judged. Beth was here because he wanted to keep her and Hana safe. The last thing he wanted was to remind them both of times when they had been intimate, both in bed and out of it.

'I'd like *a* job, Khal,' she said, rushing to paper over the cracks as he had done. 'Though I doubt I'll be here long enough. But I do have an idea.'

Why wasn't he surprised? 'Go on…'

'Well, you don't have a palace crèche, do you?'

'There's only one royal baby, as far as I am aware,' he pointed out.

'But there must be dozens more amongst the staff, and you obviously have contact with one of the greatest nursery-nurse colleges in the world. It just seemed to me…'

'Yes?' he pressed, eager to escape so he would no longer have to look into those crystal-blue eyes.

'Well, I just thought you could throw it open.'

'To all-comers?' He frowned.

'To everyone employed at the palace. It will be company for Hana, and I'm happy to help out. I could even run it for you.'

'You won't be here that long.' He could have kicked himself when her face fell.

'No, I forgot.'

She tipped up her chin. She had been carried away by a scheme she had no hope of seeing through, and in doing so believed she had made a fool of herself.

'It was just a thought,' she said, frowning.

'I'm expecting to hear that the danger has passed very soon and that you'll be able to go home.'

'Oh, good…'

Did her voice sound a little flat, or was he imagining it?

'This is nice for Hana.' She glanced around the elegant courtyard. 'But I wouldn't want her getting used to it.'

He rapped his whip across his riding boots. When he had worked out the next stage of Hana's integration into royal life, he'd let Beth know. Meanwhile, why shouldn't she enjoy the palace and all it had to offer? 'If you like riding I'll ask my groom to find you a horse so you can ride around the palace grounds.'

'Would you?'

As her eyes lit with enthusiasm, he realised Beth had mistaken this for an invitation, but what he had planned for himself was something more rigorous. 'Yes, I'll do that while I'm down there,' he said, giving his thighs a tap with the crop. 'I'll tell them to sort something out for you.'

'But aren't you riding in the grounds?'

'I have other plans. A groom will ride with you, if you like, show you around.'

'That won't be necessary, thank you,' she told him. Her eyes were wounded, though she tilted her chin in the usual way.

'Well, I'd better get on,' he said. 'I want to make the most of the daylight.' With considerable relief, he strode away.

The palace stables—why not? Even if Khal didn't want to ride with her, riding here would be a real adventure. Not that she'd go far, of course. She'd keep to the gardens as Khal had suggested.

Beth checked on Hana before she left, and was pleased to find her suggestions had been carried out to the letter. Hana was still sleeping contentedly, with the two nurses in attendance. Down in the stables, she discovered that Khal hadn't let her down. The pony they brought out for her approval was a sweet grey with a kind face, just the type of horse to give a novice confidence.

She was still wearing trousers and a shirt, and they lent her some boots with a heel to stop her foot slipping out of the stirrup, and also a freshly laundered bandana to keep the dust from her face. The grooms echoed Khal's words, telling her she must stay within the palace grounds. She was fine with that. They palace grounds were like a vast park, with plenty of opportunity to give the small pony his head.

But when she rode past one of the archways and saw the desert rolling back as far as she could see, the lure proved too much for her. She couldn't imagine any remaining insurgents would dare to come within sight of the palace. Ducking her head as she passed beneath the stone arch, she gave the guard a confident greeting as if this had all been arranged. He grew alert, as if to challenge her, but then thought better of it when she squeezed her knees to give her pony the signal to trot. She would just ride once round the palace and then return, Beth decided.

The pony responded eagerly to the promise of the desert. He carried her at a brisk pace beyond the walls, onto a shadowy carpet of sand beneath a moon in a tangerine-and-lilac sky. She rode out a bit further, and then a little further still. She felt safe as long as she could still see the palace. She was on the point of urging the pony into a controlled canter when she first caught sight of Khal in silhouette against the darkening sky. So he hadn't planned to ride in the grounds, after all. He was galloping as fast as she had seen any man ride, and his horse was stretched out like an arrow with its tail flying behind like a silken banner in the wind.

She could have sat there and watched them for hours, it was such a romantic sight. He was heading for a small fort, she noticed. What was the attraction? Beth wondered, turning her horse and trotting after him. It looked as though the crumbling building had been unoccupied for years. It was little more than an old ruin, with a yawning gap where once there must have been grand gates, and gaping holes instead of windows. It must be another one of Khal's projects, Beth guessed, squeezing her knees to give her pony the signal to move faster. She wanted to keep within range so she could admire Khal's skill on horseback. He really was amazing…

Beth tensed, hearing a sound like rolling thunder coming up behind her. Her heart fluttered an alarm as she reined in and turned in the saddle. It took her a moment to process the information, it was so surreal. It seemed that a wall of sand reaching high into the sky was sweeping towards her. And Khal wasn't simply testing his horse, Beth realised, he was riding for his life! As she must, if Hana wasn't to lose both her parents in one catastrophic incident.

She had never galloped flat-out, but now she must, it was that or become swallowed up by the sand. Pressing the little pony as hard as she could, Beth leaned forward in the saddle, gripping hanks of mane to keep her safe. Ramming her heels down in the stirrups, she prayed she wouldn't fall off. It was hard to see where she was going as the driving dust began to catch up with her. And then she saw a shadow, and realised Khal had spotted her and turned round. He was going to cross her path. He was coming for her, coming to save her, Beth realised, sobbing with relief. He was waving a warning, and pointing to the shelter of the fort. It was little enough protection, but she could see it was the only hope they had. To turn for the palace meant turning into the path of the storm. Thoughts of Hana drove Beth forward. Her baby couldn't lose both her parents!

The pony strained beneath her, moving as fast as it could, with its ears back and its eyes wild, as aware as she was that this was one race it couldn't afford to lose. 'Don't fall off!' Beth chanted to herself grimly as the sand scoured her skin and clouded her eyes, making them water. But as the roaring grew steadily louder Beth began to realize there was no hope.

But now Khal had cut across her path, and was galloping alongside her. 'Lose your stirrups!'

Take her feet out of the stirrups? Was he mad? She'd fall off! 'Leave me! Save yourself! I'll catch up.' They both knew that would never happen. But she didn't stand a chance, so at least one of them could be saved.

'Do it!' he snapped. Leaning across at full gallop, he caught hold of her reins and brought their two horses closer.

Her teeth were juddering in her jaw as she risked a glance. Khal wasn't going anywhere unless she went with him. He wasn't even going to try to save himself. She freed her feet, her scream of terror lost in a thunder of hooves as Khal grabbed her firmly round the waist. He yanked her into his arms. His horse sprang forward competitively as Beth's mount raced ahead, freed of the weight on its back, while Beth clung to Khal in a state of shock and pure relief.

He held her tight and safe in front of him as the stallion galloped for the fort. They were muscle to muscle, flesh to flesh, as he called out and thrashed the reins from side to side on its neck to urge the stallion on. Beth wasn't even sure she breathed again until they raced beneath the archway into a maze of ancient buildings, but the wall of sand followed them even there, blowing them deeper into the crumbling sanctuary. Khal dragged Beth with him as he dismounted, and her pony blundered blindly in after them. Capturing his reins as well as the stallion's, Khal led both horses as well as Beth to the shelter of a wall where perhaps they stood a chance.

'You saved my life!' Beth gasped, pressing back against the stone in an attempt to keep upright as the storm rushed over them.

'Not yet!' Khal rasped grimly, shielding her with his body, arms planted either side of her face as he yelled at her. 'What were you doing out here in the desert on your own? Don't you know how dangerous it is?'

No, she didn't, and the fierce expression on Khal's face told Beth he was thinking of another time, and another far more dreadful incident than this, an incident that had ripped out his heart. 'I'm sorry.'

'Sorry? You could have been killed.'

'Khal, please, I know I shouldn't have—'

'You know nothing,' he cut across her fiercely, and then his face contorted, and as she reached out to him he pulled away. 'Life is precious.'

'Forgive me.' But Khal wasn't interested in her compassion now, and shook her off.

'We just have to hope we get lucky and the storm veers away,' he told her grimly.

Subject closed. How she wished she could find something to say to touch the pain inside him and ease it somehow.

And the storm didn't veer away. Instead the sand and dust continued to pour into their ruined sanctuary. 'Here,' Khal said, ripping the bandana from his neck. 'Cover your pony's eyes.' Tearing off his shirt, he wrapped it around his stallion's head. Then, dragging Beth to him, he kept his arm over her head as she buried her face in his chest.

'You saved my life,' she whispered unheard against Khal's hard, unyielding flesh. She couldn't believe he'd done this for her; she couldn't believe they had survived. All she wanted to do now was thank him, heal him, save him… 'Khal, speak to me,' she begged him when the noise of the storm had abated a little.

'About what?' But, when he saw she knew and understood, and that it was no use hiding the facts from her any longer, he grated out, 'I lost her here in the desert.'

'Who did you lose?' Beth probed gently.

'My sister, Ghayda. I lost her to the quicksand. I couldn't save her…'

'Oh, Khal, I'm so sorry…' It explained so much about him. And it also told Beth that, though she loved Khal as much as she did, it wasn't enough, and that she must help him lose this heavy burden of guilt or he would never be capable of feeling again. Forgetting how he'd shrugged her off, she put her arms around him and held him, not in lust but with love and compassion, as the wind roared around them.

They seemed to stand there for hours until Khal informed her that, as he'd hoped, the storm had swung away. So it had, Beth realised with surprise as Khal eased free of her embrace. She had been so swept up in a different storm, a storm of their own making, that she hadn't even noticed. But now she felt like celebrating, because, for all the tons of sand that had poured in through the gaps in the stonework, half-burying them, they were alive, *they had made it through together!*

Beth's first thought was for Hana. 'Will they know what's happened to us at the palace?'

'You can ring them.' Khal pulled out a phone and handed it to her. 'When you're finished, I must speak to my aide-de-camp.'

Beth stared at the small mobile-phone. It seemed impossible there could still be communication with the outside world after all that had happened.

'Is Hana all right?' Khal asked the moment Beth ended the call.

'She's fine, sleeping soundly.'

It was so strange to have someone who cared as much about Hana as she did, Beth thought, as Khal delivered his information in brisk, no-nonsense Arabic. Right now she was proud to call him the father of her child. And then, perhaps because all her emotions had been stretched and tested to the limit, the most inappropriate emotion of all surfaced.

'What?' Khal said, frowning at her as he stowed the phone in his breeches.

'Do I look like you?' Beth had to press her lips down very hard to stop herself giggling, because her tall, dark, handsome sheikh had been transformed by the dust of the desert into a snowman. His thick, wavy black hair was fully coated, and his face was white too.

Khal retaliated with a scorching survey of his own. 'I don't know about me, but you could do with a wash,' he said dryly.

'Some hope of that!'

'You'd be surprised,' he said, with a slight tug of his lips that made her heart turn over.

'I certainly would,' she agreed, determined to appear cool.

'Come with me if you don't believe me.'

As Beth stared at Khal's outstretched hand, her humour gave way to emotion. 'You saved my life,' she whispered again huskily.

'And you've got guts.' His eyes shot fire into her heart, and then he laughed. 'And you look like a chimney sweep.'

And you look gorgeous even now, Beth thought. 'You don't think I'm going to go anywhere with you, do you?' she teased him. 'You could be anyone under that desert-sand face mask.'

'Could we market them at the stores, do you think?' he said, pretending to think about it. 'It's the best exfoliation I've ever had.'

Did he have to thumb the stubble on his jaw like that? 'A speciality line, maybe?' Beth suggested, enjoying the joke

'That's something we can talk about later.'

'Later?' She loved the sound of that word.

'But right now,' he said, reaching for her hand, 'It's bath time…'

'You were serious!' Beth exclaimed in astonishment as she stared at the small lagoon.

'You've never heard of an oasis in the desert?'

'Of course I have.' But this was beautiful, and she'd always thought the pictures she'd seen before must have been doctored to make things look more appealing. She couldn't imagine such lushness existed in the midst of such sun-parched nothingness. But the best thing of all was that she hadn't seen Khal so relaxed for a long time. 'Snatching your life from the jaws of death' syndrome, perhaps. But didn't both of them have every right to feel on top of the world?

'Engines?' Beth frowned, unwilling to believe anyone or anything would dare trespass upon their solitude.

'Helicopters,' Khal confirmed. 'Now they know where I am, there will be guards, guns… But don't worry—all my personal staff are trained to use the utmost discretion,' he added, seeing Beth's concern.

'And that's just another price you have to pay?'

He shrugged. 'I owe it to my people to stay alive.'

The dangers were all around him. It made her want to affirm the difference between living and life with him with everything she'd got.

He took pleasure in her wonder at their surroundings, and at the same time he was filled with an enormous sense of relief and happiness. The fact that they were alive, the fact that they were together, was all that mattered to him. The past and their disagreements seemed insignificant in the light of what they'd just been through. Going through it together and coming out safely the other side had to mean something. And it did. He hadn't realised just how much Beth Tracey Torrance meant to him until losing her had become a real possibility.

'This is the Pearl Oasis of Q'Adar,' he murmured, hardly liking to intrude on her rapt contemplation of the scene. With her chin raised, and her face in profile with the breeze fluffing out her hair, she looked so beautiful.

'The Pearl Oasis of Q'Adar,' she repeated, turning slowly to face him.

'Named for the lady Moon, who chooses to bathe here more frequently than in any other pool in the whole of Arabia.'

'And I don't blame her!' Beth told him, with her eyes full of light. 'It's so beautiful...'

He followed her gaze, to watch the crescent lantern glowing in the sky with its sprinkling of stars in attendance, and thought Beth twice as lovely. Below the moon the jagged peaks of the mountains cut sharply into the velvet sky, and lower still the oasis rippled lazily, so that the long streaks of milky moonlight reflected in its waters appeared to dance. Easing his neck, he exhaled with contentment. Standing here with Beth made him feel reborn. She made him see how beautiful this land, his kingdom, was, and how full of possibility it could be. He could forget the battles and think of a peaceful future with Beth at his side.

Beth stood in silence, drinking it in in case she never came here again. It was beyond beauty, beyond her experience, and reinforced what she already knew: that the majesty of nature far outweighed that of man. Time passed in solemn step between them, as they stood without word or explanation, and Beth felt they were growing closer all the time, floating in another world—the world of their thoughts, where possibilities were endless if you only had the courage to reach out and make them fact. She could have stayed happily all night, dreaming, but once again reality intruded and she became aware of scratchy sand in all manner of tender places. 'Do you think my clothes will dry if I take them off and rinse them?' she said, turning to Khal.

'By morning they should.'

'But doesn't it get cold in the desert at night?' Beth said, frowning.

'Not necessarily…'

CHAPTER THIRTEEN

KHAL built a big, warm fire and they set up camp around it. Their next job was to bathe the horses' eyes and make them comfortable, which Khal suggested they could do in the oasis.

'Do you mean take them swimming?'

'It's the best way to clean away all the dust and grit,' he said. 'What are you doing?'

Beth jumped as Khal turned from checking his horse's legs to stare at her. She had just been peering down the front of her shirt to see if her underwear would pass muster. Pulling her hand out, she laughed self-consciously. Khal had been half-naked for some time now. 'It's all right for a man,' she said. 'But how can I strip off?' The moment she spoke, Beth wished she hadn't. The look Khal gave her cracked the dust on his cheek. He was right. Wasn't it a bit late for false modesty?

'Please yourself,' he said, easing his powerful shoulders in a shrug. 'But I'm going swimming.'

And Beth had to admit the oasis did look tempting. She took a step back as Khal reached out. 'Your face looks sore,' he said, lowering his hand without touching her. 'The water will clean the dust away. It's what you need.'

Beth didn't answer. She only had to watch Khal's muscles

flex as he checked his stallion over to know what she needed, and it was more than a wash.

Having removed the last of the horses' tack, Khal clicked his tongue against the roof of his mouth and they followed him to the lip of the lagoon. 'I can't manage both of them,' he said. 'You'll have to come and help me…'

Beth watched transfixed as he unfastened his breeches and took them off. His black finest-cotton pants followed…

'You must have sand everywhere,' he said, turning to face her.

No wonder he had no inhibitions, Beth thought. Even in the shadowy moonlight Khal's body was magnificent, a supreme work of nature, only exceeded by his supreme lack of self-consciousness as he sprang effortlessly onto his stallion's back. 'What are you waiting for?' he said, turning to look at her over his shoulder.

For the fire to die down inside her, maybe? Though hopefully the cool water should accomplish that! Beth thought, waiting until the stallion had swum out a way. She had no idea why, when they had a child together, she should feel so self-conscious about the prospect of skinny-dipping with Khal. It was as if they were only now getting to know each other. She took her clothes off as quickly as she could, and, using the slope of the bank to her advantage, climbed up easily onto her pony's back. Squeezing her knees, she urged it into the water.

This was like something out of a film, Beth thought, as the warm breeze caressed her and the moon shone down on them. She rocked gently with surge of the pony's paddling motion, heading out towards Khal. He was right; after a grit bath this was just what she needed…he was just what she needed. And, judging by the angle of their horses' pricked ears, they thought so too.

She looked like a moon goddess coming towards him. The light was a strange mix of silver and some phosphorescent trickery conjured up by the light and the lingering heat. It gave her an aura that shimmered on her naked skin as her horse stepped out, and their mounts snickered companionably as she smiled at him.

He had been standing waiting for her, with the stallion fetlock-deep just off the shore beneath the shelter of some trees, wondering if he had ever felt so relaxed. When she reached him their mounts turned lazily towards a patch of grass that had survived the blistering heat of day beneath its canopy of leaves. Sound was contained by the mountains, and the swish of water as their horses moved through it seemed amplified, as did the hoot and scrabble of creatures of the night they couldn't see. The fantasy that they were alone in the world expanded and held firm for him. Beth's modesty was protected by her long blonde hair, which had curled damply around her nipples, allowing him no more than a tantalising glimpse of her breasts. She made no attempt to hide them, and as usual her chin was tipped at a confident angle. Anything she did she did wholeheartedly, and the way she had recovered after the storm had only increased his admiration for her.

'We can safely leave them to crop the grass,' he said, dismounting from his horse. He came to help Beth down, and then the spell broke when she looked at him, because they both knew what would happen if she came into his arms.

'Why don't we swim?' she said, pulling back.

It hurt him more to see her innocent enthusiasm change to apprehension. The depth of her hurt and uncertainty about her future in Q'Adar was reflected in her face. In all honesty there was nothing he could say to reassure her—but he had saved her once, and now he wanted to save her again, and if that meant spending time with her... 'Do you mean you want to go back in and swim without the horses?'

'That's exactly what I mean,' she said, staring past him. 'I've dreamed of swimming in the moonlight all my life, and I never thought I'd get the chance.'

'Then tonight you will.' Desire blazed inside him as he reached up for her. He could think of nothing but making her smile and relax again. He kept a safe distance between them as he lifted her down. 'Before we swim I'm going to stoke the fire, so it will blaze all night and dry your clothes.'

'I'll help you collect firewood,' she offered.

'Brushwood, dried grass, twigs, anything you can find...' The desert wasn't generous with her scraps.

When that was done, she stood with her hand on her hips, watching him. 'You make a mean fire, Sheikh...'

Enjoying the fact that she was relaxed now, he turned and gave her a mock bow. Then he saw her cheeks were blazing. They had been riding and walking in shadows, with the darkness concealing their nakedness, but like Eve she was aware of it now, and like Eve she wanted to run and hide and cover herself. He didn't want that for Beth. He didn't want her to feel ashamed, ever. It was important to him that she retained both her innocence and her pride. Reaching out, he took her hand to give her confidence, and just linking hands with her filled him with an emotion he'd never known before. They both knew this couldn't go anywhere, but while they had these few hours together why shouldn't they steal what pleasure they could?

Swimming with Khal in the moonlight was amazing. He was a much stronger swimmer than she was, but each time he overtook her he lay floating on his back, waiting for her to catch up as she thrashed energetically in the freestyle she'd learned at school.

'That was absolutely brilliant!' Beth exclaimed, finding her feet in the shallow water. But as the stones shifted she lost her balance and, lurching forward, grabbed on to Khal. He steadied her before letting go. 'It must be boring for you having to swim with me.'

'Why?' he said, lips curving into his delicious smile.

Beth changed tack rapidly. 'I've never seen a moon so bright, have you?'

'Or so many stars…' Raking his hands through his hair to move it from his face, Khal leaned back into the water, floating, and Beth thought she had never seen him so relaxed. She was relaxed too, lost in the moment, thinking about the real man: the man in front of her now, the man who had previously been concealed beneath a cloak of power. When he stood she absorbed the stillness between them. She was aching for him to kiss her, and so she did the right thing and quickly moved away.

'Now, what are we going to do?' she said, adopting a perky voice. What indeed? How to retire with her self-respect intact when she was naked? 'You'd better get out first, and I won't look,' she suggested.

'Or we could stay here a little longer,' Khal argued.

'And get cold?' Beth countered.

Khal's smile was so rare and so wicked, it made Beth doubt her self-control. 'All right, I suppose I could warm you with my wit.' The ironic expression on his face suggested not. 'Or you should just turn your back and let me get out?'

'I prefer the first option.'

'You do?'

'You offered to warm me,' Khal reminded her, slicking water off his arms.

'I did?'

'Well?' he prompted. 'I'm still waiting.'

The moment of decision had come; she couldn't keep on

ducking and diving all night, and the moment she lifted her arms towards him she was lost. The hunger inside them both had been suppressed for far too long, and as Khal dragged her to him her inhibitions fell away. 'Hold me close,' she begged him; it was she who needed warming.

'Closer than this isn't possible.'

'Yes, it is. You know it is,' Beth argued.

He did know that. Swinging her into his arms, he carried her into the deeper water where he could stand and she could not. It hardly mattered, since her legs were already locked around his waist. 'You've got me,' he murmured against her mouth.

'You'd better believe it,' she told him.

With Beth safe in one arm, he cupped her face with his hand and kissed her. She tasted like the missing part of him, and felt like it too. He hadn't realised how much he'd missed her, and he knew she must feel the same, because her feelings came pouring out in tears that he kissed away.

How could they ever get enough of each other? Even the chill of the water couldn't cool them now. She opened for him like a flower, leaning back as he eased into her, calling his name as her fingers bit into him, exhaling raggedly, eyes closed, giving herself up to pleasure.

Beth had blossomed into a woman since having the baby. She even tasted different, sweet and ripe and wonderful; everything about her was wonderful. She was hot for him, hot and wet, and her muscles gripped him with remorseless intent as he thrust deeper, taking her again and again, timing each thrust to the ebb of her sighs. He wanted nothing more than to give her pleasure. It was all that mattered to him. He wanted to watch her face and hear her moans of ecstasy, he wanted to serve her and see her dissolve into sensation; he wanted to make love to her until nothing existed for them outside of this…

'Oh, Khal, I can't hold back.'

'You don't have to.' The words had barely left his mouth before she bucked beneath him, and the sounds pouring from her lips became unfocused, unthinking and free. Free, as he longed to be.

When the storm of their love-making subsided, Khal carried her safely to the shore. 'Do you feel warm now?' Beth teased him.

'Do you?'

'I do now,' she purred as he joined her on their makeshift bed of grass.

'Then my job's done.'

As he made to pull away she drew him back. 'I see you still have the bad habit of teasing me.' She stopped, not wanting to refer back to any time that hadn't been as happy as this. It was as if they had ventured into a magic kingdom, and she wasn't ready for reality yet. 'Your Majesty,' she said, lying back to tempt him on.

'Khal,' he said, pausing for a kiss.

And even that wasn't something she could joke about. Khal's title and his position in the world carried too much weight. And that weight was all on his shoulders. 'Khal,' she amended softly, tracing the line of his hard, scarred mouth with her fingertip.

'That's better,' he said, capturing her finger and warming it in his mouth.

He drew her into his arms and made love to her slowly this time, drawing out the pleasure until it couldn't be contained. In the water they had come together like two elemental beings who knew only a primitive urge to mate, but he wanted this to be different for Beth, and for him. Maybe he wanted something to remember her by, Khal reflected, something to keep him warm, and remind him what innocence could taste like after his inevitable return to the real world. He soothed her down, and then kissed her until she told him that she couldn't wait and that her whole body ached for him again. He refused to rush and kissed his way down her body until he reached her feet, and then he massaged them until she was purring like a kitten. He turned her then to drop kisses on the backs of her knees, which made her squirm and laugh.

'I had no idea...' Her words disintegrated.

'No idea?' He was moving on to feather kisses on her pale, silky thighs.

'That my legs could be so sensitive.'

'You have so much to learn.'

'And will you teach me?'

'For as long as you are here in Q'Adar.' He felt her tense. It broke the mood. The length of time they'd have together was something neither one of them could predict.

'I want you so much.' *And not just sexually*, though she must never tell Khal that. 'I can't believe this night must end...' They lay together side by side, gazing at the stars.

'The night doesn't end until the fire goes out,' Khal murmured.

'And as you've just put wood on it...' Turning on her stomach, Beth found her cheeky smile. 'It's so special out here in the desert, isn't it?'

'I think so.'

'I thought I'd hate it. I thought it would be barren, and cruel and hard.'

'It is barren and cruel and hard.'

'But it's beautiful too.' She turned to him after a few more stolen minutes. 'We should be getting back for Hana.'

'I won't break my promise,' Khal said. Reaching for her hand, he pressed the palm to his lips. 'You'll be back before Hana wakes...'

She tried not to say anything, but as they stared at each other she couldn't hold the words back. 'And then?'

'And then life carries on as before.'

Beth's heart sank, and Khal telling her not to look so sad didn't help. She shouldn't be greedy; they'd had this night, this one magical night…

'Let's go and get the horses saddled up,' Khal suggested, springing to his feet. 'Our clothes are dry,' he confirmed, checking them out.

Reality had intruded, Beth realised, and now the dream was fading fast. There would be no more kisses and no more lingering looks as they tacked up the horses, ready to go. This was it.

Khal gave her a leg up and asked her if she felt safe before springing onto the back of his stallion.

Safe…

'Let's enjoy the ride back,' he said, sensing her dejection. They should make the most of it, because he had nothing else to offer her—and though that left him feeling deeply unsatisfied it didn't mean they couldn't enjoy every moment they had left.

CHAPTER FOURTEEN

HE STOOD outside Hana's room the next morning, watching Beth nurse their baby. They had spent the night apart, and coming here to see them both had filled him with emotion. And yet he felt shut out too. It was the loss of all the months when he hadn't been there for them. But there was a better understanding between them now, and no reason why he shouldn't raise the subject of Beth staying on as his mistress. She had mellowed since having Hana, and he was more sensitive to her needs. His timing had been clumsy before, but this time, when he showed Beth the benefits of remaining in Q'Adar under his protection, he felt sure that she would see sense.

In spite of all the uncertainty, Beth was touched by the expression in Khal's eyes when she tiptoed out of Hana's room. There was such longing in them, as well as a softness she hadn't seen before. 'Were you spying on me?'

'I was admiring your parenting skills,' Khal admitted, falling into step with her. 'Hana's so contented, and that's all thanks to you, Beth. You're a wonderful mother.'

'Thank you...' Beth felt a little glow of pride and love for him, and, without suspecting anything, accepted Khal's suggestion that they have a refreshing drink together.

'I've been thinking about our future,' he said, showing her into a shaded courtyard.

A fountain was tossing cooling plumes of rainbow spray into the air, and all around her there was something beautiful for Beth's glance to light on. She wondered if she had ever felt happier.

'It needn't be like this.' Khal's look burned into her eyes.

But it was inevitable that it would be like this, Beth thought dreamily. When you loved as much as she did, how else could it be? The world glittered with a new light; it was a better place, and everything in it jumped into clear focus when you were in love.

'I don't like to see you upset,' Khal said, drawing her out of the sun. 'I don't like to hear you talking about lawyers—and most of all,' he confessed, 'I don't like to hear myself laying down the law where you're concerned.'

'Are you telling me you're a reformed character?' Beth teased, feeling the glow of love she felt for Khal burst into flame. She felt like laughing for joy, and racing round the courtyard, spinning as she went in an effort to express the excitement and happiness inside her. She managed somehow to restrain herself and continue teasing him instead. 'So you came round to my way of thinking in the end?'

'I can't say,' Khal admitted, 'As I don't know what you were thinking.' He held Beth's gaze until she blushed and looked away. 'I'd like to think you were hoping we could spend more time together.'

'With Hana.'

'Of course with Hana,' he reassured her, 'Like a proper family.'

Beth's face lit with hope.

'That is what you want, isn't it?'

'More than anything in the world.' She couldn't believe it.

She couldn't believe Khal was telling her they could be together. But now his face had darkened, and Beth watched in concern as he stared without seeing into some place that gave him pain.

'The dust storm in the desert when I almost lost you...'

'Oh, Khal...' Remembering his confession about his sister, Beth realised Khal was not in a position to enjoy the type of joy she was feeling. Touching his arm, she stared into his face. 'You saved my life, and I can never repay you.'

He seemed surprised. 'You don't owe me anything. If I'd lost you—'

'But you *didn't* lose me, I'm here. I'll always be here for you.'

'I know you mean that.'

'I do,' Beth declared passionately. Khal, who had never revealed his feelings to anyone, was sharing them with her. She couldn't remember when she had felt so moved, or so full of love, apart from the moment when she'd first held Hana in her arms. And now her dreams had come true, and they were all going to be together like a proper family.

'Until the sandstorm I didn't realise how much you meant to me. I didn't realise what life would be like without you. And with Hana living here in the palace with us... My daughter, Hana.' Khal's strong face softened momentarily. 'Say you'll stay with me here in Q'Adar.'

'You'd do this for us?' She searched his gaze. When she thought about all the difficulties Khal would have to face, and the criticism for taking a wife from such a very different background, she admired him even more. 'You're serious about this, aren't you?'

'Never more so,' he assured her firmly. 'Hana and you are all I want. I didn't realise how far I would be prepared to go to ensure our future together. The events of last night have crystallised everything in my mind and helped me to see clearly where you're concerned.'

'Oh, Khal…' Reaching up, Beth touched his face with her soft, warm hands. 'You pretend to be so hard, but you're just like me, aren't you? We both have that empty space inside us that only one person can fill. It's recognising that person when they come along.'

With Khal's love shining down on her, and Hana safe and well, Beth knew everything would be all right. She wasn't going to waste another minute worrying about the likelihood of a Liverpool shop-girl marrying the ruler of Q'Adar. She would just get on with it as she always did. She would take instruction from Khal and his advisors. She would learn the language and study the culture and history of Q'Adar. She would seek out charities she could champion and learn how best to help them. And, most important of all, she'd help Hana to understand the richness of her heritage from both sides of the world.

'So will you stay with me, Beth Tracey Torrance?' Khal asked her gently, bringing her in front of him. 'Will you live with me and love with me?'

Trustingly holding his gaze, Beth whispered, 'You know I will…'

He wanted to reward Beth for the courage she had shown during the sandstorm, and most of all for facing up to her new life in Q'Adar with such strong-minded determination. He wanted to give her a taste of what she could expect as his mistress in Q'Adar.

'What's this, Khal?' she said, her face lighting with surprise as he brought her into his private sitting-room. He had been impatient as she'd settled Hana in her cot, having made these preparations earlier. He couldn't wait to see Beth's face when she saw all the gifts he had for her.

'Are you excited?' he said as she stared at the gift-wrapped packages. He realised she must be overwhelmed, and wanted to reassure her as she started opening them. 'If the jewels aren't to your taste, I can easily send for more—'

'More?' Beth breathed as she stared at him, and then at the tumble of jewels falling through her fingers. 'Are these real?'

'Real? Of course they're real.' He was pleased with her reaction, and this was only the start. Clapping his hands summoned a servant, who brought a bronze casket and placed it on the table where Beth was sitting. The man retired at his signal and closed the door. Reaching inside the pocket of his robe, he gave Beth a key. Instead of pouncing on the casket as he had expected her to, she frowned and turned the heavy old key over in her hands. 'Why don't you open the box instead of fiddling with the key?' he suggested. He was impatient to move on to the next part of his surprise, and had to stop himself taking the key from her and opening the box himself.

He managed to restrain himself as she fumbled with the ancient lock. He noticed then that her hands were shaking, and tried to tell himself that excitement was the cause—but her face said something else. She looked apprehensive, which made him feel mildly irritated. He couldn't understand, when he was trying to give her all the things she'd never had, why she should be hesitating.

What did all this mean? Beth wondered. Hadn't she told Khal over and over again that he didn't need to buy her, and that she didn't want anything from him? An ugly suspicion had begun to take root in her mind, and that suspicion said Khal hadn't changed, and was using his wealth to tempt her to stay on in Q'Adar. When she had already agreed to do so, Beth thought, frowning.

She prayed she was wrong as she opened the lid of the old

box. She stared inside, and didn't know whether to be relieved or not. There was nothing in it except for a bunch of keys and some photographs. 'What are these?' she said, lifting them out. The photographs showed a very grand house that appeared to be in England. Set in parkland, there was a lake to one side of it, and a garden formally laid out at the front. She told herself it probably meant nothing, and that the wife of a sheikh would have to have a grand residence—even though all she wanted was Khal and Hana and a proper family, just as he'd promised her. 'House keys?'

Khal's lips curved. 'Do you like it?'

'Is this our new residence in England?'

'I bought it for you, Beth.'

'For me...' She should be thrilled, but her guts were twisting. 'You mean we'll live here together?'

'You know I live in Q'Adar. It's for you whenever you want to return to England. I may visit you there from time to time. I don't ever want you to feel trapped here, Beth. That's why I bought it for you.'

He made it sound as if they would live part of their lives completely independent of each other. Did married couples do that?

'Once you're under my protection, you'll have to have an appropriate residence in England.'

Under his protection? Beth's apprehension grew. Were all her dreams about to come crashing down? She gazed at the discarded jewels on the table, and then at the photographs and keys.

'You made it clear you didn't like the penthouse,' Khal went on when she looked to him for answers. 'And so I bought you another property. You will need a garden, I can see that.'

'A garden?' Beth's voice was shaking uncontrollably. 'I need more than a garden, Khal.'

'And you shall have more,' he soothed. 'You will have a home here in Q'Adar, as well as a mansion in Liverpool.'

'But I don't want a mansion in Liverpool.'

'I understand this has all come as a shock to you,' Khal said indulgently. 'But as my mistress you must get used to accepting gifts.'

Shaking her head, Beth stumbled to her feet.

'And I want to give you the old fort too.'

'Khal, please…' She held out her hands; they were shaking. 'Please, stop this!'

'I thought you liked the old fort,' Khal said, frowning. 'I thought you were fascinated by its history—'

'I am!' Beth wailed, knowing if the stones had fallen down and buried her she couldn't have felt as bad as she did right now.

'Well, then?' Khal said, clearly thrown by her lack of enthusiasm.

This was not the tender lover she had known in the desert, the man who had sheltered her and saved her life. This was the ruler of Q'Adar, a man who expected his every wish to be a command, and who knew less than nothing about love.

'I'm determined to have the old fort renovated,' he went on, as if oblivious to her torment. 'And it will be good for you to take an interest in the project.'

'Good for me?' Beth clutched her chest. 'You never were talking about marriage, were you?'

'Marriage?' he said. 'What are you talking about?'

'You must think I'm naïve,' Beth said, unable to stem the tears pouring down her face. 'You'd be right—I am naïve, and stupid too.'

'Of course you're not stupid.'

'I was making plans, Khal…I'd planned everything we'd do together when we were married, for Hana, and for Q'Adar…'

'You can still do these things; I don't see what's changed.'

She laughed, a sad sound. 'I'm wasting my time thinking there's a human being under those robes, aren't I? There isn't a human being behind your title, there's just the ruler of Q'Adar—a cold, unfeeling man.' She shook him off when he tried to take hold of her. 'A man who will stop at nothing to get what he wants, even if that means trampling over those who love him.'

'Beth—'

'No, Khal!' She shook him off. 'Did you think you could stick me away out of sight in the old fort so I'd be there at your convenience, and buy my silence with a holiday home in Liverpool? No!' she warned him again. 'Stay away from me! You talked about love. You talked about how much I meant to you, when all the time you were planning this—'

'I was trying to show you how much you mean to me.'

'By setting me up in a love nest at the old fort?'

'Eventually, when the renovations were completed, I did think we could meet there—'

'Far away from prying eyes?'

'I was thinking of you.'

'And yourself too, no doubt!'

'I thought the renovation project would provide you with an ongoing interest.'

'Don't you dare patronise me, Khal. I don't need anything to keep me busy. I'm a mother, I've got Hana, and I work for my living back in England.'

'You can't just cut me out of your life,' Khal reminded her.

'And you can't ignore mine. You have no idea, do you?' she exclaimed. 'To you a relationship between a man and a woman is all about ownership and possession. For me, it's about the freedom to love unconditionally—'

'And that's the difference between us,' he cut across her. 'I'm the realist, Beth, and you're the dreamer.'

'And you dream of a warm bed and welcoming arms at the fort? No way, Khal! You can't stick me away in the desert and enjoy me whenever you have a spare moment.'

'Don't make it sound so sordid.'

'Isn't it?' She backed away from him, from his scent, from his heat, from his overwhelming presence. 'What type of role models do you think we'd make for Hana if I do as you suggest?'

'Hana is a princess of Q'Adar, and will have an army of servants—'

'Hana doesn't *need* an army of servants, what she needs is love and security.'

'And you think I wouldn't give her that?'

'I would never stop you seeing Hana, you know that, Khal. You also know I will never stay here as your mistress.'

'I've only just got Hana back, and I won't let you take her out of Q'Adar.'

'No court in the land would refuse you joint custody—'

'No court in which land?'

Beth shuddered involuntarily. The man she had so briefly known had disappeared, and she was confronting a stranger determined to impose his will on her. 'Please don't be unreasonable. This is our daughter we're talking about.'

'Exactly. Hana will live in the royal apartments, with me and with other members of the royal family.'

Beth paled as the truth sank in. 'And if you had your way Hana's mother would be housed some miles away, out of sight in the old fort? I don't think so.'

He stopped her leaving at the door. 'Where do you think you're going?'

'Away from you—to the nursery,' Beth said as her thoughts came into clear focus. 'I'm going to collect Hana, pack our cases, and get out of here—I'm going to take Hana home.'

'This is her home, and if you want to go, if you want to leave without your daughter, so be it.'

Beth could only stare at Khal in astonishment. 'You can't mean that. You can't imagine I would leave without Hana?'

'Hana's place is in Q'Adar with me, as is yours.'

'My *place*? Should I know my *place*, Khal? Is that it? Should I be grateful for all your bounty?' Beth cast a disparaging glance at the discarded jewels. 'I've never known my place, and I can't be bought. Now, open this door,' she said, rattling the handle. 'Let me out of here!'

'You can go,' he said, releasing his hold on the door. 'But Hana stays with me.'

'Stay with you? Do you think I want my daughter growing up with a stone for a heart? You think everything can be fixed with money and power, but I know it can't. I know when I'm being offered something worthless.'

'Worthless? I'm offering you a home and security!'

'Shut away as your mistress?' When he remained silent, Beth shook her head. 'It's an empty gesture, Khal. I already have a home, and Hana and I have everything we need.'

'As a royal princess of Q'Adar, Hana will need round-the-clock security, can you give her that?'

Beth paled as the helplessness of her position sank in.

CHAPTER FIFTEEN

'IT DOESN'T have to be like this,' Khal told her as Beth turned her face from his blazing stare. 'I never meant to hurt you. Beth, please listen to me. You shouldn't be so stubborn. You don't have to stand alone. You don't have to be brave all the time.'

'Yes, I do.'

As she bit her fist to stem the tears, he knew he ruled a country in which millions of people depended on him, but could see no way out of this. Having Beth stand broken in front of him was more than he could bear, and he would do anything to make it right for her. Anything except marry her, of course. He could never do that. 'What can I do to make this better for you?'

'Nothing,' she told him bluntly, recovering. 'You can't do anything. Just let me appoint a lawyer who can help me sort this out.'

'I can help you sort it out.'

'I don't want your type of solution.'

'We could live as a family here.'

'Until you were married? I won't live some charade in Q'Adar, Khal.'

'As my mistress you're not at risk,' he said pragmatically. 'You would be safe to return to the house in Liverpool whenever you wanted to.'

'And leave Hana here with you and your bride?'

Folding his hands inside the sleeves of his robe, Khal stared at her levelly. 'I suggest you go and think about this Beth…think about all your options.'

She stared at him, the man she loved—a man so changed she hardly recognised him. 'I'll do that, Your Majesty,' Beth said tensely.

She had no intention of sitting around doing nothing, or of accepting her fate as decreed by His Majesty, Khalifa Kadir al Hassan. She rang the airport and booked a flight. It was that simple. Then she went to the nursery, and, after speaking to the staff on duty, lifted Hana from her cot. She had no intention of running off or sneaking away; she would do this properly. Hana wouldn't be at risk for an instant, because she would phone the Foreign Office in England and have the appropriate security measures put in place for when they landed. She had tried reason, but Khal wasn't interested, so now she would take action. Then later in England she would appoint a solicitor to act for them.

Beth asked one of the professional nannies to accompany her. 'Just as far as the airport,' she explained as they left the palace through a side gate. She had telephoned ahead to the coach house where there were drivers on duty night and day. 'I want His Majesty reassured that Hana boarded the aircraft safely.'

The woman assured her that she would do this, and Beth thanked her before climbing into the rear of the limousine with Hana asleep in her arms

He guessed Beth would be in the nursery with Hana. When he discovered they were gone, he issued an all-points alert to close the borders. But if possible he intended to apprehend them himself. Beth's route was clear in his mind. She would try to take Hana back to England where she would feel safe. The controller on duty at the coach house confirmed this. The next thing he did was call up the limousine and tell the driver to return to the palace with his passengers immediately. When he'd done that, he'd jump in a Jeep to follow them overland while his helicopters circled overhead.

They had been driving for some time when Beth asked the driver to stop. He had been driving far too fast in Beth's opinion, and she was concerned for their safety on the bumpy road. She rapped on the glass when he didn't respond, and was alarmed when he ignored her.

'He's not our usual man,' the nanny at her side told her. 'I haven't seen him at the palace before.'

'Great.' Beth tightened her grip on Hana. Had she brought them all into danger? Now she knew why Khal had been so concerned. He hadn't wanted to frighten her, but she had gone about things in her usual stubborn way. If this was some clumsy kidnap attempt, then they were all in danger, even Khal. She had to warn him, and she must protect Hana and the nanny. But what could she do when she had no weapons to defend them, and wouldn't have known how to use them if she had? She was a stranger to the country and the driver could be taking them anywhere.

'He's taking the road to the border,' the nanny whispered, as if reading her mind.

'Then we must stop him,' Beth murmured back. All she knew was that they were in the wilderness somewhere between the palace and the airport. She rapped on the glass. When the man still ignored her, she resorted to panic measures. 'I have to change the baby's nappy now!' Beth yelled down the intercom. 'I can't do it on this bumpy road, so I suggest you stop unless you want a mess back here. Stop!' she said again, when he didn't answer. 'I think my baby's ill. You'll be held responsible if anything happens to her!'

There was a second when the limousine didn't waver, and then the brakes went on, and it slewed terrifyingly from side to side before finally screeching to a halt.

'That stone memorial,' Beth whispered to the nanny. 'Can you see it? When we stop I want you to hide Hana under your clothes, and then make for those bushes. Don't run, just walk calmly, as if you want some privacy, and don't be distracted by anything.' The woman was shaking, but Beth had to trust her now. 'Keep Hana safe until I come for you.' While she was talking, Beth was making a bundle of Hana's spare clothing, which she then wrapped in a shawl so it appeared she still had the baby. 'My maid needs to relieve herself,' she told the driver when he stopped the car.

'Good idea,' he agreed, and got out too.

It was the best opportunity she was going to get. Taking the driver's seat, Beth gunned the engine, making for the stone memorial where she could see the nanny crouching down, hiding Hana. Beth's heart was hammering as she attempted to manoeuvre the big car but she wasn't used to driving on sand. The door snapped back on its hinges as the vehicle jerked forward, and then it careered across rocks and gullies until finally she lost control of the wheel and the tyres started to spin.

Leaping out, Beth could see the tyres were buried to the wheel-wells. There wasn't a chance she could manoeuvre the limousine out of the sand now.

He changed his mind about a Jeep and took a helicopter. That way he could reach the airport before the limousine and bring Beth and Hana back to the palace without fuss.

He gazed down, as he always did when he reached that part of the desert where his guilty past lay in a patch of sand—a reminder of mistakes he'd made in his youth, mistakes that could never be repaired. It was then that he saw something moving on the ground, and hovered lower.

Wading calf-deep in sand, Beth was cutting across some scrub-land, with Hana in one arm and her other arm around the nanny, urging her to move faster, when she heard the helicopter flying overhead. She couldn't lose time staring up at it to discover if it was friend or foe. Fear was draining her strength like water through a grid, and her chest felt about ready to explode. Risking a quick glance behind them, she saw their driver who had returned to the limousine flip open a mobile phone. They wouldn't be alone in the desert for long. She had been heading back to the road hoping to flag someone down. There wasn't much of a chance, but it was all she had.

He planted the big machine on the road between the on-coming truck and the fleeing women. Beth didn't know it, but she was heading straight into trouble. There wasn't time to land and pick them up safely, so he had opted to stop the insurgents first and hold them until his troops arrived. He carried guns onboard his helicopters and wouldn't hesitate to use them.

She stopped running when she saw the dust thrown up by the helicopter as it landed. The driver was back inside the limousine now, and with impatient stamps on the accelerator was trying to blast it out of the sand.

That should keep him busy, Beth thought, wiping her face on her sleeve. 'Are you all right?' she asked the nanny, gazing intently at her charges. To her relief, Hana was sound asleep, but the young nanny was close to hysteria. She couldn't ask more of her, Beth realised, she'd asked too much already; she had to make their stand here. 'We're going back to that memorial,' she said firmly. 'And I'm going to leave you there, hidden in the bushes, where you'll be safe while I get help.'

'Don't leave me,' the girl begged, clinging to her.

'I have to go and get help. You can do this. I know you can.' There were no certainties, but Beth wasn't about to share her fears. The only thing she did know was inaction wasn't an option.

Crouching low, Beth ran towards the helicopter. Seeing Khal standing outside was so much more than she had hoped for, her legs almost gave way beneath her, but, seeing the gun in his hand, she struggled on. It was a stark reminder that this was not a fairy story or a package tour to Q'Adar, but that it was a country in the throws of rebirth, with all that that entailed. Khal was a king, Sheikh of Sheikhs, a defender of his people. She just hadn't seen the big picture before. She had judged him as she would judge some nine-to-five worker, when in reality Khal was holding a country on his shoulders, and dealing with all the new emotions Hana had brought into his life at the same time. No wonder he seemed hard. He had to be.

Swinging the gun up, he shouted, 'Beth! I could have shot you!' Grabbing hold of her, he hustled her towards the open door. 'Get in now—don't ask questions!' He could see army trucks descending on them in a pincer movement. Time to leave. He had to keep Beth and Hana alive, whatever it took. 'Where is she?'

'With her nurse in the bushes, by that memorial.'

'We'll pick them up.'

'And the driver?'

He angled his chin to the Sikorsky Black Hawk helicopters, flying fast and low across the sand to intercept the convoy. 'They'll take care of him...'

It was a terrifying situation, but with Khal's hands steady on the controls Beth felt safe. She was seeing a new side to him. This was someone in another league to the entrepreneur who had built a business empire—this was a warrior king, a true hawk of the desert, a man playing out the hand fate had dealt him with a hero's instincts. Just like his ancestors before him, Khal would fight to keep his country safe. He would fight to keep his people safe, and those he loved too. The magnitude of his responsibilities had only just hit home. All the riches and outward show didn't mean a thing compared to the riches inside a man, and she felt a great swell of love for him, this man who was a protector, as well as the ruler of Q'Adar. Her part in his life seemed miniscule by comparison to the challenges he must face.

She mustn't be selfish, Beth thought, fighting the agony inside her; she must let him go when this was over. She clutched his arm, seeing they were hovering above Hana's hiding place. Fleetingly she wondered how she could have thought him unworthy to be a father, when he was the best father Hana could ever have.

'Here?' His voice sounded metallic through the headphones, but even so she heard the purpose in it.

'Yes.'

He brought the helicopter swooping down.

'Bring her back to me safely—' But Khal had already gone. He'd barely landed the helicopter before he leapt out, and, ducking low beneath the deadly blades, sprinted away. She could do nothing now but wait tensely in her seat.

It was the longest few seconds of Beth's life, before air blasted into the cockpit and Khal was back with Hana in his arms and the young nanny clinging to him. Tears of relief poured down Beth's face when Hana was safe with her again. Khal helped the young nanny into the back of the helicopter, seeing her safely strapped in with her headphones in place, before springing in next to Beth. There was no time to reassure her, he just hit some switches, grabbed the controls, and they lifted off.

The helicopter soared above the desert, leaving the drama below them to play out. Beth could see the insurgents had been captured by Khal's troops. Perhaps she had done some good, drawing them out into the open. She hardly knew. She was seeing things she had never dreamed of seeing—and she ached for Khal, understanding now more than ever the pressures he was facing as well. Knowing the trials ahead of him, she was frightened for him, and thought his position lonely as well as dangerous.

They landed on the roof of the palace, where they were instantly surrounded by support staff and armed guards. Having ensured they were taken care of, Khal hurried away. It was a relief for Beth to have so many practicalities to occupy her: taking care of Hana, reassuring the young nanny, allaying fears amongst her staff. Everyone was tense, and it was down to her to give them confidence in Khal's ability to handle the situation. She wasn't aware of her exhaustion, there was far too much to do.

He came to the nursery to check on Hana as soon as he could get away. Beth looked exhausted, and from the confident smiles and glances he received from her staff he guessed she hadn't rested for a moment since getting back. She was busy now, making sure the young nanny had access to a phone and the privacy to call her parents to reassure them. He waited while Beth took the girl to a small ante-room, where she left her to make the call. The dark circles under Beth's eyes were a reproach for him, and he only wished he could have saved her the distress she'd endured. 'Beth...'

She looked at him distractedly for a moment. He could sense the adrenalin rushing through her veins, and knew the moment those levels dropped so would she. Then her eyes re-focused, and relief flooded in. 'Khal—are you all right?'

Always her first thought was for him. 'I'm fine,' he confirmed quickly. 'Thanks to you, we've flushed out the last pocket of insurgents and captured their leader.'

'I was wrong to put Hana at risk.'

'No recriminations, Beth, what's the point?'

'How do you stand it?'

'Q'Adar is a country in a state of change, and will be for some time. This is my life, and these are my people. I'm not going to stop until corruption is driven out, and my people can enjoy the life they deserve.'

'But not at the expense of *your* life.'

'A country is more than one life, Beth, and if I can bring stability to Q'Adar the young people who follow me will take it forward.'

'With you as their leader,' she insisted stubbornly.

Rubbing a hand across his unshaven jaw, he looked at her. 'What you did today was very brave.'

She shrugged it off. 'It was instinct, pure and simple. I was terrified.'

'That's all right.' He smiled grimly. 'So was I. It's a foolish man indeed who doesn't know fear.'

'I understand so much more now... About you, about Q'Adar.'

'What are you saying, Beth?'

'Your people need you.'

'And?'

'You always have been merciless in your need to know, Khal.'

He relaxed slightly, shifting position. 'That's how I survive.'

Beth sensed the change between them. It was a change in understanding, and in the air. It was a change that wouldn't allow her to leave him, because she could only see that as the coward's way out now.

'Well?' he pressed again, raising his brows as he stared at her.

She drew herself up. 'I need you.' She held his gaze unflinchingly. 'And, if you still want me to, I'll stay with you here, in Q'Adar, at your side.'

For a moment he didn't move or respond in any way, and then with infinite slowness, so she could relish every tiny facial muscle softening, he began to smile. It was a smile of such tenderness and longing and humour and love—and warning, too, for all the difficulties that lay ahead of them. She hardly dared breathe in case she blinked and woke up, cold in bed somewhere without him.

The gap closed between them without either of them being aware of moving, and as Khal seized Beth's hand, and brought it to his lips, he told her fiercely, 'I don't deserve you.'

CHAPTER SIXTEEN

THEY checked again on Hana and the young nanny before leaving the nursery, and then parted at the entrance to Beth's apartment, because Khal insisted she must rest.

'Take a bath,' he suggested. 'And then try to sleep for a while. I think you'll be surprised just how tired you are. If you wake in time, we'll have dinner together.'

Of course she'd wake, Beth thought, wondering what all the fuss was about. She didn't want to part now like this, not when they'd been so close to sorting out the future. But as one of the maids opened the door to her, and acknowledged him with a respectful bow, Khal told the girl to make sure Beth didn't fall asleep in the bath.

'Honestly,' Beth said, shaking her head. 'You must think I'm a real weakling.'

'Anything but,' Khal said, sweeping his strong hands down his dusty jeans as he backed away. 'But now, if you will excuse me, I think we both need to listen to our bodies and take some rest.'

'But I know you won't rest.'

'I'll take a shower.' His lips tugged up briefly in the vague approximation of a smile, and then he turned away.

* * *

Beth slept for so long and so soundly the maid had to shake her to wake her up.

'His Majesty has requested your presence at brunch.'

'Brunch?' Beth said, scrambling up. 'What time is it?'

Nearly noon the next day, Beth discovered with amazement. Taking a shower, she quickly changed into casual clothes, and then followed an attendant through the palace to the wing where the ruler of Q'Adar's private apartment was situated. She was taken through a plain-arched entrance to a part of the building that, like the man who lived there, was austere to the point of being spartan. The door that led the way into his office was a beautifully crafted, but undecorated mahogany. Khal was on the phone, and as the attendant left them, closing the door discreetly behind him, he beckoned her into the room. She could tell from his face he had something to tell her that she wouldn't like.

'You're safe to return home,' he said.

Her brain emptied. Hadn't she agreed she would stay with him?

'I was just checking everything I've put in place for you is operational.'

'But I thought—'

'I know what you said, and your offer touched me deeply, but you don't belong here, Beth, and it will be safe for you now in Liverpool. I have the co-operation of the British government. I don't want you to worry about a thing. I've even had my legal team identify three firms of solicitors for you to take your pick from—though, of course, you're free to go elsewhere if you prefer.'

She couldn't answer him. Her stomach had turned to ice; her brain had stalled too. Only one question broke through. 'And what arrangements have you made for your personal safety?' She despised the tremor in her voice.

'If I told you that, the arrangements wouldn't be secure, would they?'

Khal's lips quirked, but it was more than she could do to respond to his battlefield humour this time.

'We're living in dangerous times, Beth, and there will always be greedy, ambitious men who put their own interest above my people. It's up to me to make sure they never take hold again, and it's also up to me to keep you safe.'

'And Hana?'

'I'll drive you both to the airport first-thing tomorrow morning.'

Beth was stunned. 'You're letting Hana go?'

'It's wrong to keep a child from its mother. And, now I know a personal-protection squad has been detailed to mount a round-the-clock watch on her, I'm reassured.'

And it was wrong to take a child from a father who adored her, but as usual Khal was making sacrifices for the good of other people. She had done a lot of growing up since coming to Q'Adar, Beth realised, and Khal had taken a long journey too. Was there any greater gift he could have given her than this?

They drove to the airport the following morning in silence. There were outriders and several more cars containing armed men behind them. This was Khal's life, and she was leaving him to get on with it. She was deserting him in the middle of a situation that, whatever he said to reassure her, Beth knew still had time to run. She glanced sideways at Khal's strong, resolute face beneath his traditional headdress, knowing he would steel himself to this parting from Hana as he steeled himself to so many things.

She knew all too well what it was like to have no one in whom you could confide, and Khal was in exactly the same position. For all the apparent strength and closeness of his family, he had always protected them from the truth. As sole ruler of Q'Adar, he wouldn't share his innermost thoughts with anyone. How sad and ridiculous that their different stations in life meant they could never be close, when they were so alike in so many ways. They had so much to offer each other, and all of that was to be wasted.

With a deep sigh, she turned to stare out of the windows at the harsh realities of a land undergoing change. But, even with all the upheaval she had experienced first-hand, she could see new Artesian wells, reflecting Khal's remorseless quest for water to feed his new crops. And even with her personal preoccupations she couldn't help smiling and pressing her face against the window to wave to a group of children who had gathered to watch the passing cavalcade. Khal's responsibilities seemed endless to her, and even with a council to help him he would make all the final decisions, decisions that would affect the future of all the children of Q'Adar.

They were shown into the VIP lounge where there was no possibility of Khal speaking privately with her, or even showing the affection towards Hana which Beth was certain he longed to do. However comfortable the lounge, it seemed a sterile place to say goodbye to someone you loved. There were so many people waiting to greet him, and as always Khal made each one of them feel special. He could be gracious and gentle and genial, with his warrior self completely hidden. But it was always duty for him—duty first, duty always, even now. No wonder his people loved him and trusted him to bring them the settled existence they had so longed for.

He came over at last and addressed himself first to the female bodyguard to whom he had entrusted Beth and Hana's safety. 'Take good care of them,' he said, glancing at Beth. As the woman assured Khal that she would, Beth held Hana closer, hoping beyond hope she had the courage to keep her dignity while Khal bowed to her in the traditional Arabian salutation before turning to go. She swallowed hard on her tears as he strode from the room, followed by his attendants. She felt instantly empty and lost. Her lover, her heart, had gone; half of her had been ripped away—the better half.

He took the small, fast car they had brought to the airport for him to drive, and pushed it to the limit along the seemingly endless desert road. He didn't want to think. He didn't want anything, or anyone. He needed space and privacy to lick his wounds like an injured animal. The pain of parting from Beth and Hana was unendurable. He had dismissed his bodyguards and outriders and now he needed only one companion—and she was lying deeply buried in the sand beneath her monument.

The Ferrari slewed to a halt in a spray of sand. Backing up carefully, he parked it at the edge of the stony track along which Beth had led her tiny group to safety. But he hadn't come to relive those memories, but to remember his sister and her bright, humorous eyes.

Those same eyes had held his gaze when she'd challenged him to exchange horses with her so she could prove herself the better rider. He'd been young and full of thoughtless energy then. He had laughed at her suggestion, and had sprung down readily from his mount. She'd had the better horse. He'd known it, and had longed to test it. It was a far faster horse than his, and though she'd pressed his stallion hard his sister had fallen behind him. He had been so suffused with triumph he'd punched the air, unaware that the desert had taken her. She had tried to cut him off and had veered from the track. She had been lost, sucked down into the treacherous quicksand, a silent and terrible death.

Since then he had never shared his thoughts with anyone,

and had been closed off to feelings. He had embraced the responsibilities of Q'Adar with relief, if only because it had
meant he would never have time to feel anything ever again.
He had been so certain it would be enough and would bring
him ease, but nothing could be further from the truth. He knew
now that he only had one life, and must live it to the full as
his sister had. He had always respected Ghayda's passion for
life, and this half-life of his would have angered her, and did
no honour to her memory. He had been so foolish, so blinkered and narrow-minded...

Resting his hand on the weathered stone, he watched the giant
aircraft taking Beth and Hana home soar into the sky above his
head. 'I love you,' he whispered to his sister, and to Beth.

Normally she felt a little glow of pleasure each time she
slipped the key into the lock of her very own home. Growing
up in a series of featureless institutions had made her intensely territorial, Beth supposed. But today she felt empty.
Picking up the Moses basket, she carried Hana into the
hallway and shut the door. The adventure was over. They had
made a clean break from Khal at the airport, and now she had
to get used to life without him.

She made a determined effort to force back tears when
Faith emerged from the kitchen. 'What a wonderful surprise!'
Beth exclaimed with genuine pleasure. 'I can't tell you how
glad I am to see you. Does this mean your father's better?'

'Yes, it does,' Faith confirmed, giving Beth and Hana a
joint hug.

It made things bearable. She needed friends around her to
fill the empty spaces, though in her heart Beth knew those
spaces would never be filled.

'Shall I take Hana upstairs for you and settle her?' Faith
offered.

'I'll make us both a cup of tea while you do that,' Beth said, tenderly handing Hana over. She thought Faith looked happier than she had in a long time, and put it down to the worry about her father no longer troubling her. But Beth's smile faded the moment Faith and Hana were out of sight. She would never get used to life without Khal in it.

She made a pot of tea and then walked, pensively nursing her mug, into the sitting room…where she almost dropped it. 'Khal?' Her lungs contracted, and she had to steady herself with her hand on the back of the sofa. 'How on earth?'

'Did I get here before you?' he said, moving out of the shadows. 'I cheated.'

Even in Western clothes he was an incongruous sight in the small, neat room.

'Well, Beth… Aren't you going to say hello?'

The crease was back in his cheek, she noticed, and his gaze warmed her frozen lips. 'Hello,' she said foolishly. 'How?'

'You were in a lumbering passenger plane with a two-hour check in.'

'While you were piloting your own fast jet, and had VIP clearance.' she finished for him. She was just an ordinary girl in an extraordinary situation, Beth realised as Khal smiled faintly in agreement.

The crease in his cheek deepened. 'What's a jet between friends, Beth?'

'Friends…'

'I hope so.'

'Why are you here?' She spoke in a very small voice, not sure she wanted to hear the answer.

'Because we have unfinished business. And because I want you back,' he said after a moment.

'I can't… Not again—'

'Hear me out. I need you in Q'Adar. The country needs you.'

'Q'Adar needs me?' she said frowning.

'Wasn't it you who said that a country is more than a balance sheet?'

'But I'm an outsider; I don't know how to help.'

'You told me you had plans... The nursery, remember? And that was just the start, you said. You told me a country needs a heart. You are that heart—or you could be, if you wanted to be. And remember, I spent all my school years and most of my adult life out of the country, so I'm a stranger too. But I went back to Q'Adar, and I'm glad I did. The country needs strong leadership, Beth, or it will descend into chaos.'

'I wouldn't fall apart,' she said, eyes growing misty as she allowed herself to share Khal's dream for a moment.

'I know that. I also remember something else you said: a country needs more than strong leadership, it needs a human face.'

'But not *my* face.'

'Aren't you Beth Tracey Torrance? Aren't you the same girl who turned my world upside down? Well, Beth? Have you nothing to say? Have I found a way to silence you at last?'

'Maybe... Maybe you have,' Beth agreed.

Taking hold of her hands, Khal brought them to his lips. 'I'm asking you to come back with me...for good, this time. I know it can't be an easy decision for you, and I know I've been selfish and blinkered.'

'No,' she argued fiercely. 'You're a man who became a king, a man thrown out of his world into a dangerous situation, where you must work against the clock to bring order to Q'Adar or be destroyed in the attempt.'

'You're so wise, little Beth.'

'Not so much of the little, if you don't mind,' she said, gathering her Liverpool spirit around her. As they stared at each other, they both found it hard to hold back the warmth and relief in their eyes that said they were sharing the same space again.

'Beth Tracey Torrance, I love you,' Khal said, holding her gaze. 'And I always will, whether you agree to come back with me or not.'

'You really mean that, don't you?'

His shoulders eased in an accepting shrug. 'Fate means us to be together.'

'Fate didn't take account of my terms,' she interrupted pragmatically.

'No, but I did...'

She paused and grew serious. 'What are you saying, Khal?'

'I'm saying I let you go once before, and I will never do that again. I'm saying that I want you at my side always, and that I will meet your terms in order to achieve that.'

'But how?' Beth bit down on her lip, wanting to believe life could give them a break. But how could it, when Khal was a king and she was no one, and when she wouldn't, she couldn't, sacrifice her principles?

'If I can't live without you, what do you suggest we do?' Khal said.

Beth made a gesture of helplessness. 'I give up.'

He smiled. 'Now, that's not like you.'

'I know I couldn't live close by you in Q'Adar and see you with another family, your official family. It would break my heart.'

'My official family?' He cut across her. 'Beth, you and Hana *are* my family.' Closing his eyes, Khal spoke her name as if he wanted to brand it on his soul. 'You don't know how much I love you,' he said.

'Not enough to sacrifice your country, and I wouldn't ask you to.'

'All I need from you is to know you feel the same way I do.'

'You know I do,' Beth said passionately. 'I can't live without you, but I must. However hard we wish for things, we can't always have what we want.'

'Why can't we?' Khal demanded, bringing Beth's hands to his lips.

'It's just not our fate, our karma—'

'Rubbish!' Khal said fiercely. 'Show me a perfectly smooth path where love is concerned and I'll believe in miracles!' Cupping her chin, he made her look at him. 'Don't let me down now, Beth Tracey Torrance.'

'I don't have an answer for you.'

'But I have a question for you.'

'Tell me,' she said, ready to help him in any way she could.

'Will you marry me, Beth? Will you give your heart to me, and to Q'Adar?'

Beth's lips worked, but no sound came out. She tried to fathom it in her mind. She couldn't. 'So Beth Tracey Torrance, of no known background, can marry His Majesty Khalifa Kadir al Hassan, Sheikh of Sheikhs, Bringer of Light to his People in Q'Adar?' she said at last.

'We can marry wherever you like,' Khal said dryly.

'You're serious, aren't you?'

'Of course I'm serious. Why do you doubt me?'

'Because the picture you paint is not only improbable, it's impossible,' Beth said sensibly.

'Who says it's impossible?'

Beth shook her head as Khal drew himself up. 'Well, clearly not you, Your Majesty.'

'So, why doubt yourself?' Khal demanded.

'Because I'm no one.'

'No one?' Khal laughed as he stared down at her.

'You can't just laugh this off,' Beth protested. 'The whole world will know that I'm a shop girl from Liverpool who came to the desert and fell in love with a sheikh—they'll say I'm your plaything.'

'Not when you're my wife.'

'They'll say I slept with you and had your baby.'

'Do I care?' Khal interrupted. 'Do you care what people say?'

'I care what they say about you. It's so undignified.'

Khal's lips tugged. 'Loving you is *undignified*?'

'They'll say I got pregnant on purpose.'

'They can say what they like and be deeply envious. You can't have that much fun without getting pregnant.'

'Khal, please, this is serious—'

'No one will say anything derogatory about you in my hearing. We love each other, and that's enough. I never took you for someone who would crumble if people said unkind things about you, and I still can't imagine you allowing your life to be governed by what other people think. So if that's all that's holding you back, Beth— Or are you afraid at the thought of life with me?'

'No!'

'I understand if you are,' he said. 'I hope the dangerous times are over in Q'Adar, but there are no guarantees.'

'I can't expose Hana to ridicule.' Beth bit her lip as imaginary newspaper-headlines unfolded in her mind.

'Hana won't be exposed to anything unpleasant when we're married. I'd rather have someone true and honest and real at my side than any princess you care to name. I know I'm asking a lot of you, Beth. If you marry me you're condemning yourself to a life in the spotlight, but when the world sees you as I do, and realises how wonderful you are…'

'Beth Tracey Torrance, Queen of Q'Adar?' Cocking her head to one side, Beth stared at Khal incredulously.

'You don't see yourself as I do. You're like a breath of fresh air, and you have so much to give. You're the only person who remains to be convinced, Beth. You're never going to please everyone, so don't even try. Just do what you know to be right. And this *is* right, you know it is.'

'I'll bring you down.'

'Bring me down?' Khal looked at Beth. Far from bringing him down, she lifted him up. 'Strength isn't centred in wealth and power, it's in here, Beth.' He touched his heart. 'I need your strength, as you need mine. I'm so much more with you than I can ever be without you. You make me feel, and you make me see things differently. You give me love and laughter, and an enthusiasm for life. You took the black and white of my world and painted it in vivid colours. You make me hurt and wish and long and hope... You gave me Hana,' he finished softly.

As Khal's arms closed around her, Beth saw his tears, and was even more astonished when he knelt at her feet. 'Beth Tracey Torrance... Will you do me the honour of becoming my wife?'

'It can be a quiet wedding,' Beth suggested, now she was starting to plan something in her mind that had always seemed impossible. 'No one needs to know except us. And I'll stay in the background when we're married—' Seeing the expression in Khal's eyes, she broke off. 'What?'

'That's not what I have planned for you at all.'

That irresistible crease was back in his cheek, Beth noticed. 'What have you got up your sleeve?' she demanded as Khal stood up and embraced her.

'You'll have to wait and see. But far from hiding you away I have something quite different in mind. When I

show off my beloved wife, and our precious baby daughter,
the whole world is going to know.'

Just as Khal had promised, the world's press had assembled
for the wedding of His Majesty Khalifa Kadir al Hassan to
Beth Tracey Torrance from Liverpool. And as the ceremonial
horn of Q'Adar sounded, the Nafir, made out of copper with
its single piercing note—Beth hurried to the window to enjoy
the sight of the Sheikh of Sheikhs' loyal subjects gathered in
a tented city that housed hundreds of thousands of people on
the vast desert plain

'You look absolutely beautiful,' Khal's mother told her, as
she made the final adjustments to Beth's gauzy veil.

Then Faith carried Hana up to Beth for a kiss, and as Hana
crowed with happiness the three women shared a conspirato-
rial glance. Only they and Khal knew that Beth and Khal
were already married; a small, private ceremony for just the
two of them with plain wedding bands and no guests, other
than Faith and Khal's mother, who had acted as their wit-
nesses. The rest was between Beth and Khal and the fate that
had brought them together. But this grand wedding was at
Khal's insistence. They didn't need the pomp and ceremony,
but he wanted to show Beth off to the world, and to his
people...

Her people now, Beth thought, gazing out of the window
at the kingdom she loved. Her gaze lingered on the mountains
and the monument in front of them where she had gone earlier
that morning with Khal, just the two of them on horseback,
to lay her wedding flowers as a wreath of remembrance and
love on his sister's grave. She sensed it had been a cathartic
moment for Khal, and had brought them even closer together.

And now the time had come and, surrounded by those
who loved her, Beth walked out of her apartment and along

the corridors to the top of the grand marble staircase in the Palace of the Moon, where she looked down on the crowded assembly. Her gaze locked instantly with Khal's, and in response to his look of love she started her journey towards him.

EPILOGUE

THREE months earlier Khal had bought an emergency licence. For an emergency marriage, he'd told Beth, dragging her into his arms to tease her with kisses.

'You can't do that in Liverpool,' she'd protested, leaping up in bed in her little house.

'If the Sheikh of Sheikhs can't, then he'll find someone who will.'

'Friends in high places?'

'Relations between our two countries have never been better,' Khal had agreed, throwing Beth down on the pillows. 'I've got something for you.'

'What is it?' she demanded, starting to rifle the pockets of his casual jacket.

'This,' he said, straight-faced, handing her a box he had hidden behind his back. 'I know you can't stand jewellery.'

'Who says I can't?'

'And so I thought…'

'Khal,' Beth protested, leaping up in bed. 'What have you done?' She burst out laughing as he opened the ornate jewellery box and plucked out the 'engagement ring' he'd bought her.

'Plastic fantastic!' she exclaimed. 'How did you know it's

exactly what I wanted? Did you have it made especially for me?' Holding it up to the light, she brandished the chunky ring, pretending to admire it.

'I had to buy a lot of crackers before I found one I thought you'd like.'

'I love it, and I'll never take it off,' she assured him, over-acting terribly.

'I hope you don't mean that,' Khal said, turning serious. 'It could give a man a nasty bruise.'

'And what's this?' Beth said, as he handed her an intact cracker.

'Let's pull it and see, shall we?' he suggested, joining her on the bed.

Beth gave it all she'd got, and gasped when the contents came tumbling out. 'Is this real?' she gasped.

'Please, not that again,' Khal begged her, affecting weariness.

'Okay, it's real,' Beth agreed excitedly. 'But Khal, you shouldn't have.'

'Okay, give it back to me.'

'No—finder's keepers…'

'Let me help you, then,' he said, easing the plastic ring from Beth's wedding finger and replacing it with the most spectacular jewel Beth had ever seen. The ring was composed of a cluster of sapphires in all the colours of the rainbow.'

'Except for red,' Khal explained. 'Because red is the preserve of the ruby…'

'Oh, Khal, no!' Beth protested when he brought out yet another ring from his shirt pocket. 'You can't do this.'

'Who says?' he demanded. And now he replaced the second ring with a third, a ruby heart the size of a quail's egg.

Beth was astounded. She had never seen anything like it. The ruby heart was surrounded by the most fabulous blue-white diamonds.

'I hope you like it.' Khal said dryly. 'You can keep the plastic for every day.'

'I love it…'

'Good,' he said, and, ignoring laughing protests, he brushed the debris off the bed, threw off his clothes, and joined her beneath the covers.

The grand ceremony in the Palace of the Moon was quite a wedding, though they both knew that nothing could mean as much to them as that simple service back in Liverpool. The two weddings had reflected their very different lives, but from now on they would walk the same path, and share the same life…

Khal had been waiting for her, looking magnificent in his robes of Bedouin black trimmed with the crimson and gold of the al Hassan family, while Beth's fairy-tale gown had been picked out for her by her friends at the Khalifa store in Liverpool. She was going to keep in contact with all of them, now Khal had involved her in the business—though her brief had just expanded to embrace a country. For, when Khal placed the official wedding-band of Q'Adar on her finger, she became queen of that country. That ring would sit next to the plain gold wedding-ring he had bought for her in Liverpool, and in tribute to both their countries she would never take either ring off.

It seemed for ever that day until they were alone again. 'You didn't need to do all this for me,' Beth protested, staring out across the ocean as Khal's yacht slipped out of port. Their honeymoon would be brief but wonderful, as neither of them could bear to be parted from Hana for longer than a few days. Of course Beth wasn't to know that Khal had arranged for Hana and Faith to join the yacht when they docked at the next port. It was just one of many surprises the ruler of Q'Adar had planned for his beloved wife.

'I know I didn't have to do anything for you,' he said. 'Which is why I want to do so much for you.'

As Khal moved to brush her hair back from her face when the ocean breeze tossed it in her eyes, Beth trapped his hand in hers. 'Well, I'm very glad you did…'

'So am I…' He turned her hand and stared down at the ring she was wearing. 'The colours of the sapphire will always remind us that life is full of possibility.'

'If we take it by the scruff of the neck and shake it?' Beth suggested with a laugh.

'I couldn't have put it better myself—though right now that's not what I've got in mind…' He glanced towards the companionway that led the way to the owner's suite.

'So it's more of a passionate ruby-red-heart sort of moment?' Beth guessed, smiling up at him.

'Exactly,' Khal agreed, drawing Beth into his arms.

Desert Prince, Expectant Mother

OLIVIA GATES

Olivia Gates has always pursued many passions. But the time came when she had to set up a "passion priority", to give her top one her all, and writing won. Hands down. She is most fulfilled when she is creating worlds and conflicts for her characters and then exploring and untangling them bit by bit, sharing her protagonists' every heartache and hope and heart-pounding doubt until she leads them to their indisputably earned and glorious happy ending. When she's not writing she is a doctor, a wife to her own alpha male and a mother to one brilliant girl and one demanding angora cat.

Please visit Olivia at http://www.oliviagates.com.

To my husband and daughter. For making it possible for me to keep on dreaming, to keep on writing.

To my editor, Sheila Hodgson.
For making both activities increasingly enjoyable and rewarding.

CHAPTER ONE

LARISSA MCPHERSON was a woman in full control of her faculties, by nature, by necessity, and by vocation.

Or so she'd thought.

Anybody watching her right now would surmise that she had as much self-possession as an empty-headed, starstruck schoolgirl.

If anybody had told her when she'd arrived in Bidalya yesterday that when she headed to Az-Zufranah Royal Medical Complex the first thing she'd do would be to make a fool of herself she wouldn't have considered that worth a reply.

As it turned out, it hadn't been the first thing she'd done.

She'd first walked into the town-sized complex and let Reception know she'd arrived for her first day of work. In a minute a young woman heralded by a cloud of perfume and a toothpaste-model smile had come rushing to meet her, extending a ringed, painted-in-intricate-henna-patterns hand to her. Larissa had extended her hand, expecting a handshake, only to find herself dragged into an enthusiastic embrace and kissed once on the right cheek and twice on the left.

Stepping back from the energetic greeting, Larissa had found out Soha was another of the ultra-affable personnel organizing the executive side of the project she was here to join, those who'd turned her every minute on Bidalyan soil so far into a flawless dream. Soha told her someone would come immediately to escort her on a tour of the complex and to hand her her responsibilities for the three months she was here for.

She hadn't been able to help feeling self-conscious as she'd watched the vivacious Soha walking away. Compared to the stunning, haute couture-clad Bidalyan women she'd seen so far—those who weren't covered from head to toe, that was—she'd been feeling decidedly dowdy with her utilitarian clothes, scrubbed-clean face and practical ponytail.

Shaking her head at the unfamiliar longing for a more so-phisticated exterior, telling herself that she'd never pull off these women's ultra-sleek look and couldn't afford to invest the time and effort in achieving it anyway, she'd turned around.

And she'd seen him. Prowling from the far end of one of the street-wide, mirror-marble corridors opening into the cathedral-huge reception area, flanked by people who'd been running to keep up with his long strides. And she'd no longer been able to see anything else. Then he'd turned his gaze in her direction and something had speared into her gut and rooted her legs to the spot.

She now stood mesmerized, watching his graceful and power-laden motion, her heart hammering, her hands clammy, a current buzzing from her armpits down to her toes. She swallowed. Again.

Oh, man. Her mouth was actually watering. Worse, she just knew anybody looking at her could tell that it was. Starting with him. Then it got worse still. She could swear everything had decelerated, like one of those slow-motion scenes that em-phasized dramatic moments in movies, as if to mark the grav-ity of his presence, the enormity of his approach.

Which was a totally stupid thing to be thinking. Not to men-tion a far more stupid way to be feeling.

What was wrong with her? The hyperbole, the electricity, the breath that had shuddered out of her and now couldn't be drawn in again? It was as if she'd never seen an incredible-looking guy before.

Problem was, she'd seen tons. But that man certainly wasn't one. It would be an insult to call him anything so run-of-the-mill. He had the aura of a mystical knight, with power enough to bear mythic burdens, determination enough to forge legends. Had a face to make angels weep and a body to make the gods of old fade into insignificance...

This had gotten beyond ridiculous. She had to be having some sort of breakdown, imagining all those far-fetched things about a man who was still two dozen feet away.

But she was becoming surer he'd end up addressing her.

She dreaded it. And hoped for it. He'd probably smash the illusion with the first word he uttered. Maybe before that. She'd surely come to her senses with one good look into his eyes. She was bound to see all the flaws a male of this level of beauty invariably harbored, all the superficiality, the egocentricity. He'd probably put her off with his first presumptuous, self-satisfied smirk. And it wouldn't be a second too soon.

She couldn't afford any sort of distraction. She was here in Bidalya for a specific purpose, with the surgical trainer job she'd signed up for the means to her being here long enough to carry it out. She was here only to find out all she could about the family of the baby she was carrying!

The last thing she needed in the equation now, on her mind, interfering with her clarity of analysis and decisions, was a man. Any man. And when it was a man of this caliber...she couldn't even chart the possible damages.

OK. This had gone way beyond ridiculous. Beyond deranged. All these scenarios when the man had done nothing but look at her, head her way. He might look away at any moment, might not even stop anywhere near her, let alone talk to her. This *must* be her first taste of wayward early pregnancy hormones.

But the next second other sets of hormones were going ballistic.

The man was now a few feet away, and the slowed-down effect deepened, as if time was caught in a frame-by-frame sequence in awe of his proximity, to do his impending arrival justice.

He *was* looking at her, with an intensity and focus that penetrated her bones. He *was* going to talk to her. But it wasn't that knowledge that sent tremors storming through her. It was the awareness, the sensuality that flamed in the depths of those obsidian eyes. It was knowing she'd invited them with her runaway and blatant reaction.

For God's sake, look away.

She couldn't. His mesmeric power was something she'd never had any experience with, had no defenses against. Then he finally stopped, too close…

She felt she was suffocating. Her chest tightened, her vision began to blotch. She gulped down an oxygen-starved breath, nearly choked. She'd breathed him in. She couldn't breathe without breathing him in, his maleness, his dominance. She gulped it all down, felt it all rush to her core.

His eyes flared on a last probing, ascertaining her reaction, his welcome. Then they grew heavy with knowing, with promise as he inhaled the breath that preceded the first words. She wished she could block her ears, talk first, run away, do anything so she wouldn't hear him, loath to destroy the illusion, scared it wouldn't destroy it, would only deepen the spell.

"Who…?"

He didn't go any further. A shout ripped the air, sent both of them spinning around to its source.

"Dr. Faress."

A man was running towards them, urgency written all over him.

So her mystery man was a doctor. And his name was Faress. She got this. It meant knight in Arabic. This kept on getting worse.

What she didn't get was one word of the torrent of colloquial Arabic the man deluged Dr. Faress with. But there was no mistaking the gravity of the report he was relaying.

She did a double take as she watched the dramatic change that came over Dr. Faress's face. The sensuality and curiosity that had melted his gaze and ripened his lips evaporated, purpose replacing it, tautening his features and expression over the perfection of his bone structure.

In a few words he sent the messenger running back then turned to her, his gaze still intense, if devoid of the intimate fire that had burned in their depths moments before. So he was capable of switching off on demand, of prioritizing.

"Tell me who you are." It was a demand. Almost an order. And it felt neither presumptuous nor offensive. Not coming from him.

"I-I'm Dr. Larissa McPherson." She was genuinely surprised she could still talk. She wished *he* hadn't. Instead of shattering the illusion, the depth and richness of his tones, the darkness and potency of his accent, the virile beauty of his every inflection deepened her distress. She somehow managed to add, "I'm new here."

His spectacular winged eyebrows drew closer in the frown of someone trying to place a name and failing. "New here doing what?"

"I'm with the training program the complex is sponsoring."

God, she sounded like an idiot. And could she have been more vague? A place of such resources could, and must be, sponsoring dozens of training programs.

Sure enough, he tried to drag something more specific from her. Amazingly he got warm, if not spot on, on the first try. "You're one of Global Aid Organization's volunteer trainees?"

"No, I'm one of the surgical trainers."

"You're a surgeon?"

Now, this was his first unnecessary question. She'd said she was a surgical trainer. What else could she be? A hairdresser?

Yet she knew it had been a rhetorical question, an exclamation.

And she couldn't blame him for his stupefaction. Capable

surgeons who'd been picked as surgical trainers didn't drool over men—no matter how godlike—on sight, and they didn't stammer in their presence.

Resenting him for engendering those reactions in her, she replied tightly, "Trauma and reconstructive surgeon, yes."

Those eyes widened, those lips parted. Then both smiled and the world teetered. "This has to be fate," he drawled. "On more levels than one." Before she could make head or tail of this statement, his face turned grim, making her suspect she'd imagined the seconds-ago lightness. "There's been a pile-up on El-Eedan highway, Az-Zufranah's largest and, regretfully, most tempting for speeding, and the scene of the worst auto accidents in the last two years. Casualties in serious condition are estimated at sixty-four and rising. The first wave has already hit our ERs. In minutes they'll start sending patients to the ORs. We'll need all the help we can get. Think you're up to pitching in?"

It felt like a switch flipped inside her. Knowing that lives were in danger, that she was one of those who could help to save them, brought back the committed, resourceful, cool-under-fire person she'd been until a few minutes ago.

She straightened her shoulders, all enervation whooshing out of her body, determination and readiness flooding into its place. "Of course."

His gaze stilled on her for one of those slowed-down seconds, gauging the validity of her assurance. Then he nodded, his eyes giving no verdict away. "In that case, follow me."

She did, ran in his wake, seeing little besides him. Awareness of her surroundings finally intruded when they entered a scrubbing and gowning hall, the like of which she'd never seen. But, then, the whole complex was like nothing she'd ever seen. It felt as if it existed on some future earth where cost was no longer an issue and architecture and technology had leapt a century or two ahead and perfected the meld between esthetics, efficiency and decadent luxury.

"There's a women's hall, right through there."

She followed his pointing finger, wondering why there should be a separate women's hall, even in a country as conservative as Bidalya. Scrubbing and gowning was a unisex activity.

"Here's fine," she mumbled as she tried to catch her breath, stopped before a sink and picked up a scrubbing soap and brush.

Next moment both soap and brush went clattering into the stainless-steel sink. He'd turned his back on her and yanked his black sweatshirt over his head. He wore nothing underneath.

She snatched her eyes away, fumbled for the soap and began to scrub viciously. But it was too late. The sight of endless shoulders flowing into an acre-wide back, which in turn tapered down to a sparse waist, of steel muscles flexing and bulging under burnished skin the color of warm teak was burned into her retinas.

Now she understood why he'd recommended the women's hall. And *now* she remembered, though she hadn't worked with any, that there *were* surgeons who gowned over their underwear. Some not even that. She *wasn't* looking to see if he was one of those.

She should have followed his suggestion. She would next time.

She kept her eyes away. Not that it helped. She was still aware of his every move, his every breath as he came to stand facing her, thankfully across the five-foot partition separating the sinks. But he was so tall, six feet four or more, that she'd still get a good sight of those formidable shoulders if she looked up. She didn't. He was the one who was doing all the looking right now. She felt his eyes on her bent head and averted face, setting every inch they touched and examined on fire. She scrubbed harder.

It felt like they'd been caught in this time-distortion field for an hour when others came rushing in. The digital clock on the wall said it had only been two minutes. She recognized doctors and nurses, male and female. Two of the latter converged on him, helped him get gowned. A murmur had two more converge on her. In a minute they were gowned and she was running behind him again.

She followed him into a gigantic OR with eight stations for simultaneous surgeries. In the distance another door opened into a duplicate OR, then others after it and it felt like looking into facing mirrors reflecting images into infinity. That each OR was another high-tech setting intensified the impression. Many teams were already placing patients at each station.

Dr. Faress strode to a central position, shot out queries, in English. His people exchanged quick glances then each team answered in succession, in Arabic.

He extended a hand to her, making her move closer. "Dr. McPherson is our newest surgeon and until she picks up some Arabic, preferably not in an emergency setting, everyone will please speak English in her presence. Whether in the OR or outside it." A murmur of assent ran through the OR as he turned to her. "Now, let me translate. Main injuries are an evisceration, three closed abdominal injuries, three chest injuries and one pelvic fracture. All have compounding injuries, mainly extremity fractures. After aggressive resuscitation, on secondary survey they were all unstable, necessitating interruption of investigations and referral to us for surgical intervention."

She nodded, her eyes straying to the assortment of patients. "Do we have the latest vitals on each?"

Dr. Faress strode to the man who seemed to be organizing the transfer between ER and OR. Dr. Faress motioned to her as the man held up documents in succession because they couldn't touch them. She moved closer, read the initial diagnoses and latest values. All the crash victims were in bad shape, but the worst one was the pelvic fracture case.

"Conscious all through," Dr. Faress murmured. "No external injuries, no detection of intra-peritoneal blood but he has a tense, distended abdomen and he's in the worst hemodynamic condition." He gazed down on her, as if asking her to solve this mystery.

It wasn't one really. "They performed bedside FAST," she said. "And it only detects free fluid in the chest and abdomen and misses retroperitoneal hemorrhage on a regular basis, even massive ones, which, with a pelvic fracture, he almost certainly has."

Dr. Faress only nodded. And she knew that he'd already known that. So what had he been doing? Testing her?

He provided a nurse with the patient's typing and cross-matching info, ordered fifteen units of blood then turned to her. "We'll deal with him first." He looked over his shoulder as he strode ahead. "Dr. Tarek, you're with us. Station 3."

She rushed beside him. "How about I take care of the evisceration case while you do that?" The woman displayed the second-worst set of vitals and rate of deterioration.

"Dr. Kamel will see to her. I want you with me."

He did? Why? To see for himself if she was really up to being a surgical trainer? That her expertise went beyond the theoretical? Did he think his establishment would have hired her if she didn't have enough credentials and experience? Any other time she would have, *might* have, succumbed to his testing. But putting his mind at rest wasn't a priority now.

She tried to point this out. "There's no need to have two surgeons working on the same patient, when each of us can lead a team handling a different patient."

He only gave her an unreadable glance, though his body language made his meaning unmistakable. *Please, proceed to the case I specified. Now.*

Chagrined, suppressing the overwhelming need to rush to another patient in danger, or shove him towards one, she gritted her teeth and hastened to precede him to the indicated station.

A first glance showed her that the patient's consciousness was now compromised, although resuscitation measures were top notch and hadn't been interrupted. Urgency rose within her as she and Dr. Faress rushed through a comprehensive but necessary exam.

After minutes of exchanging findings and conclusions in muttered trauma short form, her diagnosis was confirmed. If the hemorrhage wasn't stopped immediately, no resuscitation, no transfusion would make any difference. He'd keep bleeding out and die of hemorrhagic shock.

Dr. Faress's eyes found hers. "Your course of action?"

He *was* testing her. And being very blatant about it.

Without looking at him, she turned to Dr. Tarek, who'd turned out to be their anesthesiologist. "Conscious sedation, please. We'll go for embolization of bleeding arteries under angiography."

"You don't want a pelvic CT first?" Dr. Faress raised his hand in a wait-a-second gesture. "Or opt for surgical fracture fixation or hemorrhage control?"

"No unstable patient should be taken to the scanner, as I'm sure you know, Dr. Faress." She paid him the courtesy of answering in a tone low enough for his ears only. "Also, surgically fixing his pelvic fracture won't stop his hemorrhage. And we both know open hemorrhage control mostly leads to death on the table."

There. She hoped that was a good enough answer for him.

His eyes, those black on white hypnotic tools, narrowed. She wasn't sure if it was with anger or amusement. Or was it appreciation?

A thrill passed through her when he corroborated her course of action to the anesthesiologist, hit a couple of buttons that brought an overhead angiographic machine whirring in place. He injected contrast material then they watched it bleeding in opaque clouds out of the injured arteries on the monitor.

He handed her an arterial catheter. "Go ahead."

Without a second's delay, she advanced the catheter to the first injury site, watching her progress on the monitor, then injected the material that would block the artery, sealing the injury.

It took twenty minutes to repeat the procedure in all injury sites. Finally, Dr. Faress injected more contrast material. It didn't bleed out, showing that all arteries had been success-fully sealed.

It was far from over, though. The patient had stabilized but there was still so much to do or the hard-won stability would only plunge into another spiral of deterioration.

Dr. Faress supported her opinion. "Now to the lesser dangers that can send us back to square one." Then she found out which reaction her earlier challenging answer had elicited when he gave her a melting smile and said, "Welcome to the team, Dr. McPherson. This patient is all yours."

With that, he gave her a slight nod and strode away.

She had a ridiculous urge to cry out for him to come back.

For God's sake! She'd gotten what she'd wanted, hadn't she? Recognition as a capable surgeon, and more patients treated simultaneously. *Then get to work, idiot.*

With a mental smack to her head, she plunged back into the place where she always went when she was operating on critical patients, forgetting all about herself until she pulled them out of danger.

It was two hours before she raised her eyes as her patient was wheeled away to IC, with another immediately replac-ing him. And she met Dr. Faress's eyes. He'd come back.

He didn't stay long. Only until he ascertained she'd made the right diagnosis with the current patient, took the right course of action. He helped her perform the trickiest part of the surgery then zoomed away to anther patient and another surgical team. And she realised what he was.

He was a maestro. He orchestrated what should have been chaos into a symphony of efficiency. He flitted between sta-tions, dipping into each surgery at its most critical phase, per-forming that vital step that smoothed the path for her and the other surgeons to sail through the rest of the surgery without a hitch. It wasn't only her whose hand he chose to hold. He did it with everyone, with spectacular results. It was mind-boggling with some of the conditions that they lost no one. All thanks to him.

Sure, all the surgeons she worked with during the fifteen-hour struggle ranged from competent to superior, but in such a mass casualty situation, it took more than surgical skill to pull off something like saving every patient. It took multi-tasking leadership of a level she'd never witnessed, had never known existed.

Then the crisis was over, with all patients stabilized and in IC. And he'd disappeared. Thankfully.

With the exhilaration of an impossible feat accomplished seeping from her cells, exhaustion and the despondency that was now her natural state, and which had been lifted in the surreal time since she'd set eyes on Dr. Faress, settled back on her like a suffocating shroud. She stumbled out of OR, pondering life's latest cruelty.

As if she needed more upheavals she had to meet him. Not just a man who was a phenomenon in looks and effect, but one in efficiency, organizational and leadership skills as well as in surgical ones. She was certain he was someone all-powerful here, Head of Surgery at least. She'd probably end up exposed to each of his endowments on a regular basis. Her only hope was that her training project was something he had no interest in or no time for, that contact with him would be minimal or non-existent.

With her luck? Yeah. Sure.

She staggered out of the soiled room, the women's this time, found the restrooms, tried to regain a semblance of humanity before wandering out through the gigantic edifice.

She followed signs back to Reception, thinking she'd try to get back on the right track, hopefully permanently out of Dr. Faress's path. But with every step, just making her escape tonight became the only sane option.

Her steps were picking up speed when the distressing

aromas of fresh-brewed coffee and fresh-baked pastries hit her. She swayed on her feet, moaned.

God. She was starving. It didn't help that her stomach was feeding on itself with tension. But she could wait one more hour…

A wave of dizziness put paid to that thought. She was no longer free to risk plummeting blood sugar levels. She owed it to her baby not to collapse.

Just as she turned in the direction of the aromas, another scent hit her. Even with OR overtones, it was unmistakably his.

It was her only warning before his touch on her arm followed, annihilating her balance. She stumbled, would have fallen, if not for him. Incredible speed and effortless strength took her fully against him as he steadied her back on her feet.

Gasping, her eyes tore to his face, found it inches away, the frank sensuality back in his eyes, his lips, drenching her in waves of imbalance and mortification.

"How will I beg your pardon for scaring you this way?"

She jerked away, tried to school her features, find her feet. "Y-you didn't… I'm just…tired and…and hungry, I guess…"

"Of course. You came expecting a sane first day at work and got a fifteen-hour nightmare. But I promise you, it isn't always as merciless as that." His lips twitched. "Only every other day or so." She almost squeezed her eyes, felt her bones rattling with the blast of charisma. "Let me make it up to you." He extended a hand to her, command and courtesy made flesh and bone.

Her mind screamed for her not to take it, yet she gave him her hand as if it was his will that had control of it, not hers.

With her hand lost in his, she walked beside him in a daze to an elevator which looked straight out of a science fiction film set. It didn't feel as if it moved at all, but when the stainless-steel doors slid open it was onto a different landscape. A room the size of two tennis courts with a twenty-foot ceiling and floor-to-ceiling seamless windows spanning its arched side. They were *dozens* of floors up.

It was like looking out of a plane, with Az-Zufranah and its skyscrapers sprawling in the distance, lighting up the night sky like a network of blazing jewels. She dimly realized they must be in the glass-and-steel tower that soared heavenwards in the complex.

She'd barely recovered from the breathtaking sight and elevation when the opulence hit her, the exquisite taste, the sparseness of design and the power they conveyed. Then a huge desk with a state-of-the-art workstation at the space's far end hit her with the realization that this had to be his office.

He burnt another palmprint on her arm as he escorted her across a gleaming hardwood floor covered in acres of silk Persian carpets to a deepest burgundy leather couch ensemble with a unique Plexiglas and stainless-steel centerpiece table.

A tranquil gesture invited her to sit down. When she remained standing on legs she thought would never bend again, his hand gave her the gentlest of downward tugs, causing a widespread nervous and muscular malfunction. She collapsed where he indicated.

He stood before her, above her, towering, brooding, his eyes storming through her with that probing that made her feel exposed, vulnerable. Then his lips spread. Her heart tried its best to ram out of her throat.

"If you'll excuse me for a minute, I'll just order something to eat. Do you have any preferences? Any favorite cuisine?"

"Anything with calories," she croaked.

And he laughed. Her hand came up, pressing the spasm in her chest. He really shouldn't be allowed to do that. There should be a law against such potentially destructive behavior.

She snatched her eyes off him the moment he turned around, forced them downwards. They fell on a news magazine on the lower level of the table. He was on the cover.

It was clearly a picture he hadn't posed for, a close-up of him as he directed his medical forces during a crisis, much as he had during the past hours. His face was ablaze with concentration and determination, his authority burning up the page, imposing it on the most casual browsers, entrapping their wills and fascination.

The headline read: "HRH Sheikh Faress ben Qassem ben Hamad Aal Rusheed: Healer, Innovator, Peacemaker and Leader. Where will Bidalya's Renaissance Man Steer the Region?"

It took a full minute for the import of the words to register. Then realization detonated inside her mind.

He was the crown prince.

Realization crushed down on her with each passing second, each compounding implication. Until it hit bottom. She almost moaned out loud with the impact. *He was Jawad's brother.*

This was just too much. To meet him, of all people on her very first day in Bidalya. And not only to meet him, but to go to pieces at the sight of him, to all but drool over him. He was one of the two men she'd come to Bidalya to learn about.

Faress was the uncle of the baby she was carrying.

Her dead sister's and his dead brother's baby.

CHAPTER TWO

FARESS'S lips twisted in self-deprecation.

He'd ordered "anything with calories", as Larissa put it.
Literally. More food than ten people could eat in a whole day.

He had this hope that an excess of food might mitigate the
craving to devour her.

He counted a dozen more defusing breaths before turning
to his companion, only to have this hope vaporized. One
glance and the heart that remained sedate through the worst
crises zoomed, the breath that tightened only with brutal
exertion was knocked out of him. Again. And she wasn't even
looking at him this time.

His eyes dragged appreciatively over her, almost tasting the
grace and femininity in her every line, his mind crowding with
images of tasting it for real. His body tightened. Even more.

He shifted to relieve the pressure, shook his head in
amazement. And to think he'd never gravitated towards
Western women's beauty, contrary to most men of his culture. But it seemed that was because he hadn't seen *her*. Then
he *had* and he'd known. *She* was the feminine ideal he'd
never fully imagined, never thought existed, never thought
he'd find, had now found.

He bit his lip on the rising hunger, forced voracious eyes
up from the flare of hips which even her shapeless olive pants
couldn't disguise, passed by the work-of-art hands clasped in

her lap, those hands that wielded healing and not just the thrall that had shrouded him when she'd placed one in his. He bypassed breasts that even the loose shirt of her ensemble did little to hide their ripeness. It wasn't advisable to linger there, not now. But later…

He exhaled, swept up to the exquisiteness of her face, an oval of richest cream, a focus of vitality against the darkened hues surrounding her. It was framed by a heart-shaped hairline that flowed back into glossy tresses that now suffered the confinement of a severe ponytail. From his perspective, he could see it cascading its wavy locks down to her waist, a blaze of deepest, richest red that lit up the subdued ambiance he preferred.

He drew in another shuddering breath.

Bowled over. That was how he felt. Absolutely bowled over. And to think he'd pitied the flimsy characters who imagined such hyperbole, who reacted so ferociously to nonexistent stimuli. He should have been careful with his disdain.

But he hadn't been. Thinking himself impervious to such frailties, he'd always been merciless in his judgement of people in the grips of thunderbolt attraction. And here he was, eating his every slashing statement and condescension. And loving it.

This Larissa McPherson must wield formidable magic. He'd never known such arousal at first sight. Or at all. Then he'd seen her standing at Reception and it had felt like he'd been hit by lightning that had left him at once powerless and super-powered.

It had been her eyes. Zapping him with her shock at the reaction he engendered in her, caressing him with her unconcealed wonder, gratifying him with her inability to look away. And it shouldn't have affected him this way. Women stared at him wherever he went, covetous, inviting, but their eyes and hunger on him had never thrummed self-satisfaction inside him, had mostly aroused annoyance, had rarely engendered reciprocating interest. When they did, it was a cerebral reaction. That of a connoisseur weighing up the pleasure value of what was on offer, and always finding it wanting. He'd never approached a woman, had only deigned to let those who pleased his eye enough and whom he deemed worthy the temporary distraction to do so.

Then there'd been her eyes. Those had engulfed him whole. And he hadn't only approached her, he'd barely stopped himself from pouncing on her before she dematerialized. But she hadn't.

Then he'd seen her eyes up close.

They were oceans that roiled with every heartbeat, changing hue with every thought that passed through her mind, every sensation that rippled through her body. They made him want to expose her to every stimulation there and then, so he could watch them flash through the spectrum of emotions, confessing all in spectacular, wordless color.

After her eyes had come her lips. Soft and small, flushed and plump. Parted, at a loss, reflecting his inability to apply brakes. He'd wanted them beneath his, to taste their every secret, suckle their every dimple, drain their every passion. He'd wanted them gasping in ecstasy, inviting his invasion, losing all inhibitions, clinging to his with a fever of their own.

Then she'd talked and he'd known what a siren's song sounded like. Then, as if all that hadn't been enough, she'd turned out to be a fellow surgeon. And a hell of a capable one.

She'd thrown herself headfirst into the tumult without batting an eyelid, had handled one surgery after another with all the versatility and level-headedness of a veteran surgeon, weathered the crashing waves of one extreme case after another when others had slunk away periodically for some much needed time out. She'd been the only one who'd kept up with his fifteen straight hours.

Then the woman of steel she'd become as soon as she'd donned her surgical gown had changed back into the creature of silk who'd captured his focus and sent his senses rioting, the moment no more endangered people had needed her strength and skills.

The switch was exhilarating, inflaming him with the need to witness yet another transformation, to the being of fire he knew she'd become at his touch, the one who'd match his ardor, until the conflagration consumed them both.

His gaze glided over features tailored to his every specific demand and set in a masterpiece of a bone structure, was drawn again to his foremost fascination, her eyes. Those eyes. He followed their downward gaze—and his heart contracted.

That magazine. What was it *doing* here?

With an inward groan he realized. Atef must have left it here in the hope Faress would succumb and read the unsanctioned if hugely flattering piece on him. His cousin still couldn't accept that Faress didn't share his pride over the international media's fascination with him, couldn't believe that he wasn't secretly excited about it, but was only resigned to it as part and parcel of being who he was. But while Faress had never sought or relished the attention, he hadn't exactly minded it either.

He did now. Her eyes were riveted to the damned cover.

So. She'd found out who he was. He was certain she hadn't known up till now. She hadn't recognized him on sight. Neither had she suspected his identity during the following hours. Not when he'd made it a royal decree to be addressed as Dr. Faress and never as *Somow'w'El Ameer* or Your Highness at work.

It was his reprieve from answering to the responsibilities of his inherited status, the only way to focus on those he'd chosen of his free will. It also stopped everyone from being too awed in his presence to function, created a semblance of ease in his working milieu. Not that it had been easy or was perfect. But when it had left her oblivious of his status today, he'd felt it had been worth every effort and discomfort. And now it was over.

He *had* known she'd find out sooner rather than later, but he'd hoped to remain only himself to her for a while longer. The man who'd sent awareness gushing in her system, arrhythmia into her heartbeat and imbalance into her limbs. The surgeon on whom she'd counted and with whom she'd fought alongside.

Now he'd cease to be that man and that surgeon to her and become the prince. He steeled himself against the calculation that would invade her expression, taint her body language as she estimated his net worth, the eagerness that no longer saw beyond his means and power, the coveting that had nothing to do with him and everything to do with what it meant to be coveted by him.

A breath of resignation burned out of his chest. He'd long been resigned to this, hadn't he? That along with privileges most men couldn't dream of, he forfeited what most men were *allowed* to dream of. Disinterested reactions and liaisons were foremost among those. At least he'd had her genuine interest for a few hours.

It had been nice while it had lasted.

But *no*. It hadn't been nice. It had been *glorious*.

Web'hagg'ej'jaheem...by *hell*, it should have lasted longer.

Didn't he deserve one solid day of sincerity in his life? Couldn't Fate have waited until he'd gotten one kiss, one night meant for him, Faress the man, not Faress the prince?

A discreet buzz interrupted the rising tide of bitterness.

Larissa jumped at hearing it, as if at a nearby detonation.

Why was she so nervous? Worrying about what to do next? Trying to work out how to backpedal, how to fix what she must now be thinking had been her damaging behavior with him so far?

After those first minutes when he'd felt feminine greed lashing out of her like a solar flare, sending him hurtling towards her to get scorched, the crisis had occurred and she'd switched to her surgeon side, practical, composed, detached.

In that mode, she'd afforded him only the decorum a surgeon extended to a senior one, accepted his decrees only when she'd agreed with them. She'd offered him nothing beyond equality, with the implicit understanding she only did so as long as he reciprocated in kind. And *that* had been another unprecedented and truly magnificent experience. Would she start fawning over him now?

Ya Ullah. He wouldn't be able to bear it if she did.

That he'd look into her eyes and find the confession of equal attraction and the loss of control over it gone, replaced by artifice, by calculation, sickened him, infuriated him...

The buzz sounded again and his anger spiked as he realized what it was this time. Their food.

He stalked to the door, let in their food-bearers. Sensing his mood, they hastened in with the trolleys they'd brought then almost ran out, leaving him alone with her once more.

It turned out he'd ordered food enough for ten people for *two* days.

What the hell. She'd probably be even more impressed with his extravagance. He should just urge her to eat and get it over with. He now couldn't wait to send her away.

Before he could say anything she fumbled for a silver pitcher and a crystal glass, her hands shaking so much she splashed juice everywhere but inside her glass.

"Oh, God..." She set down her burdens with a clatter, lunged for paper napkins and started to dab at the spilled juice.

When she bent to dab at the carpet he growled, "Leave it."

His terse order brought her jackknifing up, her expression so complex many of its ingredients escaped his analysis. It contained exhaustion, which was only expected. There was also anxiety, befitting his expectations. But there was no trace of the false softening he'd dreaded, the cajoling deference. There was just the opposite, a tautening, a withdrawal. But it was something else he saw, felt but couldn't credit, that stunned him. Was that...dread?

She feared him?

A vise clutched his gut at the mere thought.

He strode towards her, anxious to dispel the suspicion, and her eyes shot up to him. The trepidation there was unmistakable.

"Larissa?" He cursed himself at the jolt of pleasure her name on his lips shot through him, now of all times. "You're not well?"

She jerked her eyes away as she shook her head. "I'm fine."

She *wasn't* fine. And, *b'Ellahi*, she *did* seem afraid.

Instead of her wanting to win his favor, his status caused her fear? The idea was insupportable.

"Larissa, are you afraid of me?" Her eyes widened at his abrupt question. "*B'Ellahi*—why? You think I brought you here to have you alone to—what? Accost you?"

Her eyes went round. It took her a full minute to blurt out, "God, *no*. How can you think that? It didn't even cross my mind."

"Are you sure?" he probed, hanging on her nuances, determined to test the veracity of her claim. "Or are you just saying that because you're afraid of my reaction if you said it did?"

She seemed at a loss for words again. Then she shook her head, exhaled on what sounded like incredulity. "Look, I can keep saying I'm not afraid of you and you can keep volleying back that I could only be saying that *because* I'm afraid of you until the cows come home. So once more, and hopefully for the last time. I'm *not* afraid of you. I don't even know where you got this idea."

He folded his arms over his chest, his lips twisting. "From the stricken expression on your face, that's where. I expect a lot of reactions when people learn I'm the crown prince but you were looking at this magazine as if it had just revealed to you that you were in the same room with Jack the Ripper."

For one terrible moment, as her lips, as her whole face trembled, he thought she'd burst out in tears.

She burst out laughing instead.

He stared at her, flabbergasted, almost wincing at her

beauty as laughter overcame her, his heart kicking his ribs with each melodious peal. He'd never seen or heard anything so exquisite.

"Oh, God, excuse me," she gasped. "But you're just so far off base it's funny…" She tried to suppress her giggles, color creeping up her neck and face.

"I'm relieved you find my misreading of the situation so hilarious," he drawled, his voice heating with answering mirth, with relief, with his rising temperature. "Just what I was after."

Uncontrollable splutters escaped her containment efforts. "You're supplying comic as well as famine relief?"

He raised one eyebrow in exaggerated seriousness. "I pride myself on offering a comprehensive package to my co-workers."

And she spluttered again. Her chuckles drew out his own, even when each tinkle was tinged by the loss of control depletion wrought, twisting in his gut, tugging at his loins.

"And to put you *more* at ease, forget all about this crown-prince business. I consider myself a provisional one anyway."

That cut her laughter short, made her gape at him. "Huh?"

He didn't know why, but he needed to tell her this. "I have an older brother who's the rightful crown prince. But for reasons I won't go into now, he's left the kingdom. I prefer to think I'm warming the bench for him, as you Americans would say, and that he'll soon return and take back his rightful place."

She stared at him for another moment then wheezed again. "And that's supposed to put me at ease? Being only *second* in line to the throne of one of the most powerful oil states in the world is supposed to be less intimidating than being *first* in line?"

"Are you telling me you're intimidated?"

Her laughter spiked. "Hell, no."

He gazed at her, his heart expanding. *Ya Ullah*, she'd again pulverized his expectations. Nothing had changed. She still saw *him*, not the crown prince. His doubts had been unfounded. She was neither fawning nor intimidated. She was just being herself. Whatever chaos he'd thought he'd seen he must have imagined.

That meant he was free to resume the magic. To devour her.

And he would.

Larissa's hysterical laughter was aborted the moment Faress started prowling back to her, a predatory gleam in his eyes.

Every cell in her body surged in all-out alarm.

And she'd said she wasn't afraid of him?

She wasn't. Not that kind of fear. Not for a second.

Which might be very irrational, a scolding voice inside her tried to point out. He *was* all-powerful here, could literally get away with anything. And she was in his country, in his complex, in his den, in his absolute power. Maybe it was wise to be wary.

She wasn't. There was no doubt in her mind that he'd never harm anyone weaker than him, never abuse his power. While playboy was written all over him in phosphorescent foot-tall letters, protector was even more prominent. She'd been sure of that even before his anxiety when he'd thought her upheaval had been fear.

But upheaval was a mild word for what churned her guts into a tangled mess. And that was when shock still numbed her, when the predicament she'd stumbled into was still registering. She had no idea what it would feel like when it all hit bottom.

After being stunned by his misinterpretation she'd been enervated by the reprieve it had afforded her. Not that she could have blurted out the reason for her turmoil if it hadn't.

Yeah, *that* would have been priceless. *Oh, I'm not afraid of you, just afraid of losing my mind. I find myself falling at a man's feet for the first time in my life, find out he's all-powerful at my work, in my host kingdom—and the cherry on top? I'm carrying his older brother's baby. And by the way, the brother you hope will one day return and take his rightful place? He's dead!*

The situation was so untenable she'd almost lost control

over the tenuous leash she'd had on the ever-simmering tears, her only outlet since Claire had died, so shockingly, just three weeks ago. In the struggle to withhold the weeping jags she'd been surrendering to ever since on a regular basis until she felt she'd dissolve, she'd started giggling like a demented hyena instead. She still felt the twitches of hysteria rippling beneath the surface of a fragile, artificial composure.

God, he'd spoken of Jawad with such longing. How could she leave him living in the futile hope of his return? How could she not? She couldn't reveal her secret now. The baby's safety and future were paramount. And she had no idea if those would be best served by having Faress and the Aal Rusheeds as his family.

He came to tower above her again, his eyes now steamy slits roasting her alive, almost scorching off the tethers of control.

"So this is your final verdict?" he drawled, his exotic accent deepening. "There's not now, and won't ever be, the least awe at me being the crown prince? You don't have the tiniest fear that I might abuse my power?"

"None," she rasped without hesitation.

And he smiled. That smile that should be banned under international law. "Good." And that should be, too. That satisfied lion's rumble. "Now I will say and do anything, everything, without worrying about your interpretation."

"My interpretation?"

"That you won't fear yourself in any danger if you react as you please to my advances."

"Advances?"

He leaned down, a lazy hand reaching behind her, extracting her ponytail, bringing it thudding over her breast. It hit her nipple through the thickness of her shirt, sending a hail of stimulation to her core. She jerked, almost moaned.

She couldn't believe, let alone understand, what he was doing to her. He hadn't touched her beyond a courteous touch on her arm or hand, he'd done nothing but expose her to his sight and sound and scent, and he was teaching her what it meant, what it felt like to be at her senses' mercy. To know that they had none.

He straightened, taking a long lock with him, winding it round and round his surgeon's fingers.

Then he finally drawled, a mouth-watering smile drenching his fathomless baritone, "Do you hear an echo, or is it just me?"

She did hear ringing in her ears. He was teasing her, was coming on to her…She grimaced at the inappropriate, flimsy description. He certainly wouldn't do anything as pathetic and cheap as coming on. He'd put his intentions far better, far clearer. He was *advancing*. Like an unstoppable conquering army.

He suddenly came down beside her with a movement of such economy and grace it should have been impossible for someone of his height and bulk. Her heartbeats piled up like the vehicles had in that catastrophe they'd just finished dealing with.

He gave her a smoldering sideways glance, noting her condition with satisfied eyes. "Hmm, the echo seems to be gone." He picked up the silver pitcher, poured a glassful of pineapple juice. "This was what you were attempting a few minutes ago, wasn't it?" She stared at him mutely as he brought the glass to her lips. "Drink, Larissa. Drought relief. Part of the comprehensive service."

She didn't know how she did it, but she downed the whole thing in what felt like one gulp. He was too close, he'd emptied her lungs of air, her mind of reason. His next words emptied the world of both.

"You will come stay at my place."

The words sank, exploded like depth mines in her mind.

Shock surged to the surface in their wake, "*your place*" almost exploding out of her. She barely caught back the echoing words, croaked instead, "Uh—thanks—I—I already have an—an apartment, in Burj Al Taj…and—and it's spectacular…"

"I don't doubt the level of luxury of whatever accommodation the project provided. That's not the issue. I want you

with me." She only stared at him, too dumbstruck to even formulate a reply, flabbergasted at the speed with which everything was happening, at his sweeping advances through her
barriers. His lips tilted again. "You don't have to be *with* me,
if it's too soon for you. You can be at one of my guest houses
in my palace's grounds and be as far as a few blocks away. If
it isn't too soon, don't use irrelevant inhibitions to talk yourself out of it."

"For God's sake, we just met today!" she spluttered.

His shrug was dismissal itself. "What is time when the first
minutes tell you more about someone than years do about
others? When in hours we shared what most people live whole
lives together without sharing? Look beyond the restrictions
of custom and the expected, Larissa. Look at the reality of us,
me and you, man and woman. Nothing else matters."

He'd missed his calling, being a surgeon. He should have
been a hypnotist. A sorcerer. Then again, he was probably both.

When she kept gaping at him, he sighed, sat forward,
dragged one trolley closer, arranged a few plates and bowls
of the most incredible, hand-painted china she'd ever seen in
front of her.

He spread a deep red silk napkin on her lap then spooned
something with a browned surface and creamy depths and
brought it to her lips. She opened them without volition, felt
warm, rich sweetness the consistency of thickest cream melting over her tongue, contrasting with the chewiness of the caramelized crust and the coolness of the silver spoon. She
moaned at the sheer decadence, the brutal seduction of the
whole experience.

"You like it, hmm?" He wanted her to verbalize it? Not satisfied with seeing her almost fainting with liking it all? The
food, what he was doing to her...*especially* what he was
doing to her? He gave her a glance of all-male satisfaction,
admiring his handiwork, added another touch, wiping a lazy
finger over a smudge on her upper lip. "*M'halabeya* is made

of milk and cream and honey and ground rice. Every food group you need to replenish you now."

Her stomach wailed, loudly, for another taste. Another touch. With indulgence filling his eyes and lips, he fed her the whole bowl, eliciting almost non-stop uncontrollable murmurs of appreciation, at the care and seduction in his every move as the much-needed sustenance hit her bloodstream.

He finally drew back, his eyes heavy with so much she didn't dare name. Then he advanced again, his face nearing hers in agonizing slowness, sending all her hairs standing on end. An inch away, he parted his lips, let a gust of intoxicating breath singe her cheek before he closed his lips over the corner of her mouth. Just as the dim lights started to go out completely, he opened his lips again, swept the tip of his tongue in a warm, moist caress, licking at what must have been a smear of *m'halabeya*.

She jerked as if with an electrocuting current. It seemed this jolted something undone inside him, too. He drew away, one hand cupping her head, the other tilting her chin backward. Then he waited, his obsidian gaze tattooing her retinas.

She knew what he was asking, what he'd do if she didn't say no as her mind was screaming for her to. She had to breathe first to produce sound. And she couldn't breathe.

Growling something dark in his chest, his head descended, his lips besieging hers, detonating more depth mines in her blood. He didn't open his lips over hers, didn't breach their paralyzed seal with his tongue, just kept nuzzling her like an affectionate lion.

The he finally took his lips away an inch, groaned, as if in pain, "Kiss me, Larissa. Take what you need of me, *ya jameelati*."

"Is—is that an order?" she hiccuped, stunned that her speech center wasn't fried. "As my superior? Or as the crown prince?"

He let her go at once. She fell back in a heap on the couch. He sat for a long minute, affront radiating from him. Then he exhaled, leaned a forearm on one formidable thigh. "Out-side work, there'll never be orders between us. *If* they're not part of intimate games, that is. I wouldn't even approach you if you didn't want me as much as I want you. As we both know you do."

She wasn't even going to contest that. That would be the height of hypocrisy and coyness. Two things she wasn't equipped with. They both *did* know.

But it was impossible. On every sane and ethical basis, she had to put an end to this. Right now. She inhaled deeply.

"Listen, Dr. Faress—er…Your Highness—"

"Faress," he interrupted, terse, uncompromising. "No titles when you're addressing me, and certainly never, *ever* Your Highness. I call you by your name, you call me by mine. Now say it. I need to hear my name on your lips."

"All right. *Faress…*" She faltered, shocked at the jolt of pleasure saying his name shot through her. "It goes without saying you're used to women throwing themselves at your feet. And though I can certainly see the attraction, can't pretend not to feel it, what matters is if I act on it, and I'm not going to. Not now, not ever. This morning, right now, you just keep taking me by surprise. I never had any experience with anyone so—so potent that I just keep freezing, keep being swept along. But no matter what I want, the bottom line is I'm not here to fool around with some over-endowed, over-powerful, over-privileged crown prince!"

Silence clanged in the wake of her summation. He'd gone still, his face a heart-rendingly beautiful and unreadable mask.

Oh, God. She'd pushed her luck too far. Now he'd be angry. He might even send her packing if he believed he wouldn't have his way with her. Which, for every reason there was, he wouldn't.

After a nerve-racking moment, he threw his awesome head back and laughed. And laughed.

He finally brought himself under control, chuckles still rumbling in his chest like distant thunder. "*Ya Ullah…*I don't know which is more gratifying. Feeling you coming undone at my touch, knowing every tremor passing through you is fueled by genuine hunger, or hearing your denunciation and knowing that every word passing through your lips is fueled by genuine conviction."

So he believed she meant her rejection. Good. *She* wasn't sure she did. Which was just too infuriating. She was here to see if he was guardian material for their dead siblings' baby, not fling material. Which was no doubt what he had in mind. A very short fling. Probably a one-night stand. But at least, and unbelievably, he didn't seem to mind her rejection. She'd thought someone with his power, no matter what he professed, would be offended if even such a fleeting offer of his was turned down.

"And of course I don't mind." He'd read her mind! "I said I expect you to be totally free in your reactions to my advances. My word is considered law in most circumstances, and the first one to abide by it is myself. But advances aside, you will come and stay at my place, for as long as you're here in Bidalya."

That long? "But I already refused…" she faltered.

"You refused involvement. And while I concede your right to more time, I'm demanding that you stay at my place. Anything more is at your pace." She opened her mouth in an unformulated protest and he raised an imperious hand. "I insist. I don't know how a female doctor ended up alone at the other end of the city. There's going to be hell to pay for this serious lapse."

She found words then. "If that's your concern, you can offer me something near the complex with one or more other females."

"I can, but I won't. In my place you share my invisible protection and I have peace of mind about your safety."

"You make it sound as if Bidalya is a very dangerous place for a single woman."

"A beautiful woman living alone, even in societies where

this situation has become a fact of life, is still subject to varying levels of dangers. One of your caliber of beauty here can and will draw all sorts of unsavory attention."

"For God's sake, your women are the beautiful ones!" she exclaimed. "No one's going to give me a second glance."

"You mean like I didn't?" OK, he had a point there. *Not* that she could understand why he was giving her that attention. He went on, "And, then, our women never live alone and our men are used to their brand of beauty. You, on the other hand…" He paused, pursed his lips. "I'm not even going into the possibilities."

"You offer all foreign female doctors the same protection?"

"They're set up together in hotels and assigned guards, or live in secured compounds. Outside their residence they're told that if they breach the safety instructions we impose, they breach their contracts. You, I want with me."

OK. That was succinct. *Whoa.*

"So all you're offering me is a place to stay?" she rasped. "You don't expect anything in return?"

His smile grew bone-liquefying. "I expect everything. But not in return for anything. Ever. Only when you can't bear not giving it to me. And then all I'm offering that you can't obtain on your own is absolute security. You insisted you don't fear me." He paused. "Though here you need more than that, you need to trust me."

"I *do*."

At the swiftness, the certainty of her admission, his black eyes blazed. "You honor me."

Yeah. And you stagger me, she almost blurted out in return.

She didn't, probably because a question was overriding all her thought processes. She asked it. "But I can still say no? I can opt for what you offer every other female doctor?"

"You can say anything you like," he said. "But you won't." He cupped her cheek, aborting what would have been a vigorous nod of assent. "And though you can stay at a distance, that isn't where I'll stay. I plan on wallowing in this incredible thing we have."

She almost choked on her lungs. "We don't have anything…"

"We do. And it's undeniable, unstoppable." He leaned to brush his firm, cool lips against the scorched skin at her jaw before pulling back. "And I won't be either denied or stopped. But as I said, we'll go at your pace. My patience is legendary. Now, let's stock you up with more calories."

And for the next hour he fed her things she'd never tasted before, delicacies of his land, shared every bite with her as he told her their names and how they were made.

She surrendered to his ministrations, the urge mounting to tell him that if the baby she carried wasn't all that mattered, if her obligation to give him the best possible future by making clear, rational choices, Faress might not have needed to be patient at all.

But as it was, no amount of patience would do him any good. No matter how much she longed to, she wouldn't, *couldn't*, succumb to his annihilating temptation.

Faress didn't know how long it had been as he indulged in that most erotic experience of his life, feeding Larissa, sharing every bite with her. All he knew was that with the need for food totally sated, other hungers reigned, threatening to overwhelm his restraint. It was time to put some distance between them. Before he damned to hell all resolutions to savor this, to give her time, and seduced her here and now.

He put the fork down, cupped her velvet cheek in his large palm, feeling as if he was filling it with rose petals. He almost groaned with the surge of arousal. "Say yes, Larissa."

Another surge of color answered him before she nodded, averted her eyes. And he'd bragged about his patience?

He rose on legs stiff with leashed hunger, stalked to his desk to arrange her stay, trying not to look back at her every other step. He failed. Her effect on him was deepening.

Added to all she was, her resistance, another precedent, only made his eagerness for her mount by the second.

Ya Ullah, so this was how a bull felt with a red flag waved in front of it!

The challenge, the taunt of her indignant rejection had been almost too much to resist. He'd almost charged at her then and there, pulverized her resistance, as he had no doubt he could, would, if he wanted to. And how he wanted to.

But he hadn't. He wouldn't. He'd wait. He'd delay his gratification. She was worth every ache and frustration. There was no doubt in his mind she was the lover who'd been made to unleash his abandon, open up the endless promise of intimacy and pleasure.

She'd be the exception. He'd court her, for as long as it took. And he had every opportunity to do so with her working side by side with him, staying near, day and night, so close yet so far, heightening the torment, honing the craving. He'd wallow in her resistance as he wore it down. And when it finally crumbled...

He hit a button, grappling with his impatience for the conflagration when it did, groaned as anticipation wrenched through him. This was going to be unrepeatable.

CHAPTER THREE

LARISSA leaned her head against the upholstered side of Faress's opulent limousine, her eyes wide, gazing at the splendor of Az-Zufranah at night as it rushed by. And taking in none of it.

She could barely breathe with him so near, could feel nothing but his aura, his scent inundating her. Even though he was across the expansive eight-foot back seat, she felt as if he was touching her all over. Which he was, with his gaze.

God, he was so imposing. Everything he'd said and done had been arrogant, overriding and, if she had the mental stamina to deal with anger, infuriating. Or at least it would have been from anyone lesser. Anyone else. But from him, a superior creature in every way, one who oozed entitlement and radiated personal power and charisma, everything he'd said and done had felt so—so *right*. She'd found it exhilarating, captivating, overwhelming.

Which wasn't why she was doing this! She'd succumbed to his invitation, rather this decree, for a good reason. The best.

A voice inside her insisted again she was just emotionally exhausted, that she'd just done so because it was a blessed relief not to have to make decisions, have someone else take charge, give her a break. She smothered that voice yet again.

This opportunity he'd offered her was something she couldn't have dreamed of before coming here. Since she'd discovered that Jawad, the brother-in-law she'd worshipped and who'd died just a week before Claire had, hadn't been the orphan he'd claimed to be, but had instead been the heir to the throne of Bidalya, that she wasn't the only family the baby she was carrying for him and Claire had left, she'd been feverishly projecting the possibilities. That *was* the family Jawad had renounced, and she'd heard Bidalya's king wasn't considered a benevolent one. She owed the baby a family, but certainly not if they were a family of dictators.

When she'd found out about Bidalya hosting a unique opportunity for GAO volunteers, sponsoring their training in its state-of-the-art hospitals, she'd thought it the perfect opportunity to enter Bidalya. She'd signed up for a three-month stint as a trainer in her field and had been accepted on the spot. All she'd hoped for then had been second-hand knowledge through distant observation. It had certainly never occurred to her that she'd meet Faress on her first day here.

But she had, and he was offering her an up-close-and-personal chance to find out about him and about his family, people from a different culture, and royalty to boot, whom she knew nothing about as a people, let alone as individuals.

She *was* right to grab at the chance. What better way to gain the measure of the baby's uncle than be in his private milieu, where she was sure the real man would reveal himself?

She couldn't even presume to know anything about him yet. He was incredibly efficient as a surgeon, authoritative as a man, irresistible as a male. But that made him neither a despot nor suitable guardian material. There was far more she needed to know before she risked taking a step further.

As another voice told her it would have been enough to gauge his character at work, she silenced it saying that getting to know him in professional situations wouldn't have helped her gauge how he'd react in deeply and distressingly personal circumstances.

No. It was the best idea to be at his "place", as he'd put it. It was the right thing to do.

Suddenly he reached out, took her hand in his and tugged, bringing her half against him, where she remained in an enervated heap for the rest of what seemed like an endless drive. And she no longer knew up from down, right from wrong.

"You didn't tell me I'd be rooming with Scheherazade."

Faress gazed down at Larissa and thought this was what fire would be like made flesh, made woman.

Her hair flamed its richness in the flickering light of a dozen strategically placed oil lamps. Her lips, deepened to crimson, scorched him with promise. The rest of her, her spirit, her wit, her passion, blazed even brighter.

He smiled at her quip. After oohing and aahing over the exterior of the palace-annexed buildings with their ancient architecture, he'd felt she'd been let down by the lesser authenticity of the interiors. She'd lapsed into silence until they'd entered the guest house where she would stay. Just as he'd thought it was depletion silencing her, her eyes, exhausted as they were, had flared with pleasure.

He'd just known she'd appreciate this place. It was his favorite among all the guest houses, the one whose construction, decoration and furnishing he'd personally overseen. He'd wanted it as a special place for his special guests.

The strange thing was, since its completion, he hadn't considered anyone special enough to bring here. Now he had.

Maybe he *had* constructed this place for her.

He now watched her running a hand over the back of an Egyptian mosaic, hand-carved chair, her lips spreading at what he knew was its perfect smoothness, before she turned her attention to a spherical, glass and burnished brass lantern hanging from the ceiling with long, spectacular brass chains. The hypnotic play of light and shadows it created cascaded over her, adding an unearthly effect to her beauty, deepening her magic.

He shook his head at his ebbing control.

Then she turned to him with a smile that almost had him plunge them here and now in what he knew they were destined to drown in sooner or later.

Oblivious to his state, she picked up a hand-woven silk brocade pillow off an *areekah*, a low couch upholstered in matching fabric, ran her fingers over the delicate patterns, still smiling at him. "This place is beyond belief. It feels like a trip back in time all rolled in one with a visit to the future."

He couldn't return her smile. He ached too much. "I didn't think anyone would appreciate a literal plunge into the times of 'One Thousand and One Nights', hence the ultra-modern amenities."

"You thought right. It's amazing to walk through doors that look like they've been transported through millennia intact, only for them to swing open soundlessly with a voice recognition and fingerprint sensor. I'm sure even Scheherazade's imagination couldn't have come up with anything like this place."

He attempted a smile when all he wanted was to devour hers off her lips. "I'm sorry the authenticity doesn't extend to providing her as a roommate. But since she's not here, do you think you can stand in for her?"

"Why? Are you standing in for Scheherayar?"

"I hope I don't have anything in common with an insecure loon who had to be defused for almost three years by tales any four-year-old would have recognized as purest fantasy in a minute."

She chuckled. "I take it you despise the guy, huh?"

He raised both eyebrows. "The character who did more than the region's historical despots and madmen combined to give men around here an indelibly bad reputation? What makes you think that?"

She chuckled again. "Now that you put it so eloquently, nothing at all. So how can I stand in for Scheherazade if you're not into fairy tales? Not that I know any worth telling."

"I want you to tell me a real story. Your story."

It was as if he'd just told her he wanted her to jump into a pit full of scorpions.

She lowered her eyes as she put down the pillow, yanking away the expression of absolute panic from his alarmed scrutiny. Next second she raised her eyes again and it was gone.

Ya Ullah, was he so afraid anything would ruin the perfection that he kept imagining non-existent reactions in those eyes to torment himself with?

"It's three a.m., Faress…" She hesitated over his name, the second syllable wobbling. He barely bit back the demand for her to say it again, confidently, intimately. "I don't think it's time to recount my life story."

He stared at her, unable to believe he'd been so insensitive. He groaned. "*Aassef*—sorry for such an untimely demand. I completely lost track of time, which is your doing, of course. But this makes it twenty hours since we first met…" And it felt like it had been twenty days, weeks even. "And you've been through hell for fifteen of them, and that right after flying across the world only the day before. It's a marvel you haven't collapsed yet."

He walked to her, bent and touched his lips to her cheek, withdrew in time to see those eyes going a scalding shade of violet. It was such a bitter-sweet ache, this holding back. He'd never denied himself a woman he wanted. But, then, there'd never been anyone he'd wanted enough that he'd felt he'd been denying himself letting her go. He'd certainly never imagined feeling deprivation gnawing at him. As it was now.

And it was glorious. And maddening. And he'd better end his exposure to her before he dragged her to the floor and feasted on her.

He straightened, trying to ease the heavy throb clamping his body from the neck down. "Now I'll reprogram the door mechanism to your voice and fingerprint, teach you how to time the lock to open for the housekeepers and caterers I assigned to you when you're not around. Take tomorrow off. Or as much time as you need."

She raised her shoulders, let them drop in depletion. "If I hit the shower then bed in thirty minutes, I'll be at work at eight a.m. sharp. I just finished one of the most grueling residency programs in the States where I learned that sleep is an overrated luxury as well as something I can function at optimum without."

He scowled. "Take tomorrow off. That is an order."

"I thought you said there won't be orders except in…er…"

"Intimate games?" he drawled, imagining those games, groaning at their vividness, their effect, when she spluttered to a halt. "None as yet, *ya jameelati*. This is work-related. Get reacquainted with the concept of sleep. That's a direct order from your boss."

Her eyes became round. "You're my…?"

"Boss? You didn't know that?"

"N-no. I thought you were Head of Surgery at least, but I didn't think you'd be directly involved in the project. Actually, I was hoping you—"

"Wouldn't be?" He finished for her when her words dribbled into silence. "So you wouldn't see much of me? You hope I won't make time for you after all? Or that work will be regular eighteen-hour days and you'll be here only to crash?"

He could see his rationalizations were accurate from the mortification staining her expression. Disappointment spread like ice down his spine until she said, "That was before… before…"

"Before you got to know me a bit?" She nodded her assent. He inhaled. "I was that horrible during the crisis you wished not to see me again?"

"No, *no*." She brought both hands to her head. "Oh, please, quit interrogating me. I don't know anything any more, OK?"

He groaned again. "*Aassef marrah tanyeh, ya* Larissa. Sorry once again for testing the limits of your endurance.

Let's get you acquainted with the workings of your place, then I *will* leave you to sleep this time."

He extended a hand to her, was relieved when after a moment's hesitation she put hers there, all soft and pliable, let him guide her through the guest house. She was a quick study, getting the hang of the complex mechanisms running the place in minutes.

The last thing was the door, and after they'd reprogrammed it, she murmured and touched it open.

He stepped across the threshold, her hand still in his. He lifted it to his lips, pressed a kiss into her palm. He felt the shock wave that his touch sent through her, and the equal response it detonated inside him.

"Tomorrow you will take off, Larissa," he murmured. "Show up at work and I'll only haul you back here."

Then before he hauled her into his arms and to bed, he forced himself to turn and walk away.

Larissa watched Faress prowling away along the ingeniously landscaped pathway, tried to tear her eyes off him.

Even with his back to her, she was swooning at the sight, the very idea of him. She'd surely done her level best to feed what must be the planet-sized ego of a playboy of unimaginable scope.

She couldn't fool herself it had been her steadfastness that had sent him to his palace now. And he knew it, had once again made certain of his irresistibility. That he'd chosen to walk away had been no thanks to her. It seemed he was satisfied with the completion of phase one in his plan for her. Whatever that was.

And why should she even pretend to puzzle over that? His plan was clear. He wanted to add her to his acquisitions. Which still dumbfounded her. He was no doubt a connoisseur of women, took his pick of the world's most perfect beauties, and that he'd decided he wanted her on sight was unbelievable…

What was more unbelievable was that she was flattered out

of her mind, was fluttering so hard at the idea of his desire she was shaking all over. He had played her like the virtuoso he was, and she'd all but melted in his hands. She should resent him for that alone, for the siege he'd laid to her, the preemptive strikes he'd hit her with, one after another.

But no matter how she tried to resist him, to shake off his hypnotic effect, it was still a struggle not to run after him and blurt out the truth of who she was and why she was here.

Only his effect on her held her back. It made everything she was thinking and feeling unreliable. And with her reason shot to hell, she couldn't take any step now when she'd probably be committing an irretrievable mistake.

After all, a man like him—if men like him existed—lord of all he surveyed from birth, a man used to having people bow down to his every whim…what would he do if she told him the real reasons she was in Bidalya?

Her revelations would be a brutal blow on so many levels. A deep personal loss at Jawad's death and a huge responsibility, maybe even a threat from Jawad's unborn child's existence. She had no idea what it would mean to the kingdom's stability to introduce a male child of an estranged crown prince, a new heir to the throne. There was no telling what Faress would do in response.

What if he accused her of lying? What if, in his fury, he shed all the refinement she'd experienced so far? What if he detained her until he'd made sure of her claims? And when he did, what if his reaction and subsequent actions were extreme?

Despite his overwhelming charm, his finesse as a man and superiority as a surgeon, she sensed there was ruthlessness in him, the stamp of his royal Middle Eastern blood. She did trust him when it came to treating women, to never imposing himself where he wasn't wanted. But in extreme situations, what would a prince, on whom a whole country depended to keep order and peace, consider ethical? Ethics, morality, even basic right and wrong might be different for him than for the rest of lesser mortals.

Then came the wild card of his blatant interest in her and her reciprocating, helpless attraction to complicate everything. Instead of this being a factor to secure her a favorable reaction, gain her leniency in case of an unfavorable one, she believed it would be what turned this situation into a volatile mess. The plunge from potential mistress material into potential major troublemaker was far steeper that if she'd been a female he'd had no interest in. He'd probably be more ruthless with her on account of the thwarted expectations or the humiliation factors alone.

No. She couldn't tell him about her pregnancy. Not now. Now more than ever, she needed to stick with her original plan. She'd gather information, decide whether to tell him and his family of the baby's existence or go home without telling them and raise the child alone.

That was the thing to do. She knew it... So why were a dozen voices inside her telling her she was doing everything wrong?

Oh, God, the only truth she'd told him had been when she'd told him she didn't know anything any more.

Enough. There was one way she could think of to handle this.

Until she could tell up from down again, had found out more about him and could predict his reactions with any semblance of objectivity, she was keeping her secrets.

She took the day off. Or rather the day took *her* off.

She blinked at the digital clock on her bedside table proclaiming the time six a.m. The next day. She'd slept twenty-four hours straight. She hadn't even roused from her sleep to visit the bathroom.

Not that it should surprise her. Grief had already compromised her stamina. It was only because of the baby that she hadn't allowed it to overcome her. Now add shock, jet-lag, exhaustion, early pregnancy, the most devastating encounter of her life and the expectation of far more upheaval to come, and she should be grateful she hadn't gone catatonic.

She lay in bed, still disoriented, wondering that her eyes weren't swollen, that it had been the first time she hadn't wept herself to sleep since Claire's death, staring at the soaring, domed, whitewashed ceiling of this incredible bedroom.

Just like the rest of the guest house, it was enormous, painted in warm earth colors and furnished with the most exquisite, hand-carved and painted Middle Eastern furniture. Only the soothing light of a corner brass lantern, this time decorated with stained glass in the famous Arabian windows design, lit the room. Daylight couldn't breach the seal of the blackout curtains.

She placed a languid hand over her lower abdomen. It was too soon to feel anything. At seven weeks, there was no external evidence of her pregnancy. Yet it had changed her whole life. More, it now ruled her life. And now there was Faress…

She sprang up in bed, tearing the hand-embroidered Egyptian cotton bedspread off her suddenly steaming body.

What was Faress doing in the same thought that dwelt on what ruled her life?

She leaned forward, dropped her head in her hands.

The numbness of shock, the surrealism that had cloaked her time with Faress was evaporating. It left her feeling exposed, vulnerable. She'd never felt that way before. Not even when she'd lost Claire, her sister, her lifetime companion and best friend.

And you can stop feeling this way.

Exhaling forcibly, she rubbed her face, sprang out of bed. She'd better shower and dress. And head to work. Some action should jog her back to normal.

In an hour she was ready, her step determined as she crossed the guest house. Until her eyes fell on her reflection in the ornate full-length, mother-of-pearl-inlaid mirror at the end of the hall and her steps faltered. She groaned.

She'd dressed in a less shapeless ensemble, in a more vivid green, one of the most flattering colors for her complexion. Worse, she'd left her hair loose and it was now cascading in undulations down to her waist. Worst of all, she'd done all that unconsciously. Any guesses why?

Tossing a glance at the wall clock, she groaned again.

There was no time to change. She had no idea how she'd get to work yet, or how far the palace was from the complex. She couldn't even estimate the time the trip had taken when Faress had brought her here. Her senses had been distorted by his nearness.

She exhaled, reached into her handbag, got out a ponytail holder, swept her hair back and imprisoned it. At least she now didn't look like some wild woman.

Squaring her shoulders, she stalked to the door, activated the voice and touch sensors. The door slid open. Next second she almost slid in a heap to the floor.

Faress was approaching from the far end of the corridor of foliage and flowers, clad in casual whites and beiges, the understated elegance and light colors making him look bigger, more perfect than she remembered.

She watched with a thundering heart as he undulated towards her like a lazy lion, primal poetry permeating his every move, the seven a.m. Bidalyan sun striking dark blue highlights on his raven mane and a golden glow off his bronzed skin.

And she'd been telling herself she'd exaggerated his impact. She'd actually done a great job of diminishing it in her memory, in the hope of reducing it to manageable proportions, no doubt.

His face remained unsmiling all the way, his mood totally unreadable with his uncanny eyes and the amazing spectrum of emotions they were capable of displaying hidden behind mirrored sunglasses. But she could feel his focus like a laser beam frying her heat-regulating center, sending her temperature soaring.

He kept coming, didn't seem he'd stop, would bump into her.

She stood her ground. More out of having no volition rather than any resolve to defy his power over her. And he didn't stop.

He didn't bump into her either. He embraced her instead, the loosest of embraces, what could have been, from anyone else, the most casual of greetings. From him, it felt as he'd surrounded her, invaded her, absorbed her.

Then too late, too soon, he drew away.

"Sabah'l khair, ya jameelati." His husky whisper drenched her, his scent, the amalgam of freshness, Arabian musk and his own maleness making her dizzy with every breath she snatched. "That's good morning, my beauty. Word for word. Make note of them. Time to get you down to some Arabic basics."

Another wave of heat swept through her. "I doubt I'll ever find use for or a chance to say, *'Ya jameelati,'*" she breathed.

"But now you'll know what I'm calling you, *ya helweti*. That's my sweet." He took her hand to his lips, marked her knuckles one at a time in feathery kisses. "Had a good day's sleep?"

She winced. "You're rubbing my nose in that 'I can function at optimum without sleep' statement, aren't you?"

"You think I'd indulge in I-told-you-sos?"

She stared up at him. It was an impossibility to imagine him indulging in any pettiness of any sort, even in jest. And she'd implied he would, even if in part-mortification, part self-deprecation. The problem was, from his tone, his expression, she had no idea if he was affronted or amused.

"Uh—I'm sorry. I…" she started.

His hand came up, his forefinger touching her lips. The feeling of his firm, warm flesh touching hers struck her mute.

"I'm not," he murmured. "I love the way you don't watch what you say around me. I want you to promise me you never will."

Distress coughed out of her. "I won't promise it, I guarantee it. If you'd asked that I should, we would have had a problem."

He took off his sunglasses and his eyes flashed. She almost

squeezed her eyes shut at the intensity in his. That lasted one more second before it dissolved into teasing. "Does your guarantee include saying what comes to your mind, whenever it comes, unadorned?"

"I may not be able to hold reactions back, opinions, but as for other thoughts…"

"You mean you'd be embarrassed to voice those?" When his probing was met by her suddenly finding her shoes very interesting, a gentle finger coaxed her gaze back to him. "We'll discuss why later. For now I'll be satisfied with how well rested you look. I'm glad you rediscovered the benefits of sleep."

She nodded, relieved he'd changed the distressing subject. "Did I ever. My batteries are overcharged and I'm raring to go to work. So if you'll just let me know how to get there…"

He gave her a look of mock surprise. "You mean you haven't guessed my real motive for having you near? That it's all a ploy so we'd commute to and from work together and save fuel?"

She stared at him, elation bursting inside her. He intended to escort her to and from work on a regular basis!

Struggling to suppress her reaction, berating herself for its stupidity, its inappropriateness, she attempted a wavering smile. "Since you of all people can't be worried about fuel consumption I assume you're being environmentally conscious."

"Of course. So—are you ready?"

On the surface it sounded as if he meant ready to go to work. But she knew he meant ready for him and more of his advances.

Knowing she should say no, ask him for a separate transport, or insist she'd arrange her own, she nodded mutely.

He didn't even blink in reaction. Waiting for verbal consent? She gave it to him. A hitching, tremulous, "I'm ready."

That was another mistake, but right now she felt anything was worth the warmth that kindled his obsidian eyes.

He took her elbow in a possessive large palm, making her feel protected, coveted, steered her along the seclusion of the wide, long pathway into the open landscape of the palace's grounds.

With every step beside him, every breath that breathed him in, his virility, his uniqueness, she berated herself for breaking her promise to him so soon, so totally.

Telling him she was ready wasn't only embellishing what she said in his presence, it was an outright lie.

CHAPTER FOUR

'I WOULD be lying if I said I didn't think I'd bitten off more than I could chew, organizing this project," Faress said as he poured Larissa an Arabian cardamom coffee before taking another bite of *khobez*, the unleavened, incredibly tasty bread, dipped in *labna*, what Larissa had found out was yummy yoghurt cheese.

He'd ordered his assistants to round up the GAO trainees for a reconnaissance meeting right after he and Larissa finished breakfast. He'd insisted on having that before they started the day and, officially, the project. She'd gratefully accepted.

She'd woken up from her coma-like sleep starving. But being in such a hurry to hurtle out to work, she hadn't even considered ringing for breakfast or grabbing a bite from the guest house's overflowing fridge and kitchen. She should have insisted on grabbing something in one of the complex's five-star cafeterias and restaurants. She'd been unable to. The last weeks had depleted her stamina and sharing meals with Faress, being pampered by him, was a pleasure she had no strength to forgo.

She bit into one of the *gorrus bel'tamr*, crumbly, unsweetened cookies baked with crunchy sesame seeds, filled with chewy dates, put the tiny hourglass crystal cup especially made for drinking Arabian coffee to her lips, gulped the bitter yet mouthwatering drink with it, the way he'd instructed her to.

She sighed at the sheer decadence of the whole experience, and finally said, "So why did you organize it?"

He sat forward, flicked a crumb from the corner of her mouth with a lingering touch, watching the predictability of her response in satisfaction as he drawled, "Because, though I always donate to GAO's efforts, I was never happy that it wasn't feasible for me to be personally involved in any of their missions. Then a friend of mine, Prince Malek Aal Hamdaan of Damhoor, did sponsor and lead such a mission in his region and the urge to go out there and reach out to people in need myself welled up again.

"But as my responsibilities as Head Surgeon here and Crown Prince elsewhere weren't about to go anywhere, I decided to go for the second-best thing. At least, second best for me. It's probably much better for GAO than having me going out there myself. They've been complaining about the range and level of skills of the volunteers they have been getting lately and I decided I'd be offering the organization a more lasting contribution by addressing those problems, training those volunteers right here, where I can continue with the rest of my responsibilities."

Judging herself reasonably recovered from his last breach of her defenses, she reached for her bowl of couscous, sprinkled it with sugar and murmured, before she took a sample to her mouth, "And you're regretting your decision now? You feel you don't have time to oversee the project?"

"I certainly don't regret it. If it wasn't something I was committed to fulfilling, it would have been enough that it brought you here for me to think it my most worthwhile idea ever."

She barely managed to gulp down the grainy richness filling her mouth instead of coughing it out.

Not missing a nuance of her reaction, he smiled. "And you know the most amazing thing? You being here is not only a godsend on a personal level, it's one on a professional one, too. You are how I'm going to be able to deal with this without dropping any of the balls I have in the air."

Telling herself she was in the presence of one of history's masters of seduction, she rasped, "H-how's that?"

"Simple. You're going to be my second-in-command. We'll work out a general plan of action, then day-to-day schedules, then when I have to tend to other chores, you'll take over, direct the other trainers, oversee particulars, deal with problems and keep a progress report on each volunteer. I'll walk back the moment I can, with you updating me on everything that transpired in my absence."

She cleared her throat around a lump of stupefaction. "And, uh…how do you know I'm qualified for such a task?"

He gave an easy shrug, the very essence of certainty. "I've worked with you, that's how I know. I saw you making life-and-death decisions in a mass-casualty situation—in the worst possible conditions. I saw you implementing an incredible range of lifesaving and trauma intervention measures. I saw how cool you are, how you dealt with unknown assistants and got the best results from each. I was considering many people for this position, but none of them fulfilled all my criteria. Then you came and solved my dilemma. You're just what I want." He paused, before he added in annihilating intimacy, "Everything that I want."

She stared at him, speechless. Not because her heart had stumbled as he'd given his reasons, stopped at his blatant double entendre. It was because she wanted to scream for *him* to stop.

Every word that declared his esteem, his desire, would only be one more lash to incense him further with their memory, their humiliation, when she had to reveal why she was really here. He'd unintentionally stacked the odds against her so that even if she threw all caution to the wind and told him now, it was already too late. It had probably been too late the moment they had laid eyes on each other and her overwhelming attraction had aroused his.

A blast of alarm severed her chaos. He was frowning.

"You're not enthusiastic about this, are you?" He sat forward, tension entering his every line, his frown deepening. "I haven't even considered your reaction, didn't think for one second that it might be unfavorable."

That was what had brought on such a spectacular scowl? She didn't even want to imagine what he'd look like really enraged.

When she couldn't bring herself to say anything, he went on, his voice tight, for the first time a tinge of formality coloring it, "This position I'm offering you is far more involved than the one you originally signed on for, and it goes without saying it has all the privileges and compensations it deserves."

He thought she didn't want to take on the added responsibilities in the fear she wouldn't get paid extra for them?

This, while a reasonable assumption, enraged her.

She heaved herself up to her feet, scowled down at him. "You think I'm holding out for more money, Your Highness?"

He uncoiled to his feet, too, in the measured movements of a lethal predator, came within a breath to return her scowl, bending to reduce the foot difference in their heights to inches.

"What did you say?" This was a tone she hadn't heard from him yet, low, dangerous.

She didn't care. Taking a salaried position to do a job she had so wanted to volunteer for, and for such a staggering salary at that, was already too sore a point with her. But she couldn't afford to volunteer, with the baby coming. She had no idea how long she'd be able to work before giving birth, how soon afterwards she could resume working, and this job ensured a desperately needed financial security until she sorted herself out. She still felt terrible about accepting money to take part in such a great cause. He'd just pressed all her buttons and she wanted to lash back.

She said through gritted teeth, "If you think I'm bargaining for—"

He cut her off, his voice lower, more dangerous, "Not that."

She faltered now. "You mean when I said 'Your High—'"

He swooped down like an attacking eagle. She didn't have time to blink, think, to brace herself.

She didn't need to. Not against any force. His lips landed on hers in a hot, moist seal, enveloping, dissolving, his tongue delving into her open mouth in thorough possession.

She heard a sob, knew it was issuing from her only when she felt it tearing out from her very foundations, quaking them. An answering jolt swept through him, buzzing like a high-voltage current from the hands clamping her arms. She shuddered all over as if with an electric shock. He bit into her lower lip, stilled its trembling in a nip so leashed, so carnal it tore through her far more than a blood-drawing bite would have. She cried out into his mouth, opening hers wider, deepening his invasion.

Just as she felt she'd come apart, he tore his lips away, severing their embrace with something harsh erupting from his gut, wrenching a harsher sound from hers.

The moment he freed her she stumbled back, collapsed into the nearest seat. She would have burned to ashes if she'd remained within his aura one more second.

He neared her again, bent, an imperative finger below her chin demanding her gaze. She met the blaze in his eyes, shriveled with shyness, with the scorching desire to surge up and into him again, take his lips, surrender hers, long and hard and assuaging.

"Call me 'Your Highness' again," he said, tones clipped, "and I'll stop you the same way."

And he considered that a threat? When women would fight tooth and nail to elicit even a long look from him? Was it possible he thought that was punishment?

Though maybe he did feel it *was* punishment for her. The worst possible kind. He just had no idea why it was.

He took off his jacket, threw it on the couch he'd vacated moments ago for their confrontation, tore a few of his shirt buttons open, giving her a glimpse of bronze skin sprinkled with silky black hair. Was he burning, too?

He swung towards her, dipping his hands deep in his

pockets, drawing her unwilling greed and rising mortification to the evidence of the raging arousal of his formidable body.

Muttering a curse in Arabic, he took his hands out of his pockets, brought both up to his nape, linked them there, tipped his head back, stared at the ceiling for a few moments.

Then he exhaled. "I assume you have other reasons for not wanting the position I'm offering you?"

"Who said I don't want it?" she croaked, again stunned at the resilience of her speech faculties. "You just assumed that. Why? Because I didn't jump up and down right on the spot? Well, excuse me, but it takes a woman a few minutes to adjust her mindset from being one of many surgical trainers to suddenly being at the helm of the full project—at least second-in-command of said project."

His gaze sharpened on her. "You mean you accept?"

Her mouth twisted in self-deprecation. "If only not to ruin a perfect record."

One eyebrow arched at her. "And that means…?"

"It means I ended up somehow accepting all your offers, all those dizzying, blindsiding mixes of imperious commands, cajoling demands and fait accompli decisions, didn't I?"

He moved closer until his leg nudged her knee. "You are in danger of being kissed again, and this time for real."

She jumped up, put a few feet of breathable air between them. "You mean that wasn't a real kiss?" she gasped. She was done for if he ever hit her with the real deal. Which he mustn't. *Mustn't.*

And he had to go and answer her rhetorical question. "No. You'll know when I kiss you for real. From your reaction right now, you'll go up in flames, and I can't wait for them to scorch me."

Burning with mortification, she couldn't let him get the last word here. "If I've realized anything in the past couple of days, Your Highness…" She jumped out of reach when he growled and lunged for her. She put the breakfast trolley between them. "It's that no one has diagnosed you since you no doubt overwhelm everyone. So it falls to me to tell you that, while you have every reason there is to be full of yourself, it doesn't mean it's healthy. You're so addicted to your own power you should consider rehabilitation. Think of it as a sort of detox."

He stared at her in stupefaction.

Just as she thought she'd stepped over the line, he threw his head back, exposed her again to what had to be the most fantastic sight on earth. Him in the grips of uncontrollable mirth.

"Ya Ullah…" He tried to speak between helpless guffaws. *"Entee mozth'helah*—you're just incredible. If I'm addicted then you're definitely the cure, *ya'yooni."*

She bit her tongue so she wouldn't ask what *ya'yooni* meant.

"I'm glad you find my psychoanalysis so entertaining," she mumbled, struggling with arrhythmia, rephrasing his earlier similar comment. "Just the reaction I was after."

He stalked to her again, his intention of giving her that *real* kiss blasting off him.

She held out a hand. "Faress…please, don't." That slowed him down. But he kept coming, his face alight with such passion that it made agitated words spill from her lips. "You—you probably think I was just spouting prudent-on-a-first-meeting modesty that wasn't meant to last a second meeting. And from women's reaction to you—hell, from *my* reaction—you have every right to think this. So, yes, if you want an admission, you overwhelm me. But I don't want you to. If we're going to work together as closely as you suggest, please, stop trying to ratchet up the intimacy between us. If you don't…" She faltered for a second then blurted out, "I'll have to leave!"

That made him stop, evaporated all heat from his face.

A long moment later, during which she felt he'd given her a full body and mind scan, solemn, almost grim, he muttered, "Is there someone else?"

"What? No, *no…"* The denial burst out of her before she

gave herself a mental smack. Why was she so anxious to deny the charge? She rushed on, in a less fretful tone this time, "But that's not the only reason a woman—"

He cut her off, tension visibly draining out of him. "That's the only reason I consider. If there's no prior claim to your emotions and fidelity, no other reason is good enough to stop me from claiming you for myself."

"Good enough according to whom?" she groaned.

He gave her a new look, full of reason and open-mindedness. "Convince me how good your reasons are. Tell me."

Tell him? Yeah, sure.

Instead she tried to search for something feasible to explain the reluctance he knew had nothing to do with what she really wanted. Finding nothing even remotely so, she groaned. "You are going to make me leave, aren't you?"

His eyes flared. "I would do anything to stop you leaving."

"Then, please, Faress—I can't handle this kind of pressure."

In answer, he reached for her and all resolution and self-preservation ebbed out of her. He kept his embrace undemanding and it only stormed through her defenses more.

He smoothed a gentle hand over her hair, in soothing, hypnotic strokes. "I am sorry, *ya jameelati,* if I am going too fast for you. But whatever hit us both, my reaction is not to struggle against it, but to rush to the very center of its overpowering gravity towards you. It's the way I'm made. But to let you get your bearings, I'll slow down."

"I want you to *stop*, Faress."

"No." This was said with the most indulgent of smiles. And was there any wonder? With her asking him to stop in a breathless quaver that all but begged him to brush her demand aside, give her what she really craved, more and more of him. "I will slow down. This is all I can promise you."

"Faress…"

"I won't be near you and not say and do what your nearness inspires and arouses me to say and do. But you will be the one to tell me you're ready for the next step. Now give me your decision. Will you stay? Will you be my right hand?"

She nodded, then groaned. "Now I know how you run a country. You compel everyone to do what you want as if by magic, and have them totally convinced and happy doing it, too."

His smile was an amalgam of relief and mischief, yet another in his fibrillation-inducing repertoire. "I don't exactly run the country single-handedly, *ya helwah*," he teased. "We do have a king and a thousand royals around. But where I do run things, like in this complex, the trick is to know what everyone wants that works with what I want then put people where I think they'll fulfill that best. This way everyone ends up working extra hard because it's in their best interests too, freeing me to concentrate on what I'm best at, being a surgeon, and everybody ends up happy."

She sighed. "And from what I've seen of the complex, your strategy is yielding spectacular results. Something this effective just has to be wicked."

"Oh, I'm wicked. Wickedly effective." He gave her cheek the softest pinch. "Now, before I jinx myself so everything I touch devolves into anarchy, let's get to work, number one."

They got to work. For the next few days they made up their schedule, adjusted it a dozen times before finally settling into a steady, productive, if mind-numbingly exhausting rhythm.

She'd at first thought the whole thing too daunting a task. Faress was offering such an unprecedented opportunity it seemed everyone who'd ever wanted to volunteer had found this the best time to do so. Three hundred and fifty trainees were way more than she'd expected. And their role was to prepare them, mostly medical professionals who'd drifted away from practice with enough updated medical and surgical skills to function in the field.

It had seemed more daunting when she'd shot her mouth off and, instead of arguing with her, Faress had entrusted her with picking the fourteen she'd directly train. The others she only oversaw in rotation with him over the other two dozen trainers' shoulders.

Now she was with the four she judged could move into a real trauma surgery scenario. The other ten of her team were watching from the Plexiglas-walled, soundproofed observation rooms ringing the OR a level up. When the surgery began, their viewing experience would include monitors transmitting the recording of the surgery from video cameras in the hi-tech ceiling mechanisms, as well as through endoscope-mounted ones. Later they'd each have a DVD of the surgery to study, then there'd be discussions of what had gone on, alternate ways to have done each step in various conditions of preparedness, and when hopefully everything had gone well, discuss what couldn't have and what to do in each scenario.

"Can anybody tell me why Es-sayed Hamed El-Etaibi here…" Larissa gestured towards their sedated patient, a dark, overweight man who looked ferociously upset even in sedation "…though he took a thirty-foot fall to break both femurs in a dozen places, and as he yelled before morphine dissipated his pain and consciousness, on his birthday too, is still a lucky man?"

Larissa looked from one of her assistants to another as they surrounded the OR table.

"He's lucky because he's still alive?" Helal Othman quipped.

She gave the lanky forty-year-old with a hawk's face and sharpness an assessing glance. He could do better than that. He was brilliant and had been the first one she'd picked as best suited for involved trauma surgery training. He was a Damhoorian general surgeon who'd taken a sharp detour into the stock market over ten years ago and who'd decided he wanted to get back into the medical world, if only as a volunteer. But he was also a clown and he couldn't pass up any opportunity to make a joke.

She smirked at him. "Any more medically specific reason to consider him lucky, other than steady life signs?"

Before a sheepish Helal could come up with a more serious answer, a drawl broke out from behind her. "Because he's got you working on him?"

Faress. Oh, God. She didn't jump. Somehow.

"Uh, it remains to be seen if that's lucky." She turned to Faress, hoping it wasn't too apparent she wanted to whoop with pleasure that he'd come after all. She'd joined him for his morning surgery list as she now did every day, only starting her training schedule after the lunch-break when he'd always done his best to join her. Today he'd said not to expect him.

But he was here. *Here.* Walking in those leashed-power steps, making the shapeless blue surgical gown look like the height of virile haute couture.

She somehow managed to murmur what she thought a reasonably cool and professional, "Glad you could make it." Then before she made a fool of herself by absorbing his sight like a starstruck idiot, she turned to her trainees. "But he's really lucky for a specific reason, which I hope you figure out, or I'll know that my course on 'Gift horses in trauma and the thankful trauma surgeon' has entered one ear and exited from the other."

Her four assistants hadn't recovered from Faress's entrance yet. But besides the awed stares, they were also casting curious glances from him to her. Speculation about the nature of their relationship was running rampant throughout the complex.

At last, her oldest assistant, Patrick Dempsey, an Australian sixty-three-year-old grizzly bear with a gooey center, an obstetrician who'd decided to retire, then continue his life as a volunteer, seeking training in the field of surgery that had always fascinated him, said, "Let's see…the first gift horse is when we're certain what a trauma case *does* have, no matter how bad, since in trauma it's always worse if we're not sure. In Mr El-Etaibi's case, what he does have is a diaphragmatic rupture…"

Larissa cocked her head at him. "I only *said* he does."

His salt-and-pepper bearded jaw fell open. "He doesn't?"

She shrugged. "You tell me if I was telling the truth."

"Well, you were," Patrick started. "All his signs—"

She cut in, "Were mostly inconclusive and misleading."

"Yeah, that's true," he conceded. "But his investigations—"

She cut in again. "Abnormalities in X-rays aren't conclusive in diaphragmatic rupture without abdominal organs in the chest cavity. CT and MRI are also inaccurate in such conditions."

"So you didn't diagnose him?" Patrick looked stymied. "You were just testing to see if we'd know that you couldn't have?"

She shrugged again. "You tell me."

"You didn't diagnose him." That was the only woman around, Anika Jansen, a thirty-five-year-old Dutch former surgical nurse, with tons of theoretical and practical surgical knowledge. "You have a strong suspicion and that's why you're performing a video-assisted thoracoscopy. If your suspicion is right, you'll turn the diagnostic procedure into a surgical one and repair the tear."

Larissa beamed at the lovely blonde, proud of her knowledge and reasoning powers, and simply glad to have another woman and such a kindred soul around. Though all the men were perfect gentlemen, too much testosterone got to her sometimes.

"That is a perfect answer," Larissa said. "And the course of action you should adopt in almost all suspected diaphragmatic rupture cases if at all possible…" She paused with an apologetic glance at Anika. "But this answer isn't perfect here, since I *am* certain what he's suffering from. VAT will only have a surgical role here. So what does he have? And how did I know? Take another look at his history and investigations and tell me."

They shuffled to gather over the patient's file, leaving her without the safety net of their focus and all alone in Faress's.

He moved towards her, shrinking the gigantic hall, emptying it of air. And that when he only came to stand in her first assistant's position across Hamed. He kept his distance in public, physically. Not that it stopped people from speculating. It was the vibes they generated. She sometimes felt they were tangible. It was impossible for others not to feel them.

He let go of her eyes to sweep his over their patient, his expert gaze missing nothing. A murmur brought a nurse streaking forward to leaf through a copy of Hamed's file for him.

"*Shokrun*," he murmured after a few absorbed moments and the nurse closed the file and moved away. His eyes went back to the patient. "That's one angry man. A stable one who can still take a turn for the catastrophic. A baffling enough case to give your team's clinical knowledge a trial by fire. Great choice." He raised his eyes, the usual intimacy filling them still something she couldn't face. "I found myself unexpectedly free and came over. It's only fair to hold your hand on your first big outing with your charges when you hold mine every day in my lists."

"As if I do," she breathed, her mind filling with images of all the times he'd held her hand, scorched it in caresses and kisses. "As if you need anyone to hold your hand."

"You do, and I do need an intuitive, fluent, resourceful first assistant. And you're the best I've ever had."

Now she was in danger of spontaneously combusting. Or would that be arson? Since he was setting her on fire?

"Uh—right." She cast blind eyes away from his entrancing face. "Anyway, that's no big outing. Even had they been trauma surgeons, with the staggering advances in the time they've been away from practice, I wouldn't have risked their involvement yet. As it is, they're just observing and assisting in minor stuff."

"You're still the only surgical trainer who thinks her team ready for even that in only two weeks."

"It's because I'm the only surgical trainer who was lucky enough to pick the cream of the crop of trainees." He gave her that indulgent smile he always did when she bragged about her team's skills. Her heart responded with the usual kick against her ribs. "I can't believe it's been two weeks already."

His eyes blazed a few degrees hotter. "They feel like two hours. And two years. Either way, they passed like a dream."

Not where their work was concerned, they hadn't. The dream was every excitement-filled, emotion-charged moment with him. And that he meant the same about being with her...

"So you think they'll solve your puzzle? You haven't confused them too much?"

His murmur made her blink. His smile made her certain she'd been looking at him with her thoughts written all over her face.

She cleared her throat. "I'm confident a good look at the facts will lead them to the truth."

He gave her team an assessing look. "And you know what? I now share your confidence. You're blessed with the ability of gauging people's worth. I for one thought Helal, while brilliant, was too much of an undisciplined clown, and Patrick, while methodical and thorough, was too much of an uncooperative grouch. I had reservations about the rest, too. But your evaluation was correct. They're topping all theoretical training charts, and if their practical simulation scores keep up, every one of the fourteen you picked to train yourself will be the first we hand back to GAO with our seal of approval."

Heat rushed to her head at his validation. She'd felt a similar rush when, in spite of his skepticism, he'd so graciously let her make her picking decisions.

She'd agonized over the ones she'd picked. As she was only twenty-seven, they were all much older than her. She'd only ever trained interns and junior residents at most her age or a bit older.

Faress had declared age was irrelevant, that they'd recognize ability and follow the lead of experience. That glowing testimony had only made her even more scared she'd fall flat on her face.

She'd started her basic surgical skills refresher course with an unhealthy dose of trepidation, only for their terrific attitude to dispel it in an hour. They'd made a great team from day one.

At her silence he pouted. "You won't jump on my concession?"

Her mouth twisted, mostly at her reaction to his pout. "You think you're the only one who doesn't indulge in I-told-you-sos?" At the flare in his eyes she rushed to add, "Not that I'm not glad you think they'll be the first to be ready. As long as you don't expect this to be within the next two and a half months."

"Of course not. You can take as long as you deem necessary to get them ready for the field."

There he went again, talking as if it went without saying that she'd stay way longer than her contracted three months!

But she couldn't even dream of that. She was counting down to one of two moments, both leading to her departure. Either she confronted Faress and his family over her baby and left, leaving them to consider how to take part in his life, or she didn't and left before her pregnancy became visible. She couldn't even bear to think of a confrontation with Faress over it.

She was searching desperately for a way to avoid what he was after, an assurance she'd stay indefinitely, when her assistants walked back to flank both her and Faress and saved her.

Obviously displeased that he hadn't obtained what he wanted, at least to her hypersensitive senses, Faress tore his gaze away from her, turned it on them. "Well, don't leave me in suspense. Why is *Es-sayed* Hamed deemed lucky by your illustrious trainer?"

"Let's present the first gift horse, Dr. Faress," Anika said, fluttering like all females fluttered in his presence. "He does have a diaphragmatic tear. Larissa knew that from his paradoxical breathing. With no multiple rib fractures, the only other reason could be rupture and paralysis of one side of his diaphragm."

"And the reason he's lucky," Helal put in confidently, "is that it's on the left side, where tears are usually isolated."

He gave her a look that said, *You're right to be proud of them.* Out loud he said, "I'm impressed. Truly. Well done."

As her assistants shuffled their pleasure at his praise,

Larissa thought she should end this before his agitating effect rendered them useless, as he almost did her.

"And while *Es-sayed* Hamed is nowhere within the danger zone time-wise," she said, "always get on with your intervention while you have plenty of time on your side."

She turned to Dr. Tarek, who'd become her constant anesthetist companion. "Switch to general anesthesia, please, Dr. Tarek. Turn him to his right side, please, Patrick, Tom."

As they did as she directed, Faress came to stand behind her, looking over her shoulder as he'd been doing each time he wasn't the primary surgeon while she assisted, or vice versa.

She took a steadying breath, made the first incision between the ribs, introduced the tiny fiber-optic thoracoscope through it, all the time detailing her technique for her viewers. She advanced the stapler through another incision. Soon she visualized the tear and started to staple it shut.

As they watched the injury being sealed on the monitors, she felt Faress's readiness to help if she needed him, felt his bolstering presence enveloping her.

And though she told herself she was being maudlin and stupid, questions kept revolving in her mind.

When she left, what kind of injury would tearing herself from all that, from him, inflict?

And what would it take to seal it?

CHAPTER FIVE

"KEEP walking. I'm abducting you."

Faress watched Larissa jump and whirl around, her eyes snapping up, slamming into his pseudo-menacing ones.

Elation fizzed in his blood as emotions chased away the melancholy she lapsed into when she thought herself safe from scrutiny.

He was now certain she'd recently suffered a loss. Too huge to come to terms with, too raw to talk about.

But instead of making him obey his need to tear down her barriers, satisfy his painful curiosity and absorb all the pain she harbored, it made him hold back, in respect for the sanctity of her suffering, until she gathered enough stamina to seek his solace.

But *enough*. It wasn't time she needed. It was him. Losing herself in his arms would be the best medicine. Tonight he'd end the frustration, start her healing. He had a night of magic planned for them.

Though if she insisted it was still too soon, he'd have to wait…

He believed he wouldn't have to.

She stumbled back a step, leaned on the wall.

"I said keep walking, *ya jameelati*," he drawled again, coaxing, hunger turning his voice into a bass rasp.

"Aren't you afraid that with the advance warning I'd make

a run for it?" she breathed, her eyes helplessly clinging to his lips.

He put a hand on each side of her head. "You know you don't want to escape me. Now we'll walk out to the airfield and I'll fly you to my hideaway. You haven't been to Bidalya until you've spent a night in our desert, under the full moon."

Her breath came faster now, the rise and fall of her perfect breasts pouring magma into his veins, his head flooding with images of suckling them, branding them, devouring them.

"Full moon?" The strident murmur seemed for her own ears only. "I arrived on a full moon."

And how he remembered. It had been one of his theories that day, that the full moon had had a role in his hyper-reactions. But when they'd become even more so on exposure to her, he'd known. The only magic had been hers. Her.

"Yes. You've been with me for four glorious weeks."

Next second she was at his feet in a heap.

It took him another second for the blast of fright to detonate in his mind. *"Larissa!"*

He swooped down on her, his hands flailing over her, all medical knowledge evaporating at seeing her limp and senseless.

He barely registered the gathering mob around him, felt nothing but panic suffocating him, the need to restore her almost rupturing his skull.

"Dr. Faress, let us take care of her."

"No." He roared at whoever had dared make the suggestion. Then he was scooping her up in his arms and running.

She had to be all right. She had to be.

He couldn't live otherwise…

Larissa opened her eyes. It took her a moment to realize what had happened, where she was.

She'd fainted. For the first time ever. And she couldn't *believe* where Faress had her now.

She was in the new multi-million-dollar IC, the first patient in it, hooked to half a dozen monitors. He was leaning over her, his eyes drilling anxiety into her. And he was about to plunge a needle into her vein. No doubt to extract blood for investigations. *No.*

She yanked her arm away, scrambled up in bed, started snatching off leads.

"Lie down, Larissa," Faress growled. "And give me your arm."

She shook her head. "I'm fine. Really."

"You're not fine or you wouldn't have fainted. And what's this? The fearless surgeon afraid of a needle prick?"

She swung her legs off the bed. She had to get out of there. "Aren't you going overboard over a slight fainting spell?"

"You were out for fifteen minutes. I don't call that slight."

She attempted a wavering smile. "Maybe it was an act to escape your intended abduction."

He gave her a disparaging pout. "Even if I believed you can act to save your life, which I don't, you can't fake tachycardia. Your heart was hurtling at 170 per minute." His eyes flared at the memory, his voice thickening. "You scared the hell out of me."

Her heart hurtled once more at his impassioned confession.

She escaped his attempt to make her lie down again. "My blood sugar must have suddenly dropped," she gasped. "Stop fussing, *please*."

He unfolded to his full height, scowled down at her. "You didn't eat lunch when I was called away, did you?" She grabbed at his explanation, nodded. "And you've been skipping meals every time I didn't make sure you ate. You *are* losing weight."

"Isn't that every woman's dream?"

"It shouldn't be yours. You can't improve on perfection."

She coughed in distressed incredulity. "That hyperbole aside, if I ate every meal the way you have me eating, you'll have to roll me around before long. I got busy and I thought

I could skip a meal. Evidently not. So, I promise, no skipping meals from now on. Can I go now?"

"No, you can't. You're staying the night. As for being too busy to eat, that tears it. You're working too hard. I'm cutting your workload to half."

"Now, be reasonable, Faress. I'm only working eight hours per day. What will I do with myself if you cut them to four?"

"You mean while waiting for me to come to you? Rest, read, shop. You have carte blanche to do anything in the kingdom."

Her lips twisted. "That's too generous, Your Highness, but—"

He swooped down on her, his lips clamping hers in all-out possession. Just as she sobbed, surrendered, let him surge inside her mouth, devour her, his pager beeped.

He withdrew, breathing harshly. "You're *not* saved by the beep. Leave the glucose line in and eat the food I'll send you. All of it. I'm returning as soon as I'm done. And I'm staying in the complex overnight, so don't think you can slink away."

With one last fierce kiss, he let her go and rose to his feet. Larissa's eyes clung to him until he disappeared then they squeezed shut as she trembled with the reprieve.

She couldn't have borne him finding out she was pregnant that way. She had to tell him herself. If she told him at all.

And she'd been just thinking how her first trimester had passed smoothly! Then he'd reminded her she'd been here four weeks and she'd read his intention for tonight to be *the* night and everything had gone blank, no doubt seeking to escape the confrontation she was now dreading.

As it was, her faint *had* solved the immediate problem. He was so concerned, his plans to push their relationship to the next level were seemingly on hold.

"You're pregnant, aren't you?"

Her eyes snapped open, her gaze slamming up at the whispered words in shock.

She only found Patrick, standing above her, his face the

essence of kindness. She groaned. Leave it to an obstetrician with over three decades' experience to recognize her condition. She could only nod.

"And you don't want...anyone to know." She heard Faress in place of that "anyone" loud and clear. She nodded again. He sat down beside her. "What are you doing about your antenatal checks?"

She let out a tremulous breath. "I haven't been getting any. I'm afraid if I do, it would get around."

"Not if I'm your obstetrician, it won't. Let's set up a schedule right now. And get that first check under way."

"Oh, Patrick." She clung to his hand with a sob. "Thank you."

He squeezed her hand and gave her a huge wink. "Oh, you won't thank me when you see the list of dos and don'ts I have for you."

A week later, on the first day Faress allowed Larissa to work a full day, she was in her office, that gigantic, postmodern space he'd allocated to her, surrounded by her team who used it as their hangout, when Helal walked in.

"Did you hear about the latest human rights breach the good king of Bidalya committed yesterday?"

Larissa's heart took a now-familiar plunge to the pit of her stomach. Not another rumor, she groaned inwardly.

"I wonder where you hear these things." Anika raised her head from her laptop and mumbled, "I haven't met one Bidalyan who has anything bad to say about King Qassem."

Helal gave her a pitying glance. "You haven't met Bidalyans, you've met people who work in this complex. You think they'd speak out against their worshipped employer's father?"

"I do go out after work, you know?" Anika smirked.

"And it doesn't surprise you no one has anything derogatory to say about the king? Where in the world does a ruler have his people's complete admiration and support?"

"In your country?" Anika shot back.

"It's Prince Malek who had that, and he abdicated. Our regent is fine, but he isn't perfect. And we can say that in Damhoor, privately or publicly, and not get arrested."

Anika gave him a ridiculing glance. "So every Bidalyan who has criticized the king has been arrested?"

"Many have. The king is intolerant and senile, and hasn't heard the twenty-first century is well under way."

"Let's say he's no angel," Tom Gerard countered. He was an American neurosurgeon who after a twelve-year rehabilitation following a near-fatal accident had decided to return to medicine as a volunteer. His ordeals had tempered him with infinite tolerance and insight. "But what ruler hasn't been accused of that? Here I can see no reason for the sweeping majority of Bidalyans to be dissatisfied with theirs. The average Bidalyan lives like a king in a country that's a marvel of modern advances and constant development."

"So they should shut up when their rights are breached if they don't toe the line?" Helal shot back. "And it isn't him who's responsible for all the security and prosperity. It's Prince Faress and his modernizing, innovating team of royal cousins. The king is just an old despot Prince Faress barely keeps in check nationally and keeps hidden internationally."

"Just don't let him hear you say that." Patrick slapped Helal on the back. "Dr. Faress, I mean. Calling him *Prince* Faress here."

Larissa couldn't let one more word or speculation add to her turmoil and indecision.

She got to her feet. "How about you keep your crusading powers for the areas of the world that need it, Helal? *When* I whip you into a good enough trauma surgeon, and when Bidalya, where we're all subsidized guests, salvages the other areas of your surgical prowess? And how about I find out if your unquestionable knowledge extends to damage control surgery?"

Everyone burst out laughing at Helal's chagrin before he joined in then proceeded to make an outrageous joke of the

whole situation all through their session. Larissa went along
with the rampant teasing, if only to cover up her tumult.

Though she'd stopped Helal short, her own information-
gathering had validated his words *and* her initial fear of
Jawad's father. Every source said that while the king wisely
presented Faress to the outside world as Bidalya's advanced,
peace-advocating, benevolent front, let him and the younger
generation of his royal family forge Bidalya's foreign policy
and take it to its current prosperity, Faress couldn't be everywhere, was engrossed in his medical role. A lot slipped under
his radar, while the king still ruled absolutely and sometimes
most unwisely in many internal affairs.

So when…if…she revealed her secret and the king's
reaction was worse than anything she'd ever feared from the
reasonable, refined man Faress was, would Faress be able to
counteract it? And even if he did, was it wise to let that kind
of man be the baby's grandfather, the one with the most say
and sway in his life? Could she possibly tell Faress only?
What would that achieve? Except alienation from him and
nothing at all for the baby? Without the king's knowledge,
Jawad's heritage wouldn't be passed on.

Despondent, more undecided than ever, she staggered out
at the end of the session. *Oh, God, Faress, where are you?*

He'd never been away longer than four hours at a time. But
yesterday he hadn't spent the evening with her, hadn't taken her
home. And today he hadn't escorted her to work. He'd canceled
his morning list, had told her to substitute it with her training
session. He'd called her at one p.m. to say he'd be a bit later. It
was now four p.m. That made it twenty-four hours since she'd
last seen him. She still kept expecting, *hoping* he'd materialize
like he always did, her heart dropping a beat out of every three.

He didn't.

She entered the ward where they shared scheduling cases
each day on dragging feet, grief hitting her the hardest it had
since she'd set foot in Bidalya, almost doubling her over.

Faress had been giving her no chance to dwell on how lost she felt without Claire, her confidante, advisor and the surrogate mother who'd made losing both their parents when she'd been only twelve survivable. The roller-coaster of emotions he'd plunged her into had distracted her from burning with rage at fate for depriving her, depriving the world of such an incredible being. But all it had taken had been a day away from him for her to revert to her misery before she'd laid eyes on him.

Deprived of his borrowed vitality and stability at a time when the support of preoccupation was temporarily removed, memories, anguish hit her with the force of an eviscerating blow.

Just as she stumbled with it, another thought struck her, sending her first taste of real nausea welling up her throat.

What if Faress had decided she wasn't worth more of his time or attention?

He'd kept his promise after all, had slowed down. Not that she felt he had. If she'd thought he'd overwhelmed her at first, she should have reserved judgment a bit longer. He was an unbelievable amalgam of old-world chivalry and contemporary sophistication and charisma, all entrenched in true superiority and profound benevolence. What she'd seen of him then had been but a taste of a humbling human being.

But maybe he'd been withdrawing, not slowing down. And if this was true, was today the beginning of the end?

She should be hoping it was.

As long as he pursued her, she was trapped, couldn't find an opening to even broach the subject of the baby. But if he was cooling now, he might develop the detachment that would avail her of an objective hearing. Her one chance was if he was forgetting about her in the heat of another conquest and...

She couldn't bear thinking he was forgetting about her.

But he *wasn't*. She had last week to prove it! And just yesterday he'd still been lavishing passion and hunger, respect and admiration on her...

So how could she confront him, pulverize all that?

Oh, God, she'd trapped herself on a one-way road to damnation the day she'd withheld the truth from him.

Pressure built inside her, desperate for an outlet, until she prayed her skull would burst. It didn't, the pressure not finding release even in the tears that clogged her eyes.

Oh, Claire. What shall I do?

As if in answer to her plea, an answer boomed in her head. *Tell him the truth.* Now. *Come what may.*

Withholding it any more meant sinking deeper into the unintentional deception, ending up looking far worse in his eyes once it came out. And it had to come out. She owed it to him that she told him all, her situation, his brother's fate and his unborn nephew's existence. She could only pray he'd understand, be lenient with her, kind to his flesh and blood.

Taking several deep breaths until she started feeling lightheaded, she turned around—and almost stumbled.

He was walking through the ward's door, his gaze catching hers at once with *that* look in his eyes. The look to dive into and never resurface from. The look that told her all her hopeful dread had been unfounded, that instead of cooling he was now like a heat-seeking missile, locked onto his course and unswerving.

Except if she told him something drastic. Like the truth.

But until she did, he wasn't stopping. Conquerors of his caliber only became unwavering with a difficult target.

She stood transfixed, watching him eliminating the distance between them, grateful for the tiny favor of being in public. It was only there he didn't touch her, his aversion to public displays of affection a personal predilection, she was sure, not one imposed by the conservative culture or his status.

Then he spoke and she almost collapsed at his feet.

"Did you miss me, *ya jameelati*?"

Faress heard the gruffness of his voice, had no control over it, didn't want to control it.

Why should he? He wanted her to hear it, see it, how he'd hungered for a sight of her after an endless day of deprivation.

He hadn't expected an answer to the question he'd used for a caress, an embrace. But she gave him one, an overcome nod as her eyes stormed through an unprecedented array of hues.

Elation stormed from his depths. She'd missed him. Like he'd missed her. He couldn't believe how he'd missed her.

But then again, he believed nothing more. Her spell had been tightening over his senses from that first look. She wasn't only the female who appealed to everything male in him, she was the doctor whose skills and work ethic enthralled the doctor, the wit and mind that spellbound the intellectual, and the overall character who'd earned the admiration and respect of the man.

He was used to recognizing talent and assigning responsibility to the capable. But he'd never had anyone surpass his expectations like she had, never counted on anyone as unquestioningly as he'd come to count on her.

From the moment he'd unloaded most of his burden of the project onto her shoulders, she'd amazed him. She'd taken his plans and tightened them up, kept fine-tuning them. The project was turning into a great success and it wouldn't have without her. She kept surprising him, keeping up with him like no one ever had, his most valuable surgical partner to date, enhancing his efficiency, saving him untold time and effort while saving priceless lives and preparing others for doing the same. He delighted in their intuitive rapport and the complementing array of skills they possessed and exchanged.

Then there were the precious personal times that gave him his first taste of true happiness.

He'd at first surrendered to the immense emotions she evoked in him without trying to identify them. It had taken her collapse, feeling dread tearing at his insides, despair at imagining a life without her, to know what they were. That transporting, transfiguring malady called love.

Instead of being appalled by his diagnosis, he was elated. Yes, this was love. And it wasn't a malady but an enhancement of life. And it had claimed him whole when he'd always thought it a fiction, when he'd been resigned he'd one day wed for duty.

Now he'd wed for love. And who more worthy than her to bestow his heart, faith and honor on? She was a being without equal, and he would be the proudest man on earth to call her his, to pledge himself hers. No matter the opposition. Or the price.

He now stopped himself with all his will so he wouldn't cleave her to him. He'd never been one for exhibiting emotions. Now he realized he'd never had any to exhibit. She'd changed that. In private, he lavished intimacies on her. In public he barely held them back, so he wouldn't compromise her image as a lady and a professional or her status as his deputy.

But a day apart had turned the certainty of his emotions into urgency, made him unable to wait to proclaim them, to draw her admission of equal involvement with him.

He touched her, powerless to stay away, needing to absorb her tiredness and all her troubles. He needed *her*, must have her, soon, and for ever. He groaned with it all. "And how I missed you."

Larissa lurched at Faress's touch, at his words, raised her wavering gaze to his, and the tears that had been accumulating inside her almost burst out under pressure.

This was the last look of warmth and craving and indulgence, and, oh, God, respect, trust, untainted by doubts and resentment, she'd ever see in his eyes. She drowned in it, flayed herself with it, then inhaled the breath to fuel the words that would deprive her of it all...

"Somow'w'El Ameer Faress*!"*

The shout shot through her, severing the last of her control.

Worry flared in Faress's eyes at her shuddering reaction and he tightened his grip on her arm. Next second the man who'd shouted for him almost barreled into him, snatching his focus away.

Faress swung around to him, took hold of him to steady him, give him an anxious shake. "Speak, *ya rejjal!*"

The man burst out in agitated Arabic and Larissa felt each word jolt through Faress like a bullet. Her anxiety surged with his until she cried out, "What is it?"

Faress turned to her, his whole face working. "It's my sister Ghadah and my niece, Jameelah—they've been in a helicopter crash."

CHAPTER SIX

THE trip on board Faress's flying hospital to the accident scene was a nightmare. As much of a nightmare as the trip Larissa had made just eight weeks ago, to her own sister's accident scene. The only difference was that on that trip she'd already known what to expect. Her sister had already been dead. They'd been certain.

She'd still torn through the bleak, freezing roads with one idea filling her head. That they'd been wrong, that her sister was only gravely injured, her life signs so weak they'd hadn't been able to detect them. That she could still save her.

They hadn't been wrong. Her sister's death had been instantaneous. Larissa had wondered ever since if she'd meant it to be, to make sure Larissa would have no chance to pull her back from death's jaws, like she had countless trauma victims.

But Faress's sister and niece were still alive. They could still save them. *If* they reached them in time.

She clamped her jaw against yet another geyser of debilitating frustration.

It had been fifteen minutes since they'd taken off. They were supposed to reach the crash scene in fifteen more. But each second as she'd watched Faress go through hell was a brand-new definition of the word. The need to ward off his anguish, to help his loved ones was making every second a lifetime. It wasn't making it any more endurable knowing her role would come later.

Her blood had chilled in helplessness as she'd watched the rescue efforts via satellite feed on half a dozen monitors in the communications cabin, keeping totally still so as not to distract Faress.

He hadn't paused for breath ever since they'd come on board, barking constant directions, orchestrating the efforts of the teams extricating the victims from the wreck. She'd lived his distress as Ghadah and Jameelah had been, by necessity, the last ones to be extracted, reliving her own horror and agony on watching her sister's lifeless body being pulled out from the twisted hulk of metal that had been her car.

Both the pilot and Ghadah's assistant were suffering from minor injuries. But the co-pilot was dead, of what had clearly been instantly fatal multiple injuries. Ghadah's and Jameelah's injuries were life-threatening. It was a small mercy both weren't suffering from significant external injuries. She couldn't stand to imagine he could have seen his loved ones like she'd seen her sister.

His voice was rising, developing a terrible, jagged edge that tore across her hyper-extended nerves, the bellows of a cornered lion, of a man losing his mind, as he directed those installing initial lifesaving measures. If she was going crazy, needing to be taking care of them herself, she could only imagine what he was going through, and only because she'd once been there herself. It was unbearable, feeling his suffering.

She looked out of the window at the dunes racing past, stretching to the horizon, the declining sun melding their variegated magnificence with that of azure skies tinged with all the hues of the spectrum to paint a landscape of unforgiving beauty.

Tears accumulated behind the dam of all that stopped her from giving in to their release. Foremost was her need to be Faress's strong right hand in his life's darkest hour. She wouldn't let the echoes of her own ordeal render her less than perfectly useful to him.

"Larissa." Faress's call brought her out of her struggles, dissipating any weakness, had her beside him in a second, ready for anything, his to command. He took her shoulders in a steely vise, looked down at her with eyes gone wild with foreboding.

"You'll see to Jameelah and I'll see to Ghadah. The moment either of us stabilizes their charge and is sure she can hold for even minutes without intervention, we'll go to help the other with the less stable one."

She clutched his arms, her heart torn at seeing him so shaken, so vulnerable. "We'll save them, Faress," she pledged.

He gritted his teeth, gave a curt nod, before he drew her to him, ground stiff, trembling lips to her forehead.

The moment the helicopter descended, he let her go, exploded around and through its hundred-foot length to its door at the tail, shouting orders left and right. He knocked the door open, jumped out of the helicopter when it was still some feet off the ground. At the last moment before she jumped out in his wake she remembered.

She couldn't. She could fall, hurt the baby.

With a bursting heart she waited as the door that turned into four steps whacked the ground as the chopper came to a standstill on the ground. She negotiated the steps then ran across what felt like an impeding sea of powdered gold.

In seconds she was beside Faress who'd fallen to his knees between his unconscious sister and niece.

At her first look at them her heart convulsed, her pain at seeing them this way soaring for their distressing resemblance to Faress.

Ghadah was what her name proclaimed her to be, a beauty, Faress's feminine equivalent, a statuesque, queenly woman of overpowering femininity. Jameelah lived up to her name, too. Beautiful. Clearly Faress's flesh and blood, what his daughter would look like one day…

She bit her lip hard, drawing blood as she swooped down on Jameelah. Faress had forbidden intubation attempts. With both maximum suspicion head and neck injury cases, he couldn't risk anyone less skilled than them handling it. She wasn't waiting until they were inside the helicopter.

Faress validated her decision, rasped, "We intubate here."

Without missing a beat they both reached for intubation instruments, had Ghadah and Jameelah intubated within minutes, the difficult procedures proving his fear had been justified.

Then each raced into an initial survey, exchanged clipped, shorthand trauma findings, each painting a grave diagnosis and a possible bleak prognosis.

In minutes he raised his eyes to her, his urgency making him terse. "Let's get them to surgery."

Then everything overlapped. Securing Jameelah for the transfer, running beside her and then ahead, directing assistants, installing her in the fully equipped surgical station, connecting her to a dozen monitors, injecting her with contrast material, watching radiographic images, getting a definitive diagnosis.

All the time it felt she was sharing every second with Faress, her lungs burning on the same bated breath, her throat closing on the same mounting desperation as he rushed through the same sequence with Ghada, but reaching a far worse diagnosis.

After resuscitation, she left her assistants performing crucial investigations on Jameelah and raced to his side.

Faress snatched a look up at her before returning feverish eyes to Ghada, his hands a blur as he instituted one measure after another, calibrated one machine then the next, obtaining more and more readings and images.

Larissa gave him the report his single burning glance had asked for. "Jameelah has blunt abdominal aorta injury, consistent with a seat-belt injury, has a contained if growing pseudo-aneurysm. Aggressive fluids are correcting her shock so far."

Faress's shuddering exhalation agreed with her decision to leave Jameelah to come to his aid with Ghada. Though the ten-year-old's injury could turn catastrophic, with the pseudo-aneurysm bursting and causing fatal internal hemorrhage if not controlled at once, Ghada was the one in graver danger right now.

Unable to speak, Faress's agonized gaze led hers to the monitor transmitting images from an overhead X-ray machine.

Larissa barely caught back a cry. Ghada had four pulverized thoracic vertebrae!

Even before she snatched burning eyes from the catastrophic injury to images detailing Ghada's thoracic and intracranial injuries that made her a multi-trauma nightmare, Larissa had seen enough to plunge her into despair. Whatever they did now, Ghada would probably be crippled for the rest of her life.

But that was no consideration right now. They had to save her life. And then her spinal cord might be intact. Her lack of reflexes on initial survey could be transient spinal shock. They had to take care of the immediate dangers.

"We'll deal with the thoracic hemorrhage first?" she asked. Faress's answer was practical, as with a face turned to stone and motions as precise as an automaton, he made his first incision between Ghada's ribs. He was going for a thoracotomy. There was no place for minimally invasive techniques here. She handed him a rib spreader, waited until he placed it then took over, needing to spare him being the one to saw his sister's chest open. He let her without a word, raised the rate of blood transfusion to maximum, demanded ten more units then suctioned what seemed to be an unending fount of blood out of Ghada's chest cavity.

They explored and repaired the lung and great vessels injuries in record time. But it seemed nothing they were doing had any effect. Ghada's vital signs deteriorated steadily.

They rushed through closure, immediately turned to her subdural hematoma evacuation. They'd gone through scalp and skull opening, were working in tandem like a perfectly oiled machine, suctioning blood, irrigating clots and cauterizing bleeding vessels when Faress suddenly spoke, his voice as thick and ghastly as the clotted blood they'd evacuated from Ghada's injuries.

"The sandstorm came out of the blue, lasted long enough only to take the helicopter down. Ghadah was on her way back from her husband's grave in his home town. It's the first time she let Jameelah go with her. It's why she's here, like this, instead of in the emergency compartment, being treated for simple fractures."

Larissa raised horrified eyes to him. "Faress..."

"She wasn't wearing a seat belt," Faress grated, his voice fracturing, agony made sound, for her ears only, even though Ghada was beyond hearing him. "She must have left her seat to wrap her body around Jameelah to protect her. And she did. Jameelah was on the side that sustained the most damage. She would have been killed on impact like the co-pilot. Ghada gave her life for her daughter."

"Oh, God, Faress don't say that. We'll save her..."

"We'll fix her injuries. We *have* fixed them. But don't you see?" His tattered groan broke her control, her resolution not to keep looking at what would undermine her stamina. She looked now at Ghada's monitors, each testimony to a life ebbing by the second. "She's letting go." He raised eyes crimson with fear, drowning in despondency. The cautery probe Larissa was holding crashed to the floor. She barely felt her assistant pushing another into her nerveless hand as Faress's words pummeled her. "She feels what surviving means, that her life as she knows it is over, that she won't be the mother and princess she was and she'd rather die. I know that. I know *her*."

"No, Faress," she sobbed. "She'll live, for Jameelah...for you...for herself..."

Ghada gave her answer to that. She flatlined.

"Defibrillator," Faress roared, had it in his hand charged and ready in seconds, roared again, any resignation scorched away in a blast of terror and determination, "Clear."

The first shock had no effect. Neither did the second. Or third.

And in a fifteen-minute exacerbation of horror, a seizure of desperation, nothing did.

Then there was silence.

Larissa felt as if the very world held its breath, as if time itself had stopped, in recognition not only of such a loss but in awe of the magnitude of grief it inflicted.

Faress stood there, his shocked gaze riveted to his sister's battered form, the shell that no longer housed the woman who'd shared his life from childhood, whom he clearly loved with all of his being.

An eternity later, he moved. Everyone in the compartment lurched out of their paralysis. He reached out and time expanded, magnifying each motion as his hand touched Ghada's lifeless cheek. Gasps of stifled horror spread like wildfire. Then he bent, put his forehead to his sister's, closed his eyes on a shuddering exhalation.

Someone burst out crying. A commotion erupted as others rushed the woman out of Faress's hearing. Not that he seemed to be aware of anything around him. Larissa staggered towards him and the world blinked out. It came back again, to the floor rising up to meet her. At the last moment hands caught her, pulled her up to her feet, but she only saw him, distorted, rippling, through a hot, wet barrier, frozen in the last communion with Ghada, oblivious to everything, a prisoner to the brutality of his unendurable loss.

Suddenly high-pitched bleeps blared, tearing Larissa out of the well of crushing anguish. *Jameelah's monitors.*

Strength and focus surged into her with dizzying suddenness as she exploded to Jameelah's side, met Dr. Tarek's reddened eyes.

"Deepen sedation and regional block," she croaked. "We can't risk general anesthesia."

Tarek nodded, jumping on the reprieve of the need for his skills. Larissa gasped more orders, preparing for the open laparotomy it would take to reach Jameelah's injury and repair it. In a minute she stood poised to start.

She couldn't bear to intrude on Faress's grief, but he was the best surgeon around. She needed him. Jameelah needed him.

"Faress."

At her desperate call he swung up, his empty gaze meeting hers. She meant to say, *I need you.* She couldn't produce a sound, mouthed the entreaty.

He turned his eyes back to Ghada, touched her hand. Larissa saw his lips move, as if he was talking to her. Her heart seized in her chest, but she couldn't afford to give the tragedy one more moment, couldn't wait to see if he'd be able to bring his turmoil under control long enough, well enough to be of any help.

She made the first incision in Jameelah's abdomen, rasped to her first assistant, "Start the cell-saver, get as much blood as you can."

She knew the helicopter's blood bank couldn't have enough blood to cope with the enormous amounts Jameelah would need until they got her hemorrhage under control, not after the amounts they'd used up already. With a cell-saver machine they'd collect, clean and save Jameelah's blood for re-transfusion.

"Cell-saver won't provide a product of good enough hematocrit value to correct Jameelah's hemorrhagic shock on its own."

Faress. He'd come. Oh, God…

He went on, his face impassive, his voice dead, "Get twenty more units of O-neg."

One of the nurses said, "We have only eight more units."

"I'm O-neg," Larissa said, her voice wavering beyond her control. That made her a universal donor. And though she was pregnant and would usually be unable to donate, she knew there was no risk, when she'd replace what she donated the same day.

Faress's eyes went to her and she thought she saw the Faress she knew, beneath the suffocating layers of unspent suffering, communicating with her, needing her.

Then he turned away. "Lamyaa, see if anyone else is O-neg. Get a blood collection bag for Larissa."

"Make it two," Larissa said. "Just put the volume back into me. I'll get a transfusion as soon as we're back at the complex."

Something like anxiety disturbed the deadness in his eyes. Then he nodded. "Get me two over-the-needle catheters, 18 gauge." Those were in his hands in seconds. He approached her, for the first time since she'd known him depriving her of eye contact. He placed each catheter into the sides of her neck to keep her arms free for the surgery. His technique was so perfect she barely felt the needles piercing her skin.

They found two more O-neg people among them. With two units from each, as well as the cell-saved blood, they'd cover Jameelah's needs.

Without missing a beat, Faress turned to Jameelah, widened the incision Larissa had made, placed self-retaining retractors, until they had maximum visibility and reach. Gritting her teeth against the reality of the little body she was invading, she reached in, pushed the intestines to the side, exposing the aorta for him as their assistants struggled to siphon off a horrifying amount of blood. It took endless minutes before he cross-clamped the aorta, stopping it, only for a feverish race against time to start. All through the procedure her assistant blotted tears instead of sweat.

It took thirty minutes to repair the aortic tear, three times that to explore Jameelah's abdomen for other possible injuries then close her up.

At last Faress took a step back, stared down at Jameelah, for the first time looking at her face. Silence reigned throughout the compartment again. Now the field of surgery had been covered, Jameelah looked like she was sleeping peacefully. Her mother lay dead a dozen feet away. Another wave of empathy and pity crashed through Larissa. This time she let it, no longer trying to slow down the cascade of tears.

The flow became a deluge when Faress bent to his niece,

repeated the heart-rupturing gesture of putting his forehead to hers, like he'd done with her mother.

She thought she heard him say, *"La tkhafi, ya sagheerati, ana baadi ma'ek."*

Don't be afraid, my little one. I'm still with you.

The following days were beyond nightmarish.

Only Faress keeping her close made them endurable. Larissa would have gone out of her mind away from him, fearing for his sanity after having Ghada slip through his fingers. She burned with needing to offer support, jumped at the chance to be of use when he delegated to her the task of addressing foreign correspondents, giving his formal statement covering his sister's death. He had enough on his hands, being the surgeon in whose hands she'd died, the crown prince responsible for major public announcements, and the brother who'd had to inform his family of his sister's death.

It had been then she'd had her first sighting of his father and had been shaken to her foundations.

In her line of work she dealt with grieving parents all the time, had seen people from resigned to manic. But the king's reaction to the news of his daughter's death was horrifying. He was. All her fears of him had multiplied as she'd watched Faress struggle to contain his rage and grief.

Then the first devastating crest passed and Faress still had to deal with the funeral and with a grieving nation. Princess Ghada had been a truly beloved princess and her passing reverberated throughout the kingdom like an earthquake.

All through they shared Jameelah's vigilant follow-up, her constant improvement the only ray of light in the catastrophe. But that was dimmed by the dread of having to face her with the news of her mother's death. Faress decreed it wouldn't be until she was back to full health, trusting no one but himself and Larissa near her when he let her surface from sedation.

Everything settled into pervasive resignation until two

weeks to the day they had lost Ghada Faress declared that they'd resume their schedule, that work and other patients waited for no one.

With a battered heart Larissa hoped preoccupation would help him to regain his balance, start to heal his wounds.

That first day back at the complex was like going to Ghada's funeral all over again. Everyone was subdued, and around Faress silent, tense, in respect for his loss and continued suffering.

That night, going back to the palace, Faress held her hand. Larissa tore her eyes away from his profile, berating herself for obsessively watching for any chink in his suffering where she could enter and offer something, anything that might help alleviate even a wisp of it.

She stared at the magnificence of the most advanced city she'd ever seen, one that gave the impression it had all been erected whole that day to the most lavish standards, while constantly evolving with extreme-concept projects that rose between soaring mirrored buildings without disturbing the perfectly realized surroundings. She failed to be impressed tonight. Any pleasure in her surroundings had been extinguished along with Ghada's life. Living with Faress's grief was turning everything into torment instead.

Faress as usual walked her to her guest house. At her door, he took her in a fierce hug that lifted her off her feet, then he abruptly let her go before she could cling, and walked away so fast he seemed to dissolve into the night.

She stood transfixed for endless minutes, swaying, shaking, struggling for breath. And she knew. She had to go after him.

She staggered through the extensive, ingeniously landscaped and lit grounds, her awe rising even now at what permeated them—the entitlement of the all-powerful prince Faress was, the subtlety of the man and the sensitivity of the surgeon. In the distance rose the sprawling stone palace that spoke of all that and everything else that Faress was.

She felt his guards' invisible eyes monitoring her every move, relaying them ahead to forward stations. She wondered if they'd stop her until they asked Faress how to deal with her intruding outside her permitted territory.

They didn't stop her, and when she was on the steps leading to the columned patio, footmen seemed to appear from nowhere, rushed to open the gigantic double doors for her, treating her with all the deference they'd offer Faress himself.

She wobbled into a circular, columned hall that sprawled under a hundred-foot-high stained-glass dome, swayed as the doors were closed soundlessly behind her. Her gaze slammed around but there was no one there to meet her and in her hectic state and the subdued lighting she got only impressions of a sweeping floor extending on both sides, felt a male influence, Faress's, in décor and furnishing, a virile presence, his, permeating the place. Her nervous gaze ended up where thirty-foot-wide marble stairs rose a dozen feet before reaching a spacious platform that extended each side of the upper floor.

Suddenly her gaze dragged to the top of one side and her heart kicked. A shadow detached itself from the depth of darkness, moving soundlessly into the light.

Faress. Haggard and heart-wrenching in the first indigenous garb she'd ever seen him in, a black robe, an *abaya*, trimmed in gold thread. He looked as if he'd stepped out from another world, another time, almost supernatural in mien and impact. But it was the fevered emotions radiating from him that shook her.

She ran up, needing to be near him, stopped a step beneath him, shaking, her tears flowing free, her larynx a fiery coal. "I *hurt* for you…" she wailed. "As much as I hurt for myself when I lost my own sister to a senseless accident, too, just before I came here. She—she was everything to me…"

His nostrils flared, his jaw muscles bunched. Then the rawness that had replaced all emotions in his eyes melted in a flare of empathy.

"Did you have a chance to fight for her?"

She hiccuped a tearing sob at the enormous emotion thickening his voice. She shook her head, sent tears splashing over her lips, her forearms, the floor.

"Then your loss is even worse, arriving too late, deprived of the chance to try to save her, or to even say goodbye."

"Oh, God, no, Faress, arriving too late was like a single bullet to the heart. Not like the hail that shredded you as Ghada slipped through your fingers. The hope, the dread, the desperation, the crushing responsibility. Oh, God, Faress, the way you suffered, still suffer, I can't bear it!"

Something unbridled detonated in his eyes. She cried out at its impact, reached out trembling hands, offering all that she was, if it would only alleviate a portion of his suffering.

He took her up on her offer, bent and swept her up in his arms. Then the world moved in hard, hurried thuds, each one hitting her with vertigo, the pressure of emotion almost snuffing out her consciousness.

Then she was sinking into a resilient surface, into cool softness, enveloped by his scent, shrouded by dim lights and incense, by virility and craving.

He came down half over her and she moaned with the blow of stimulation, emotional and physical, of her first real contact with him, her first exposure to the full measure of his ferocity, his hunger.

He rose over her, his hands trembling in her confined hair, releasing it, spreading its thickness beneath her, then burying his face in it and breathing her in hard. "I couldn't have survived the past two weeks without you, Larissa, *habibati, hayati, abghaki, ah'tajek...*" Then he took her lips.

He'd called her his love, his life, had told her he wanted her, *needed* her. And if it had been possible to let him take her very life to fill his needs, she would have surrendered it. She surrendered what she could now, all of herself.

He must have felt the totality of her offer, plunged deeper into her mouth until she felt him touching her essence, drawing it into him, his tongue thrusting in furious rhythm, deep and carnal, each plunge riding a growl of insatiability, sending molten agony to her core, carrying on it his dominance, his imperiousness, his surrender and supplication.

Then his hands were everywhere, down her length, fusing her to him, on her buttocks, pressing her against his steely erection, in her elasticated waistband, dragging her T-shirt out then over her head, on her flesh beneath, sending a high-voltage current streaking through her to the rhythm of his feverish stroking before both hands circled her waist, raised her against the headboard, bringing her confined breasts level with his face. Then he buried it there, nuzzled her fiercely.

She cried out with the excess of sensation, with seeing the dark majesty of his head against her bursting flesh. Overcome, she let her hands fulfill the fantasy she'd thought would remain one for ever, burying their hunger in the luxuriance of his mane, pressing his head harder to her.

He rumbled something deep and driven, the sound spearing from his lips directly into her heart. Then he tore himself from her convulsing grip. She cried out as if he'd wrenched her hands off.

Before she could flay herself for being so wanton that she might have appalled him, he spread her on her back again, captured her hands in one of his, stretched her arms above her head. She twisted in mortification, turned her face into sheets laden with his scent, unable to withstand his burning scrutiny.

"Look at me, *ya galbi*." His demand overrode her will and distress, drew her eyes to his. She lurched at the darkness there, the pain. "Let me see you, feel you, your beauty, your vitality…"

And she understood. He needed to feel her life, to counteract the horror of losing someone so loved, so alive, so senselessly.

Needing to offer her body, her very life for his pleasure, his comfort, she arched up, let him undo her bra, expose breasts turgid with pregnancy and arousal.

"Ma ajmallek ya galbi…anti rao'ah…" He closed trem-

bling hands on her breasts and she arched off the bed in a shock of pleasure, making a fuller offering of her flesh. He tore his *abaya* off, half exposing a body chiseled from living granite by virility gods and endless stamina and discipline.

Her awed hands trembled over his perfection. "How beautiful you are… *You* are the wonder…"

He caught her hands again, spread her arms wide at her sides. "Explore me, lay claim to my every inch later, Larissa, later."

He growled as he swooped down on her, rubbed his hair-roughened chest against her breasts until she thrashed beneath him, bucked. Then he bent, opened his mouth over first one breast then the other, as if he'd devour her. Between long, hard draws on each nipple that had her writhing, sobbing, begging, he told her exactly that. That he wanted all of her now. *Now.*

"Bareedek kollek, daheenah, habibati. Daheenah."

She lay powerless under the avalanche of need as her clothes disappeared under his urgency. The spike of ferocity in his eyes at his first sight of her full nakedness should have been alarming. It only sent her heart hurtling with shyness, with pride that her sight affected him that intensely, with the brutality of anticipation. Her moans became keens as he sought her womanhood, his fingers parting her, sliding between her folds, his face contorting on something primal when he felt the heat and moistness of her readiness. She convulsed on the pleasure, hazing with it, with failing to imagine what union with him would bring if a touch unraveled her body and mind. Her stifled cries harmonized with his rumbles, the sound of his steel control snapping.

He came over her and the feel of him, his mass and maleness and power between her legs melted all her heart, all her insides, each thrust at her core through the last barrier of clothes wrenching more pleas from her depths. He rose to both knees to free himself, his lips spilling feverish worship into hers, proclaiming her soul of his heart, raggedly confessing his need to be inside her. *"Roh galbi, mehtaj akoon jow'waki…"*

And she couldn't bear not having him inside her, couldn't bear the emptiness he'd created inside her, couldn't… couldn't…

Oh, God! She *couldn't*.

She went rigid, almost wailed, "Faress, please, *stop*…"

CHAPTER SEVEN

LARISSA felt her plea pummeling Faress.

He lurched and his hand stilled, his lips froze on her neck. Tension buzzed through every muscle imprinted on hers. Then slowly, so slowly, he rose above her, his face taut, his breathing harsh, his eyes unreadable.

He'd be justified to think she'd been leading him on, to even disregard her flimsy demand, give her what her body was screaming for.

But she had no doubt he wouldn't. Faress would never impose himself on her, on any woman. Not even after she'd led him on. But how she wished she could tell him to forget her outburst, to just take her, now.

But she couldn't let him take her, share ultimate intimacies with her, not under false pretenses. And it would be just that with him still ignorant of the truth. He probably wouldn't want to come near her when he finally learned it.

But how could she tell him now? Ghada's death had nearly destroyed him. How could she tell him that he'd lost his brother too? The brother he kept talking about with such love and longing? Jawad's death had been over two months ago, but to him it would happen the moment he learned of it. She couldn't inflict another beloved sibling's death on him now.

She could only do one thing. Beg his forgiveness.

She didn't hope she'd obtain it. She'd given him the first

reason to think the worst of her. And just thinking she'd lose his good opinion brought on again the tears that had dried in the heat of her hunger.

"Faress, please, forgive me, I needed to be with you, b-but I—I…" And she could say no more.

Faress raised himself on arms so stiff they wouldn't have felt more painful with an infarction. But the agony was the urge to fill their emptiness with her beloved body.

He filled his sight and senses, his memory, with her instead as she lay spread beneath him, beyond his fantasies, lush and vital and all female, his female, aflame in the dark solitude of his bed, exposed and vulnerable and the most overwhelming power he'd ever known. Her power over him was absolute. And she was cradling him in the only place he'd ever call home, the moist heat of her welcome unraveling his sanity.

But what was shriveling his heart was the sight of her tears, tears of distress again, the pummeling memory of what she'd come here confessing, sharing. Her similar, mutilating loss. The loss he would have given anything to discover, to heal. And what had he done when she'd finally worked up the fortitude to talk about it, if only under the pressure of catastrophic circumstances and the need to offer *him* solace? He'd swept her to his bed.

And she'd begged *his* forgiveness. *Ya Ullah.*

He should be the one on his knees, asking hers. If she hadn't asked him to stop, he would have been lost inside her now, minutes away from release. And it didn't matter that he knew he would have given her the same pleasure. What mattered was that he'd snatched at her the moment she'd offered herself, rushed her seduction, short-changed her cherishing, would have turned their long-craved, their *sacred* first time together into a frenzied mating. The first time she hadn't even been here offering.

He carefully lifted his body from the cradle of hers, shuddered at the sensations even severing contact with her detonated inside him. But mostly at feeling the same brutal desire eating through her, wrenching at his, clamping his loins in agony, such a contrast with the agitation shaking her all over and the shyness spreading peach through her cream.

And he knew. What he now realized he'd known all along but had never dwelt on. What everything about her, every word and look and tremor since they'd met had been telling him.

She was a virgin. He was certain. No man had ever plundered her pleasures.

Alhamdolel'Lah... Thank God she'd stopped him. The crime of rushing not only their first time but hers would have been irretrievable.

But she *had* stopped him. And now he couldn't stop pride from surging in guilt's wake. Though her sexual experience hadn't even been an issue with him before, though he liked to think he'd left the elemental possessiveness of his heritage behind, now he knew she had none, he couldn't help the rush of exultation that his mate would know no other man's touch.

But if, without experience, she'd responded to him, enslaved his senses this way, he couldn't even imagine what it would be like, what she'd do to him once he initiated her into the rites of passion, swept her into the abandoned realms of sensual decadence, once she applied all that genius and skill to becoming a mistress of the arts of pleasure as she was in the arts of healing.

But it wasn't time to torment himself with those projections. It was enough now that he knew. He'd be her first. And her only.

Only not now. Only when he could offer her all of himself untainted by grief, by any form of emotional dilution. It had to be soon. It would be.

He swung his legs to the floor, reached for the cover he'd tossed aside in preparation for entering the bed that had been a barren desert strewn with thorns until she'd come, the bed he needed her to never leave. He turned back to her, started to slide the cover over her, feet, then legs, going up, hearing the whisper of rich cotton gliding over richer velvet skin, savoring her every jerk, every moan betraying her enjoyment, her torment. When he reached her waist, he gave in, took more suckles of the breasts that had re-whetted his appetite for life. The music of her gasps, the intoxication of her squirming, the hands that, in spite of her intentions, clamped his head to her engorged-with-need flesh, begging his devouring, and the scent of her arousal sent blood crashing in his head, thundering in his loins.

It took all his will to end his feast of her, tuck the cover beneath her armpits, covering up her temptation. Then he dropped kisses across one shoulder, up her neck to her lips then down the other side. Her trembling was constant by the time he withdrew.

He soothed her, smoothed his hand over the luxury of her incredible tresses. "It's me who begs your forgiveness, *ya rohi*. You came here so magnanimously offering me haven from my turmoil and I took your offer where you didn't mean it to go. Not yet. And justifiably so. When I take you, not one second of my possession of you, my pleasuring of you will be tainted by any need but my need for every inch of you, every quiver, every cry, every satisfaction. I won't take you when the need for solace in your arms is an ingredient that mars the purity, the ferocity of my need for you."

A strangled sound escaped her, and he swooped to take it into him, opening his lips over hers.

"I admit," he muttered between deep, then deeper plunges into the maddening fount of her taste, "Though it's an impossibility not to be aroused to the point of pain at the mere thought of you, my need for your haven is as great now." He withdrew to fill his sight with her, her beauty ripened with need for him, to make his urgent request. "Will you bestow it on me?"

Her tears flowed heavier as she held out shaking arms to him. On a groan of sweetest relief and triumph, he filled them, came down beside her. He turned her to her side, plastered his chest to her naked back, then wrapped himself all around her, filled his aching limbs with her preciousness, settled into another form of intimacy to what his body was roaring for.

And if he'd needed proof of how much he loved her, this was it. Just holding her permeated him with the peace he'd thought he'd never experience again, with a feeling of invincibility, brought him far more pleasure than all his life's previous intimacies combined. But, then, she *was* his life's first true intimacy.

Larissa had been awake for a few minutes. She kept her eyes closed.

She didn't want the sight of her surroundings to distract her from savoring the memories of her life's most incredible night.

Faress had not only not been angry at her contradictory behavior, he'd left her in awe of his control again, in agony at his trust, exonerating her, even apologizing for almost taking what she'd offered so fully.

Then he'd bestowed another privilege on her, letting her offer him solace. For hours she'd lain awake, scared of wasting one second of experiencing him, listening to his every breath, her heart vibrating to his every heartbeat as he'd lain awake too, fully aroused yet drenching her with tenderness. It had been beyond any intimacy love-making could have imparted, a sharing of such profundity she hadn't known two separate beings could share.

She didn't know when sleep had claimed her, but it was clear it had, and it had been her life's most peaceful and rejuvenating.

She lay savoring the imprint of his every inch on hers even now he wasn't there, finally knowing one thing.

Everything would work out. She just knew that when she judged it possible to burden him with the truth, he'd understand why she'd withheld it, would let her be there for him in yet another loss and everything would eventually end up resolved for the best.

She opened her eyes. Only because the need to see him again had built to an unmanageable level. And because she had to get ready, get *dressed* before he came back.

She jumped out of bed, *his* bed, ran across the gigantic, almost spartan room, snatched the clothes he'd folded with care on the back of an armchair by a matching desk with just a laptop on it and streaked to the door she hoped was the bathroom.

It was. The most incredible place she'd ever been. An honest-to-goodness *hammam*, his own Turkish bath. Three interconnected halls, with the middle one she'd just entered ringed by arches supported by a dozen tapering columns, sprawling beneath a soaring dome with stained-glass windows that created an otherworldly half-light. Below the dome was a raised marble platform of purest white that seemed to glow in the unearthly illumination. This had to be the hot room, the equivalent of a sauna.

Images invaded her mind, her nerve endings, of Faress, naked, lying face down on the marble as steam swirled around his magnificent body, his muscles glistening, their tautness after their exhausting days relaxing under her hands as she rubbed him down, hands and lips lost in tactile nirvana as she tasted him, tongue and teeth overdosing on virility made flesh. Then he turned to her, yanked her to him, plastered her to his slick, heated flesh, let her feel what she'd done to him before laying her down on the marble, spreading her, coming over her...

Sounds outside jerked her out of her erotic haze. He might have returned! And she was standing here in his bathroom, naked and almost reverting to a fluid state with hunger for him.

With the breath knocked out of her she rushed in search of a shower cubicle, found it, turned on perfect-temperature water, stepped inside, her blood tumbling with arousal at the elaborate images her mind generated, of sharing this place's pleasures with Faress. Suddenly her blood congealed as the images turned vicious, showing him sharing it with other women, maybe many at once...

No, *no*. He wasn't like that.

But even if he were, who was she to presume to judge him? He treated her with all the chivalry of a knight of the desert, the elevation of a born prince, but he only wanted her for a lover, would never want her for more. Wouldn't want her at all when he learned the truth. She had no claim on him. Would never have any. Even if his claim on her was for life and beyond and... Oh—oh...

Oh, God.

She should have known. What had been happening to her since she'd laid eyes on him. It wasn't only that he'd bowled her over and she wanted him like she'd never known she could want. It wasn't only that his company had been what had kept her sanity together, what had suppressed her grief and fear of the future. It wasn't only that she'd counted on his collaboration and advice to center her, to extract from her a level of efficiency she hadn't known she was capable of. It wasn't only that she'd gotten so dependent on his support she knew she'd feel its loss like a crippling physical one.

That was all true and had been horrible enough.

But the truth was far more so.

She loved him.

All the way to no return, with everything in her.

Knowing herself, she should have realized her unprecedented reaction to him *had* been love at first sight.

But she'd never believed it could ever happen to her. Though, heaven knew, she should have. Hadn't Claire fallen in love with Jawad the same way? Hadn't that love turned out to be not only real but the only absolute reality in her life? The one thing that had overpowered her love of everything and everyone, her love of life itself? Hadn't it been the reason she'd died?

And she was so like Claire. Why had she believed she'd be different in that?

She should have run away after those first days, before his

spell had become total, unbreakable. She should have found some other way to solve her dilemma.

But she hadn't. She'd stayed, greedy for more of anything with him, drowning in him. And though he wanted her, had last night lavished loving endearments on her, she knew they had been nothing more than what the passionate man he was had lavished on the woman he'd craved in the heat of lust. She couldn't dream her overriding feelings for him could be reciprocated. He was beyond such hopes.

She laid her forehead on the cool marble wall, suffocating with yet another head-on crash with merciless reality.

She'd lost everything loving him, any chance of happiness or even peace. She'd never have anyone else in her life, let alone love again. But she would have realized that sooner or later. Realizing that now made no difference.

And then none of this had been about her in the first place. This was all about Claire's and Jawad's baby.

And if she told Faress, assured the baby's future, and Faress still wanted her, she'd take anything he offered, for as long as he offered it. She only hoped he wouldn't be too angry with her, cut her off, or at least opt out of any liaison with her in fear of complicating his relationship with someone he'd have in his life through his brother's baby. She hoped he'd realize that when he chose to end it, she'd bow out, never cause him any discomfort.

Drawing in painful breaths, she reached for a bar of rich white soap and began lathering his loofah with it, trying to bring her tumultuous emotions under control.

She failed. Everything here smelt of him, felt like him, each whiff, each vibe sending her into spiraling misery and sensory overload. *Just get out of here...*

She stumbled through a slapdash shower, was dressed and desperately gulping steadying breaths in under five minutes.

She heard nothing outside, had probably imagined hearing the noises before. But now she *felt* him outside.

She tried to school her features, her emotions. She'd rush out and throw herself in his arms if she didn't get those under control.

With one last inhalation, she stepped out. Knowing she was fighting a losing battle, that her feelings must be emblazoned all over her face, she walked towards him as he stood by the desk, indescribable in tight-fitting black pants and white shirt, looking down in absorption at an open file. Her heart ricocheted in her chest in anticipation of seeing new levels of intimacy, no matter how superficial and transient in his eyes after last night.

At her approach, he turned.

Her heart stopped. Then it almost burst.

This wasn't Faress. This was a stranger.

An incensed stranger looking at her out of his eyes.

She groped for the armchair's support, swayed, her eyes prisoner to the rage in his, her soul burning with it.

She'd left it too late. She'd lost her chance to be the one to tell him the truth.

He'd somehow found out.

Faress stared at Larissa, rage and disillusion consuming him.

The woman he'd fallen in love with, the *only* woman he'd ever fallen in love with, laid his heart in her hands, at her feet.

A liar. A manipulator. A merciless cheat.

He'd found out just an hour ago. As she'd slept in his bed in the aftermath of what he'd believed to be his life's first true intimacy. He'd left her side unquestioning that he'd found the other half of his soul, that she'd saved his sanity by her empathy and magnanimity. He'd intended to come back to her with his mother's betrothal anklet, kneel at her feet and offer his heart and honor, his life and beyond.

He had it in his pocket now, felt as if each priceless stone studding it was a prism focusing his agony into an unerring laser targeting his heart, shriveling it, his reason, charring it.

But what almost sent him over the brink was the destruction of his last hope. He *had* been clinging to it, even in the face of all evidence. He *had* been hoping he'd face her with his fury and disillusion only to see her innocence in her eyes, in confusion and hurt. But what he saw there was her realization that he'd found her out, her admission that her crimes were grave enough to warrant any punishment.

He saw *fear* in her eyes for the first time. And he knew.

The woman he loved with everything in him had never existed.

So that was why she'd never told him more...*anything* about herself. *Ya Ullah,* how had he never grown suspicious when she'd steered him so masterfully away from anything that could give him clues about her life?

"Faress..." His name on her lips quaked through him. Still. He gritted his teeth against her siren's song, made overpowering now with the imploring quaver braiding through it. "Please...let me..."

He turned on her, crimson blotching his sight, black eclipsing his heart and reason. "Let you what? Lie to me some more?" At her gasp, the way she squeezed her eyes as if against a mortal blow, he lost it. "Let *me,*" he bellowed, feeling the shards of his shattered heart shredding his ribcage, "spare you the effort of coming up with more lies. Which were never lies, of course, just omissions of the truth. Isn't that what you wanted to say? Now, do you want to know how luck betrayed you? When you could...*would* have gotten away with it for ever? It was because Ghada died."

The tears filling her stricken eyes spilled at hearing Ghada's name, splashing down her velvet cheeks. Everything in him roared with the need to reach for her, comfort her, ward off the pain he was inflicting. Then a lacerating voice lashed him.

You're inflicting nothing. Anything you see or feel from her now is part of the ongoing pretense.

He went mad with pain. "It was only because she died that I broke my promise to Jawad. You know, the insane pledge he made me take? What made you so sure I would never tie you to him?"

"Faress, no, please," she sobbed. "I didn't—"

"Didn't know that he made me pledge to never look for him?" he cut her off, his voice shearing, terrible, unrecognizable. "That he'd contact me only on condition that I remained ignorant of his whereabouts, his life? You want me to believe you didn't know he renounced our ways and his family, abdicated his birthright, hid from us for the last eight years? You let me talk and talk about him and all the time *you knew*."

She nodded, her lips trembling so hard they constantly escaped her teeth's efforts to still them. Acknowledging the truth of his words, or only his right to believe them under the circumstances? If the latter, *was* there another explanation…?

Ya Ullah, he still believed there'd be extenuating circumstances? That she'd turn out not to be the fraud the facts revealed her to be?

Incensed further by his inability to overcome her spell, he ground out, his voice butchered, the howl of a mortally wounded beast, "Too bad for you I broke my pledge. Because Ghada died and I thought he should know. Because even though you made me believe I could share my loss with you, she still wasn't a part of you. Because she was a part of *him* and I needed him to share *her* loss."

At this Larissa's silent tears spiked on a hot, sharp lament, a lance penetrating his heart with the force of a heart attack.

He ignored the agony, hurtled on, "Too bad for you I needed him, needed my older brother. So I searched for him. And an hour ago, I got this."

He slammed his open palm down on the file that had taken his one remaining sibling from him, just as it ended all his hopes and pulverized his heart. The desk splintered under his agonized fury.

Larissa was weeping openly now, the sight of her desolation, her false, self-serving desolation skewering through his skull with another wave of rage and misery.

"He hid so well in the new land he'd made his home, even my intelligence service got hazy information on his life there. He was so afraid that if anyone knew where he was, our father would too, and he would tear him away or, worse, poison his life there, end his happiness, even harm his beloved. He even feared telling me. *Me.*" And he'd go insane with regret, with guilt, for the rest of his life that he hadn't overridden that fear, disregarded it and *made* Jawad share his self-made privileges. Now it was too late. Too late. He roared with it all. "And just when I did what I should have done years ago, found him, I learned that he died in his self-imposed exile, sick and alone." Larissa shook her head, hiccuped, one hand extending to quake its negation. "You're trying to say he wasn't alone? That he had a loving wife at his side? Yes, I had an indistinct photo of his wife. A woman with flaming red hair and a willowy body. *You.*"

She staggered, collapsed where she stood with the wrath of his last shout, ended up on the floor, clinging to the chair he'd kept between them so he wouldn't reach for her, touch her and lose what remained of his mind and control. He was close enough with her looking up at him with those miraculous eyes wild with shock.

Why shock? Why now? And he even assumed this could be real? From the woman who'd lied so seamlessly, whose very vibes had sworn to him of her inexperience in the ways of the flesh? When she'd been his brother's for eight years? In a marriage that, from the little Jawad had told him of the woman he'd left the whole world for, had been blazingly sensual? And it had remained so till the day he'd died. Otherwise Jawad would have come back to them.

The woman he worshipped body and soul was the same woman Jawad had worshipped the same way…inconceivable, unendurable…

He went down on his haunches. Unable to stand any more. Unable to stand seeing her at his feet this way when he should relish it. He didn't, felt every nerve punishing him with the need to haul her up, carry her to the bed they'd shared all night, turn back the clock, wipe his memory clean.

He flayed his stamina for a minute, watching her tears, imagining them changing color in her distress.

Then he groaned, "*B'Ellahi,* why did you come here?"

She shuddered, wiped a trembling hand over her wet lips, started to open them. Did she think he wanted an answer? Could bear listening to her adding to the lies?

"I'll tell you why," he grated across her first wavering syllable. "You came here intent on getting the wealth and privileges you married Jawad for. You must have been enraged when they never materialized, when Jawad threw away all he was born into in his pursuit of your love and a so-called normal life with you. You must have lasted that long with him only in hope you'd one day get an unimaginable return on your investment of years of putting up with his infatuation and acting the part of the devoted wife and lover—a life as a queen."

She kept shaking her head, jerking with each word soaked with the venom of his agony as if with the lash of a whip, her tears splashing his hands, wetting the hardwood floor.

Her distress corroded him as if it were real. But it could only be the distress of a criminal caught in the act and fearing retribution, or at least the loss of her projected gains. After the unparalleled effort she'd put into her flawless charade, too. Appealing to him on every level, projecting the illusion of the soulmate who instinctively knew him down to his last impulse and thought, who shared his views and goals, who understood and appreciated him like he'd never been, would never be, understood or appreciated…

Ya Ullah… How could he live with the loss of all that?

Losing both his siblings was more endurable. He retained

so much of them, their love and their integrity, his love for them, faith in them, memories of them.

But with Larissa he'd lost everything. He'd been stripped of all he'd had before he'd known her. She might have lost a gamble, a highest-stakes one, but she'd cost him everything worth having.

Feeling the deadness of resignation invading his being, he welcomed it, hurried it on as he rasped, "So when Jawad died without giving you what you wanted, you went for plan B. With his extensive knowledge of me at your disposal, you came here armed with all you needed to lay your trap, aiming to capture another Aal Rusheed brother, this time one in his full power, one capable of handing you the world. Too bad for you that you failed."

Each word of rage, of pain, each look of disillusion and disgust had been a knife twisting in Larissa's vitals. But that summation, that verdict was a mortal blow she couldn't survive.

She had to ward it off, fought the muteness, choked out her only defense, the truth. *"I only came here for the baby."*

At the word "baby" Faress staggered up and backwards as if blown away by the force of a detonation, only the collision with the now-askew desk aborting his momentum. He looked at her with the same shocked eyes that had acknowledged Ghada's death. Worse, with the eyes of someone looking at the woman who'd just shot him in the heart.

After a mutilating stretch of harsh-breathing, bone-quaking silence he finally rasped in a voice that felt no longer like sound, but like pain, like bleeding, "You have a baby?"

She'd already blurted it out, but to have to elaborate on it, detail the specifics, when he looked down at her that way…

Another geyser of tears flowed out of her eyes. "N-no…I'm—I'm pregnant…f-fourteen weeks n-now…" Then she broke down.

It could have been an hour while Faress stood frozen,

looking down at her as if at an impossibility, a monstrosity, while she surrendered to the crushing breakers of misery.

When they finally receded enough, after they'd made sure she was within a breath of unconsciousness, she had to state another part of the truth. For the record. She had no hope for amnesty.

"I thought Jawad was an orphan. I—I only found out who he really was after he died. And when I came here and met you, I had no idea who you were until I saw that magazine…"

She choked on another wave of desolation, fell silent.

At length, he talked, his voice a dead monotone, "So you came here, signed up for this job, and didn't know I was the current crown prince, and your boss?"

She raised her gaze to him, hoping to find a glimpse of the Faress she knew. There wasn't. He was gone. She still had to make this stranger understand how things had developed.

She forced in a trembling inhalation. "Jawad and Claire died within a week of each other and the weeks afterwards… they were a nightmare. I was pregnant and suddenly alone and I had to rearrange my life around having the baby with no help and with a job like mine. I was desperately looking for alternative career paths when I discovered the baby did have a family. But I couldn't contact you, I thought it might be a mistake. I—I haven't heard good things a-about your father, and your family *was* the family Jawad had cut all relations with. But since I didn't know what drove him away I thought I'd try to find out for myself if it had been something serious because I owed it to the baby to try to give him a family. I took this job knowing only that it was in Bidalya where I could gather information about your family before deciding whether to approach you or not. And then I met you and it all spun out of control. But I did it all for the baby. And I-I'm still not sure if it would be in his best interests to have the Aal Rusheeds for a family…"

"His?" he interrupted, his eyes obsidian chips of steel. "You talk as if you think it's a boy."

"I—I know it is," she stammered. "I had a maternal blood test. Jawad wanted to know." A memory detonated, of Jawad's face as he'd made that demand, drained, emaciated but laughing, excited. "He had a relapse…leukemia, and after the treatment cycle had an infection. He was sure he'd beat it, like he had so many times before, so he wanted to know which gender to shop for the minute he was out of hospital, which he estimated to be by the time the test became possible. But he never made it out… He—he died the very next day."

Something horrifying scraped from the depths of Faress's chest as he dropped into the chair, the sound of his brother's death congealing into reality, another scar gouged in his psyche.

She fought off the horror, the need to rise and throw her arms around him, rid him of all his agony, his rage, at whatever cost to her. She choked on instead, "I still had the test at six weeks, felt as if he'd know w-when I did…"

Faress exploded to his feet, his eyes crazed with pain and rage beyond control. "What a poignant tale," he snarled, vicious, almost inhuman. "What a perfect angel."

Her heart nearly burst out of her ribs. Oh, *God*…

She shouldn't have told him about the baby, should have left Bidalya with her secret intact!

His fury, his contempt were so annihilating, they might reach explosive levels if she tried to defend herself any further.

Her only consolation was that she hadn't told him the whole truth. And as long as he believed she was Jawad's widow, she had some power. He wouldn't think any better of her if he learned she wasn't. His accusation would still stand. The sister of Jawad's widow could as easily aspire to be a queen, using the privileged information gleaned from Jawad about him as an entrapping weapon. If she confessed now, he'd only know she had less claim to the baby than he thought, and would most likely snatch him away the moment he was born.

If he did, the baby would be the king's to raise, and she'd seen the evidence of the king's brand of upbringing in Jawad.

Even if he had been the most loving, sensitive man on earth, he'd suffered deep grief, had been scarred, and she now knew it had been his father who'd scarred him.

Faress had survived his father unscathed, but he was infinitely stronger than Jawad, than anyone she'd ever known. And then, being the younger son, the king probably hadn't focused on him. Also, from what she'd heard, Faress's mother had been a powerful woman who'd kept the king in check before Faress. She'd probably been the buffer who'd kept Faress and Ghada from their father's influence. But she hadn't been able to protect her firstborn, his heir, whom he'd pressured and twisted to his heart's content.

But the baby, if Faress took him away, would have no mother to fight for him. And no matter how loving Faress was, as she'd seen him with Jameelah, he was simply too busy to take a real part in the baby's upbringing. He would be at the mercy of an unreasonable old man, have no more maternal care than the indifferent service of distant female relatives and servants.

She couldn't let that happen. No matter what the cost. To her.

"So...no more fabrications?" She jerked at Faress's rumble, that of a lion about to pounce. "No more rewriting of history to make yourself into the selfless, steadfast heroine you've been playing so far? You stand by your story that you didn't come here to get what you wanted all along from Jawad from me?"

She swallowed past the jagged rock that had replaced her larynx, tried to no avail to slow down the flow of tears. She knew they were incensing him further.

"I have no way to prove to you I didn't know anything about you," she whispered. "But even if you think I did, how could I have predicted your reaction when you saw me?"

"Because you had trapped one Aal Rusheed brother before," he growled. "You had him sell out his world, his soul for you. You thought you'd have the same effect on his brother. And I'm sure if it hasn't worked out that way, you had a back-up plan."

His contempt, after she'd had his respect, his trust, pulped her, left her helpless. She tried one last time for the least ex-oneration, a drowning woman's grab at a straw.

"Your anger, your suspicion," she rasped, "are the result of my actions. But none of them was premeditated. It's been like living on a roller-coaster since we met and most of the time I haven't known if I was coming or going. I couldn't tell you at first for the reasons I told you, because I had no idea what kind of man you were. But the better I knew you, the longer I put it off, the harder it got. I was...*am* still afraid of your father, and I was more afraid every day of your reaction...*this* reaction, and I kept sinking deeper into unintentional decep-tion. But I was going to tell you, come what may, just before Ghada's accident. Then I couldn't tell you, couldn't inflict another sibling's loss on you."

He stared down at her for so long she had a crazy hope he might actually be lost in thought, considering her words.

Then he spoke, and her world came to an end.

"I should be in your debt for such solicitude," he drawled, his voice cold, pitiless, far more devastating than the earlier volcanic emotions. "But I'm so ungrateful I choose not to be-lieve a word you said, or will ever say. You have lied about *ev-erything* so far. You're lying now. With Jawad ill with a disease whose treatment would have damaged his fertility, what are the odds that the child you're carrying is his? Whatever they are, I don't care either way. Right now I care about one thing. That you get out of here. I never want to see you again."

CHAPTER EIGHT

THE flight attendant gave Larissa a pained attempt at a smile as she told her to fasten her seat belt.

Larissa couldn't blame her. A blurred look in the mirror on her way out of Faress's guest house had shown her a blotched, swollen zombie. She'd cried all through the sixteen hours it had taken to organize her departure from Bidalya. She might still be crying now. She was too numb to tell.

After Faress had left her in a heap on his bedroom floor, she'd stumbled back to the guest house somehow, phoned the airport and booked the first flight home. She'd left everything but her passport and credit card behind, had left at once and spent the hours till her flight slumped in a seat against a wall in the furthest corner of Az-Zufranah's airport.

She'd spent every minute telling herself it was for the best for the baby. That Faress, by not believing her and kicking her out of Bidalya, had made for her the decision she'd been agonizing over. That this assured the baby would be safe from his grandfather. She'd tried to tell herself she'd done what she could, that no matter how differently she might have handled this it would have all ended the same way. She'd now be the baby's whole family, should be satisfied she'd tried to give him a family, even if she'd failed. Even if she'd damaged herself irrevocably while doing so…

I never want to see you again.

Faress's icy, final decree had felt like a death sentence. A fatal blow. But she had to live. At least to exist. For the baby.

A fresh wave of desolation rolled through her. She tossed in her seat, the seat belt against her now-larger stomach constricting. She reached uncoordinated hands to loosen it and it struck her.

Something was wrong here. Their first layover was in London. Seven hours from Az-Zufranah. Though she'd been lost in a timeless zone of misery, it couldn't have been that long since take-off. So why had the flight attendant asked her to fasten her seat belt again?

She waited until the woman walked briskly by her seat and called out to her, "Excuse me…why are we fastening our seat belts?"

The exquisite Bidalyan flashed her a wary smile, as if she was afraid Larissa would start bawling all over her. "We've been recalled to Az-Zufranah airport. The pilot already announced it."

Larissa now remembered hearing the pilot's nasal droning in a few languages. She hadn't caught one word of any. "Recalled? Why?"

The woman shrugged. "Crown Prince Faress's orders."

Larissa gasped. The brunette excused herself and rushed away in alarm, leaving Larissa to struggle with another debilitating surge of agitation. He'd recalled the plane. Why?

She couldn't even imagine his intentions. Any projection carried hope. Hope was far more mutilating now. Despair was at least unambiguous, final, certain.

But hope had a way of springing up where it shouldn't. Of taking hold on non-existent foundations. And for the next half-hour, until they landed, it took her on a ride into yet another brand-new hell.

She sat in her seat, frozen, hypersensitive, until a ripple of gasps and exclamations spread from the business-class section.

She lurched into the aisle, investigating the source of disturbance. And there he was.

Faress.

He saw her at once, too.

With unfathomable eyes fixing on her, he strode towards her, regal in step and dress, towering, beyond description, like an avenging angel, all in white, from the flowing ankle-length *tobe* to the gold-trimmed *abaya* covering it, to the *ghotrah* headdress to even the usually black *eggal* keeping that in place. His bronze skin glowed against all the pristine whiteness, incandescent even in the atrocious cabin lighting.

It hurt, on every level, seeing his beauty, feeling his uniqueness, knowing what she'd lost, what she'd never have.

It was a good thing she was drained or she would have bawled at the sight of him, like the flight attendant had been afraid she would.

He stopped a foot away. Then, in silence, he extended a hand to her. Her eyes gushed. So she wasn't drained after all.

Or tears and misery were simply unending…

Faress sat on his eastern terrace facing a subdued Larissa across the table laid with their elaborate, untouched breakfast.

He'd been trying to keep his eyes off her ravaged beauty, off the uneven rise and fall of her ripe breasts below yet another shapeless outfit, off the glossy fire-fall around her strong, now defenseless shoulders where the cool dawn breeze was combing its invisible fingers, making *his* fingers itch to replace them. He'd been trying to find distraction in the vista that usually imbued him with peace, the magnificent daybreak desert that spread into the horizon after the oasis of his palace grounds ended.

He found no distraction, no peace now. He knew he'd never find them again. Not without her.

He was still reeling. Too many losses, too brutal, too overwhelming, paralyzed him, mind and soul. But after the first tidal wave of discovery, of agony and jealousy and disillusion had devastated him, after suspicion and betrayal had shattered his reason and control, painted everything in ugliness and sordidness, starting with her, it had started to recede.

He'd found himself at her guest house, needing to look into her eyes once more, needing to find closure. At her door he'd known what he'd been there for. Just to find *her* again. And with her the only possible continuation of his life.

What he'd found had been everything she'd brought to Bidalya. Everything she'd left behind.

She hadn't hung around, like the woman capable of such an elaborate charade as he'd accused her of perpetrating would have done. That woman would have known such rage as he'd shown indicated an involvement of surpassing magnitude. A fatal weakness to be exploited, forged in time into unconditional surrender, one he would have been all too eager to offer, to atone for all the malice that had spilled from his lips.

But she hadn't waited to strike while he was at his most unstable, most vulnerable. She'd left. She'd used the hours during which he'd ridden into the desert, when a blanket order not to be disturbed had blocked reports of her departure.

He could have considered her leaving at once, leaving her belongings behind, to be further manipulation. One guaranteeing him to panic, pursue her with carte blanche offers. He hadn't. He'd seen something die inside her at the finality of his contempt, his rejection. Many things had died inside him lately. He'd forever recognize the inimitable loss in others now. He'd recognized it in her. She'd left, never to return.

So he'd given the order ensuring her return then had lain in her unmade bed, to breathe what would make air breathable again—her scent. It had permeated him, bringing back their night in his bed, eclipsing the following fateful morning. And all his pain and jealousy and disillusion had started to fade. And he'd realized.

He didn't care. Why she'd come here or whose baby she was carrying. She had made him hers, and her baby was as precious to him as his own just because it was hers. Whatever the truth was, there *had* been extenuating circumstances, over-whelming enough to force her into the secrecy she'd maintained and the lies she'd told.

Then as the peace just her memory brought defused more of his upheaval, he surrendered to her echoes around him, to her essence embedded inside him, psyche and soul. He relived their weeks together, the ordeals, the collaboration, the companionship, the breathless anticipation, the boundless hunger, the unadulterated pleasure, the full, absolute *life* of each moment in her company.

And he knew. He knew *her*, from that first moment.

She had hidden the truth, but she hadn't lied.

But having his faith restored in her had only made it worse.

He would have given both arms for her to have been lying, to have been anybody else's. But she'd belonged to Jawad...!

He'd worshipped Jawad, had been gutted over his estrangement, was now devastated over his death. How could he still covet Larissa, knowing she'd been his brother's woman, was now the mother of his unborn child?

And what about her? Before yesterday he'd been certain her emotions had mirrored his. But now he knew what he did, could she have possibly switched from loving Jawad, *mourning* him—which must be a major part of her grief, mixed with her anguish over her sister—to loving *him*? Could he *want* her to, so fast? If she had, what did that say about the depth of her emotions?

He had believed the overriding magic that had enslaved him had enslaved her as quickly, as fully. But what if she was just fickle? Worse, what if he was deluding himself so he could hang onto her and the baby, the last thing he had of his brother?

But if she wasn't the woman he believed her to be, *was* the baby his brother's? That could be proved easily enough, but just the thought of seeking proof made him soul-sick. But, then, he'd already acknowledged he didn't care, that it was enough it was *her* baby. Still, the idea that she might be lying about something so vital, the ramifications...

Her soft inhalation brought him out of his turmoil, caressed his insides, scraped his every nerve ending.

"Faress, I need to tell you…"

He raised his hand, aborting her overture. They'd parted on his vicious words. The first words to be uttered now also had to be his. They might be a grave mistake, but he could do nothing but obey his heart's conviction, risk them.

He inhaled. "It's I who needs to tell you that I went mad with grief and shock yesterday. I now do believe you are carrying Jawad's baby. As a doctor you must have been fully aware of the effects of chemo and radiation therapy on his fertility and you must have frozen sperm beforehand. You got pregnant via IVF?"

She only nodded. He was silent for a moment, fighting back the welling of scorching regret that Jawad hadn't lived long enough to see the baby he'd craved.

He exhaled, resigned by now to the sick electricity arcing through him. "You didn't handle the situation well, but you do have legitimate grounds for your fears, so that makes the course you chose somewhat justifiable. I hope you'll forgive my accusations."

"Oh, God, Faress, it's me who…"

He raised his hand again. He had to get this out in one go. He kept his eyes fixed on a point in the horizon behind her. "I've given the situation a lot of thought. I've found only one solution. You must marry me."

Faress felt the dry proposal, the imperious command gash him on its way out. This wasn't how he'd dreamt of offering himself to her. But everything had changed. For now he had to claim her and Jawad's child as his own, protect them, offer them all the privileges that should have been Jawad's if not for their father's injustice. Larissa had come here looking for her baby's heritage and family. This would be the immediate reason she'd accept his proposal. Then when one day they both managed to bury Jawad, they could let their emotions surface past the grief and the guilt…

He gritted his teeth against the surge of desire and desolation. *Ya Ullah*, would he ever be able to forget? Would she?

He forced his eyes back to her to read her reaction. What he saw threatened his sanity. It was beyond endurance, watching the precarious control she'd been maintaining over herself coming undone, seeing her in the grip of such profound heartbreak.

Was this her grief over Jawad surfacing in full measure at last? Was she desolate over loving *him*, consumed by guilt for letting go of Jawad so soon? Or was it because she only wanted him, when her heart and soul belonged with Jawad still, the guilt far more lacerating for him being Jawad's brother?

Desperate to ameliorate her anguish, to lessen the emotional impact, the intimate implications of his proposal, he rasped, "I wouldn't have proposed this now if you weren't pregnant. And I am destined to marry for duty anyway, to produce heirs. And you've already proved fertile…"

Her weeping only got worse. He measured the magnitude of his stamina. It was three minutes of watching Larissa dissolve in misery. Then it snapped.

"I presume these aren't tears of relief?" he grated. She shook her head on another ragged sob. "You mean you refuse?" She nodded, her sobs slowing, as if she was running out of power.

He stared at her bent head, relief washing over him. She was still committed to Jawad, wasn't inconstant, as he'd feared.

Next moment a new surge of rage and devastation crashed on him.

If her refusal was final, that meant she didn't want him at all. So what had the past weeks meant? She'd said no to his advances at first, but every look and breath and word since had only been saying not yet. So had her desire been faked? And if so, why? She still loved Jawad, had only wanted what was rightfully hers and her baby's, then she'd stumbled on him and thought if he was smitten enough, he'd give her what the

Aal Rusheeds owed them? But she didn't want it if he was included in the bargain?

Ya Ullah, was that how men lost their minds?

But he wasn't just any man, and he couldn't risk losing his. The repercussions would be unspeakable.

He got to his feet and stormed away, down the steps, tore toward his stables.

If he rode hard enough, fast enough, far enough, he might outrun all the agony and heartache.

Larissa watched Faress receding through solid sheets of tears, her consciousness wavering as anguish pummeled her.

He believed her about the baby being Jawad's. Probably only because he believed she wouldn't be so stupid to lie about something that could be proved so easily. His coldness had barely covered the volcano of precariously leashed resentment and rage, he'd barely treated her with the restraint he thought he owed her as his brother's widow. And if he found out that she wasn't, now that his feelings for her, whatever they were, had been destroyed, worse, reversed, she could lose the baby.

Then just as she'd thought this made it even more vital that he never found out, conceding that anything she suffered was a small price to pay to keep the baby, that she'd try to arrange something with Faress so that the baby would grow up knowing his heritage and, if possible, his family, Faress had delivered the killing blow.

Looking as if he'd turned to stone, as if this was the most repugnant thing he'd ever had to do, he'd made his marriage offer.

At that moment she'd seen into the center of her being.

She'd found it wrapped around the dream she hadn't dared let herself formulate. It had erupted then, fully formed, the dream of belonging to Faress pulverizing her every cell with longing and futility, with imagining every emotion, every sensation, every spark of thought and joy and life of an existence as his wife.

And he'd offered her the dream in the form of a nightmare. It had ruptured her heart.

She was surprised it hadn't for real. But she had the debilitating pain and despondency to thank for stopping her from taking this mess into irretrievable reaches.

They'd stopped her from snatching at his offer, come what may…

"Have you heard the latest catastrophe?" Helal strode into Larissa's office, tossing the rhetorical question around. His answer was the tension in the room rising another notch. Everybody in the kingdom had heard by now. Helal went on, serious, almost agitated, "*B'Ellahi*, first Princess Ghada and now Prince Jawad. I pray this curse doesn't run in threes."

Everybody exchanged uneasy glances. The idea of Faress being the next stricken Aal Rusheed *had* crossed their minds.

Larissa's stomach heaved, her abused heart smashing itself against her ribs as if it would ward off the insupportable dread.

"I heard he was married to an American woman," Tom said. "I don't know why, but I got the impression she didn't survive him."

"If they're both dead," Anika said, shuddering, "thank God they had no children."

"Actually, it's lucky for the non-existent child for another reason," Helal asserted in his all-knowing way. "Other than the kinder fate of being orphaned."

This jogged Larissa from her numbed fugue. She squinted at Helal. "What do you mean?"

Helal elaborated. "If Jawad had fathered a son, by the law of succession of Bidalya, he would have superseded Prince Faress as Crown Prince. And then the king would have fallen on him like he did on Prince Jawad, to mold him into his vision of what a crown prince should be. At least Jawad had a few years of freedom from his father's oppression, and hopefully happiness, before he died. He also had the king for an oppressor when he was a younger and more reasonable man. A child wouldn't have stood a chance."

Larissa regretted asking. She regretted coming to the complex at all today.

She'd come yesterday to check on Jameelah, had kept up a bright façade even knowing it had been goodbye. She should have gone straight to the airport then. But she hadn't been up to making another escape yet. Then she'd found Faress's message on her return to the guest house, demanding her presence at work today.

She'd come running, desperate to see him under any pretext. Not that she had. She'd found him nowhere.

She'd dragged her feet to her team, and all but Helal had been tactful enough not to ask her about her absence the previous day, and her ravaged appearance now.

They'd just finished their list and she was resigned that Faress had asked her to come only to do the job he was paying her for.

Right now she wasn't up to having her team treat her office as their hangout. She opened her mouth to ask them to leave her alone, closed it. He was here.

Faress. Filling her door, filling her world.

Everything fell away on a wave of searing longing. If only…

"I'll see you in my office," Faress said, his voice clipped, formal, for the first time ignoring the others.

She rose to her feet as if on strings, her team disappearing from her awareness as she followed him.

In minutes she was in his office, all the memories of the best times of her life here, with Faress indulgent and carefree and spontaneous, sweeping through her. Could she one day begin to endure the loss?

He prowled in tight figure eights like a caged lion before her as she slumped on the couch where he always had her sit.

Suddenly he growled, "Why did you refuse my marriage offer?"

The question shot through her heart. The answers almost erupted out of it.

Because you're offering it to a woman who doesn't exist any more, not to me, as a tribute to your brother, a duty to your unborn nephew. Because I can't have you under false pretenses even though I'm dying to have anything of you. Because you only hate me now, would hate me more if you knew the truth…

Instead, her answer was tears gathering in her eyes again.

Faress's black eyes flashed with something like… anxiety? Fear?

Of *course* it was neither. It had to be annoyance with her for resisting his plans when he'd set his mind on them.

Whatever it was, he pressed on, "Larissa, you must reconsider. Think of your baby. You came here looking for his best interests, and this *is* the best thing for him. This is the only way he'll be raised in his privileges and surrounded by his family, with a mother *and* a father."

"A father…?"

"Yes. I will proclaim the baby mine. He will be my heir."

Larissa stared at him, flabbergasted.

She'd automatically assumed he'd be the baby's guardian. She'd thought that he intended later to have heirs with her as she'd already proved fertile, as he'd pointed out, and one fertile woman was as good as another when it came to fulfilling his royal duty.

But he wanted to claim the baby as his firstborn heir. Why?

Suddenly Helal's comments flashed in her mind, knocking the breath out of her.

Was it possible he was doing this to stop her baby from preceding him in the succession?

The suspicion lasted all of two seconds. And the verdict was an incontestable *no*. She'd never believe Faress was capable of anything underhanded or petty.

And then even if the baby did have precedence over him,

Faress would be acting Crown Prince and, if the king died, regent, until the baby came of age. Not that any of that was even an issue to her.

If Faress proclaimed her baby his, he might not get all of his birthright, but he'd be a prince, would have the family she couldn't give him. And no matter how cold Faress was with her now, any child would be the luckiest on earth to have him as a parent.

But if she told him she wasn't the baby's mother now, he'd rescind his marriage offer. How would he claim the baby then? He could only do that by revealing the truth, that he was Jawad's. And again that would leave the baby motherless. Which was unthinkable.

But he'd already implied that it didn't matter to him who he married as long as she produced heirs, that he only wanted to give the baby both a mother and a father. So would she be committing too huge a crime if she took up his offer to be the baby's mother? Maybe he might even want her again someday…

She raised her abused eyes to his tense, distant face, the face of the stranger he'd become. And she knew. No matter what happened, and even if he wanted her physically, he'd never treat her with tenderness and respect again. If she married him, the only crime she'd be committing would be against herself. She'd be consigning herself to a living hell.

But she didn't matter. Only the baby did.

Feeling like she was jumping into the abyss, she finally nodded.

"You accept?"

His dark, dead voice reverberated in her ears. She nodded again, rasped, "Can you tell me what to expect? What you expect?"

Something agonized seized his noble features. Then it was gone, leaving his face an impassive mask.

His voice was as expressionless when he said, "We will

have a ceremony when the forty days of mourning Ghada are over. As for expectations, heirs are what all royal marriages are about. I expect nothing until it's time for a second child."

CHAPTER NINE

"I MUST say it's testament to your progress." Faress inclined his head at the four people milling around him before he transferred his starving eyes to the focus of his world. "And more to your trainer's proficiency that you're here assisting me in one of any surgical team's toughest tests, consecutive surgeries on the same patient."

At his praise, Larissa raised disturbed eyes the blue of his kingdom's twilight skies, lashed him with lust and longing.

She said nothing. She would have before. But she'd stopped talking to him. Beyond necessities and stilted answers to direct questions.

And it had been agony. He'd come to depend on her wit and interaction and counsel for everything from well-being to entertainment to decision-making. Deprived of communication with her, he felt raw, hollowed, cut adrift.

And it was his fault.

Going mad with wanting her, loving her, knowing that she should be taboo to him, with her withdrawal and pain incensing him, more misery crushing him, rejected, guilty, he'd taken refuge in being cold and distant.

She was done appealing to him, had only taken her cue from him. It was as if she turned herself off around him.

Then she'd accepted his proposal as if she had been submitting to a death sentence, had asked what to expect as if asking how he'd carry that sentence out, and his heart, his sanity, had shattered.

Instead of telling her that he'd wait, for ever if need be, until Jawad's memory relinquished its hold over their hearts and psyches, he'd implied that their marriage wouldn't be a real one, ever, that he'd only seek her intimacy to produce heirs.

He'd been trying ever since to retract that insanity. He still couldn't bring himself to voice what he hoped for. Jawad's memory, his own guilt over wanting his woman, his fear of only pushing her to a final, vocal rejection, held him back. So he resorted to actions, showing her that he couldn't get enough of her everywhere in his life. She responded, with something like her former warmth, only around Jameelah…

He tamped down the surge of emotions, for the thousandth time during the past week questioning the sanity of his decision to continue working together, even more closely than before.

He now included her in all his surgeries, delighting in guiding her to wider fields, astounded at the speed of her uptake, the precision with which she adjusted her surgical knowledge to new procedures, the range of specialties she'd gained experience in before settling on trauma surgery. He even included her team now so she wouldn't spend time away from him. His one excuse was that they were ready, no less than his other secondary assistants.

His gaze caressed her face, regret gnawing him when she averted hers. A rush of oppression flushed through him as he muttered, "A quick review of *Es-Sayedah* Enayat's condition, please, Larissa."

Larissa nodded, snatched her reaction further away from his starving scrutiny, her gaze restless on her team. "*Es-Sayedah* Enayat is a 69-year-old who presented last night with severe chest pain. Investigations revealed blockage of two coronary arteries and carcinoma of the esophago-gastric junction. Faress decided to go for simultaneous transhiatal esophagectomy for tumor removal and an off-pump coronary artery bypass."

"Off-pump?" Helal exclaimed. "Beating-heart surgery? Isn't that still controversial?"

Faress was for once grateful for Helal's contentiousness. It dragged his focus back to his surgical and teaching role, distracted him from counting Larissa's breaths, striving to analyze their cadence for clues to what was going on in the mind she'd closed to him.

Before he could answer Helal, she overtook him, "You think it's safer to employ the conventional cardio-pulmonary bypass? Why? What are the benefits of stopping the heart during surgery?"

Helal cleared his throat, looking like a grade-six student who knew he was about to impress his teacher. "An arrested heart provides surgeons with a still field, no blood while they place the coronary artery grafts, and an empty flaccid heart that can be manipulated easily to expose all coronary branches."

Helal's usual opponent, Anika, spoke up, "Sure, it's easier, surgically speaking, but CPB leads to significant side effects which are cause enough to go for any other viable procedure."

Faress's heart itched in jealousy as Larissa smiled at Anika, one of those smiles of wordless appreciation she'd once lavished on him. It was a good thing she was bestowing it on a woman. A man would have been in grave danger had he been the recipient.

"Exactly," Larissa said. "Those side-effects resulted in a revival of the beating heart technique. Today up to 20 percent of bypass surgeries are performed off-pump. And with *Es-Sayedah* Enayat, a high-risk patient, it upped off-pump from preferred to indicated."

She snapped a glance at him, asking if she was doing a good job. He wasn't up to anything beyond a nod. He was a half a thought away from grabbing her and ravishing that mouth that so elegantly wrapped around each informed syllable.

Instead, he exhaled, decided to contribute a few insights before they started. "The key to a successful OPCABG is effective cardiac stabilization, reducing cardiac motion either by pressure or suction devices. This is a huge advance from the days when slowing the heart was induced for a quieter heart. Bidalya is making those devices widely available to all GAO surgeons."

"But why are we performing both surgeries at once?" That was Patrick, the bear of a man he now obsessively sought out to discuss Larissa's and the baby's status. "Wouldn't it have been better to remove her cancer first, medically manage her coronary insufficiency, then schedule her for a later bypass?"

Faress looked at Larissa, delegating answering to her, and was again skewered in the gut by the absence of her vivaciousness, her spontaneity. He wished, each second, that he could erase the past two weeks, return to ignorance, let Jawad live again in his mind and heart, disentangle the memory of his worshipped brother from the reality of his beloved, have his Larissa back.

She inhaled. "From the latest evidence, simultaneous surgeries on a stable patient reduce post-operative and long-term complications. Not to mention cost. As field surgeons they should be your choice whenever possible, to make the most difference to each patient while you can."

Faress considered that perfect wrap-up the ideal point to end the educational session. "We'll go for a curative resection of the lower third of the esophagus and upper third of the stomach," he said. "Then do the CABG next. Larissa and I will keep up a running commentary and I'm sure you won't be shy about asking questions. Be ready to perform any step along the way."

And for the next seven hours, in the tension of an always-precarious endeavor and the exhilaration of being with Larissa in the depth of their element, Faress forgot everything.

During the procedures, he felt Larissa's eyes on him often.

Each time he rushed to meet them, anxious for direct contact, only to have them escape, leave his cold and abandoned. But once, at the very end, they didn't.

And what he saw there, the desolation, the yearning...

Ya Rubb, was that how much she mourned Jawad, missed him?

If she'd loved Jawad half as much as *he* loved her, it was.

At that moment, to spare her that much suffering, he wished he'd been the one who'd died.

In another week, Larissa was sure she wouldn't survive.

Ever since Faress had made his intentions clear, her waking and sleeping existence had turned into a parade of night-mares, projecting a life alone as he sought his intimacies else-where. Until he needed another heir and came to her, slaked his lust in her body, if only for the purpose of impregnating her, before discarding her again. And she'd have no choice, living for ever in a hell of jealousy and deprivation, for the baby's sake.

She would have surrendered to the despair, adopted it as her new outlook in life, if not for the torment of confusion Faress kept her in.

He kept her closer than ever at work, too close, the man she'd fallen in love with, the leader and healer to be followed, worshipped, once again extending her public esteem, focusing on her with an intensity that seared her soul with a deeper brand of ownership, even made her hope he might be consi-dering making the best of the compromise he'd made. Yet he said nothing. And she couldn't survive the insecurity, the un-certainty for much longer...

"I can't put it off any longer."

Larissa's heart contracted, wouldn't expand again. *Faress*.

Oh, God. She'd been staring at him all along. But now he'd spoken, she didn't have to ask him to elaborate.

Jameelah was ready to be discharged. It was time to tell her.

She gulped down an upsurge of scorching pity, nodded. "Will you be with me?"

Oh, God, the way he'd said that! The sheer depth of need, dread and suffering!

And if that was all he needed from her, solace and support, it would be enough. It was a good enough cause.

She could stop herself from reaching out to him as easily as she could stop her heart. She took his hand, squeezed it between both of hers. His jaw muscles bunched. Then his other hand enveloped both of hers in the grip of a man clinging to a lifeline, the pressure assuaging, engulfing, emptying her heart of blood, filling her with strength for him to draw on, to supplement his boundless one.

A long, full glance told her he understood, and appreciated it.

Then he turned and walked with her to Jameelah's suite.

Larissa was no stranger to horrific emotional injury and loss. With all her loved ones dead, with the only man she'd ever love alienated for ever, she thought nothing could be more brutal.

Then came the harrowing chore of informing Jameelah that she'd lost her remaining parent.

All else seemed to pale in comparison.

She felt Faress's echoing devastation as they struggled to contain Jameelah's first explosion of denial and grief, the hysterical accusations that they were lying, the screams for her mother, the manic struggles to run in search of her. They restrained her, sedated her, huddled over her, warding off what they could of her agony.

After the first tidal wave had wrung the weeping girl dry, she and Faress sat next to her on the bed, forming an impenetrable shield around her, caressing and soothing her. Then as the girl sagged into their embrace, surrendered to shock and exhaustion and chemical relief, Larissa raised her eyes to Faress's. And the tears that had just slowed down gushed again.

His face was wet, his eyes reflecting the hell his niece had been plunged into. With a cry of distress she reached a quaking hand to his face, wiping away his tears. He surrendered to her ministrations, pressed his face into her palm, a deep groan bleeding from his chest. Their eyes meshed in deepest empathy, in communion.

Then he reached for her, his large hand cupping her head, bunching in her hair, transfixing her. Then he took her, fused her to him, his tongue seeking her passion and life, devouring her, invading her, demanding that she join her flesh to his, that she surrender all her pain and take his, share it, halve it, exorcize it.

Then, just as it started, it ended.

He withdrew, breathing hard, his eyes scorching down at her, passion and pain staining his every feature. Then his eyes clouded on another brand of pain, one that left her gasping with confusion and anxiety, before withdrawal stole any flicker of emotion from them. He tore them away and she plummeted in a void of deprivation as he curved his body around Jameelah.

Choking on her pulped heart, she withdrew her arms from the sleeping girl, relinquished her to his care.

At the edge of the bed, Faress's hand clamped her arm, gentle, fierce, inexorable, tugged her back.

Nerveless, she fell back on the bed as he sat up, dwarfing both her and Jameelah. In heartbreaking tenderness he curved her and Jameelah together until they were almost a single entity. Then he came around, stretched his formidable body behind her, slipped his arms and legs beneath and above them, containing them both in his all-encompassing embrace.

She lay inundated by him, hugged around Jameelah, her tears a constant stream wetting the girl's hair, trickling down her now sunken cheek, trembling for hours as Faress stroked bonding pathways between their huddled bodies, his protection flowing in caresses over her and both ravaged and unborn child of his lost siblings, alternating ragged kisses between her and Jameelah, murmuring Arabic of such complexity she understood none of it beyond the certainty that it was prayers. And pledges.

"You must promise first!"

Larissa gazed up at the beautiful sight before her, her heart booming in thankfulness. Two weeks after her discharge from hospital, Jameelah, resilient and intensively nurtured by her and Faress, was back to normal. Physically at least.

In a palest yellow cotton silk *jalabeyah*, her mahogany hair hanging in glossy waves down to her hips and surrounding a face of smoothest olive skin and loveliest features, she was now standing over her, somber, demanding her promise for her honest opinion of some of her artwork. Before she ventured to show her any.

"I promise, *ya habibati*," Larissa said, the endearment as usual flowing from her heart. "I will always tell you the truth."

The girl gave her the uncertain look of someone who was loath to expose her dabbling to others yet longing for feedback and deciding to throw caution to the wind.

Larissa watched her spin around, gathering her long *jalabeyah* in one hand as she rushed to her activity room, her every move and line a pleasure to watch, her every breath a reason for gratitude.

Ever since she'd had the privilege of helping to save her life, she'd forged a profound connection to her, formed of Jameelah's bond with Faress, Jameelah's own exquisite nature and the pull of her own blood now coursing in Jameelah's system. And she knew the connection was reciprocated.

She'd come to know so much about her in the past two weeks, every day bringing more proof of sensitivity, brilliance and thoughtfulness that were rare, not only at her age but in anyone of any age. Larissa also got glimpses of her wit, sensed her innate exuberance. But those were now buried. It would take much longer for those traits to resurface.

She'd been with her at Faress's palace every day, adjusting her schedule for breakfasts together every morning and early enough dinners to allow for a couple of hours before Jameelah's bedtime every night. In part, she'd been reveling in her company, in another, striving to tide her over the worst of her mourning.

And Jameelah had tided her over the worst of hers.

That had been until Faress had also adjusted his schedule and became a constant part of their time together.

She craved having him near, but she'd almost demanded he leave her alone with Jameelah, to make his own time with her. It was too much, having him in such proximity, in such an emotional, family-like setting. For there, for Jameelah's sake, he reverted to the spontaneous, indulgent man he'd been, including her in his cosseting of Jameelah.

Then when Jameelah left for bed, he reached for her, as if compelled, his touch tinged with an obsession that ignited hers, his kisses draining her of reason and essence, only to pull away, a look of regret and revulsion twisting his face.

She stumbled deeper in chaos, obsessing over explanations.

She only came up with one. Each time his unappeased hunger for her body overcame his discretion and intentions, he ended up hating her more, hating himself for his lapses. But he'd later remember that she was too valuable to him, if only for his dead siblings' children, and he'd resume his efforts to return to warmth and ease with her. Until the next kiss...

But what made her suffering and turmoil fade into insignificance was Jameelah. And the baby growing inside her. They were the suns in the perpetual night her existence had turned into.

"Hadi walla hadi?"

Larissa stirred with a jerk, instantly translating Jameelah's question in her mind. This or this?

She marveled at both paintings. And bled at both. They

showed such talent, such a sense of balance and beauty, such an eye for detail and a hand capable of translating what that eye perceived. But the pain there, the loss…

One was of an empty bedroom, a woman's, full of everything that spoke of taste and prosperity, everything arranged in painful order, indicating no life there, turning the bedroom into a shrine. The other was of a cliff overlooking the sea with a little girl sitting there alone, tiny and lost in the vastness.

Fighting the suffocation of pity, she forced tears back and pleasure in Jameelah's artwork to surface on her face. "*Habibati*, they are each a masterpiece."

Jameelah's black eyes faltered on uncertainty, then a sparkle lit their depths. "Really?"

"They would be for someone twice your age. But they're unbelievable for a ten-year-old. When did you complete them?"

"At school. I can't go to physical education classes since… since the accident, so I go to the art room."

"You should go more often. Do you have more work?"

"Loads." Suddenly she wilted, tears blossoming in her eyes. "Mama had loads of paintings too, but hers are like magic. She's the one who taught me how to draw and paint. She was teaching me how to do perspective and shadows before…before…"

Larissa hugged her, kissed her eyes, wiped away the tears that had escaped, the tears that always seemed poised to brim over. "And she taught you so well, and now every time you put a pencil or a brush to paper or canvas, you'll make magic, too. And every time people look at it, they'll feel happy, like I am now. Your mother gave you an incredible gift."

Jameelah stared at her with those eyes that so resembled Faress's, as if trying to decide if she could believe all that.

Then a tremulous smile broke on her dimpled lips. "So you don't have a preference?"

"Actually, I do. But it's not because it's better drawn.

They're both amazing. But the cliff scene is so incredible, you make me feel the salt wind on the girl's face and in her hair, the rumble of the waves breaking on the rocks, the heat of the sun beating down on her. It's as if it's all real."

"It is real. It's…it *was* Mama's favorite place in all the kingdom."

"You see?" Larissa rushed on to interrupt Jameelah's renewed agitation. "You re-created it so faithfully you did more than make it *look* real. A photo does that. You made it *feel* real. You are a true artist."

Jameelah's wobbling chin stilled as Larissa talked. Then it started again. "It's called Ras Algam. Mama went there with Baba, then when he died and I grew up, she took me…"

And there was no question the girl sitting huddled under the outcrop of rock was Jameelah, left behind in the world by both her parents. Larissa hugged her again, trying to control the gush of emotion. "Will you take me some time?"

Jameelah blinked, the tears receding. "You want to go?"

"I'd love to go. Can we have a picnic?"

Jameelah's brightness dimmed again. "By the time I'm well enough and autumn comes, when we can go, you may be gone."

Larissa wanted to cry that she'd never go, that she'd always be there for her. But the promises caught in her throat.

She had no way of knowing if she would be. Thirty-six days of Ghadah's forty days' mourning period had passed and Faress hadn't mentioned any preparations. He hadn't even mentioned his offer again.

He'd probably decided to withdraw it, was thinking of some other way to keep his brother's son. He'd probably realized he couldn't tie himself to a woman he didn't love. He must be thinking of when he finally met the woman he wanted to marry and have children with, what an injury he would have done her and himself tying himself, for whatever reason, to Larissa.

Even if he went through with his plans, she might not be able to survive being near him and estranged from him. She might end up running away. How could she promise the bereaved girl that she'd stay, when she might end up leaving her, too?

"*Khali* Faress!"

Larissa jerked at Jameelah's exclamation. She'd been staring at her as she'd struggled for something truthful to say, now saw her dejection dissolve in the sheer pleasure that was reserved for Faress.

She swung around, her heart shaking her apart as Jameelah rushed to meet him, swallowed the surge of longing as he opened his arms wide, his stride eating up the ground to contain Jameelah that much sooner. But what slashed her was his smile, so welcoming and unfettered. A smile he'd once lavished on her. Never again.

"*Kaif Jameelati?*"

Her heart fired. Her eyes flew in a shock of hope to his, met them over Jameelah's head and realized. He'd meant Jameelah. He was asking how his beautiful one was.

He kept his eyes on her as he hugged Jameelah with as much exuberance as she hugged him. Then with utmost care for her recent injuries, he swung her up in his arm, walked toward Larissa with Jameelah clinging around his neck, her head buried in his chest. It was clear Faress had always been her most loved relative after her mother, the man who'd been her father figure all along.

He sat down beside Larissa, and every cell in her body surged at his nearness as he took Jameelah nestling into him, threw his other arm along the couch's back, an inch from Larissa's. In a moment his arm obliterated that inch.

It lay there on her shoulder, as if waiting for something. The shudder that shook her seemed to be it. His arm tightened, drawing her into him, hugging her as he did Jameelah, sat sweeping caresses over them.

She lay in his embrace, enervated, listening to the most potent, world-shaking sound she'd ever heard. His heartbeats.

He sighed, a sound of contentment playing havoc with hers, tilted both her and Jameelah's faces up to him. "So what have my ladies been up to in the two hours they managed to have without me?"

She stopped herself from surging to catch his words in her lips somehow. Next second, mortification clogged her throat.

She *would* end up begging him. And when he rejected her...

Jameelah hugged him more securely. "We've been starving."

He exhaled. "Don't make me feel more guilty than I already am, *ya sagheerati*. Keeping you waiting was something many people found out I don't take kindly to tonight."

Larissa's heart itched at the remorse in his voice. She'd already known any child, anyone, would be the luckiest person on earth to have Faress's love. But the full scope of that luck was unfolding with each moment, each word, each action. And she couldn't bear it that he might be thinking he'd let Jameelah down even fleetingly. She had to rid him of any shadow of discomfort.

She breathed, "Actually, we couldn't decide what to eat."

He chuckled, his heavy-lidded gaze now focused on lips still tingling with the kiss she hadn't dared to take.

"Never fear. I'm here to feed my girls." He turned to Jameelah. "How about we raid the kitchen and whip up something Larissa has never eaten before?"

Jameelah sat up, her eyes brightening. "Can we make *harees*? And *maasoob* for dessert?"

Faress laughed. "*Maasoob* is in, *harees* is out, if we want to eat tonight." He turned to Larissa, explained, "*Maasoob* is *khobez*, cut in small pieces, mashed with banana and sugar and caramelized in butter. Done in minutes. *Harees* is veal and chicken cooked with whole wheat and a dozen spices and then served on fried crunchy *khobez*. Very tasty, but it takes hours, maybe a whole day."

"Now I'm really starving!" Larissa exclaimed.

"We can make *matazeez* instead," Jameelah suggested. "It

has meat and tomato sauce and okra and aubergine and cour-
gette and this stuff that looks like ravioli…"

"Oh, please, stop," Larissa moaned. "I'll eat anything now."

Laughing again, Faress heaved up to his feet, pulling them
both up. "Let's take pity on Larissa, Jameelah, and not tell her
about *el marassee*, *el aggut*, and *el gareesh*."

Jameelah was excited now, as alive as Larissa had ever seen
her. "We can make them on Friday when we have all day!"

At the mention of Friday, she met his eyes, saw his instant
awareness of what it was. Their supposed wedding day.

Seeing tension leaping back in his eyes again, she knew.

He'd decided not to go ahead with it. But he still hadn't found
an acceptable alternative. He wanted Jawad's baby, and he
wanted her to be Jameelah's surrogate parent with him. And he
wanted her body. And he still couldn't come up with a solution
that didn't include marriage to assure him of having all that.

On realizing she'd sunk so far she'd been yearning to
become his sham wife, now wanted to offer to be anything
else so she'd be with him and the children, the world that had
brightened with the magic of his ease and seeming return to
intimacy dimmed again.

CHAPTER TEN

"The packs are stuck. More saline please, Anika," Faress murmured.

Anika at once complied, soaking the packs around the liver so Faress could remove them without yanking on the fragile tissues, causing renewed hemorrhage.

"Turn up the heat, Tom, please," Larissa said without removing her eyes from his fingers. Tom pushed up the dial of the electric blanket their patient lay on. "And raise IV fluid temperature to 108 degrees."

"Two more units packed red blood cells and coagulation factors," Helal told one of the nurses. He was one of the team now working on a patient with multiple abdominal injuries.

Faress nodded his corroboration and the nurse hastened to comply. Hypothermia and coagulation failure and the vicious circle of deterioration they initiated were the cause of death in multiple abdominal trauma. No care to avoid their development was too much. Larissa and her team were going by the book.

"I still can't believe *Es-sayed* Anan here lasted through the first stage of damage control surgery," Patrick said as he helped Faress remove the last of the packs. "And is now well enough to be back for definitive repairs just a day later."

Larissa's team had had their first unassisted, unsupervised surgery yesterday when Larissa hadn't been able to come to work. Another pile-up on the highway had made Faress decide to test them out with three surgeries he thought Larissa had well prepared them for. They'd come through with flying colors.

"Perfect first-stage management, Tom, Helal, Patrick, Anika," Faress said after he and Larissa finished exploring the abdomen. "We wouldn't have done better."

"Thanks", "Yeah, we're good", "We were *lucky*" and "We just have the best trainer" were murmured in succession, a true reflection of each respondent's character.

Then silence fell as they collaborated on working on one of the man's injuries. Faress worked with Patrick and Tom on the intestinal injuries, Larissa, Helal and Anika took the spleen.

When they came to the hardest and most delicate part of the surgery, the removal of the vascular shunt, the rest left him and Larissa to it, went back to lesser assisting roles.

"Medial rotation of the liver, Anika," Faress murmured.

"Suction. And more exposure of the portal triad, Tom." Larissa's request was tranquil, her movements as she repaired the vessels a blur of fluency and assurance.

He could hardly believe that just yesterday he'd exploded to Larissa's side with nightmares crashing in his head, transporting a lab's and investigative unit's worth of portable kits and instruments to her bedside, not even thinking of taking Patrick with him. His heart still stopped when he remembered how he'd found her lying there pale and too scared to move.

It had taken both of the experienced surgeons a frantic time and every investigation they could think of to realize she hadn't been miscarrying but had had a touch of enteritis, which had responded promptly to mild medications.

The relief, the poignancy of knowing Jawad's baby was safe, that she was, had given way to the arousal of being near her on the bed he'd once lain in absorbing her echoes, with her now in it shaken, relieved, equally aroused...

Only the memory of her depressed apprehension when Friday—which was now tomorrow—had come up that night with Jameelah had stopped him from reaching for her.

He'd been waiting for her to express the least interest in his plans for their upcoming marriage ceremony. But she evidently still thought of the event with the same resignation of serving a life sentence.

"Warm, stable. He's going to be fine. He's all yours, guys. Close him up."

Larissa's assessment dragged his focus back to the moment, made him step back to join her in watching the others perform a meticulous closure. Afterwards they checked their patient's vital signs then Anika and another nurse took him to IC and Larissa walked ahead with the rest of her team to the soiled room.

He followed, devouring her as she stripped off her scrubs, her clothes stretching over her curves, clinging to her, the barely detectable mound where her baby was growing healthy and strong, her bun unraveling, her hair thudding down her back…

It was no good. He *was* going out of his mind. This was far stronger than he was. And each night he succumbed, snatched her in his arms, against his resolutions and good intentions. And each time she responded and he'd forget anything had ever gone wrong between them. Then he'd see that haunted, pained look in her eyes, and he'd have a reality check.

Feeling guilty and heartsick, he forced himself to withdraw. And burned. He shouldn't be craving her every minute of every day like that. He despised his weakness, couldn't help but have episodes of bitterness towards her for engendering it in him, for wanting him so soon, for only wanting him and not loving him.

Then he shared with her again and she conquered him again. Then she went further, extended her healing and generosity to his bereaved Jameelah, and gave her, and him, in the times of closeness and poignancy they spent together, a family, a renewed will to live. Now he had a taste of what was to come, he wanted it all, the family, the children, her, body and soul…

The forty days were over today. He'd intended to inform

his father of his plans long before now. But he hadn't yet made them. He couldn't bring himself to with Larissa in this state. Couldn't bring himself to tell her that if she didn't want their marriage to be real eventually, she had to say no. Couldn't risk she'd say it.

But he wouldn't marry her and remain away from her. Jawad's memory wouldn't hold him back for ever, but if it would her, she'd better...

"Dr. Faress, Dr. Larissa..." A nurse came in, panting. "*Ameerah* Jameelah is in the prep room."

He tore his eyes from the nurse, sought Larissa's, shared his shock. Then they exploded in motion.

In a minute they entered the hall where surgical cases were prepped before being rushed to the OR, found Jameelah standing in the middle of the floor, looking smaller, lost.

Larissa's breath was knocked out of her at the sight of Jameelah.

She'd been crying, her eyes swollen, feverish.

Oh God, what was wrong now?

She reached her first, swept her in a fierce hug. "*Habibati,* are you OK?"

Jameelah nodded as Faress took them to one side of the hall.

"How did you get here, *ya sagheerati?*" he asked, his voice gentleness and indulgence itself.

"I told Hassan to drive me here after school." She looked up at Larissa with wavering eyes. "I—I wanted to make sure you remembered our—our cooking date tomorrow..."

Larissa's heart convulsed. "Of course, I do."

"It's just you didn't come yesterday..."

"I was sick, *ya habibati.*" She'd woken up with cramps, and they'd sent her crying for Faress. Not Patrick. When she'd needed help, he was all she'd been able to think of. She still couldn't believe the speed with which he'd responded, the mini-hospital he'd transferred to her bedside, the magnitude of his anxiety.

It had turned out to be nothing, but he'd insisted she stay in bed the rest of the day. They couldn't be too careful. She'd agreed. She'd been useless anyway in the aftermath of anxiety, and the further blow of having him so caring only to have him withdraw again.

"But you didn't come for breakfast today," Jameelah insisted.

That sounded like an accusation. She had to tread carefully. "I was tired after yesterday. I woke up after you went to school."

Jameelah was ready with an argument. "But you came to work."

Larissa measured her words. They were the truth, but she had to be careful how to phrase it. "I woke up feeling better and, knowing you were at school, I came here. And I'll come home right after work. And tomorrow we have a date, a whole day together, like every weekend, *ya habibati*. I can't wait for your *gareesh*."

"You may be sick again," Jameelah mumbled.

"I won't be. It was nothing serious. But, darling, please…"

At that moment the doors whooshed open and an incoming casualty was wheeled in. At the sight of the woman on the gurney, Larissa's blood froze. Her external injuries were extensive. And she had an uncanny general resemblance to Ghadah.

A glance at Faress showed his equal dread what this might do to Jameelah's fragile mental condition. She tore her eyes away, rushed Jameelah out of the room, feeling Faress rushing after them, being detained at the door.

"Was Mama hurt like that?" Jameelah's voice wobbled, her tears streaming again.

"No, no," Larissa groaned. "It was inside she was hurt. But she didn't suffer."

"Will *Khali* Faress operate on the hurt woman?"

"Yes, *ya habibati*, but you must go home now…"

Jameelah clung to her just as Faress exploded out into the corridor to join them. "Come with me."

Just as Faress's hand squeezed her shoulder, telling her he didn't need her there now, Anika came out of the hall, running.

"Dr. Faress, Dr. Larissa—she has cardiac tamponade, already fibrillated once!"

Larissa knew the emergency thoracotomy needed for that was one procedure her team wasn't proficient in yet, and no other surgeon was free to give Faress the help he'd need. She exchanged desperate looks with Faress. He gave her a terse nod.

"Prep her. We're coming," Larissa called back, then turned to Jameelah. "*Habibati*, I have to take care of that woman."

"So when will you be home?"

"I don't know exactly when we'll finish…"

Insecurity and panic flared in Jameelah's eyes. "You're not coming, are you? You're not coming to see me ever again!"

Faress tried to intervene. "Jameelah, that is not true. We're both coming home right after we finish here."

Jameelah turned eyes full of fear and accusation on him. "You're just saying that. You didn't come yesterday either."

"I was with Larissa, treating her—"

Jameelah's cry cut him off. *"You'll stop coming, too."*

Larissa's heart gave a sickening lurch as she met Faress's anguished gaze. He went down on his haunches, bringing his eyes level with Jameelah's. "I'm never going to stop coming, *ya sagheerati*. But this woman will die if we don't help her. And you want us to help her, don't you?"

Jameelah looked from him to Larissa then burst out crying.

Faress hugged her. "We'll send you home now, *ya Jameelati*, and we'll come rushing to you as soon as we're done."

Larissa surrounded her with Faress, bent to kiss her, whispered the promise, "Both of us."

Feeling Jameelah's tension drain away, Faress straightened, barked orders arranging for both her return home and the surgery. Larissa stood long enough to see Jameelah being escorted out then raced with Faress to tend their casualty in a blur of urgency.

It was three hours before they rushed back to the palace, their trip an even more agitated experience than their daily ones had become.

Minutes before they arrived, Faress received a phone call that turned him to stone beside her.

He barked something explosive then snapped his phone shut.

He turned to her, his eyes wild. "Jameelah has disappeared."

They arrived to chaos. All the invisible people Larissa sensed and never saw were swarming over the palace grounds.

A man in black, clearly Faress's security co-ordinator, came rushing up to them.

"You will all answer for letting her slip your surveillance," Faress hissed, dread making him frightening. Larissa shuddered, her already compromised composure teetering. Faress gathered her to him, bolstering her.

The fierce-looking man bent his head, unable to meet Faress's volcanic gaze. "*Somo'ak*… Her guards just returned. They lost track of her car on the way from the complex, thought Hassan had sped ahead. When they arrived here to find she hadn't arrived, they combed the city, hoping to find her. They didn't, had to come clean. As Hassan didn't try to alert them, we're suspecting a plot, a kidnapping."

"Then you're fools as well as incompetents," Faress growled. "Insight into people's characters is a security professional's number-one asset and since you're clearly lacking in it, it's time we re-evaluated your careers, Bassel. Hassan worshipped *Ameerah* Ghadah, dotes on Jameelah. He'd give his life for them. Why do you think I trusted him with them in the first place? Don't compound your negligence. Find her."

Then with Larissa flying in his wake, he exploded into a desperate search for her himself, contacting his extensive family, ordering each member to search for her, turning her quarters inside out for clues, his anger and suspicion rising by the second as he expanded the search from a local to a national one.

At one point he groaned to Larissa, "If only it was an abduction, I'd be sure to get her back. Enemies would know not to harm her, and that I'd pay of my flesh to get her back."

But no calls came. There was silence, ignorance. Nothing. After a horrific night of futility, dawn came.

Faress was standing by Jameelah's bedroom window, rigid, staring out at skies turning indigo.

Larissa watched him, her tears internal now, drenching her soul. She wouldn't show him her tears. And she wouldn't cry for Jameelah. She was fine. She *had* to be.

But she couldn't bear feeling his guilt, his dread destroying him all over again. She would have multiplied hers a hundred times if she could only have spared him.

"That night I came late," he suddenly said, his voice a bass grate of anguish. "I stood in the doorway and watched you. You were so absorbed in what you were discussing, you weren't aware of me. I couldn't hear you either, not what you were saying, just your murmuring and cooing. And it was the most beautiful thing I've ever seen, ever heard. That night I thought, Ghadah can find peace, knowing the daughter she lived for won't be lost with her death. Now I may have really lost her…"

Larissa raced to him, her arms convulsing around him from the back, cried, "You won't lose her, we won't." She staggered back. He swung around, reached for her, anxiety blazing on his face. She reached back, gripped both his arms. "I think I know where she is. That night she showed me a painting she made of her mother's favorite place. It's called…called… Oh, God…"

His eyes feverish with hope, he ran calming hands over her head and face. "Breathe, *ya habibati*, concentrate."

She racked her brains. Then it came to her in a flash. "It's Ras Al… Ras Al…"

His obsidian eyes flashed. "Ras Algam?"

She jumped in his arms. "*Yes*. That is *it*. I have a feeling she went there, to feel close to her mother.

Hope solidified into certainty in his eyes as he grabbed her arm, already running. "Let's find her."

They found her. They also found out how she'd made it there. Her driver, Hassan had driven her there.

At seeing Faress, he fell to his knees before him.

"Ameerah Ghadah came to me in my sleep," Hassan sobbed. "She told me she wanted to see her daughter. And when Jameelah asked to come here, on the fortieth night of her mother's passing, I knew this is where and when *Ameerah* Ghadah wanted to see her. The night was still and warm and I thought *ameerati es-sagheerah* would be safe here. I had blankets and food in the car and I promised not to tell you before noon. I know my punishment will be severe…"

"Silence," Faress ground out, his face shuttered on extreme control, his eyes feverish on the cliff where Jameelah was a barely visible sleeping heap. "I'll see to you later."

Then he was striding to the cliff.

Larissa kept up with him. "She came last night looking for me, Faress. I was the one to whom she showed the painting of this place, the one she fears will abandon her. Her crisis right now is focusing on her mother and me. And, knowing her, this isn't a cry for attention. This is serious. Let me go to her, alone."

Faress looked down at Larissa. In the sunlight reflected off the stormy sea and white sand, though pale and exhausted, she took his breath, his soul away.

And he conceded her point. With Jameelah this vulnerable, it was the woman who'd started to fill the void of Ghadah's loss who was the most likely to get favorable results.

He took her hand, pressed a kiss laden with gratitude into her palm, nodded. She gave him a wobbly smile then turned and strode up the slope leading to the cliff.

In minutes she was up there. His heart thundered as he watched Jameelah waking up, scrambling to her feet and rushing away from Larissa's solicitude. And close to the edge. Too close.

And he ran, breathless, keeping out of sight, scared out of his mind that his appearance and any more agitation might tip Jameelah over the edge.

He circled them, climbed on top of the outcrop of rock overlooking the recess where Jameelah had spent the night. He was calculating he could take the fifteen-foot jump, reach Jameelah in under five seconds, if the worst came to the worst, when he heard Larissa's voice. Compassion incarnate.

"Your mother loved you, even when she was late or away. It's the same with me and Faress. We'll always come back to you."

"No, you won't. *Mama is never coming back now*," Jameelah cried, her usually tranquil voice shrill.

Larissa kept her voice soothing. "No one can beat death, *ya habibati*. But it will take that to take us away from you."

"So you won't mean to leave me, but you will, like Baba and Mama. And if death will take everyone away and then me, why shouldn't it take me now?"

Faress's heart burst with the need to jump down and snatch her away from the edge. That wasn't a hypothetical question. She *was* contemplating it. Larissa had been right about the necessity of treating her with the caution of defusing a bomb.

But how would she defuse such an explosive question?

"We all know we'll die, *ya habibati,* and it makes life so much more precious," Larissa said seriously, no trace of condescension in her words or voice. "And we want to live it with the people we love. And it is horrible and heartbreaking that you lost your parents. But life gives as well as takes. You're much better off than most people still. You can do so many things in your life, make such a difference to the world, help so many people, like your mother did. You're a princess, you have a family…"

Jameelah stomped her feet over and over in a fit of frustration. "I *don't*. They pretended to care about me to please Mama, and now to please *Khali* Faress. Everyone else is paid to be nice to me, or they want something from being nice to me. I only have *Khali* and now you…maybe…"

Faress's heart compressed. She'd realized the burden of being royalty too early. *Ya Ullah*, what would Larissa say to that?

"You have me, no maybes," she said, her voice brooking no argument. "And it *is* enough to have only one or two people in the world who truly love you, *ya habibati*. And you never lose the people you love when they die. They're still with you, part of who you are. I lost my mother and father at the same time and I still remember and love everything about them. I was older than you are now but I had no one to truly love but my sister. Then I lost her, too, just before I came to Bidalya. But God is giving me what's making her loss bearable. A baby."

"A baby? You mean you're having a baby?" Jameelah looked her up and down in stupefaction. "But your belly isn't big!"

"Oh, it will get bigger and bigger now." Larissa's hands stroked her stomach lovingly. Faress's whole being seized with love and tenderness, for her and for the baby growing inside her. She took a step towards Jameelah, who took an instinctive step back. That froze Larissa, almost burst Faress's head in fright. The only thing that stopped him from jumping was knowing that five seconds wouldn't be enough if Jameelah took one more step back.

Larissa looked around, as if she was struggling for the best thing to say now. Then she exhaled. "I want to share a secret with you, Jameelah. Can you promise to keep it?" Jameelah nodded warily. "My baby is a boy, and he's your cousin."

After a moment of incomprehension, the most amazing transformation came over Jameelah's face. "He's *Khali* Faress's!"

Larissa hesitated just a second before nodding. "Now you'll have another person to love and who'll love you. You'll be his big sister and I'll need all your help with him. And there's one thing you can give him that I can't. I'm hopeless at art and I so hope you'll teach him the magic that your mother taught you."

Faress squeezed his eyes, an agony of love and pride and gratitude for all that Larissa was and did clamping his chest, would have brought him to his knees if he wasn't already on them. She'd found the only thing to drag Jameelah from the abyss of despair. A focus outside herself, someone to nurture, a cause.

Sure enough, Jameelah's tears dried, her face coming alive as she bombarded Larissa with questions. "When will you have him? Can I suggest names for him? Please, don't call him Omar or Fahad. I have *six* atrocious second cousins with those names."

Still asking questions, Jameelah moved away from the edge. Larissa rushed to meet her halfway. Faress began to breathe again.

And it all happened at once.

The cliff edge crumbled beneath Jameelah's feet. She screamed, stumbled, fell flat on her face. A shout rang out of Larissa as she lunged after her, caught both her wrists at the last moment. Faress exploded into motion, felt his muscles tearing, saw nothing but Larissa beginning to slide with Jameelah's weight and the rolling rocks beneath her, didn't even feel the impact this time when he flung himself after her, clamped her ankles.

He pulled them back, their combined weight nothing to the force of his love, snatching them, the two who made up his world, from danger.

He carried them to safety, his arms convulsing around them, his lips spilling a fever of gratitude and love all over them.

They both buried themselves in his chest and wept.

"She's still sleeping." Faress turned to Larissa as he closed Jameelah's door. She'd fallen asleep on the way back and hadn't stirred when he'd carried her to bed.

Larissa nodded, lingering shock in her eyes, wringing his heart. He bent and swept her up in his arms.

She clung to him all the way to his quarters, her head on his heart, alive and unharmed. *Ya Ullah*, alive, unharmed.

He could have lost her. She would have given her life to save Jameelah. And he would have only flung himself after her and all that remained of his siblings.

And he knew. There wasn't the tiniest bit of jealousy or bitterness left in him that fate had chosen to make her Jawad's before him. His love had grown truly unconditional.

And there was no guilt either. His brother had loved her beyond reason, for every reason, as she deserved to be loved. And so did he. Jawad had lived for her, had died in her arms, and, knowing him, the all-loving man he'd been, he would have wanted her to live her life to the full, to find love and passion again. And she had, with him, and it no longer mattered how fast it had happened. It had, and he wasn't postponing making her his, becoming hers, one more minute. Seconds had ended Ghadah's life, could have lost him Larissa and everything he lived for. Each minute was no longer something he could afford to waste, waiting on the caprices of custom or the insubstantial rites of guilt.

The time was now. And for ever.

He placed her in reverence on his bed, his eyes never leaving hers in the lights he kept dimmed to counteract the glare of the rest of his existence, saw them reflecting the turbulence of the sea where he'd almost lost her today.

With a moan warding off the memory, he came down half over her, needing to feel her, her life, her reality. Memories crashed inside him still, of every moment he'd known her, of the only time he'd had her here, the heart-bursting expectation of pleasure beyond his knowledge and her overwhelming surrender.

This time she didn't surrender, she went far beyond overwhelming him. She sabotaged his reason, surging into him, bringing him fully over her, taking the brunt of his passion, containing it in limbs that clamped him body and will, fingers that unraveled his flesh and control, meeting his crushing kiss halfway, her lips, full and fragrant, mashing against his, her tongue invading his mouth in turn, flooding him with her taste and her passion, snatching at his, turning the kiss into a full rehearsal of the mating they'd soon lose themselves in, multiplying its force, deepening its madness, sharpening its pleasure to pain.

He thrust at her, tongue and loins, blind, out of his mind, heard his frenzy harmonizing with hers in a duet of rising voracity. She thrust back, offering, demanding, undulating beneath him, her heat even through their clothes igniting consecutive fuses inside him, until their mimicking of their love act turned into distress, writhing desperation. He was overloading, she was...

He tore his lips from hers, roared at the separation, at the convulsion that went through her with his loss, at the sight of the full measure of his ferocity, his insanity reflected in the depths of eyes gone purple. He shuddered in unison with her with arousal turned into agony, the need for fusion becoming damage.

One shaking hand gathered both of hers when they reached for him, dug into his flesh, tugged at his hair, hurrying his impact, imprisoning them above her head. His other tore her out of her clothes, shredded what slowed him down, the rising music of her cries of stimulation, of impatience urging him on.

Then she was naked beneath him, velvet resilience and total hunger sending the beast inside him howling. He swooped down on her, mouth clamping nipples larger than before, darker, better instruments for her torment and pleasure, for his, hands kneading riper breasts. Her cries became keens fractured by indrawn distress, her hands lurching out of his containment, grabbing at him, shattering the last of his restraint. He boosted her pressure, mashed his face into her mounds, into the firmness of her abdomen that had barely begun to succumb to the expansion of pregnancy...

An image hit him like a gut punch with its clarity, its tangibility. Larissa, riper, bigger, with him kneeling between her thighs, thrusting, caressing her womb from inside with his manhood as he caressed it from outside with his hands...

Growling incoherently, he rose over her, tore his shirt off flesh that would burn if it didn't mesh with hers, now...*now*. One hand went to release himself, the other dipping two fingers inside her, all he could do in his extreme to ascertain her readiness.

She flinched as if he'd stabbed her, grabbed his hand.

Then her sob tore through him. "Faress...I *can't*..."

He blinked, paralyzed with the sight of pain and panic flooding her face. Blood crashed against the walls of his arteries with the sudden halt, making the world flicker, his hands shake as he forced both to withdraw, one from his body, one from hers.

But he couldn't accept her rejection this time. Her desire for him was indisputable, and her emotions were involved. With her reticence with him from day one, he had no idea how involved they were, could only hope for a fraction of his own involvement.

All that was left was for him to dispel her demons as he'd dispelled his, release her from the shackles of guilt and make her embrace their new life together.

"Larissa," he started, his breathing labored, frustration shredding through him, the need to see her delirious and open for him once more an even bigger pain. "I know, as Jawad's widow..."

She twisted in his arms as if he'd backhanded her, looked up at him as if she expected an axe would swing down and lodge in her heart.

Then she rasped, "I'm not."

CHAPTER ELEVEN

"I'M NOT his widow," she repeated, her whisper thicker, more impeded. Faress stared at her, certain his mind had disintegrated. Her trembling hand reached for the cover, dragged it over her nakedness. "The photograph you saw, that was my sister, Claire. She looked almost like my twin. She was Jawad's wife."

He staggered up to his feet.

Larissa wasn't Jawad's. *She wasn't Jawad's.*

Before the elation had a chance to batter through him, another shock detonated. He choked on it. "Then the baby isn't…?"

And Larissa delivered another blow, her face contorting, her voice raw. "Oh, God, Faress, no, he *is* Jawad's."

He sagged onto the foot of the bed. If this was Jawad's baby, and she was his widow's sister, that meant…

Larissa scrambled to him on all fours, panicked, reading where confusion was tossing him, blurted out, "No, no, Faress… He's Claire's!"

He stared at her, overcome, demolished, mute.

She choked on. "Claire and Jawad tried to conceive for years, until they were told it was hopeless. Claire was unable to carry a pregnancy beyond a few weeks. Then Jawad got sick and Claire begged me to be a surrogate mother to their baby. I would have done anything to make Claire and the man she worshipped, and I loved like the brother I never had, happy."

A moment of congealing shock passed before she struggled on.

"Just as we discovered IVF had worked, Jawad died. And his loss killed Claire, literally. She drove her car over a bridge a week after his funeral." She gulped a broken breath. "I—I panicked at first. The soon-to-be single mother of a child who, instead of handing to his parents, I'd have to raise alone when I had a job that had me almost living at the hospital. The first days after Claire died, I broke down, fell prey to all sorts of crazy ideas. Adoption, termination..."

He inhaled a taxed breath. She rushed on, "It was just shock! Those were never options. Then with each hour my concerns died and my feelings for the baby grew. Then as Claire's loss became a reality, I clung to the baby even more as it was all I had left of her. Then I had to sort out Jawad's papers and found out who he was. The rest I've already told you."

Silence throbbed, expanded. Inside Faress's head there was a crashing ocean of realizations. They deluged him, conquered him, paralyzed him. He stared into her abused, anguished eyes.

Could there be relief, *eshg,* like that?

But something was wrong here. Very wrong.

"There could be only one reason you kept silent," he rasped. "You feared you'd have less claim on him as only his next of kin. You feared I'd take control over him. You feared *me*."

"No." She shook, her tresses rioting around her shoulders. "Not you. Not after I got to know you. I feared your father. After—after Ghadah, when I saw him, I—I wanted to leave, without telling you about the baby at all. Then you found out part of the truth, were so angry, so agonized over Jawad, I did fear your reaction if I told you the rest. Then you accused me of coming here to—to trap you, and I defended myself, told you about the baby. When you said you didn't believe it was Jawad's, I was almost relieved, so I'd just get out of here, keep him, knowing I'd tried and failed to give him a family. Then

you brought me back and offered to marry me because you naturally assumed I was the baby's mother…"

She stopped and bit her lip. "I had no illusions that I lost your respect, was afraid if I revealed I had no more claim on the baby than you, you'd take him from me. I was scared he'd end up under your father's thumb, abused like Jawad, raised by hired help while you were too busy to take a real part in his upbringing and…and…"

"And what?" He rose to his feet, struck to his core. "After all we've been through, after you saw me with Jameelah, you still thought I'd leave the baby to my father's mercies and servants' cold care?"

Her whole face shuddered, her swollen eyes squeezed shut. "God, no…Faress, please, I'm sorry…so much was at stake. Then came Jameelah, and I was scared I'd have to leave her, too, if you sent me away. When you didn't mention marriage again, I kept hoping you'd offer me another solution that would make it possible for me to stay and be part of both their lives. I—I don't know what I was hoping for. I was overwhelmed, afraid any step I took in my condition would be the wrong one…

"But—but I've told you now. Now you know I am not genetically his mother, that I withheld the truth, accepted an offer of marriage you made only because you were ignorant of it. And though I did it only for the baby, I'll understand if you don't show me any leniency. But it's not me you should consider here. Please, let me be a part of the baby's life. I am the closest person to his mother he can have. Feeling him growing inside me, I do feel he's mine, yet for being Claire's and Jawad's, for being yours too, he's just *too* precious and I can't bear to think he'd…he'd…"

And she wept as if she'd start weeping blood at any second.

He stared at her, his heart cracking in his chest, his world blackening again. She thought he could take her baby from her? And the baby was all she cared about? And now Jameelah? She'd been hoping he'd forget about his marriage offer?

It could have been an hour when she finally whispered a broken, "Please, Faress…say something."

He sagged on the bed. "*Ya Ullah,* what do you want me to say? That I won't deprive you of your child or Jameelah, or deprive them of you, their surrogate mother? How can you know me so little you even have to ask, to worry?"

Her face flushed with such mortification it caused him physical pain. "Oh, God, I keep making this worse. I believe you're the most noble, caring, protective man on earth, Faress, and all my fears stem from knowing how badly I abused your trust…"

He couldn't hear that, bear that. "You were protecting your child. To the same end, I'd do far, far more than hide a few facts and consider myself justified."

Her tears turned off, her eyes flooding with such relief it was equally painful to behold. "Oh, Faress, thank you."

"*Arjooki.*" He muttered his agonized plea. "*Never* thank me."

She bit her lip, her eyes almost black now. "Have you thought how I can stay here, be a part of the children's life? Now there won't be a marriage…"

"There *will* be a marriage."

"Oh, so you still intend to…for them…" She nodded, to herself it seemed, like a little girl talking herself into swallowing foul-tasting medicine. "But it won't be a real one."

Feeling like he was knowingly stepping into quicksand, he gritted, "It *will* be."

Larissa jerked at his intensity, her whole being surging with hope. It deflated next second. He meant sex. Of course.

She tried to bring the nauseating tremors arcing through her under control. She would grab at anything he had to offer her, and be thankful for it. She shouldn't even fantasize about more. She should take her own advice, the advice she'd given Jameelah earlier. She was so much luckier than most people. She'd end up having her baby and Jameelah. And the memories of their intimacies when Faress no longer wanted her.

"Just now, I guess you still want me. And I—I want you, too. I only stopped you now, and before, because I couldn't let you make lo—" Her heart stopped for three long beats, aborting the words, and any hope she could ever say them to him. "Uh…h-have sex with me when you didn't know the truth. And when it's over…"

The grimness that had turned his face into stone deepened. "Over?"

"This part of our relationship, I mean…" Oh, God, she couldn't start crying again. Couldn't let him suspect the magnitude of her emotions. He might fear she'd become a liability instead of the helpmeet he thought he was acquiring. She believed it was her reticence so far that made him believe he could trust her to accept her role in his life, the transient place in his bed, that made it possible at all to offer her what he had.

And here she was, laying down the terms of the agreement, delineating how the woman in her would come to life, burn bright with his passion and nearness before she turned to ash and only the doctor and mother remained.

She turned blind eyes around the room, unable to look at him as she propositioned him. "It can be as short as you wish, which, with me pregnant, will probably be very short. And then, after just once you may find out I wasn't worth the trouble after all."

She had to stop. She sounded desperate. As she was. And this wasn't the way to convince him that when he'd had enough of her, she'd let go. She inhaled, strove for her long-lost composure.

There was one last point she wanted to lay to rest.

"About what you said, about me wanting wealth and privileges—I wouldn't know what to do with either. That may sound laughable as I'll be sharing yours to some degree by default, but that's unavoidable as long as I live here for the children's sake. But I won't take anything else. My tastes are simple and my needs are few, and I always made my own living and I wouldn't change that for anything. I—I just want some time with you."

"Just some time," Faress echoed as he moved closer.

She closed her eyes, let his approach permeate her. Maybe she was deluding herself. Maybe she wouldn't know how to give him up when it was time to do so. Maybe she should tell him to forget it.

She couldn't. She had to be his, be with him, if only once.

She leaned back in bed under the onslaught of arousal, not meeting his eyes so she could bring herself to say this. "I want one night, Faress…tonight. Then I'll retreat from your life, un-until you want another heir. You won't see or hear from me, except as a caregiver of the children, and at work."

Suddenly he snarled, "You want one night? And another when I want another heir? Well, *I* don't."

Her eyes flew up, saw his beloved face working, every muscle in his perfection bulging as if straining under a crushing weight.

"But I thought you wanted me, too…"

"I don't *want* you." This was roared.

Oh, God. He'd just wanted relief, didn't want her specifically. Even that was gone. She wouldn't even have the memories.

Her heart imploding, tears scouring down her cheeks, she dragged the cover around her nakedness, staggered to gather her ruined clothes. "I…I'll just go…"

She turned, blind, finished, and found him blocking her path, emanating such intensity she swayed.

"Not before you do one thing for me. Explain something. If one night is all you want, what was everything I felt from you all those months? It all made sense when I thought you were Jawad's, your reticence, your resistance. It almost killed me with guilt and jealousy and regret, until I conquered it, knew only that what we share matters. But if this is how you feel, I no longer know if we shared anything. *Ana majnoon?* Am I crazy? Did I imagine all that?"

"Faress…" she choked, reeling.

He kept advancing on her, driving her back until she grate-fully felt the wall's support. "Or do you think you can give me all this…uniqueness, then tell it was all for one roll in bed and I wouldn't mind? Why? Because you think I change women as often as I do surgical gloves? Or do you think I'm invincible? I must be a casualty or a child or someone who needs your help for me to deserve your care and caring? I only warranted those when I was devastated and fit those criteria? Now I'm back on my feet, you've moved on to other causes, satisfied that your part is done? Well, it's not. You still have one more mission on my behalf. If you don't need me to exist, then use all that healing and compassion of yours and cure *me* of needing *you* to exist."

She staggered, her heart long burst with every word he'd uttered, everything she felt radiating from him. Everything she'd never let herself fantasize about. Everything she still couldn't let herself begin to believe. "B-but you said you don't want me…"

He smacked his palm against the wall by her head. "I *don't*. Wanting is a grabby, empty, flimsy emotion. And I don't love you either. Love is still too limited and flawed. I don't even worship you. That too can be built on blind, groundless delusion. *Ana aashagek*. Do you know what *eshg* means?" She stared at him, everything inside her still, tears and heart-beats and thought. This was too momentous, too astounding. One single tremor would snap her hold on consciousness. "Everyone says it's all combined, multiplied. But to me it means I have faith in you. That I'd die for you and far worse. That I lust for your every breath and move and inch, crave your well-being and appreciation, depend on your existence and counsel, flourish, *live* with your nearness."

She sagged to her knees, flailing arms hugging his legs, her head resting on one of his thighs, the rising tide of shock and disbelief and elation beyond her ability to process, to withstand.

He felt the same. *He felt the same.*

* * *

Faress stared down at Larissa, his reason and reasons made flesh, kneeling at his feet, flailing as if in a hurricane, whimpers scraping her throat as if in a seizure of prayer, clinging to him as if to a last hope. His immediate impulse was to kneel before *her*, prostrate himself for her mercy. But the sight of her was overpowering, everything flaring from her depths to impact him, psyche and soul, plumbing the reaches of love and devotion. Of *eshg*.

He allowed himself moments, let her storm him, filled himself with her. The cover pooling on her thighs exposing the sweep of a graceful back and flared hips in a pose out of his deepest erotic fantasies, the flames of her hair cascading over one shoulder, raining between his rigid thighs, her face, her working lips almost buried in his painful erection.

He took all he could then snapped, hauled her to bed, covered her with his limbs and lips and debilitating relief and gratitude.

When the extreme of emotion leveled out, she lay in his arms, her eyes on his, and he knew how much of herself she'd been withholding, wondered if he could survive being exposed to her full reality, didn't mind if he didn't.

Her hand trembled on his cheek, in his hair, joy streaming from her eyes. "Will you believe me when I say, me, too, oh, *God*, me, too? All you said? And a whole life full of what I feel for you, and yet more that I'd do for you? You won't ever think I'm exaggerating to…to…?"

"To enslave me? I deserve to be punished for ever for this outburst of insecurity, but I throw myself at your mercy. I was bleeding, was telling myself anything I would listen to, to stop tearing myself apart demanding you."

Indulgence spread her lips, melted him, a tremor of awe in her touch and gaze. "It worked too well on me. I was so afraid that anything that showed you how I feel would be proof you were right. It's still so hard to let go of the dread."

"Let it go, I beg of you. If you're fond of my sanity. I said it but I never believed it. I believed anything you said even when all the evidence was against you. Now my belief is absolute. You've earned it, for ever. So say it, *ya maaboodati*. Have mercy and say it."

Her eyes stilled on his with the solemnity of a revelation, her voice steadying with the firmness of a pledge. "You're beyond hope and dreams, *ya habibi*, and it has nothing to do with who you are. It's what you are, everything I look up to and am awed by. Everything I never thought my children could be blessed enough to have in a father, everything I can only dream my daughter would find a fraction of in the man who'll have her well-being in his safekeeping. You're just too much. I never dared hope you could feel for me anything like I was feeling for you, couldn't believe anyone, let alone me, could aspire to hold your heart. Dying for you would be too little. But I first want to live for you."

And for the first time in his life Faress knew what it meant to feel humble. To feel blessed. He could die now and his life, his happiness would be complete.

He lowered his head, closed his eyes, touched his forehead to hers, groaned, "*Ya rohi*, I had so much to help me become what I am. It's you who are too much, it's I who realize I shouldn't have been so arrogant as to be sure I could hold your heart. But knowing that I do, I have nothing more to ask or expect of this life."

A sob and a convulsive tug brought his lips to hers, inundating him with hunger and more and more confessions.

He wallowed in the deepening certainty for as long as he could stand it. Then emotional confirmation gave way to the demands of the flesh. He imprisoned the hands that branded him, tore her cover away. She lurched with what looked like shyness mixed with arousal, shuddered with the impact of his *eshg*.

He smiled his satisfaction at her reaction before he even touched her, just reading his intentions. And that when she had no idea what he had in store for her yet.

He rained caresses from shoulders to buttocks, a path of

torment from gasping lips to begging-for-his-mouth nipples. "I've been waiting for you my whole life, *ya hayati*. I hope you'll forgive the haste when I gulp you down whole. I promise you a lifetime of everything, but now I must devour you."

She twisted in his arms, sat up, grabbing the cover again, looking flustered.

He frowned. "You fear my urgency? You think I'd be rough, wouldn't dissolve you with pleasure?"

Larissa gave a distressed laugh. "If I craved your urgency any more, you'd have to defibrillate me. And I dissolve with pleasure just looking at you. It's just there's one last thing I need to tell you, and I'm not sure how you'll react, as it's really ridiculous, with me being eighteen weeks pregnant, but I'm…" She paused as she struggled with what looked too much like embarrassment. Then, looking as if she was expecting him to start laughing, she burst out, "I'm a virgin."

He stared at her. Just stared.

The heart that had stopped in surprise now began to rumble, like the breakers of his kingdom's seas on its shores in a storm.

She mumbled on, "Since I was a little girl, I've always wanted love. Then Claire found Jawad and I was more adamant I either had the same, that totality of desire and understanding and commitment, or I didn't want anything at all. Then I thought having their child would be…" Her color rose, her eyes fluctuated among half a dozen distressed hues. "I don't know how to say this so it won't sound stupid, but it seemed like an equally worthy cause to…to offer my body to."

Faress moved, measured, controlled. Otherwise he would ravage her until he'd finished her. That would come later.

Now he took the midnight blue cover she held to her body like a shield, and slowly, so slowly, dragged it down.

"I knew it." He laid her back, spread her, took in every shudder as his voracity singed her. "In my blood, my bones. Your flesh, your essence called to me, from that first moment, demanded mine, decreed my surrender, predestined my enslavement, pledged yours. Now you'll have everything, your goal of sharing your first intimacy, all our intimacies, in the absoluteness of *eshg*, then you'll have this most treasured baby. And I'll have you both, miracles from *Ullah* I'll live my life striving to deserve. And with Jameelah and any more children you can give me, I'll have the world and beyond."

Larissa was shaking so hard her teeth rattled. "Faress, please, I can't breathe…" And it did seem she couldn't. She was gasping, looking faint. "My heart…it'll stop…if I don't have you, if you don't take me. Don't torment me any more… please, please, now…"

"*Umrek, ya rohi*, command me, and I'm yours." He came over her, parted her trembling thighs, slipped a careful finger inside her, felt the truth of her words. She was flowing for him. She thrashed, attempted to clamp him to her. He soothed her frenzy, trying to mask his own, rein it in, took her buttocks in one hand, tilted her to him as his other roamed her, in wonder, in ownership. He brought his shaft to her body's scorching entrance, rested there, struggling with the elemental need to plunge, seek her depths, go home.

Gritting his teeth, he began to invade her, her trust, her hunger, her beauty open before him, her constant pleas a continuous current fusing his insides.

The feel of her attempting to open to accept him, knowing that he'd cause her pain before he gave her pleasure, the concept of finally merging with her, and that she *had* been made for him, had waited to find him, made him almost weep.

"Please, Faress, make me yours…" she wailed.

There was only so much he could take.

He surrendered to her, to a fraction of the need, pushed into her, going blind with the burst of pleasure, the tightness of her velvet vise enveloping him. The tears he'd never thought he'd shed after Ghadah and Jawad welling in his eyes at feeling the hotness of her blood mix with that of her arousal, at the measure of the gift she was bestowing on him, at her attempts to smother the sharpness of her pain.

He stilled in her depths as she arched off the bed with the shock of his invasion, shuddering, praying the worst of it would pass quickly. *"Samheeni, ya rohi."* He panted his agitation, adjusted his position to maximize her comfort, roamed her ripeness with soothing, worshipping hands and lips. "Forgive me...I'll make it up to you in a lifetime of pleasures..."

"No, no..." she moaned, rigidity draining out of her beloved body. "I've waited my life for this, for you, but never dreamed, *never...*" Her fingers dug into his chest, his shoulders, bringing him down to her, forcing him to stroke deeper into her. She cried out this time, a hot sharp sound that tore a growl out of him. He heard exultation mixed with the pain now, his heart booming with relief, pride.

She thrashed her head, never taking her eyes off his, letting him see every sensation ripping through her, her flaming hair, her paleness brightening with her rising pleasure, burning up the darkness she lay on.

"You're magnificent inside me," she panted, her voice smoky, the exhilaration thickening it sending another tidal wave of arousal crashing through his body. "Never knew so much pleasure existed. Give me all of you, *ya habibi*, love me, take me."

"Aih, ya rohi, et'mataii..." He rumbled to her to take her fill of pleasure as he began to feed her hunger more of him, struggling as the slide inside her gripping heat sliced through him, still afraid she couldn't accommodate all of him. He watched in awe and receding sanity as she accepted more of him, arching, offering, abandoned. Then she was weeping, her cries rising as she snatched for him, seeking his lips in another exercise of abandon, her core throbbing around his invasion, pouring a surplus of welcome, demanding more of him. He couldn't believe she'd reached fever pitch so soon. But, then, so had he. And he had to obey her.

He withdrew then plunged, burying himself all the way inside her. Her scream ripped through him as her body convulsed. Then she shattered around him, her fit shredding her screams. The knowledge that he was pleasuring her, fulfilling her, boiled his seed in his loins, her wrenching tightness tearing his answering orgasm from depths he'd never known existed.

With the wish that one day his seed would take root in her womb too, produce another child of their own flesh and love, he jetted inside her, causing her paroxysm to spike. One detonation of ecstasy after another rocked him, her, held them in a closed circuit of over-stimulation, their eyes locked together in shock at sensations so sharp it felt they'd cause lasting damage. They plateaued until she was sobbing, he grunting, clinging together, dissolving in each other, at the mercy of a merciless first.

When he felt his heart would never restart, the convulsions of release gave way to the flooding warmth and weakness of satiation. He felt her melt around him, awe and cell-deep satisfaction glowing on her face.

"Marati," he rumbled against her lips as he twisted around, bringing her lying on top of him, maintaining their merging.

"Your woman, yes…oh, yes…" Her voice was different, awareness-laden, smug, overcome. She opened her lips over his heart. It almost rammed out of his ribs for a direct kiss. Then she bit into him, delicate, devouring. *"Rejjali…?"*

"Ya Ullah, bedoon shak," he groaned, feeling she'd uprooted his heart, taken it into her possession. "No doubt ever, your man. And everything else you need me to be, for ever."

She raised her head, her hair raining all over his chest, in her eyes everything he'd live for from now on. "I knew the first moment I saw you that my body had been made to sing when yours was near. It was like I'd turned into a living tuning fork with your vibe the frequency that sets me off. But I still had no idea what I've been missing. Now I am kicking myself I didn't surrender to you the first moment you wanted me."

He stroked her, turned her to lie beside him, in more comfort. "It wouldn't have been like that at first. This...cataclysm we just shared was all emotional, and we needed to go through all that we did to achieve this pinnacle."

She gave him such a smile, no inhibitions, no uncertainties, awakened, gaining in confidence. She'd become annihilating when she realized her full power. He couldn't wait to be devastated.

"I achieved that emotional pinnacle a long time ago," she whispered, between kisses all over his chest. "I should have snatched at you then. But my excuse is I had no idea it could be anything like this. No imagination or fantasy could have done what you did to me, what you gave me justice. But if it was a fraction as life-changing for you as it was for me, and you knew it would be, how did you not take me long ago? What's your excuse?"

"My excuse is that I had no idea it could be like this. I only had experience with sex..." She moaned, bit into him, punishing him for daring to have shared his body in meaningless physical release with others. He'd let her punish him, long and elaborately. "I had no idea what love, what intimacy, what dark, raging, blinding, transfiguring passion can be like. What the woman I was created for would do to me with her hunger, her surrender." She shuddered, more bliss seeping from her eyes to splash his chest. He bit one nipple, the body that hadn't subsided surging to full need as she blossomed under his hunger, undulating in a sinuous dance of urgency and demand and submission.

"Faress, *habibi*, take me again. Don't make me wait."

"You're sore. You can't take me again."

"I can. I want the pain and anything else. I just want to experience everything with you, feel your weight on me, feel you inside me, stretching me, dominating me, until I'm finished, complete. Just take me, come inside me, fill me, *ya habibi*."

In answer to her pleas, Faress sprang out of bed in one impossible movement, then bent to carry her as if she weighed no more than ten pounds, not her now substantial one-forty.

She cried out and he gave her a devilish smile. "All good things, all mind-blowing pleasure come to she who waits."

He was taking her to his *hammam*! She nearly fainted with the surge of images and the pangs of hunger they elicited.

He strode into the otherworldly hall, placed her on the glowing white marble platform, making her feel he was placing a priceless work of art on a pedestal. He suckled on each nipple, then gestured to her to stay in place as he walked away.

He came back with steam already billowing around him, a colossus of virile beauty stepping from the shroud of myth and time, and amazingly, unbelievably, hers.

The half-light worshipped endless shoulders and chest, muscled arms, defined abdomen and muscled thighs flanking a manhood whose sight rattled her with arousal and amazement that she'd been able to accommodate all that power and potency.

She lay back, struck mute, her mouth watering, her insides cramping, dizzy with the aftershocks of the transfiguring experience in his arms. The pleasure had been enough to overcome her, but the concept, the reality of his possession, the force of his passion, the heights of his generosity…! She'd metamorphosed in those minutes. She'd become a new creature, truly his.

In her recklessness she'd demanded him again. She had no idea if she'd survive those heights again or, as she suspected, something even fiercer, more uninhibited.

He came to stand over her, the purity of his emotions emblazoned on his face. "I claimed you, *ya galbi*," he said, raggedly. "Gave myself to you." Suddenly his solemn lips turned wicked. "And now…I pleasure you."

And as his hands slid over her now slick flesh, seeking her secrets, finding triggers she hadn't known she had, teasing, igniting, life expectancy became a serious issue.

CHAPTER TWELVE

FROM the depths of Faress-filled dreams, dreams that had failed to even mimic the wonder of him, the magic he'd exposed her to, Larissa opened her lips to his reality, to his cosseting, his ownership. She surfaced from the luxury of their mouths mating to the face, the smile, the reason of everything she'd wake up every morning for, as long as she lived.

"Aroah sabah fi hayati, ya hayati," he murmured, caught her answering delight in his lips again before moving his possession down to her core, tasting and teasing her in another soothing invasion, what he'd exposed her to a dozen times during the night.

"I need no more healing, Faress, just come inside me…" Her sobs choked on another heaving climax.

He came up after completing her pleasure, satisfaction and pride blazing, hunger so ferocious it cleaved into her. But she knew, no matter how she begged him, he wouldn't take her again. He was determined her next time would be pure bliss.

He drowned her in his embrace, his hardness against her side betraying the magnitude of his need, his control. He sighed. "The most incredible morning of my life, for certain, my life."

"Ahebbak, ya habibi, aashagak." She surged in his arms, sought his lips, his treasures, greedy, awed hands seeking his potency as she invaded the fount of his taste with all her fervor,

moved beyond her ability to contain it, her heart pouring into him. "That you exist, that I am yours...*aahen ya habibi*..."

He surrendered to her ministrations, her ownership, magnanimous with his demonstrations, his hypnotic eyes never leaving hers as he let her see how much, how far in her power he was, roaring his surrender, convulsing in his pleasure.

Afterwards they lay stunned yet again at the depth of their connection, its unending promise.

Suddenly trepidation started to seep through her nerves.

This was too incredible. Could life offer something of that magnitude and not exact equal and opposite payback?

Then they heard the buzz.

She felt Faress stiffen, the eyes drenching her in *eshg* draining of all expression. She choked on her heart. "What is it?"

He took her trembling lips, but it wasn't a kiss. It was a pledge. It scared her even more.

"It's nothing you should worry about, *ya rohi*," he said. "Go to work if you like today. I'll catch up as soon as I'm done." Then, with a final caress, he left her arms.

In minutes he was dressed and gone.

It was the king. He'd summoned Faress. She'd put two and two together after he'd gone.

Going crazy wondering what was going on, Larissa decided to go to work. Even if she wasn't up to working today, her team would keep her sane until she saw Faress again.

It was after breakfast, during another debate between Helal and Anika, the other blazing, if decidedly different in tone romance developing during the project, that she learned some vital truths, about Jawad's history and the current situation.

"After your all-knowing assertions last time, Helal..." Anika cocked an eyebrow at him "...I did some research. And it isn't true that a male child of Prince Jawad's would have become crown prince instead of Dr. Faress. You should do your homework before you shoot your mouth off."

"Oh?" Helal dropped beside her, his eyes promising retribution. "And what new 'facts' have you uncovered? When nobody in the kingdom talks about why Prince Jawad was supplanted by Prince Faress as crown prince?"

Anika smirked. "I told you you're not talking to real Bidalyans, Helal. The ones I talked to told me it hadn't been made public, but everyone knows the king was enraged when Jawad refused to enter into the state marriage he'd arranged for him, insisted on marrying the woman he loved. The king stripped him of his titles and wealth, even threatened to 'deal' with the woman who presumed to seduce his heir, hoping it would bring him to his senses. But what Jawad did was disappear. When the king failed to locate him and drag him back, in a fit of rage over his son's insubordination he issued another royal decree that Jawad and his line would forever be denied right of succession."

Larissa squeezed her eyes, hot shame and mortification clogging her throat. The baby had been denied all his rights. This meant Faress was actually reinstating them by claiming him as his. And she'd been so stupid, so suspicious. She'd doubted his intentions, no matter how fleetingly.

"If this is true, Ani," Patrick rumbled, "then let's hope Dr. Faress doesn't anger the old man and accept the marriage of state I hear he's pushing down his throat."

"Logic says that even if he doesn't," Tom interjected reasonably, "the king can't disown him, too. He's out of heirs. Princess Ghadah only had one daughter."

"Logic? You clearly know nothing about the old fossil," Helal scoffed. "If Prince Faress thwarts him, he'd throw the succession to any cousin. Probably the most inept one, just to spite Faress."

Larissa stopped listening. Suspicion mushroomed in her system, congealing to a heart-snatching certainty in seconds.

Faress was risking his birthright to have her and the baby.

And she knew what that pledge before he'd left had been. He'd been telling her nothing would stop him from having them.

She didn't know what she said to her team as she ran out. She only knew she had to stop Faress from throwing everything away.

She tried to reach him on his cellphone as she raced to the king's palace, to no avail.

On arrival, she was received with all the deference a royal guest would receive. It had to be on Faress's orders.

But it was too late. Faress was already with the king.

She begged the one who seemed like head of security to transmit an urgent message to Faress. Hesitating to interrupt his king's private audience with his son, yet bound by that son's orders to answer her every request, he consented to try.

Minutes passed until she felt she'd start running through the palace, yelling for Faress, any second.

The man suddenly reappeared. "Dr. McPherson. You're to be admitted into the king's presence."

"But I just need to talk to Prince Faress…" she faltered.

The man bowed his head. "You're summoned to the king's presence by *Somow'w'el Ameer* Faress's orders."

She staggered behind him in chaos. Why had Faress done that? She didn't want to see that man, and more so with every step through his palace's impossible opulence, pompous and extravagant where Faress's was tasteful and prosperous.

Her stomach roiling with anxiety, she walked into the king's stateroom. The first thing she saw was Faress, striding towards her, his eyes fierce, his jaw set. She had no idea how she stopped herself from throwing herself into his arms.

Acutely aware of his father's presence, his rage, her chaos spiked when Faress embraced her.

"I'm loath for you to witness this," he murmured against her lips, "but I couldn't leave you outside."

"Is this the harlot come to take my one remaining offspring?"

This couldn't be the voice of a man. It was the roar of a wounded monster. Larissa started in Faress's arms, felt him stiffen as he whirled around.

"Have a care, Father," Faress rumbled, his voice as low and as frightening as his father's explosive fury. It gave the older man pause.

Then his rage spiked as he stormed towards them, as big as Faress, bulkier. He must have been as handsome once, but his volatile ruthlessness furrowed his good looks, made him forbidding, sinister.

"I know who your harlot is, Faress," the king raved. "Did *you*? Or did she con you like her harlot of a sister conned Jawad?" At uttering Jawad's name something crazed came into his eyes. He roared, "Jawad. Dead. Ghadah. Dead. And this...this..." He made a snatch at her. Her heart hit the base of her throat. Faress's lightning move intercepted his father. As she staggered out of the man's reach, Faress grabbed his father's arms, overpowered him with steady power until the older man stood grunting with effort, shaking with frustration, pain and rage.

"I know what you're going through, Father..." Faress started, a pained look on his face at his father's devastation.

"You know nothing," the king snarled, sounding even more deranged. "They were just your siblings. They were my first-born, my hope, my little girl, the balm of my soul. Tell me you know what I'm going through when you bury two children."

"I know what you're going through," Faress insisted. "I almost lost everyone I hold dear yesterday, and I know I would have been driven to extremes if it had come to pass. But you're the one who deprived us of Jawad, so own up to it."

After a long wrestling look between father and son, the king relinquished what he knew was a losing match, turned his disturbed and disturbing gaze on Larissa.

"You... I'm not letting you take my only remaining son. I'm throwing you out of Bidalya." He turned his rabid eyes on Faress. "And you had better not intervene."

Faress held his father's gaze and weighed his options. He'd never seen him like this. The certainty of Jawad's loss, his guilt over his role in it all was tampering with his sanity. If he told his father Larissa was carrying all they had left of Jawad he might relent. But with his father so unstable, he couldn't risk him going into another fit of royal retribution, insisting on still disowning Jawad's son as well, or, worse, snatching him away from Larissa and banning her from seeing him ever again. There were no options really. His father, though he bled for him, had forfeited his right to his family.

"Oh, I wouldn't intervene, Father." He felt Larissa's start. He grated on, "I'd only leave with her. Larissa isn't only the woman I love, she's my wife, already pregnant with my heir. I've only been waiting for the proper time to take our vows again in the Bidalyan tradition, wanted you to be part of a family that will give you a new daughter and a grandson. But you can cling to your irrationalities. Like Jawad, my first loyalty and duty is to the woman who owns my heart. Exile her and you'll never see me again either."

"Then get out of my sight, both of you," the king thundered. "Out of my kingdom."

Faress merely gave his father a small bow, wrapped his arm around her and walked her out.

Larissa remained in shock all through the rush to the palace to collect Jameelah then to the airport to board one of Faress's private jets.

They were in the air and the bewildered if excited Jameelah had fallen asleep in one of the jet's two bedroom suites when Larissa finally caught Faress between his continuous phone calls.

"I can't let you do this to yourself or to Bidalya," she blurted out. "You were born to be king and I won't let you sacrifice yourself for me and my baby."

He pulled her onto his lap, nuzzled her neck. "I was born to be yours, your man and the father of our children. I was born to fight to my last breath for you. You're already my wife before

God. I don't care about being Bidalya's crown prince or future king. I only want to be your knight and king of your heart."

She squirmed, tried to slow down her descent into his thrall. This had to be resolved. "You'll always be that. But you don't have to give up anything to have me. I'm yours for ever, and will live for the time when you can be with us." He just shook his head and she got desperate. "You can't throw away your birthright like Jawad did!"

His gaze stilled on her until she felt he'd penetrated her down to her marrow. Then he asked, "Did it ever seem to you that Jawad was unhappy? In the years of his marriage to your sister, did you feel he had any regrets?"

She closed her eyes, knowing he'd cornered her.

"Not for a second," she admitted thickly. "Through the trials of infertility and terminal illness, I never saw a man happier or more in love than Jawad."

"You're *looking* at that man." His voice was certainty itself. "But unlike Jawad, I have extensive wealth and status independent of my royal position. We'll go wherever we want, set up our humanitarian operations, our hospitals and research centers and be productive and happy together for the rest of our lives."

Everything he said humbled her, made her delirious with elation. But she was still oppressed at the massive privileges he was throwing away to be with her.

She tried again. "*Habibi*, I'll give my life, every minute of it, to make you happy, to deserve your love and faith. But you don't have to marry me. Your love is all I want from life…"

His mouth, passionate and overriding, silenced her. Then he murmured, "You're having all of me. For ever. Any objections?"

Larissa could no longer find any.

Drowning in his arms, she came out of her haze of happiness to the sound of the jet landing. A glance outside the jet confirmed one thing. They'd landed back in Bidalya!

It had to be the king's doing.

Next moment, her deduction was confirmed. The king appeared on the screens of Faress's video conferencing facility.

The king looked haggard, defeated. He started immediately as soon as Faress opened the channel.

"I can't lose another son, *ya bnai*. And Bidalya can't lose the man best suited to be its king. I want you back and I want you to start the restructuring plans you've been proposing."

Then he was gone.

Faress stared at the blank screen for a while. Then he turned to Larissa, serious, intense. Her heart thumped.

He exhaled. "My father really knows how to offer bait when he wants to. He just offered me what I thought he'd never agree to. To start reorganizing the rule in the kingdom now, in his lifetime, so that by the time I come to reign, the monarchy will have far less power and I will have far less to do as king, so that I can continue being a surgeon."

She was stunned. "Oh, God, Faress. That's huge. And so exciting. And scary."

"Indeed. And I'll need all the help I can get to organize my time. And who better than you? You showed me new levels of time efficiency, and efficiency in general. Will you be my personal advisor, my official right hand in all things medical?"

Larissa flung herself at him, took his lips, rained kisses in a fever over his beloved face. "I'll be anything you want. Anything. I'll take on the whole world, take the most grueling tests, perform the impossible, for ever."

He took over until she was trembling, writhing.

"You already did that and then some, *ya rohi*," he growled, then swung her in his arms, heading for the other bedroom. "Not in a hurry to leave the jet, are you?" She shook her head frantically. He chuckled as he locked the door behind them.

A long time later, they were moaning their completion, watching stars outside the window twinkling in the inky sky, when he suddenly groaned.

"You make me forget the world." He rose over her. "But

we must make plans for our wedding. When would you like to have it?"

Snuggling into the heaven and haven of his arms, she chuckled. "Any time before I'm in labor would be good."

EPILOGUE

FARESS managed that, barely.

Because of the changes Faress had to put in place before the wedding took place, Larissa shocked the world by showing up eight months pregnant in the internationally broadcast marriage ceremony, and in a conservative country like Bidalya to boot.

Bidalya's crown prince and the proud and magnificent groom in traditional ceremonial garb rose from their matrimonial *kousha* and announced that this was a belated public ceremony, that their marriage had taken place a year ago, and that there would be another ceremony on the birth of their first child. He proclaimed that both days would become national holidays.

Then he turned, winked at the distraught with excitement Jameelah, before coming to stand above Larissa.

Suddenly, he knelt. The crowds went wild.

Ecstatically wrecked, Larissa barely managed not to fall at his feet in a heap, remembering the decorum she was supposed to show as a princess of Bidalya. Faress produced an anklet right out of Ali Baba's treasures, took her green silk moccasin-like clad foot, raised it, placed a fervent kiss on her exposed flesh. The crowds roared like a raging storm with approval.

Looking into her drenched eyes, he whispered, for her ears only, "*Maaboodati*, my goddess, I give you everything that I am." Then he snapped the anklet in place.

He stood up, pulled her to her wobbly feet, supported her swaying, heavily pregnant body all through endless, hyper-charged minutes of waving to the crowds.

Finally the public celebrations started, and he seated her, sat down beside her, pride and ever-increasing *eshg* blazing in his obsidian eyes.

Giggling, going to pieces, Larissa gasped, "The way we left things, those two holidays you proclaimed will be too close together. Little Jawad is probably days from making his entrance into the world."

Faress took her clammy hand, kissed it. "And next year at the same time, we may even have a little Claire to crowd the month with one more national holiday."

Choking up even more, Larissa tried not to break down with happiness. "In the interests of interspersing those, we have to plan a bit. I'd love to have a winter baby."

"You can have everything you want," he declared, his eyes vowing. "Whenever you want it, and a baby in each season. I want to fill my world with little replicas of you."

And Larissa shocked the world again.

She threw herself at him, her emotions and passion and gratitude for all that he was boiling over in an all-the-way kiss.

She dimly heard the roaring of the crowds reaching a crescendo. And realized.

Not only were public displays of affection frowned upon here, this was Faress's personal inclination. He'd kissed her hand and foot in tenderness and chivalry, but the kiss she was giving him was right out of their erotically abandoned encounters.

She'd compromised his image, started her life as his princess proving how unsuitable she was for the role...

She jerked out of his arms. "Oh, God, I'm sorry Faress..."

He pulled her back, his laughter the very sound of delight and arousal. Then he kissed her again. This time he really gave the crowds something for their eyes to pop over.

When he at last let go of her lips, he kept her ensconced in his embrace, an ecstatic mass of agitation. And *eshg*.

Tilting her face up to him to let him see it all, she saw his own *eshg* in his eyes as he murmured, "This is the…"

"This was the best wedding gift you could have given me, *ya roh galbi*. Showing me in front of the whole world that nothing matters but me. Worry about behaving with all the decorum of a princess in public…tomorrow. Now let's give the world a royal wedding that will make history."

And he took her lips again.

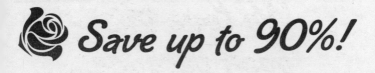

 *Special Offers*

Every month we put together collections and longer reads written by your favourite authors.

Here are some of next month's highlights— and don't miss our fabulous discount online!

On sale
20th January

On sale
20th January

On sale
3rd February

On sale
3rd February

Under the scorching heat of the desert sun
these powerful princes' thoughts turn
to seduction!

CLAIMED BY THE Desert SHEIKH

Three exotic and compelling books
by three exciting authors:

SUSAN MALLERY
SUSAN STEPHENS
OLIVIA GATES

The Sheikh Collection
4 exciting volumes!

Available in January 2012

Available in February 2012

Available in March 2012

Available in April 2012